Thomas Power O'Connor

Napoleon

Thomas Power O'Connor

Napoleon

ISBN/EAN: 9783337349905

Printed in Europe, USA, Canada, Australia, Japan

Cover: Foto ©Andreas Hilbeck / pixelio.de

More available books at **www.hansebooks.com**

NAPOLEON

BY

T. P. O'CONNOR,

AUTHOR OF "SOME OLD LOVE STORIES."

LONDON: CHAPMAN AND HALL, Ld.

1896.

F. M. EVANS AND CO., LIMITED, PRINTERS,
CRYSTAL PALACE, S.E.

PREFACE.

I HAVE thought of various methods for presenting these Essays in a collected form. The first and most natural suggestion was that I should, after a careful comparison of their conflicting points of view, and an assortment of their statements, present to the reader a final estimate and a finished picture. I found it impossible to adopt this course. Napoleon had so many sides; was not only so contradictory in himself, but produced such contradictory impressions on different people, that it lay far beyond my power to make one consistent picture of him, and to decide with anything like confidence between testimony at once so contradictory and so authoritative. The plan to which I have been driven, then, is to present these Essays pretty much as they originally appeared—which means that I have made myself the interpreter, and not the judge, of the witnesses and of the evidence. I am conscious of the disadvantages of such a plan; but, on the other hand, it has its compensations. The reader will have ample material for forming his own judgment: Napoleon, too, will be presented in his vast many-sidedness; and finally, there will probably be in the reader's mind, after hearing all these conflicting voices, a nearer approach to a just and accurate estimate of Napoleon than if he had read any one set of witnesses, or if he had been confronted with a self-confident judgment on the final merits of the evidence. No human character is mathematical in its lines; and historical characters especially are much less consistent, either in their goodness or their badness, than their admirers and their foes represent. The final picture of Napoleon which these Essays will leave in the minds of the reader will, I expect, be somewhat blurred, inconsistent—perhaps even chaotic. The picture, perhaps, will be for all this the nearer to reality.

CONTENTS.

CHAPTER I.

CHAPTER II.

CHAPTER III.

Contents. ix

CHAPTER IV.

CHAPTER V.

CHAPTER VI.

Contents.

CHAPTER IX.

CHAPTER X.

NAPOLEON.

CHAPTER I.

TAINE'S PORTRAIT.*

I BEGIN the series of portraits by giving that of
Taine. It is the most finished and the most
powerful. Indeed, I know scarcely any portrait
in literature in which there is more dazzling
literary skill; but it is a portrait by an avowed
and a bitter enemy. It is too peremptory and too
consistent; above all, it is a portrait drawn by
what I may call a literary absolutist—the artist
who insists that human figures should follow the
rigidity of a philosopher's scientific rules.

I.

NAPOLEON AN ITALIAN.

THE first point which Taine brings out is that this
mighty despot, who ruled France as she had never
been ruled before, was not even a Frenchman.
Not only in blood and in birth, but in feeling he

* "The Modern Régime." Vol. I. By H. A. Taine.
Translated by John Durand. (London : Sampson Low,
Marston, & Co.)

B

was an Italian. He remained, in some respects, an Italian all his life. In Taine's eyes, too, he is not only an Italian, but an Italian of the Middle Ages. "He belongs," says Taine, "to another race and another epoch." And then, in a series of wonderful passages, Taine traces back the heritage of Napoleon to those men and those times. "The man-plant," says Alfieri, "is in no country born more vigorous than in Italy," "and never," goes on Taine, "in Italy was it so vigorous as from 1300 to 1500, from the contemporaries of Dante down to those of Michael Angelo, Cæsar Borgia, Julius II., and Macchiavelli." In those times great personalities fought for crowns, money, and life at one cast, and when they succeeded, established a government remarkable for splendour, order, and firmness. This was the period of great adventurers — great in battle, great in council, great in courage, great in imagination, great in their love of the arts. All these qualities are reproduced in Napoleon.

"He is," says Taine, "a posthumous brother of Dante and Michael Angelo; in the clear outlines of his vision, in the intensity, coherence, and inward logic of his reverie, in the profundity of his meditations, in the superhuman grandeur of his conceptions, he is, indeed, their fellow and their equal. His genius is of the same stature and the same structure; he is one of the three sovereign minds of the Italian Renaissance, only, while the first two operated on paper and on marble, the latter operates on the living being, on the sensitive and suffering flesh of humanity."

II.

HIS ITALIAN TEMPERAMENT.

ANALYSING Napoleon's temperament, Taine also finds that it belongs to another race and another epoch. "Three hundred years of police and of courts of justice," "of social discipline and peaceful habits," "have diminished the force and violence of the passions natural to men," but in Italy, at the period of the Renaissance, those passions were still intact.

"Human emotions at that time were keener and more profound than at the present day; the appetites were ardent and more unbridled; man's will was more impetuous and more tenacious; whatever motive inspired him, whether pride, ambition, jealousy, hatred, love, envy, or sensuality, the inward spring strained with an energy and relaxed with a violence that has now disappeared. All these energies reappear in the great survivor of the fifteenth century; in him the play of the nervous machine is the same as with his Italian ancestors. Never was there, even among the Malatestas or Borgias, a more sensitive and impulsive intellect, more capable of such electric shocks and explosions, in which the roar and flashes of the tempest lasted longer, and of which the effects were more irresistible. In his mind no idea seems speculative and pure; none is a simple transcript of the real, or a simple picture of the possible; each is an internal eruption, which suddenly and spontaneously spends itself in action; each darts forth to its goal, and would reach it without stopping were it not kept back and restrained by force."

Of this Italian explosiveness of nature, Taine gives scores of examples. This conception of Napoleon's character differs fundamentally from many of our preconceived notions; and from the idea of himself which Napoleon was able to convey in public and to all who did not know him intimately during his lifetime. "The public and the army regarded him as impassive;" in his battles "he wears a mask of bronze;" in "official ceremonies he wears a necessarily dignified air;" and in most pictures of him which I have seen, one gets the impression of a profoundly immutable calm. But the real Napoleon was altogether different from this. A more sensitive, restless, irritable nature never existed. His emotions are so rapid that they intercept each other, and emotion irresistibly compels immediate action.

"Impression and expression with him are almost always confounded, the inward overflowing in the outward, the action, like a blow, getting the better of him."

"At Paris, towards the end of the Concordat, he says to Senator Volney, 'France wants a religion.' Volney replies, in a frank, sententious way, 'France wants the Bourbons.' Whereupon he gives Volney a kick in the stomach, and he falls unconscious. On his being conveyed to a friend's house he remains there ill for several days. No man is more irritable, so soon in a passion, and all the more because he purposely gives way to his irritation; for, doing this just at the right moment, and especially before witnesses, it strikes terror—it enables him to extort concessions and maintain obedience; while his explosions of anger, half calculated, half involuntary, serve him quite as much as they relieve him, in public as in private, with strangers as with intimates, before constituted bodies, with the Pope, with cardinals, with ambassadors, with Talleyrand, with Beugnot, with anybody that comes along, whenever he wishes to set an example or 'keep the people around him on the alert.'"

His unfortunate wife is one of the greatest victims of this violence, and even at the moment when she has most right to complain.

"At St. Cloud, caught by Josephine in an act of gallantry, he springs after the unlucky intruder in such a way that she has barely time to escape; and, again, that evening, keeping up his fury, so as to put her down completely, 'he treats her in the most outrageous manner, smashing every piece of furniture that comes in his way.'"

And here is another example of the way in which he treats his Ministers.

"A little before the Empire, Talleyrand, a great mystifier, tells Berthier that the First Consul wanted to assume the title of king. Berthier, in eager haste, crosses the drawing-room full of company, accosts the master of the house, and, with a beaming smile, 'congratulates him.' At the word 'king' Bonaparte's eyes flash. Grasping Berthier by the throat, he pushes his head against a wall, exclaiming, 'You fool! Who told you to come here and stir up my bile in this way? Another time don't come on such errands.' Such is the first impulse, the instinctive action, to pounce on people and seize them by the throat. We divine under each sentence, and on every page he writes, outbursts and assaults of this description; the physiognomy and intonation of a man who rushes forward and knocks people down."

III.

IN DÉSHABILLE.

AND then there come some striking pictures of Napoleon in his study and his dressing-room—where we see him in *déshabille* and as the natural man. It is not a pleasant picture—indeed, the whole impression one gets from this study of Napoleon is brutal, revolting.

"When dictating in his cabinet he strides up and down the room,' and 'if excited,' which is often the case, 'his language consists of violent imprecations and oaths, which are suppressed in what is written.' But these are not always suppressed, and those who have seen the original minutes of his correspondence on ecclesiastical affairs find dozens of them of the coarsest kind. . . .

"When dressing himself, he throws on the floor or into the fire any part of his attire which does not suit him. . . . On gala days, and on grand ceremonial occasions, his valets are obliged to agree together when they shall seize the right moment to put something on him. . . . He tears off or breaks whatever causes him the slightest discomfort, while the poor valet who has been the cause of it receives a violent and positive proof of his anger. No thought was ever carried away more by its own speed. 'His handwriting,' when he tries to write, 'is a mass of disconnected and undecipherable signs ; the words lack one half of their letters.' On reading it over himself he cannot tell what it means. At last he becomes almost incapable of writing an autograph letter, while his signature is a mere scrawl. He accordingly dictates, but so fast that his secretaries can scarcely keep pace with him. On their first attempt the perspiration flows freely, and they succeed in noting down only the half of what he says. Bourrienne, De Méneval, and Maret invent a stenography of their own, for he never repeats any of his sentences ; so much the worse for the pen if it lags behind, and so much the better if a volley of exclamations or of oaths give it a chance to catch up."

IV.

HIS ITALIAN LOQUACITY.

ONE generally associates extraordinary military genius with taciturnity ; and there is also a disposition to regard reticence as an inevitable accompaniment of great force of will, and of genius in action. There are many good people who really think that Mr. Gladstone cannot be regarded as a man of genius in action for the reason that he has talked so much throughout his life. A study of Napoleon will dissipate this idea; never was there a talker so incessant, so impetuous, so daring. Here, again, his Italian origin reveals itself. Italy is the land of improvisation, and over and over again Taine applies to Napoleon the Italian term "*improvisatore.*" This is his description, for instance, of Napoleon speaking at a Ministerial Council :—

"Never did speech flow and overflow in such torrents, often without either discretion or prudence, even when the outburst is neither useful nor creditable ; subject to this inward pressure the improvisator and polemic, under full headway, take the place of the man of business and the statesman. 'With him,' says a good observer, 'talking is a prime necessity; and, assuredly, among the highest prerogatives, he ranks first that of speaking without interruption.' Even at the Council of State he allows himself to run on, forgetting the business before the meeting; he starts off right and left with some digression or demonstration, some invective or other for two or three hours at a stretch, insisting over and over again, bent on convincing or prevailing, and ending by demanding of the others if he is not right, 'and in this case, never failing to find that all have yielded to the force of his argument.' On reflection he knows the value of an assent thus obtained, and, pointing to his chair, he observes : 'It must be admitted that in that seat one thinks with facility !' Nevertheless, he has enjoyed his intellectual exercise and given way to his passion, which controls him far more than he controls it."

v.

AND HIS SENSIBILITY.

IT is, however, one of the contradictions of this extraordinary character, that he has moments of intense and almost ingenuous sensibility. "He who has looked upon thousands of dying men, and has had thousands of men slaughtered, sobs after Wagram and after Bautzen at the couch of a dying comrade." "I saw him," says his valet, "weep while eating his breakfast, after coming from Marshal Lannes' bedside ; big tears rolled down his cheeks, and fell on his plate."

"It is not alone the physical sensation, the sight of a bleeding, mangled body, which thus moves him acutely and deeply ; for a word, a simple idea, stings and penetrates almost as far. Before the emotion of Dandolo, who pleads for Venice his country, which is sold to Austria, he is agitated and his eyes moisten. Speaking of the capitulation of Baylen, at a full meeting of the Council of State, his voice trembles, 'and he gives way to his grief, his eyes even filling with tears.' In 1806, setting out for the army and on taking leave of Josephine, he has a nervous attack, which is so severe as to bring on vomiting. 'We had to make him sit down,' says an eye-witness, 'and swallow some orange water. He shed tears, and this lasted a quarter of an hour.'" The same nervous crisis came on in 1808, when he was deciding on the divorce. "He tosses about a whole night, and laments like a woman. He melts and embraces Josephine ; he is weaker than she is. 'My poor Josephine, I can never leave you!' Folding her in his arms, he declares that she shall not quit him. He abandons himself wholly to the sensation of the moment ; she must undress at once, and lie beside him, and he weeps over her ; 'literally,' she says, 'he soaked the bed with his tears.'"

VI.

HIS MOMENTS OF COWARDICE.

IT is also this extreme sensibility which accounts for those few moments of abject cowardice that stand out in the career of one of the most fearless human beings who ever lived. He himself has always the dread that there would be a breakdown in the nervous system—a loss of balance. "My nerves," he says of himself, "are very irritable, and when in this state, were my pulse not always regular, I should risk going crazy." But his pulse does not always beat regularly.

"He is twice taken unawares at times when the peril was alarming and of a new kind. He, so clear-headed and so cool under fire, the boldest of military heroes, and the most audacious of political adventurers, quails twice in a Parliamentary storm, and again in a popular crisis. On the 18th of Brumaire, in the Corps Législatif, 'he turned pale, trembled, and seemed to lose his head at the shouts of outlawry. . . . They had to drag him out . . . they even thought for a moment that he was going to faint.' After the abdication at Fontainebleau, on encountering the rage and imprecations which greeted him in Provence, he seemed for some days to be morally shattered ; the animal instinct asserts its supremacy; he is afraid, and makes no attempt of concealment. After borrowing the uniform of an Austrian colonel, the casque of a Prussian quartermaster, and the cloak of a Russian quartermaster, he still considers that he is not sufficiently disguised. In the inn at Calade 'he starts and changes colour at the slightest noise;' the commissioners, who repeatedly enter the room, 'find him always in tears.' 'He wearies them with his anxieties and irresolution;' he says the French Government would like to have him assassinated on the road, refuses to eat for fear of poison, and thinks that he might escape by jumping out of the window. And yet he gives vent to his feelings and lets his tongue run on about himself, without stopping, concerning his past, his character, unreservedly, indelicately, trivially, like a cynic and one who is half crazy. His ideas run loose and crowd each other like the anarchical gatherings of a tumultuous mob; he does not recover his mastery of them until he reaches Fréjus, the end of his journey, where he feels himself safe and protected from any highway assault. Then only do they return within ordinary limits, and fall back in regular line under the control of the sovereign intellect, which after sinking for a time, revives and resumes its ascendency."

This strange, tasteless loquacity of Napoleon—without dignity, self-respect, or decency—is one of

the many features in his character which must
always be remembered if one wishes to have a
clear and full conception of him. I shall, by-and-
by, bring out the severer and more sinister aspects
of his nature; for a moment let me lay stress on
this smaller, and what I might call more frivolous,
side of his character; it adds grimness to his more
fatal and awful qualities. Some of his sayings at
the period to which I have just referred cannot
be transferred to the chaste pages of an English
book. Taine is justified in speaking of Napoleon
as giving under such circumstances "a glimpse
of the actor and even of the Italian buffoon;"
and it was probably this aspect of his character
conjoined to others — this petty buffoonery in
association with almost divine genius — which
suggested the felicitous title of "Jupiter Scapin,"
applied to him by M. de Pradt, who knew him
well. To this same M. de Pradt Napoleon spoke
very plainly after the return of the disastrous and
terrible expedition to Russia; in these reflections
he appears "in the light of a comedian, who,
having played badly and failed in his part, retires
behind the scenes, runs down the piece, and
criticises the imperfections of the audience." This
"piece" which had sent hundreds of thousands to
violent death!

VII.

NAPOLEON'S FAMILY.

NAPOLEON'S father, Charles Bonaparte, was weak and even frivolous, "too fond of pleasure to care about his children," or his affairs; he died at thirty-nine of cancer of the stomach—"which seems to be the only bequest he made to his son, Napoleon." His mother was altogether of a different type—a type, too, thoroughly Italian. "Serious, authoritative," she was "the real head of the family." She was, said Napoleon, "hard in her affections; she punished and rewarded without distinction good or bad; she made us all feel it."

On becoming head of the household "she was too parsimonious—even ridiculously so. This was due to excess of foresight on her part; she had known want, and her terrible sufferings were never out of her mind. . . . In other respects this woman, from whom it would have been difficult to extract five francs, would have given up everything to secure my return from Elba, and after Waterloo she offered me all she possessed to retrieve my fortunes."

Other accounts of her agree in saying that she was "unboundedly avaricious;" that she had "no knowledge whatever of the usages of society;" that she was very "ignorant, not alone of 'French' literature but of her own." "The character of the son," says Stendhal, "is to be explained by the perfectly Italian character of Madame Lætitia." From her, too, he inherited his extraordinary courage and resource. She was _enceinte_ with her great son at the very moment of the French invasion, and she gave birth to him "amid the risks of battle and defeat. . . . amidst mountain rides on horseback, nocturnal surprises, and volleys of musketry." "Losses, privations, and fatigue," says Napoleon, "she endured all, and braved all. Hers was a man's head on a woman's shoulders."

The sisters of Napoleon are also remarkable in their way—though, as often happens, what is strength in the men, degenerates in them into self-destructive vice.

"Passion, sensuality, the habit of considering themselves outside of rules, and self-confidence, combined with talent, predominate in these women as in those of the fifteenth century. Elisa, of Tuscany, had a vigorous brain, was high-spirited and a genuine sovereign, notwithstanding the disorders of her private life, in which even appearances were not sufficiently maintained. Caroline of Naples, without being more scrupulous than her sister, 'better observed the proprieties; none of the others so much resembled the Emperor.' 'With her all tastes were subordinated to ambition;' it was she who advised and prevailed upon her husband, Murat, to desert Napoleon in 1814. As to Pauline, the most beautiful woman of her epoch, 'no wife, since that of the Emperor Claudius, surpassed her in the use she dared make of her charms; nothing could stop her, not even a malady attributed to her dissipation, and on account of which we have often seen her borne on a litter.'"

This, perhaps, is the most effective and deadliest blow at Napoleon in Taine's terrible indictment. If to this despot had been apportioned the female belongings of a man in, say, Ratcliff Highway, we should know what it implied. It would imply a family of brutal, predatory, foul instincts. The inheritors of such instincts would, in the case of the men, be the denizens of gaols; in the case of the women, would swell the ranks of prostitutes.

It is healthy, though not wholly comforting, to be reminded of the similarity of human nature through the vast differences of human rank and fortunes. To those who are fearless realists like Taine, there is a sombre joy in penetrating through trappings and robes to the naked animal beneath. Reflect for a moment that behind the flowing Imperial robes at the High Altar in Nôtre Dame, there is a nature, which in other circumstances would be clothed in the garment of a violent convict; that these beautiful, delicate, richly - bedizened women, whom Napoleon and chance have placed on thrones, are of the same mould as that brawling drab who is being haled to the prison, or lies, broken and beaten, in the bed of a hospital!

All the brothers of Napoleon were likewise re-markable in their way; and finally, the family picture is completed, and Napoleon's character is also indicated by what Napoleon himself says of one of his uncles. He "delights in calling to mind one of his uncles who, in his infancy, prog-nosticated to him that he would govern the world because he was fond of lying."

VIII.

NAPOLEON'S BEGINNINGS.

MOODY, rancorous, hating the French as the conquerors of his country, Napoleon as a youth looked on the events of the French Revolution with the detachment of a foreigner. In 1792, when the struggle between the monarchists and the revolutionists was at its height, he tries to find "some successful speculation," and thinks he will hire and sub-let houses at a profit. On June 20 in the same year he sees the invasion of the Tuileries, and the King at a window placing the red cap on his head. "*Che Coglione !*" (What a cuckold!) he exclaims, and immediately after, "How could they let the rabble enter! Mow down 400 or 500 of them with cannon-balls, and the rest of them would run away."

"On August 10, when the tocsin is sounding, he regards the people and the King with equal contempt; he rushes to a friend's house on the

Carrousel, and there, still as a looker-on, views at his ease all the occurrences of the day; finally the *Château* is forced, and he strolls through the Tuileries, looks in at the neighbouring cafés, and that is all. He is not disposed to take sides; he has no Jacobin or Royalist impulse. His features, even, are so calm as to provoke many hostile and distrustful remarks, 'as unknown and suspicious.' None of the political or social conditions which then exercised such control over men's minds have any hold on him. . . . On returning to Paris, after having knocked at several doors, he takes Barras for a patron—Barras, the most brazen of the corrupt; Barras, who has overthrown and contrived the death of his two former protectors. Among the contending parties and fanaticisms which succeed each other, he keeps cool and free to dispose of himself as he pleases, indifferent to every cause, and caring·only for his own interest. On the evening of the 12th of Vendémiaire, on leaving the Feydeau Theatre, and noticing the preparations of the Sections, he said to Junot: 'Ah, if the Sections would only let me lead them! I would guarantee to place them in the Tuileries in two hours, and have all those rascals of the Convention turned out!' Five hours later, denounced by Barras and the Convention, he takes 'three minutes' to make up his mind, and instead of 'blowing up the representatives,' he shoots down

Parisians like any other good *condottiere*, who, holding himself in reserve, inclines to the first that offers, and then to whoso offers the most, prepared to back out afterwards, and who finally grabs anything he can get."

And it is as a *condottiere* that Taine regards Napoleon to the end. From this point of view he surveys his whole career, and here is the result of the inspection :

" He is like a *condottiere,* that is to say, a leader of a band, getting more and more independent, pretending to submit under the pretext of public good, looking out solely for his own interest, centreing all on himself, general on his own account and for his own advantage in his Italian campaign before and after the 18th of Fructidor. Still he was a *condottiere* of the first class, already aspiring to the loftiest summits, ' with no stopping-place but the throne or the scaffold,' 'determined to master France, and Europe through France, ever occupied with his own plans, and demanding only three hours' sleep a night'; making playthings of ideas, people, religions, and governments; managing mankind with incomparable dexterity and brutality ; in the choice of means, as of ends, a superior artist, inexhaustible in prestige, seduction, corruption, and intimidation ; wonderful, and far more terrible than any wild beast suddenly turned on to a herd of browsing cattle. The expression is not too strong, and was uttered by an eye-witness almost at this very date, a friend and a competent diplomat. ' You know that, though I am very fond of the dear General, I call him myself *the little tiger*, so as to properly characterise his looks, tenacity, and courage, the rapidity of his movements, and all that he has in him which may be fairly regarded in that sense.'"

IX.

HIS POWER OF COMMAND.

POOR, forlorn, discontented, at first sight insignificant in figure, and without any employment, Napoleon in these early days might have been passed by without much notice. But it is a singular thing that the moment he attains any position, people at once, involuntarily, even strongly against their will, recognise and bow down before his calmly arrogant capacity. There are, for instance, two portraits of him at the period in his existence just following that to which we have now reached, and both give the same impression— the one is by Madame de Staël, and is in words; the other is by Guérin, a truthful painter. Madame de Staël meets him at a time when, having gained some victories, she and the public generally are sympathetic towards him; and yet, she says, "the recovery from the first excitement of admiration was followed by a decided sense of apprehension." He had then no power, and might any day be dismissed, and "thus the terror he inspired was simply due to the singular effect of his person on all who approach him."

"I had met men worthy of respect, and had likewise met men of ferocious character; but nothing in the impression which Bonaparte produced on me reminded me of either. . . . *A being like him, wholly unlike anybody else*, could neither feel nor excite sympathy; he was *both more and less than a man*; his figure, intellect, and language bore the impress of a foreign nationality. . . . Far from being reassured on seeing Bonaparte oftener, he intimidated one more and more every day. . . . *He regards a human being as a fact, an object, and not as a fellow-creature.* He neither hates nor loves: *he exists for himself alone*; the rest of humanity are merely ciphers. . . . Every time that I heard him talk, I was struck with his *superiority*. It bore no resemblance to that of men informed and cultivated through study and social intercourse, such as we find in France and England; his conversation concerned *the material fact* only, like that of the hunter in pursuit of his prey. His spirit seemed a cold, keen sword-blade, which freezes while it wounds. I realised a profound sense of irony which nothing great or beautiful could withstand, not even his own fame, for he despised the nation whose suffrages he sought."

X.

AN EARLY PORTRAIT.

AND now, here is Taine's description of the Guérin portrait :—

"Now, notice in Guérin, that spare body, those narrow shoulders under the uniform wrinkled by sudden movements, the neck swathed in its high twisted cravat, those temples covered by long, smooth, straight hair, exposing only the mask, the hard features intensified through strong contrasts of light and shade, the cheeks hollow up to the inner angle of the eye, the projecting cheekbones, the massive protuberant jaw, the sinuous, mobile lips, pressed together as if attentive, the large clear eyes, deeply sunk under the broad arched eyebrows, the fixed oblique look, as penetrating as a rapier, and the two creases which extend from the base of the nose to the brow, as if in a frown of suppressed anger and determined will."

" Add to this the accounts of his contemporaries who saw or heard the curt accent, or the sharp, abrupt gesture, the interrogating, imperious, absolute tone of voice, and we comprehend how it was that the moment they accosted him, they felt the dominating hand which seized them, pressed them down, held them firmly, never relaxing its grasp."

Admiral Decrès, who had known him well in Paris, learns that he has to pass through Toulon on his way to take up the command of the army in Italy. He rushes to see an old acquaintance :—

"'I at once propose to my comrades to introduce them, venturing to do so on the grounds of my acquaintance with him in Paris. Full of eagerness and joy, I started off. The door opened, I am about to press forward,' he afterwards wrote, 'when the attitude, the look, and the tone of voice suffice to arrest me. And yet there was nothing offensive about him ; still this was enough. I never tried after that to overstep the line thus imposed upon me.' A few days later, at Alberga, certain generals of division, and amongst them Augereau, a vulgar, heroic old soldier, vain of his tall figure and courage, arrive at head-quarters, not well disposed towards the little *parvenu* sent out to them from Paris. Recalling the description of him which had been given to them, Augercau is abusive and insubordinate beforehand :

"'One of Barras's favourites ! The Vendémiaire General ! A street General ! Never been in action ! Hasn't a friend ! Looks like a bear, because he always thinks of himself ! An insignificant figure ! Said to be a mathematician and a dreamer !' They enter, and Bonaparte keeps them waiting. At last he appears with his sword and belt on, explains the disposition of the forces, gives them his orders and dismisses them. Augereau is thunderstruck. Only when he gets out of doors does he recover himself and fall back on his accustomed oaths. He agrees with Massena that 'that little —— of a general frightened him.' He cannot comprehend the ascendency 'which over-awes him at the first glance.' "

One instance more will suffice. General Vandamme, an old revolutionary soldier, still more brutal and energetic than Augereau, said to Marshal D'Ornano, one day when they were ascending the staircase of the Tuileries together, "My dear fellow, that devil of a man" (speaking of the Emperor) "fascinates me in a way I cannot account for. I, who don't fear either God or the Devil, tremble like a child when I approach him. He would make me dash through the eye of a needle into the fire!"

XI.

HIS POWER OF WORK.

FROM almost the very first, Napoleon makes no secret of his final purposes. Let us study the causes which enabled him to so successfully use men and events to carry out these designs.

First among these are his extraordinary powers of work and of mastering and remembering all the details of every subject which can come under the notice of a commander or a ruler. When one reads the record of his gifts in this respect, one is for the moment tempted to forget all his crimes, and to feel that he honestly earned his success.

Take him, for instance, at the Council of State:

"Punctual at every sitting, prolonging the session four or six hours, discussing before and afterwards the subject brought forward . . . informing himself about bygone acts of jurisprudence, the laws of Louis XIV. and Frederick the Great. . . . Never did the Council adjourn without its members knowing more than they did the day before, if only through the researches he obliged them to make. Never did the members of the Senate and Corps Législatif, or of the tribunal, pay their respects to him without being rewarded for their homage by valuable instructions. He cannot be surrounded by public men without being the head of all, all forming for him a Council of State."

Here is another picture of him which tells the same tale:

"'What characterises him above them all,' is not alone the penetration and universality of his comprehension, but likewise and especially 'the force, flexibility, and constancy of his attention. He can work thirteen hours a day at a stretch, on one or on several subjects. I never saw him tired, I never found his mind lacking inspiration, even when weary in body, nor when violently exercised,

nor when angry. I never saw him diverted from
one matter by another, turning from that under
discussion to one he had just finished or was
about to take up. The news, good or bad, he
received from Egypt did not divert his mind from
the civil code, nor the civil code from the combinations which the safety of Egypt required.
Never did man more wholly devote himself to the
work in hand, nor better devote his time to what
he had to do ; never did mind more inflexibly set
aside the occupation or thought which did not
come at the right day or hour ; never was one
more ardent in seeking it, more alert in its pursuit,
more capable of fixing it when the time came
to take it up.' "

The best description, after all, of the working
of the mind is his own. "Various subjects," he
said, "and affairs are stowed away in my brains,
as in a chest of drawers. When I want to take up
any special business, I shut one drawer and open
another. None of them ever get mixed, and
never does this incommode me or fatigue me.
If I feel sleepy I shut the drawer and go to
sleep."

XII.

THE POWER OF TAKING PAINS.

THIS genius has not only the power of constant
work, but also of taking infinite pains. It will
be seen that nothing in which he succeeds is in

the least degree the result of accident.　Here is a description of himself which will bring this out :

"'I am always at work.　I meditate a great deal.　If I seem always equal to the occasion, ready to face what comes, it is because I have thought the matter over a long time before undertaking it.　I have anticipated whatever might happen.　It is no genius which suddenly reveals to me what I ought to do or say in any unlooked-for circumstance, but my own reflection, my own meditation. . . . I work all the time, at dinner, in the theatre.　I wake up at night in order to resume my work.　I got up last night at two o'clock.　I stretched myself on my couch before the fire to examine the army reports sent to me by the Minister of War ; I found twenty mistakes in them, and made notes which I have this morning sent to the Minister, who is now engaged with his clerks in rectifying them.'"

He wears out all his Ministers by this incessant power of work.　When Consul, "he sometimes presides at special meetings of the Section of the Interior from ten o'clock in the evening until five o'clock in the morning."　Often, at St. Cloud, he keeps the Councillors of State from nine o'clock in the morning until five in the evening, with fifteen minutes' intermission, and seems no more fatigued at the close of the sitting than when it began.

"During the night sessions 'many of the members succumb through lassitude, while the Minister of War falls asleep.' He gives them a shake and wakes them up. 'Come, come, citizens, let us bestir ourselves; it is only two o'clock, and we must earn the money the French people pay us.' Consul or Emperor, he demands of each Minister an account of the smallest details. It is not rare to see them leaving the council-room overcome with fatigue, due to the long interrogations to which he has subjected them ; he disdains to take any notice of this, and talks about the day's work simply as a relaxation which has scarcely exercised his mind."

XIII.

HIS MASTERY OF DETAIL.

ALL this work would be useless if it had not been backed by a mind which had an almost miraculous power both of absorbing and retaining facts and details.

" In each Ministerial department he knows more than the Ministers, and in each bureau he knows as much as the clerks. 'On his table lie reports of the positions of the forces on land and on water; he has furnished the plans of these, and fresh ones are issued every month.' Such is the daily reading he likes best. 'I have reports on positions always at hand: my memory for an

Alexandrine is not good, but I never forget a syllable of my reports on positions. I shall find them in my room this evening, and I shall not go to bed until I have read them.' "

And the result is that he knows all the positions on land and at sea—the number, size, and quality of his ships in or out of port, the composition and strength of his enemies' armies, every detail of every ship and of every regiment, better than the naval commanders or staff officers themselves. Added to this, he has a marvellous power of remembering topographical facts ; he can revive at will an inner picture of every detail at any distance of time. And this extraordinary result follows :

" His calculation of distance, marches, and manœuvres is so rigid a mathematical operation that, frequently, at a distance of two or four hundred leagues, his military foresight, calculated two or four months ahead, proves correct, almost on the day named, and precisely on the spot designated."

An even more remarkable example occurs when M. de Ségur sends in his report on the coast line. " I have read your reports," he says to M. de Ségur, "and they are exact. Nevertheless, you forgot two cannon at Ostend," and he pointed out the place, "on a road behind the town." " I went out," naturally exclaims M. de Ségur, "overwhelmed with astonishment that among thousands of cannon distributed among the mounted batteries or light artillery on the coast, two pieces should not have escaped his observation."

In March, 1800, he punctures a card with a pin, and tells Bourrienne, his secretary, four months before, the place he intends to beat Mélas at San Juliano. "Four months after this I found myself at San Juliano with his portfolio and despatches, and that very evening, at Torre-di-Gafolo, a league off, I wrote the bulletin of the battle under his dictation." Similarly in the campaign against Austria :—

"Order of marches, their duration, places of conveyance or meeting of the columns, attacks in full force, the various movements and mistakes of the enemy, all, in this rapid dictation, was foreseen two months beforehand and at a distance of 200 leagues. . . . The battlefields, the victories, and even the very days on which we were to enter Munich and Vienna were then announced, and written down as it all turned out. . . . Daru saw these oracles, fulfilled on the designated days up to our entry into Munich; if there were any differences of time and not of results between Munich and Vienna, they were all in our favour. . . . On returning from the camp at Bologna, Napoleon encounters a squad of soldiers who had got lost, asks what regiment they belong to, calculates the day they left, the road they took, what distance they should have marched, and then tells them : 'You will find your battalion at such a halting-place.'   At this time the army numbered 200,000 men."

.   And here is another passage, which also gives an idea of the immense and practical grasp of this intense mind :

" 'There is nothing relating to warfare that I cannot make myself. If nobody knows how to make gunpowder, I do. I can construct gun-carriages. If cannon must be cast, I will see that it is done properly. If tactical details must be taught, I will teach them.'   Hence his competency at the outset—general in the artillery, major-general, diplomatist, financier, and administrator, all at once and in every direction. Thanks to his fecund apprenticeship, beginning with the Consulate, he shows Cabinet clerks and veteran Ministers who send in their reports to him what to do. 'I am a better administrator than they are : when one has been obliged to rack his brains to find out how to feed, maintain, control, and animate with the same spirit and will two or three hundred thousand men, a long distance from their country, one soon gets at the secrets of administration.'   He takes in at a glance every part of the human machine. He fashions and manipulates each in its proper place and function ; the generators of power, the organs of its transmission, the extra working gear, the composite action, the speed which ensues, their final result, the complete effect, the net product; never is he content with a superficial inspection; he penetrates into obscure corners and to the lowest depths, 'through the technical precision of his questions,' with the lucidity of a specialist."

XIV.

HIS GRASP OF CHARACTER.

AN equally astonishing power of his is that of penetrating into the minds of men ; he is, Taine says, " as great a psychologist as he is an accomplished strategist." " In fact, no one has surpassed him in the art of defining the various states and impulses of one or of many minds, either prolonged or for the time being, which impel or restrain men in general, or this or that individual in particular ; what springs of action may be touched, and the kind and degree of pressure that may be applied to them. The central faculty rules all the others, and in the art of mastering man his genius is found supreme."

" Accordingly at the Council of State, while the others, either legislators or administrators, adduce abstractions, Articles of the Code, and precedents, he looks into natures as they are—the Frenchman's, the Italian's, the German's ; that of the peasant, the workman, the noble, the returned *émigré*, the soldier, the officer, and the functionary —everywhere at the individual man as he is, the man who ploughs, manufactures, fights, marries, generates, toils, enjoys himself, and dies."

Taine dwells on the wonderful power, which, too, Napoleon derives from his Italian blood, of describing his thoughts. "His words," says Taine, "caught on the wing, and at the moment," are "vibrating and teeming with illustration and imagery." Here is a sample: "Adultery is no phenomenon; it is common enough—*une affaire de canapé*. . . . There should be some curb on women who commit adultery for trinkets, sentiment, Apollo and the Muses, etc."

Here are several others:

"'You Frenchmen are not in earnest about anything, except, perhaps, equality; and even this you would gladly give up, if you were sure of yourself being the first. . . . The hope of advancement in this world should be cherished by everybody. . . . Keep your vanity always alive. The severity of the Republican Government would have worried you to death. What started the revolution? Vanity! What will end it? Vanity again. Liberty is merely a pretext. Liberty is the craving of a class small and privileged by nature, with faculties superior to the common run of men; this class may, therefore, be put under restraint with impunity; equality, on the contrary, catches the multitude.' 'What do I care for the opinions and cackle of the drawing-room; I never heed it. I pay attention only to what rude peasants say.'"

"His estimates," says Taine, "of certain situations are masterpieces of picturesque conciseness."

"'Why did I stop and sign the preliminaries of Leoben? Because I was playing *Vingt-et-un* and was satisfied with twenty.' His insight into character is that of the most sagacious critic. 'The "Mahomet" of Voltaire is neither a prophet nor an Arab, only an impostor graduated out of the École Polytechnique.' 'Madame de Genlis tries to define virtue as if she were the discoverer of it.' (Of Madame de Staël), 'This woman teaches people to think who never took to it or have forgotten how.' (Of Châteaubriand, one of whose relations had just been shot), 'He will write a few pathetic pages and read them aloud in the Faubourg Saint-Germain; pretty women will shed tears, and that will console him.' (Of the Abbé Delille), 'He is wit in its dotage.' (Of Pasquier and Molé), 'I make the most of one, and made the other.'"

It is partly this power of grasping the thoughts and intentions of others which helps to make him such a general. Again and again the point must be insisted upon—that his victories were not happy accidents, but the final link in a long chain of reflection, work, knowledge, and preparation. All this is summed up in a picturesque phrase by Napoleon himself:—

"'When I plan a battle,' said he to Roederer, 'no man is more pusillanimous than I am. I magnify to myself all the dangers and all the evils that are possible under the circumstances. I am in a state of agitation that is really painful. But this does not prevent me from appearing quite composed to people around me; I am like a woman giving birth to a child.'"

It is also a necessary part of this system that he should be always looking ahead, and this aspect of his character is also set forth with picturesqueness by himself:

"Passionately, in the throes of creation, he is thus absorbed with his coming greatness; he already anticipates and enjoys living in his imaginary edifice. 'General,' said Madame de Clermont-Tonnerre to him one day, 'you are building behind a scaffolding which you will take down when you have done with it.' 'Yes, madame, that's it,' replied Bonaparte; 'you are right, I'm always living two years in advance.' His response came with 'incredible vivacity,' as if it were the result of a sudden inspiration, that of a soul stirred in its innermost core."

XV.

WHAT HIS MEMORY HELD.

AND then Taine proceeds to give some notion of all that was contained in this single brain, and, powerful as the summing-up is, it will yet be seen that it necessarily falls short of all that Napoleon had to know and remember.

"He has mentally within him three principal atlases, always at hand, each composed of ' about twenty note-books,' each distinct, and each regularly posted up. The first one is military, forming a vast collection of topographical charts as minute as those of an *état-major*, with detailed plans of every stronghold, also specific indications of the local distribution of all forces on sea and on land—crews, regiments, batteries, arsenals, storehouses, present and future resources in supplies of men, horses, vehicles, arms, ammunition, food, and clothing. The second, which is civil, resembles the heavy, thick volumes published every year, in which we now read the state of the Budget, and comprehend, first, the innumerable items of ordinary and extra-ordinary receipt and expenditure, internal taxes, foreign contributions, the products of the domains in France and out of France, the fiscal services, pensions, public works, and the rest ; next, all administrative statistics, the hierarchy of functions and of function-aries, Senators, Deputies, Ministers, Prefects, Bishops, Professors, Judges, and those under their orders, where each of these resides, with his rank, juris-diction, and salary. The third is a vast biographical and moral dictionary, in which, as in the pigeon-holes of the *Chef de Police*, each notable personage and local group, each professional or social body, and even each population, had a label, along with a brief note on its situation and antecedents, and therefore its demonstrated character, eventual disposition, and probable conduct. Each label, or strip of paper, holds a summing-up; all these partial summaries, methodically classified, terminate in totals, and the totals of the three atlases combined together thus furnish their possessor with an estimate of his disposable forces. Now, in 1809, however full these atlases, they are clearly imprinted on Napoleon's mind; he knows not only the total and the partial summaries, but also the slightest details; he reads them readily and at every hour; he comprehends in a mass, and in all pàrticulars, the various nations he governs directly or through some one else; that is to say, sixty million men, the different countries he has conquered or overrun, consisting of seventy thousand square miles; at first France increased by the addition of Belgium and Piedmont; next Spain, from which he is just returned, and where he has placed his brother Joseph; Southern Italy, where, after Joseph, he has placed Murat; Central Italy, where he occupies Rome; Northern Italy, where Eugène is his delegate; Dalmatia and Istria, which he has joined to his empire; Austria, which he invades for the second time; the Confederation of the Rhine, which he has made and which he directs; Westphalia and Holland, where his brothers are only his lieutenants; Prussia, which he has subdued and mutilated, and which he oppresses, and the strongholds of which he still retains. Add to this a last mental tableau, representing the Northern Seas, the Atlantic, and the Mediterranean, all the fleets of the Continent, at sea and in port, from Dantzic to Flessingen and Bayonne, from Cadiz to Toulon and Gaëta, from Tarentum to Venice, Corfu, and Constantinople."

And, finally, there is this fact to be considered: that all this did not only extend over a small portion of his lifetime. General Grant worked prodigiously, and had an extraordinarily close and intimate knowledge of all the details of his army; but then the Civil War of America lasted for but four years. But think of the duration of Napoleon's career—think how many there were of those days and nights packed full of feverish, incessant, wild work.

"The quantity of facts he is able to retain and store away, the quantity of ideas he elaborates and produces, seems to surpass human capacity, and this insatiable, inexhaustible, immoveable brain thus keeps on working uninterruptedly for thirty years."

XVI.

HIS IMAGINATIVENESS.

Now I take him on another side of his character—the side which ultimately led to his ruin — that is, his imaginativeness. He has accomplished a tremendous amount; he has undertaken even more; but "whatever he may have undertaken is far surpassed by what he has imagined." For, great as was his practical power, "his poetical faculty is stronger." This poetical faculty it is which ultimately saved his enemies, for "it is too vigorous for a statesman"; "its grandeur is exaggerated into enormity, and its enormity degenerates into madness." And then Taine reproduces some of his wild dreamings, to which he gave vent when the moment of expansion was on him, and his brilliant Italian vocabulary was at the service of his excited imagination; as, for instance—he is talking to Bourrienne:

"' Europe is a molehill; never have there been great empires and great revolutions except in the Orient with its 600,000,000 of men.' The following year, at St. Jean d'Acre, on the eve of the last assault, he added: 'If I succeed, I shall find in the town the pacha's treasure and arms for 300,000 men. I stir up, and arm all Syria. . . . I march on to Damascus and Aleppo; as I advance in the country my army will be increased by the discontented. I proclaim to the people the abolition of slavery, and of the tyrannical government of the pachas. I reach Constantinople with armed masses. I overthrow the Turkish empire; I found in the East a new and grand empire, which fixes my place with posterity, and perhaps I return to Paris by the way of Adrianople, or by Vienna, after having annihilated the House of Austria.' "

XVII.

DREAMS OF A NEW RELIGION.

ALL this is before he has become Consul and Emperor; but even after he had reached the pinnacle of power the dream recurs again and again. "Since two hundred years," he said at Mayence, in 1804, "there is nothing more to do in Europe; it is only in the East that things can be carried out on a grand scale." And then, giving way to that extraordinary imagination of his, he says:

"'I created a religion; I saw myself on the road to Asia mounted on an elephant, with a turban on my head, and in my hand a new Koran, which I composed to suit myself.' "

This idea of founding a religion, and so exercising the same tyrannous influence on the future generations of men, as that which he exercised over his own generation, is a dream that constantly haunts him. Paris is to be the centre of the world. "I mean that every king shall build a grand palace in Paris for his own use. On the coronation of the Emperor of the French these kings will come and occupy it; they will grace this imposing ceremony with their presence, and honour it with their salutations." This is grandiose enough, but it is not all; the future of the soul still remains; and as he cannot make a new Eastern Empire and a new Koran, he must get at Europe through the Pope. The Pope must give up Rome and come to live in Paris permanently. And then the Pope will rule the conscience of the world, and Napoleon will rule the Pope. "Paris would become the capital of the Christian world, and I would have governed the religious world as well as the political world."

I put down all this not merely to the insatiable love of power, but to profound, unfathomable contempt for mankind, which made it delightful to the imagination of Napoleon to think of their grovelling in their folly before him long after he had gone. Here is a further example of this spirit:

"'I come too late; there is no longer anything great to accomplish. I admit that my career is brilliant, and that I have made my way successfully. But what a difference to the conquerors of antiquity! Take Alexander! After having conquered Asia, and proclaimed himself to the people son of Jupiter, with the exception of Olympias, who knew what all this meant, and Aristotle, and a few Athenian pedants, the entire Orient believed him. Very well; should I now declare that I was the son of God Almighty, and proclaim that I am going to worship Him under this title, there is not an old beldame that would not hoot at me as I walked along the streets. People nowadays know too much.   Nothing is left to do.'"

And this imagination and poetic power are to be found in his private as well as his public concerns. For instance, he is superstitious: "He was disposed to accept the marvellous, presentiments, and even certain mysterious communications between human beings."

"I have seen him," writes Madame de Rémusat, "excited by the rustling of the wind, speak enthusiastically of the roar of the sea, and sometimes inclined to believe in nocturnal apparitions; in short, leaning to certain superstitions."

"Méneval notes his crossing himself involuntarily on the occasion of some great danger or the discovery of some important fact. 'During the Consulate, in the evening, in a circle of ladies, he sometimes improvised and declaimed tragic tales, Italian fashion, quite worthy of the story-tellers of the fifteenth and sixteenth centuries. . . . As to love, his letters to Josephine during the Italian campaign form some of the best examples of Italian passion, and are in most piquant contrast with the temperate and graceful elegance of his predecessor, M. de Beauharnais.'"

XVIII.

HIS COURT.

I TURN now to another and a different side of his character. It is part of his intense love of power that everybody about him must be perfectly dependent on him. "He considered himself," said an Italian diplomatist who had studied him for many years, "an isolated being in the world, made to govern and direct all minds as he pleased." By-and-by, I shall describe how he carried out this in the case of men; for the moment, I shall deal with the exercise of this passion in reference to women.

There had been despots in France before Napoleon; for instance, the sway of Louis XIV. was absolute; but then in him, as in most monarchs, there were two sides. As monarch and man of business, he was one thing; but when he was engaged in social duties, he was head of his house; "he welcomed visitors, entertained his guests, and that his guests should not be automatons, he tried to put them at their ease." He did not, above all things, "persistently, and from morning to night, maintain a despotic attitude;" quite the reverse:

"Polite to everybody, always affable with men and sometimes gracious, always courteous with women, and sometimes gallant, carefully avoiding brusqueness, ostentation, and sarcasm, never allowing himself to use an offensive word, never making people feel their inferiority and dependence, but, on the contrary, encouraging them to express opinions, and even to converse, tolerating in conversation a semblance of equality, smiling at a repartee, playfully telling a story—such were his ways in the drawing-room. . . . Owing to education and tradition he had consideration for others, at least for the people around him, his courtiers being his guests without ceasing to be his subjects."

But Napoleon will have none of this. He borrows from the old Court "its rigid discipline, and its pompous parade;" but that is all.

"'The ceremonial system,' says an eye-witness, 'was carried out as if it had been regulated by tap of drum. Everything was done, in a certain sense, in double-quick time.'

". . . This air of precipitation, this instant anxiety which it inspires, puts an end to all comfort, all ease, all entertainment, all agreeable intercourse. There is no common bond but that of command and obedience.

"'The few individuals he singles out—Savary, Duroc, Maret—keep silent and transmit orders.'"

And then comes this truly odious picture of Napoleon's Court:

"'Through calculation as well as from taste he never relaxes his state'; hence 'a mute, frigid Court . . . more dismal than dignified; every countenance wearing an expression of uneasiness . . . a silence both dull and constrained.' At Fontainebleau, 'amidst splendours and pleasures,' there is no real enjoyment or satisfaction, not even to himself. 'I pity you,' said M. de Talleyrand to M. de Rémusat; 'you have to amuse the unamuseable.' At the theatre he is abstracted or yawns. Applause is interdicted; the Court, sitting out 'the file of eternal tragedies, is mortally bored . . . the young ladies fall asleep, people leave the theatre gloomy and discontented.' There is the same constraint in the drawing-room. 'He did not know how to appear at ease, and I believe he never wanted anybody else to be so. He was afraid of the slightest approach to familiarity, and inspired every one with the fear of saying something offensive of his neighbour before witnesses. . . . During the quadrille he moves around amongst the row of ladies, addressing them with trifling or disagreeable remarks,' and never does he accost them otherwise than 'awkwardly and as if ill at ease.' At bottom he distrusts, and is ill-disposed towards them. It is because 'the power they have acquired in society seems to him an intolerable usurpation.'"

And if any picture could be more odious than this, here is another more odious still:

"Never did he utter to a woman a graceful or even a well-turned compliment, although the effort to do so was often apparent in his face and in the tone of his voice. . . . He talks to them only of their toilet, of which he declares himself a severe and minute judge, and on which he indulges in not very delicate jests; or, again, on the number of their children, enquiring of them, in rude language, whether they nurse them themselves; or, again, lecturing them on their social relations. Hence there is not one who does not rejoice when he moves away. He often amuses himself by putting them out of countenance, scandalising and bantering them to their faces, driving them into a corner, just as a colonel worries his canteen woman. ' Yes, ladies, you furnish the good people of the Faubourg Saint-Germain with something to talk about. It is said, Madame A., that you are intimate with Monsieur B., and you, Madame C., with Monsieur D.' On any intrigue chancing to appear in the police reports, ' he loses no time in informing the husband of what is going on.' He is no less indiscreet in relation to his own freaks; when the affair is over he divulges the fact and gives the name; furthermore, he informs Josephine of its details, and will not listen to any reproach. ' I have a right to answer all your objections with an eternal "Moi!" ' he says."

XIX.

HIS RUDENESS.

NAPOLEON'S awkwardness with women was the theme of everybody who knew him intimately, and observed him closely. One of these says:

"It would be difficult to imagine any one more awkward than Napoleon in a drawing-room. . . . 'I never heard a harsher voice, or one so inflexible. When he smiled it was only with the mouth and a portion of the cheeks; the brow and eyes remained immovably sombre. . . . This combination of gaiety and seriousness, had something in it terrible and frightful.' On one occasion, at St. Cloud, Varnhagen heard him exclaim over and over again twenty times before a group of ladies, 'How hot!'"

This awkwardness of men of action when with women is not at all uncommon. There are examples even in our own day. "Small talk" is really a difficulty with men whose whole being is intent on great enterprises and on the ruling of men. Napoleon, living always two years ahead of himself—with all these images and recollections of terrible battle-fields, great combinations, world-wide empire—found it impossible to attune his mind to the trifles of the hour.

His restless, vivid, and realistic mind seems, indeed, always under an unpleasant restraint in

civilian surroundings. A good deal of this is
doubtless due to the fact that all his training
had been in the guard-room and at mess, and
many of his acts and expressions have the fine,
full-flavoured tone of the soldier. Hence his
dislike to all the conventions of society. Says
Taine:

"It is because good taste is the highest attain-
ment of civilisation, the innermost vestment which
drapes human nudity, which best fits the person,
the last garment retained after the others have
been cast off, and whose delicate tissue continues
to hamper Napoleon: he throws it off instinctively,
because it interferes with his natural utterance,
with the uncurbed, dominating, savage ways of the
conqueror who knocks down his adversary and
treats him as he pleases."

Napoleon himself was not slow to avow with
characteristic frankness his feelings on the subject.

"'I stand apart from other men. I accept
nobody's conditions, nor any species of obligation,
no code whatever, not even the common code of
outward civility, which, diminishing or dissimu-
lating brutality, allows men to associate together
without clashing.' He does not comprehend it,
and he repudiates it. 'I have little liking,' he says,
'for that vague, levelling word politeness, which
you people fling out whenever you have a chance.
It is an invention of fools who want to surpass
clever men; a kind of social muzzle which annoys

the strong and is useful only to the mediocre. . .
Ah, good taste! Another classic expression which
I do not accept.' 'It is your personal enemy,'
says Talleyrand to him one day; 'if you could
have shot it away with bullets, it would have
disappeared long ago.'"

XX.

HIS AGGRESSIVENESS.

His hatred for all the conventions of society
comes out in his intercourse with other nations
and other monarchs. His diplomacy was as
different from that of all other times and men
as anything else. His everlasting desire to command is unchecked for a moment by good feeling,
good taste, any of the finer sensibilities which
influence the ordinary man.

"His attitude, even at pacific interviews,
remains aggressive, and militant; purposely or
involuntarily he raises his hand, and the blow is
felt to be coming, while, in the meantime, he
insults. In his correspondence with Sovereigns,
or in his official proclamations, in his deliberations
with Ambassadors, and even at public audiences,
he provokes, threatens, and defies; he treats his
adversary with a lofty air, insults him often to his
face, and loads him with the most disgraceful
imputations; he divulges the secrets of his life in
private, of his study, and of his bed; he defames

or calumniates his Minister, his Court, and his wife; he purposely stabs people in the most sensitive part; he tells one that he is a dupe, a betrayed husband; another that he is an abettor of assassination; he assumes the air of a judge condemning a criminal, or the tone of a superior reprimanding an inferior, or, at best, that of a teacher taking a scholar to task."

Instance after instance can be given of this, as for instance :

"After the battle of Jena, 9th, 17th, 18th, and 19th, there is, in the bulletins, comparison of the Queen of Prussia with Lady Hamilton, open and repeated insinuations, imputing to her an intrigue with the Emperor Alexander. 'Everybody admits that the Queen of Prussia is the author of the evils that the Prussian nation suffers. This is heard everywhere. How changed she is since that fatal interview with the Emperor Alexander. . . . The portrait of the Emperor Alexander, presented to her by the Prince, was found in the apartment of the Queen at Potsdam.'"

XXI.

HIS TREATMENT OF HIS MINISTERS.

IN Taine's picture, Napoleon is so overbearing towards his Ministers, that it seems incredible that he could have got any man to serve him—except that the love of power and office, as well as of money, will always give to rulers plenty of tools to assume and even to love the badge of servitude.

In his dealings with his Ministers, Napoleon proceeds on a plan—a plan which was impossible to any one except a man of hard and un-generous nature. "His leading general principle," says Taine, "which he applies in every way, in great things as in small ones, is that a man's zeal depends on his anxiety."

"For a machine to work well, it is important that the machinist should overhaul it frequently, which this one never fails to do, especially after a long absence. Whilst he is on his way from Tilsit 'everybody anxiously examines his con-science to ascertain what he has done that this rigid master will find fault with on his return. Whether spouse, family, or grand dignitary, each is more or less disturbed; while the Empress, who knows him better than any one, naïvely says, "As the Emperor has had such success, he will certainly do a good deal of scolding!"' . . . In fact, he has scarcely arrived when he gives a rude and vigorous turn of the screw, and then, 'satisfied at having excited terror all round, he appears to have forgotten what has passed, and resumes the usual tenor of his life.'"

The experience of M. de Rémusat, Prefect of

the Palace, and one of his most devoted servants,
is the same.

"When the Prefect has arranged 'one of those
magnificent fêtes in which all the arts minister
to his enjoyment,' economically, correctly, with
splendour and success, Madame never asks her
husband if the Emperor is satisfied, but whether
he has scolded more or less."

XXII.

THE DEPENDENCE OF THE MARSHALS.

As Napoleon trusts to no principle in his
Ministers but fear and self-interest, he takes
elaborate precautions against their ever becoming
independent of him. In this respect he shows a
delight in the degradation of human nature
that sometimes almost appals one — it is as
though the hideous sneer of Mephistopheles
were transferred from the pages of the poet to
the more moving drama of human life. Take,
for instance, Napoleon's treatment of his Marshals. He claimed to "be sole master, making
or marring reputations" according to his personal
requirements.

"Too brilliant a soldier would become too
important; a subordinate would never be tempted
to be less submissive. To this end he plans
what he will omit in his bulletins, what alterations
and what changes shall be made in them. It

is convenient to keep silent about certain victories, or to convert the defeat of this or that Marshal into a success. Sometimes a General learns from a bulletin of an action that he was never in, and of a speech that he never made."

When the General complains, he is given the right to get rich by pillage, or has a title bestowed upon him. But even yet he does not feel the grasp of the iron hand of Napoleon removed.

"On becoming Duke or Hereditary Prince, with half a million or a million of revenue from his estate, he is not less held in subjection, for the creator has taken precautions against his own creatures. 'Some people there,' said he, ' I have made independent, but I know when to lay my hand upon them and keep them from being ungrateful.' In truth, if he has endowed them magnificently, it is with domains assigned to them in conquered countries, which ensures their fortune being his fortune. Besides, in order that they may not enjoy any pecuniary stability, he expressly encourages them and all his grand dignitaries to make extravagant outlays; thus, through their financial embarrassments, he holds them in a leash. 'We have seen most of his Marshals, constantly pressed by their creditors, come to him for assistance which he gives as he pleases, or when he finds it for his interest to attach some one to himself.'"

There is an even deeper depth than this :—

"'He carefully cultivates all the bad passions . . . he is glad to find the bad side in a man, so as to get him in his power.' The thirst for money in Savary, the Jacobin defects in Fouché, the vanity and sensuality of Cambacérès, the careless cynicism and 'the easy immorality' of Talleyrand, the 'dry bluntness of Duroc,' the 'courtier-like insipidity of Maret,' 'the silliness' of Berthier; he brings this out, diverts himself with it, and profits by it. 'Where he sees no vice he encourages weaknesses, and in default of anything better, he provokes fear, so that he may be ever and continually the strongest. . . . He dreads ties of affection, and strives to alienate people from each other. . . . He sells his favours by arousing anxiety, and he thinks the best way to attach individuals to him is to compromise them, and often, even, to ruin them in public opinion.' 'If Caulaincourt is compromised,' said he, after the murder of the Duc d'Enghien, 'it is no great matter; he will serve me all the better.'"

XXIII.

HIS HATRED OF INDEPENDENCE.

IT is a necessary part of this horrible system that all Napoleon's Ministers must surrender all their independence of judgment; their one law must be his will and his interest.

"If his scruples arrest him, if he alleges

personal obligations, if he had rather not fail in delicacy, or even in common loyalty, he incurs the risk of offending or losing the favour of the master, which is the case with M. de Rémusat, who is willing to become his spy, reporter, and denunciator for the Faubourg Saint-Germain, but does not offer at Vienna to drag from Madame d'André the address of her husband, so that M. d'André may be taken and immediately shot. Savary, who was the negotiator for his being given up, kept constantly telling M. de Rémusat, 'You are going against your interest; I may say that I do not comprehend you!'"

This Savary was one of the most contemptible and villainous of Napoleon's agents. Napoleon himself said of him: "He is a man who must be constantly corrupted."

"And yet Savary, himself Minister of the Police, executor of most important arrests, head manager of the murder of the Duc d'Enghien, and of the ambuscade at Bayonne, counterfeiter of Austrian banknotes for the campaign of 1809, and of Russian banknotes for that of 1812, Savary ends in getting weary; he is charged with too many dirty jobs; however hardened his conscience, it has a tender spot; he discovers at last that he has scruples. It is with great repugnance that, in February 1814, he executes the order to have a small infernal machine prepared, moving by clockwork, so as to blow up the Bourbons on their return to France.

'Ah,' he said, giving himself a blow on the forehead, 'it must be admitted that the Emperor is sometimes hard to serve.' "

And the final result is that Napoleon drives from his Court and his Cabinet every man of sense and honour. " Independence of any kind, even eventual and merely possible, puts him out of humour; intellectual or moral superiority is of this order, and he gradually gets rid of it."

" Towards the last he no longer tolerates alongside of him any but subject or captive spirits; his principal servants are machines or fanatics— a devout worshipper like Maret, a gendarme like Savary, ready to do his bidding. From the outset he has reduced his Ministers to the condition of clerks, for he is administrator as well as ruler, and in each department he watches details as closely as the entire mass; accordingly he requires simply for head men active scribes, mute executioners, docile and special hands, no honest and free advisers. 'I should not know what to do with them,' he said, 'if they were not to a certain extent mediocre in mind and character.'"

And the result is the deadening in him of all real human feeling.

" Therefore, outside of explosions of nervous sensibility, 'he has no consideration for men— other than that of a foreman for his workmen,' or, more precisely, for his tools; once the tool is worn out, little does he care whether it rusts

away in a corner or is cast aside on a heap of
scrap iron. Portalis, Minister of Justice, enters
his room one day with a downcast look, and
his eyes filled with tears. 'What is the matter
with you, Portalis?' inquired Napoleon. 'Are
you ill?' 'No, sire, but very wretched. The
poor Archbishop of Tours, my old schoolmate——'
'Eh, well, what has happened to him?' 'Alas,
sire, he has just died.' 'What do I care? He
was no longer good for anything.'"

XXIV.

HIS ESTIMATE OF HUMANITY.

SURROUNDED by such creatures, it is not un-
natural that the original and instinctive cynicism
of Napoleon's nature should be aggravated. In
the end, all faith in anything but the base and
the selfish in human nature disappeared. His
scepticism was not affected as it often is—it was
genuine conviction. Nay more, it was almost a
fanatical faith—a faith that was one of the chief
causes which led to his final destruction. Everybody who knew him agrees in describing this
disbelief in anything but the base in man as a
fixed idea.

"'His opinions on men,' writes M. de Metternich, 'centred on one idea, which, unfortunately,
with him had acquired in his mind the force of an
axiom; he was persuaded that no man who was

induced to appear on the public stage, or who was merely engaged in the active pursuits of life, governed himself or was governed otherwise than by his interests.' According to him, man is held through his egoistic passions, fear, cupidity, sensuality, self-esteem, and emulation; these are the mainsprings when he is not under excitement, when he reasons. Moreover, it is not difficult to turn the brain of man; for he is imaginative, credulous, and subject to being carried away; stimulate his pride or his vanity, provide him with an extreme and false opinion of himself and his fellow-men, and you can start him off, head downwards, wherever you please."

This theory of Napoleon sometimes finds difficulties in its way. There, for instance, are Lafayette and others, who have given proof of disinterestedness, loyalty, and zeal for the public good. But Napoleon is neither dismayed nor converted; whenever he meets such a man he tells him to his face that he regards him either as a conscious or a self-deceived impostor.

"'General Dumas,' says he abruptly to Mathieu Dumas, 'you were one of the imbeciles who believed in liberty?' 'Yes, sire, I was, and am still one of that class.' 'And you, like the rest, took part in the Revolution through ambition?' 'No, sire; I should have calculated badly, for I am now precisely where I stood in 1790.' 'You are not sufficiently aware of the motives which prompted you; you cannot be different from other people; it is all personal interest. Now, take Massena. He has glory and honours enough; but he is not content. He wants to be a prince like Murat or Bernadotte. He would risk being shot to-morrow to be a prince. That is the incentive of Frenchmen.' 'I never heard him,' said Madame de Rémusat, 'express any admiration or comprehension of a noble action.' 'His means,' says the same writer, 'for governing men were all derived from those which tend to debase them. . . . He tolerated virtue only when he could cover it with ridicule.'"

His disbelief in anything but the base was, as I have said, one of the causes of his downfall, for it led to some of his grossest miscalculations; or, as Taine well puts it:—

"Such is the final conception on which Napoleon has anchored himself, and into which he sinks deeper and deeper, no matter how directly and violently he may be contradicted by palpable facts; nothing will dislodge him, neither the stubborn energy of the English, nor the inflexible gentleness of the Pope, nor the declared insurrection of the Spaniards, nor the mute insurrection of the Germans, nor the resistance of Catholic consciences, nor the gradual disaffection of the French. The reason is, that his conception is imposed upon him by his character; he sees man as he needs to see him."

XXV.

HIS JUDGMENTS ON HIMSELF.

HIS miscalculation arises from another cause—the excessive imagination, which so often led astray that cold, calculating, splendid mind. "The Emperor," said M. de Pradt, that keen observer of him, whom I have often quoted already, "is all system, all illusion, as one cannot fail to be when one is all imagination. Whoever has watched his course has noticed his creating for himself an imaginary Spain, an imaginary Catholicism, an imaginary England, an imaginary financial state, an imaginary *noblesse*, and still more, an imaginary France."

A curious thing about him is that occasionally he has glimpses of his own faults and of the verdict which will be passed upon him. Take, for instance, his judgment upon his treatment of his subordinates :

"He was heard to say, ' The lucky man is he who hides away from me in the depths of some province.' And another day, having asked M. de Ségur what people would say of him after his death, the latter enlarged on the regrets which would be universally expressed. 'Not at all,' replied the Emperor ; and then drawing in his breath in a significant manner indicative of universal relief, he replied : ' They'll say, *Ouf !* ' "

And here is another self-condemnation :

"On reaching the Isle of Poplars, the First Consul stopped at Rousseau's grave and said : ' It would have been better for the repose of France if that man had never existed !' 'And why, citizen Consul ?' 'He is the man who made the French Revolution.' 'It seems to me that you need not complain of the French Revolution.' 'Well, the future must decide whether it would not have been better for the repose of the whole world if neither myself nor Rousseau had ever lived.' He then resumed his promenade in a reverie."

And from the outset of his career, he boldly proclaims his selfish purposes.

"' Do you suppose,' says he to them, after the preliminaries of Leoben, 'that it is to aggrandise Directory lawyers, such as the Carnots, and the Barras, that I triumph in Italy? Do you suppose, also, that it is for the establishment of a republic? What an idea! A republic of thirty million men! With our customs, our vices, how is that possible? It is a delusion with which the French are infatuated, and which will vanish along with so many others. What they want is glory, the gratification of vanity — they know nothing about liberty. Look at the army! Our successes just obtained, our triumphs have already brought out the true character of the French soldier. I am all for him. Let the Directory deprive me of the cockade and

it will see who is master.   The nation needs a
chief, one who is famous through his exploits,
and not theories of Government, phrases, and
speeches by ideologists, which Frenchmen do not
comprehend.' "

And when he is recommended to make peace
and end the war in Italy, he says :

" ' It is not for my interest to make peace.
You see what I am, what I can do in Italy.
If peace is brought about, if I am no longer at
the head of the army which has become attached
to me, I must give up this power, this high
position I have reached, and go and pay court to
lawyers in the Luxembourg.   I should not like to
quit Italy for France except to play a part
there similar to that which I play here, and the
time for that has not yet come—the pear is not
ripe.' "

XXVI.

THE CAUSES OF HIS FALL.

FINALLY, his desire to rule the whole world brings
Napoleon to his fall.   He has been such a scourge
to humanity that humanity rises up in revolt
against him.   He has taken Spanish, Italian,
Austrian, Prussian, Swiss, Bavarian, Saxon, Dutch,
as well as French lives; the nations hate him as
much as their monarchs.

" Unquestionably with such a character nobody
can live ; his genius is too vast, too mischievous, and

all the more so because it is so vast. War will last as long as he reigns; it is in vain to reduce him, to confine him at home, to drive him back within the ancient frontier of France; no barrier will restrain him, no treaty will bind him; peace with him will never be other than a truce, he will use it simply to recover himself, and, as soon as he has done this, he will begin again; he is in his very essence anti-social. The mind of Europe in this respect is made up definitely and unshakeably. One petty detail alone shows how unanimous and profound this conviction is. On March 7th, the news reached Vienna that he has escaped from the Island of Elba without its being yet known where he would land. M. de Metternich, before eight o'clock in the morning, brings the news to the Emperor of Austria, who says to him, 'Lose no time in finding the King of Prussia and the Emperor of Russia, and tell them that I am ready to order my army to march at once on France.' At a quarter-past eight M. de Metternich is with the Czar, and at half-past eight with the King of Prussia; both of them reply instantly in the same manner. 'At nine o'clock,' says M. de Metternich, 'I was back. At ten o'clock aides flew in every direction countermanding army orders. . . . Thus was war declared in less than an hour.'"

XXVII.

THE INSTABILITY OF HIS RULE.

AND not only is Europe united against him, but his own country at last ceases to have any faith in him. Those who are immediately around him are soonest convinced that his day must come to an end, and that with such a despotism as his, abyssmal ruin is the foredoomed and inevitable result. It shows a strange lack somewhere in Napoleon's character and mind that he was always blind to consequences, which the commonest and the dullest man around him could see. I suppose that this is one of the penalties which men of inflexible and resistless wills have to pay for their great powers—the same fearlessness, the same tenacity, the same determination to succeed which make them, are also the very qualities which finally mar them. We have seen in Irish political history a remarkable and tragic example, in our own time, of how the same great qualities, which commanded success against gigantic odds, brought failure when the power to calculate the odds had been submerged by the inflexible will, imperious temper, and deadly and unyielding tenacity of purpose.

All those near Napoleon or at the centre of affairs, like Metternich, saw, as I have just said, that the fabric raised by him had not a single element of durability.

"M. de Metternich," says Taine, "by way of a political summing up, expresses the following general opinion: 'It is remarkable that Napoleon, who is constantly disturbing and modifying the relations of all Europe, has not yet taken a single step towards ensuring the maintenance of his successors.'"

As time went on this opinion of Metternich is confirmed, and gradually it spreads to Napoleon's *entourage*.

The diplomat adds, in 1809: "His death will be the signal for a new and frightful upheaval; so many divided elements all tend to combine. Deposed sovereigns will be recalled by whilom subjects; new princes will have new crowns to defend. A veritable civil war will rage for half a century over the vast Empire of the Continent of Europe."

In 1811, "Everybody is convinced that on the disappearance of Napoleon, the master in whose hands all power is concentrated, the first inevitable consequence will be a revolution." At home in France, at this same date, his own subjects begin to comprehend that his dominion is merely temporary, that the Empire is ephemeral and will not last during his life; for he is constantly raising his edifice higher and higher, while all that his building gains in elevation it loses in stability. 'The Emperor is crazy,' said Decrès to Marmont, 'com-

pletely crazy.　He will ruin us all, numerous
as we are, and all will end in some frightful
catastrophe.'"

And the curious fact is that even Napoleon
himself takes, "in lucid moments," as Taine
put it, "the same view."

"'It will last as long as I do.　After me,
however, my son may deem himself fortunate if
he has 40,000f. a year.'　How often at this time
(1811) was he heard to foretell that the weight
of his Empire would crush his heir.　'Poor child,'
said he, looking at the King of Rome, 'what an
entanglement I shall leave you.'"

XXVIII.

HIS OBSTINATE EGOTISM.

BUT it was only in lucid moments that Napoleon
was able to see this clearly; as a rule he was
the slave of his imagination; and no disaster,
no combination of Kings, no superiority of
forces, could abate his self-confidence or curtail
his schemes.　Almost to the last he persisted
in believing that everything would end as he
desired.

And, in the meantime, how is it with France?
At last, even the inexhaustible courage and patience
of the people are coming to an end.　But Napoleon
persists.　The more the people groan, the more

of them are killed, the heavier becomes his hand, the greater the exactions, the more unsparing the conscription. Between January and October in the year 1813, 800,000 men had been raised. Other levies followed, and altogether 1,300,000 men were summoned in one year. "Never," says a writer of the time, "has any nation been thus asked to let itself be voluntarily led to the slaughter-house." Young men were torn from their wives the day after marriage, from the bedside of a wife in her confinement, from a dying father or sick child. "Some looked so feeble that they seemed dying;" and one-half of them died in the campaign of 1814. Self-mutilation became common; desertion still commoner. It had taken a long time; but Napoleon had at length exhausted France.

But Napoleon held out still; uncowed, unmoved by these awful catastrophes.

"'What do they want of me?' said he to M. de Metternich. 'Do they want me to dishonour myself? Never! I can die, but never will yield an inch of territory! Your sovereigns born on the throne may be beaten twenty times over and yet return to their capitals. I cannot do this, because I am a *parvenu* soldier. My dominion will not survive the day when I shall have ceased to be strong and, consequently, feared.' In fact, his despotism in France is founded on his European omnipotence; if he does not remain master of the continent, 'he must settle with the *corps législatif.'* . . .

"'I have seen your soldiers,' says Metternich to him, 'they are children. When this army of boys is gone, what will you do then?' At these words, which touch his heart, he grows pale, his features contract, and his rage overcomes him. Like a wounded man who has made a false step and exposes himself, he says violently to Metternich: 'You are not a soldier! You do not know the impulses of a soldier's breast! I have grown up on a battle-field, and a man like me does not care a —— for the lives of a million men.'"

Nor did he, for here is the final record of his rule of France:

"Between 1804 and 1815 he has had slaughtered 1,700,000 Frenchmen, born within the boundaries of ancient France, to which must be added, probably, 2,000,000 of men born outside these limits, and slain for him under the title of allies, or slain by him under the title of enemies. All that the poor enthusiastic and credulous Gauls have gained by entrusting their public welfare to him is two invasions; all that he bequeaths to them as a reward for their devotion, after this prodigious waste of their blood and the blood of others, is a France shorn of fifteen departments acquired by the Republic, deprived of Saxony, of the left bank of the Rhine, and of Belgium, despoiled of the north-east angle by which it

completed its boundaries, fortified its most
vulnerable point, and, to use the words of
Vauban, 'made its field square,' separated from
4,000,000 of new Frenchmen which it had
assimilated after twenty years of life in common,
and, worse still, thrown back within the frontiers
of 1789, alone, diminished in the midst of its
aggrandized neighbours, suspected by all Europe,
and lastingly surrounded by a threatening circle
of distrust and rancour."

CHAPTER II.

THE ESTIMATE OF A WORSHIPPER.*

I HAVE not paused in my quotations from Taine to point out where I think the author has been unjust to Napoleon. As I have indicated, that would be contrary to the *rôle* I have given myself of interpreter rather than critic. Besides, I am about to give a picture of Napoleon drawn by a worshipper in immediate succession to this tremendous indictment by an enemy; and the unbridled eulogy will be the best antidote to the unsparing attack.

I.

MÉNEVAL.

ANYBODY acquainted with Napoleonic literature will know that Madame de Rémusat's Memoirs form the groundwork of Taine's picture; and especially in those portions which describe life at Napoleon's Court.

* Memoirs to serve for the history of Napoleon I. from 1802-1815. By B. de Méneval. Translated by N. H. Sherard. (London : Hutchinson.)

I heard a clever Frenchman once, when discussing the famous Memoirs of Madame de Rémusat, quote what I thought an excellent comment upon them. The Memoirs, said the commentator, were clever, but they were the Memoirs which might have been written by a *femme de chambre*, " and I do not love domestics," added this critic, " who speak badly of their masters." M. de Méneval was a servant of Napoleon, but he does not speak badly of his master. I cannot read these Memoirs—indiscriminate in their praise, partial, uncritical, not very luminous—I cannot read them without feeling that Méneval was a downright good fellow. To Méneval Napoleon is always the hero; always right, always high-minded, always unselfish, always wronged. I need scarcely say that this is not the view of Napoleon's character which even the most benevolent student of his career can adopt; but do you suppose I am going to find fault with our good Méneval for this? There are some people who forgive anything to intellect; my tendency is to forgive anything to heart. I have always regarded a good disposition as much more attractive than a good brain. And, then, I like people who have the talent of admiration. Carlyle exploded the doctrine that nobody is a hero to his own valet, with the pertinent remark that perchance that was the fault of the valet. For my part, I always look with a certain suspicion on a man who has not the power of admiration. It marks, I think, not a superiority, but an inferiority of temperament.

II.

A HERO WORSHIPPER.

OUR friend Méneval, as I have said, had the bump of admiration in a remarkable degree. He would perhaps have been a better writer of Memoirs if he had been a less fervent worshipper ; but let us forgive the good fellow for his defects in style because of the pleasant impression he leaves of himself. He was introduced to Napoleon by Joseph Bonaparte. He was not very eager to enter into the service of the great captain. "I did not," he says, "feel myself at all capable of filling the post for which he intended me, and confessed that I feared the loss of my independence." But it was of no avail :

"On the morning of the second of April Joseph Bonaparte gave me a letter from General Duroc, who wrote to tell me that the First Consul could receive me at five o'clock in the afternoon of that day. I was obliged to accept an invitation which was really a command. General Duroc conducted me to Madame Bonaparte, who received me with exquisite grace and politeness. She was kind enough to talk to me of the business which had brought me to the Tuileries. I was encouraged by her kindness to tell her the objections I felt

to a gilded chain. She succeeded in making me
agree to remain three years only with the First
Consul. I should be free to retire at the end of
that time, and she assured me that the First
Consul would reward me with an honourable post,
and further undertook to gain his consent to this
arrangement. I mention this circumstance to
show with what cleverness she could enter into
the feelings of others, and appear to share their
illusions. On reflection I had no reason to hope
that the First Consul would agree to a bargain
of this kind, or would, indeed, approve of my
dictating terms. Madame Bonaparte did me the
honour to say that I must be her guest at dinner
that night. A moment after Madame Louis
Bonaparte entered the drawing-room, and the
conversation became general. In the meanwhile
time was passing."

III.

NAPOLEON APPEARS.

AND now Napoleon makes his appearance. His
entrance, like everything else this strange creature
does, is effective :

"At last, at about seven o'clock, the sound of
hurried steps on the staircase, which led to the
room in which we were sitting, announced the
arrival of the First Consul. Madame Bonaparte
introduced me to him. He condescended · to
receive me with a kindness which at once dissi-

pated the respectful awe in which I stood. He walked rapidly into the dining-room, whither I followed Madame Bonaparte and her daughter. Madame Bonaparte made me sit next her. The First Consul spoke to me several times during dinner, which only lasted twenty minutes. He spoke of my studies, and of Palissot, with a kindness and a simplicity which put me entirely at my ease, and showed me how gentle and simple this man, who bore on his forehead and in his eyes the mark of such imposing superiority, was in his private life. When I returned to the drawing-room we found General Davoust. The First Consul walked up and down the room with him, conversing, and a quarter of an hour later disappeared by the stair-case from which he had come, without having spoken to me on the matter for which he had ordered my attendance."

This whole picture is so like Napoleon; the hurried entrance, the equally hurried dinner, and then the resumption immediately after of the interrupted threads of work. Let us go on :

"I remained with Madame Bonaparte until eleven o'clock. I had asked her to be so good as to tell me whether I should go away, thinking that I had been forgotten. She told me to remain, and assured me that the First Consul would send for me. True enough, a footman came to fetch me. I followed him down a long passage to a staircase by which we reached a little door, at which he knocked. There was a wicket in this door, which I examined with curiosity. My state of mind was such that I seemed to be outside the place of eternal imprisonment, and involuntarily I raised my eyes to see whether I could not read over the door that inscription of Dante's, '*Lasciate ogni speranza voi ch' entrate.*' An usher, who had looked through the wicket, opened the door after some words with the footman, and I was shown into a small drawing-room poorly lighted. Whilst I was being announced I cast a rapid glance around the room, being anxious to acquaint myself with what was to be my prison. The furniture consisted of some chairs covered with green morocco, and a very luxurious roll-top writing-table, which was loaded with gilt bronze ornaments, and inlaid with rosewood mosaics representing various musical instruments. I afterwards learned that these pieces of furniture had belonged to Louis XVI. It was subsequently sent to the *garde meuble* as useless. A low book-case ran round one side of the room. Some papers were scattered on the top."

IV.

MÉNEVAL STARTS WORK.

" I WAS announced, and immediately afterwards was ushered into a room, where I saw the First Consul seated behind a writing-table. A three-branched flambeau, covered with a shade, cast a strong light on the table. The rest of the room was in the shade, broken only by the light from the fire on the hearth. The First Consul's back was towards me, and he was occupied in reading a paper, and finished reading it without taking notice of my entrance. He then turned round on his chair towards me. I had remained standing at the door of his cabinet, and on seeing him turn round I approached him. After having examined me for a moment with a piercing glance, which would have greatly intimidated me if I had seen it then for the first time, he told me that he wished to attach me to his service, and asked me if I felt myself strong enough to undertake the task which he proposed to confide to me. I answered him with some embarrassment, with the commonplace remark that I was not very sure of myself, but that I would do all in my power to justify his confidence. I kept my objections to myself, because I knew that he would not like them, and, besides, the way in which he had received me at dinner had considerably weakened them. He did not seem dissatisfied with my answer, for he rose from his seat and came up to me smiling, rather sardonically, it is true, and pulled my ear, which I knew to be a sign of favour. He then said to me, 'Very well, come back to-morrow morning at seven, and come straight here.' That was all the [conversation which preceded my admission into [this sanctuary, which I pictured as a sort of place from which nothing but invisible oracles proceeded, accompanied by lightning and thunder. Such was the very simple investiture by which I received a post, the responsibility of which seemed so terrible that, when it was proposed to me, I could only think of it with terror. After this short audience, and this laconic dialogue, the First Consul made a sign with his hand which I took for an order to withdraw, and left me to go into an adjoining drawing-room, where no doubt, some business awaited him. Slightly reassured by the simplicity of this commencement I went back the way I had come, preceded by my guide, who had waited for me outside the door. Nothing but solitude and silence reigned in the dimly-lighted corridors through which I passed. I met nobody on my way out, except a sentry placed at the gate of the inner court."

V.

FIRST DICTATION.

OUR poor Méneval, who was then only twenty-four years of age, went home to bed, but had a sleepless night. He was probably relieved when the night was over, for, as he goes on to say :

"I got up before daybreak, and made my way to the Tuileries, arriving there before the

appointed hour. I rather feared that I should
not be able to find my way in the intricacies of
the palace, and that I should have difficulty in
explaining to the sentries who I was, and was
very much surprised at the ease with which I
made my way to the door through which I had
passed the previous evening, and which I recognised by the wicket in it. As soon as he saw
me the usher showed me into the cabinet, which
was empty. The First Consul was in his drawing-
room with the Minister of Finance, M. Gaudin,
who afterwards became Duc de Gaëte. I sat
down at a table which stood in the embrasure
of a window, and waited for nearly two hours
for the return of the First Consul. He arrived
at last, holding a paper in his hand. Without
appearing to pay any attention to my presence
in his study, just as if I had always been there,
and had always occupied the same place, he
dictated a note for the Minister of Finance
with such volubility that I could hardly understand or take down half of what he was dictating.
Without asking me whether I had heard him
or whether I had finished writing, he took the
paper away from me, and would not let me
read it over, and on my remarking that it was
an unintelligible scribble, he said it was on a
matter well known to the Minister, who would
easily be able to make it out, and so saying,
he went back to the drawing-room. I never

knew if M. Gaudin was able to decipher my writing. I feared that the paper might be sent back to me, and that I might be asked to explain what I had written, which would have been quite impossible. I never heard any more about it."

A PORTRAIT OF NAPOLEON.

MÉNEVAL had little more to do on this eventful day of his life, and pauses to give us a portrait of Napoleon as he then was. The date, it will be remembered, was 1802, and Napoleon was still First Consul:

"Napoleon was at that time moderately stout. His stoutness was increased later on by the frequent use of baths, which he took to refresh himself after his fatigues. It may be mentioned that he had taken that habit of bathing himself every day at irregular hours, a practice which he considerably modified when it was pointed out by his doctor that the frequent use of hot baths, and the time he spent in them, were weakening, and would predispose to obesity. Napoleon was of mediocre stature—about five feet two inches—and well built, though the bust was rather long. His head was big, and the skull largely developed. His neck was short, and his shoulders broad. The size of his chest bespoke a robust constitution, less robust, however, than

his mind. His legs were well-shaped, his foot
was small and well-formed. His hand, and he
was rather proud of it, was delicate and plump,
with tapering fingers. His forehead was high and
broad, his eyes gray, penetrating, and wonderfully
alert ; his nose was straight and well-shaped.
His teeth were fairly good, the mouth perfectly
modelled, the upper lip slightly drawn down
toward the corner of the mouth, and the chin
slightly prominent. His skin was smooth, and
his complexion pale, but of a pallor which denoted
a good circulation of the blood. His very fine
chestnut hair, which, until the time of the expedition to Egypt, he had worn long, cut square,
and covering his ears, was clipped short. The
hair was thin on the upper part of the head, and
left bare his forehead, the seat of such lofty
thoughts. The shape of his face and the *ensemble*
of his features were remarkably regular. In one
word, his head and his bust were in no way
inferior in nobility and dignity to the most
beautiful bust which antiquity has bequeathed
to us. Of this portrait, which in its principal
features underwent little alteration in the last
years of his reign, I will add some particulars
furnished by my long intimacy with him. When
excited by any violent passion his face assumed
an even terrible expression. A sort of rotary
movement very visibly produced itself on his
forehead and between his eyebrows; his eyes

flashed fire; his nostrils dilated, swollen with the inner storm.   But these transient movements, whatever their cause may have been, in no way brought disorder to his mind.   He seemed to be able to control at will these explosions, which, by the way, as time went on, became less and less frequent.   His head remained cool.   The blood never went to it, but flowed back to the heart.   In ordinary life his expression was calm, meditative, and gently grave.   When in a good humour, or anxious to please, his expression was sweet and caressing, and his face was lighted up by a most beautiful smile.   Amongst familiars his laugh was loud and mocking."

At this period of his life, Napoleon, says Méneval, "was in the enjoyment of vigorous health."   He had just been cured by Corvisart of that cutaneous disease which he had contracted from the gunner whose work he did at the siege of Toulon.   Napoleon had neglected at the time to undergo treatment:

"In the carelessness of youth, and being entirely absorbed in his work, he had neglected to undergo any treatment.   He contented himself with some remedies which only caused the outward signs of the disease to disappear, but the poison had been driven into his system, and caused great damage.   This was the reason, it was added, of the extreme thinness, and poor, weak look of Napoleon during the campaigns in Italy and Egypt."

Mr. Sherard, the editor and translator of these volumes, quotes appropriately here the statement from Stendhal that a lady who met Napoleon several times in April and May, 1795, spoke of him as "the thinnest and queerest being I ever met," and "so thin that he inspired pity."

VII.

NAPOLEON AT TABLE.

MÉNEVAL confirms what other writers have told us of the Spartan simplicity of Napoleon's method of daily life:

"He dined with Madame Bonaparte and with some persons of his family. On Wednesdays, which were the days of the Council, he kept the Consuls and the Ministers to dinner. He lunched alone, the simplest dishes being served, whilst for drink he contented himself with Chambertin diluted with water, and a single cup of coffee. All his time being occupied, he profited by the lunch hour to receive the people with whom he liked to converse. These were generally men of letters or artists."

As has already been seen, there were none of the elaborate precautions around the Palace of the Tuileries which in those stormy times one might have expected in the case of a great ruler. There

were, nevertheless, plenty of conspiracies against
Napoleon's life. Napoleon had a "conviction of
the impotence of . . . conspirators," "a conviction produced either by his confidence in
his destiny, or by his contempt for danger."
But when at last an attempt was made to
kill him by an infernal machine—which exploded a few seconds after his carriage had
passed, and wounded nearly eighty people—
he for a time consented to precautions and
to rigorous measures. But this was not long
continued—he fell back into his usual feeling of
security, ceasing to trouble himself about the
dangers which might menace his person :

"He even listened with impatience to the
reports on this subject which were transmitted to
him by the police or by the persons around him ;
he needed all his calm ; he made no change in his
habits, and continued his work without allowing
himself to be turned aside from his path. When
I entered the Consular Palace, I did not see any
of those precautions which denote suspicion and
fear."

VIII.

LIFE AT MALMAISON.

AT La Malmaison Napoleon's life was even more
homely :

"He used to spend the hours which were not
taken up by work, exercise, or shooting, with

Josephine. He used to lunch alone, and during this repast, which was a relaxation for him, he received the persons with whom he liked to converse on science, art, and literature. He dined with his family, and after dinner would look in at his cabinet, and then, unless kept there by some work, would return to the drawing-room and play chess. As a general rule he liked to talk in a familiar way. He was fond of discussions, but did not impose his opinions, and made no pretension of superiority either of intelligence or of rank. When only ladies were present he liked to criticise their dresses, or tell them tragical or satirical stories—ghost stories for the most part. When bed-time came Madame Bonaparte followed him to his room. Napoleon wasted very little time in preparing for the night, and used to say that he got back to bed with pleasure. He said that statues ought to be erected to the men who invented beds and carriages. However, this bed into which he threw himself with delight, though often worn out with fatigue, was quitted more than once during the course of the night. He used to get up after an hour's sleep as wide awake and as clear in his head as if he had slept quietly the whole of the night. As soon as he had lain down his wife would place herself at the foot of the bed, and begin reading aloud. As she read very well he took great pleasure in listening to her. At La Malmaison Napoleon used to spend the moments

which were not taken up in his work-room in the
park, and there again his time was not wasted."

IX.

JOSEPHINE'S OCCUPATIONS.

MÉNEVAL was fond of Josephine ; but this picture
he gives of her is not very flattering :

"Josephine spent her time as she chose. She
received numerous callers during the day. She
used to lunch with some friends, and with new
and old acquaintances. She had no accomplishments, did not draw, and was not a musician.
There was a harp in her apartment on which
she used to play for want of anything better
to do, and it was always the same tune that
she played. She used to work at tapestry, and
would get her ladies or her visitors to help her.
In this way she had made the coverings for the
furniture in the drawing-room at La Malmaison.
Napoleon approved of this busy life. The re-
establishment of peace with England had allowed
Josephine to correspond with some English
botanists and the principal London nurserymen,
from whom she received rare and new plants and
shrubs to add to her collection. She used to
give me the letters from England, written in
connection with this business, to translate into
French. At La Malmaison, Josephine used to
visit her fine hothouses regularly and took great

interest in them. In the evening she would take the backgammon board, a game she was very fond of, and which she played well and quickly. Family theatricals were also played at La Malmaison in a little theatre which accommodated about two hundred spectators. Eugène Beauharnais, who excelled in footman's parts, and his sister Hortense, were the principal actors, not only by rank but by talent. . . . Napoleon was regularly present at the performances, which consisted of little comedies, and thoroughly amused himself. He took pleasure in praising or criticising the actors' performances. His remarks, which were often words of praise, and which were always interesting, showed what an interest he took in these spectacles. On Sundays there were little balls given, at which Napoleon used to dance. He found a charm in this patriarchal life. In his retreat at La Malmaison, Napoleon appeared like a father in the midst of his family. This abnegation of his grandeur, his simple and dignified manners, the pleasing ways and gracious familiarity of Madame Bonaparte had a great charm for me."

"There was a harp in her apartment on which she used to play for want of anything better to do, and it was always the same tune that she played." What a delightful picture of this strange, empty-headed, frivolous, attractive creature! I suppose when Napoleon at twenty-six was paying court to her, this harp did duty as an evidence of her numerous accomplishments.   Poor Josephine! She made the most of herself; but why not?

X.

MÉNEVAL CHARMED.

MÉNEVAL, it will seem, was a good deal happier in his new position than he had expected:

"I could not conceal my surprise at finding such simplicity of habits in a man like Napoleon, who from afar seemed so imposing. I had expected to find him brusque, and of uncertain temper, instead of which I found him patient, indulgent, easy to please, by no means exacting, merry with a merriness which was often noisy and mocking, and sometimes of charming *bonhomie*. This familiarity on his part did not, however, awake corresponding familiarity. Napoleon played with men without mixing with them. He desired to put me entirely at my ease with him, from the very first days of my service, and, in consequence, from the very first I felt no embarrassment in his presence. Doubtless he impressed me to some extent, but I was no longer afraid of him. I was fortified in this state of mind by all that I saw of his pleasant and affectionate ways with Josephine, the assiduous devotion of his officers, the kindliness of his relations with the Consuls and the Ministers, and his familiarity with the soldiers."

XI.

THE SHADOW OF A CRIME.

I MAKE a big skip in the Memoirs, and come to a striking description of the day which followed the execution of the Duc d'Enghien :

"La Malmaison presented a sad spectacle that day. I can still remember the silence which reigned that evening in Madame Bonaparte's drawing-room. The First Consul stood with his back against the mantelpiece, whilst Madame de Fontanes read from some book, of which I have forgotten the name. Josephine, with a melancholy look and moist eyes, was seated at the far end of a couch; the persons in attendance, very few in number at the time, had withdrawn into the neighbouring gallery, where they conversed in whispers on the topic which absorbed all minds. Some people came from Paris, but struck by the doleful appearance of the room, remained standing at the door. The First Consul, anxious or pre-occupied, or listening attentively to what Madame de Fontanes was reading, did not appear to notice their presence. The Minister of Finance remained standing in the same place for a quarter of an hour without being spoken to by anybody. Not wishing to go away as he had come, he approached the First Consul, and asked him if he had any orders to give him; the Consul made a negative gesture in reply."

XII.

NAPOLEON'S POWER OF WORK.

As time went on, and Napoleon became involved in his great wars, the demands upon his energies were greater. His power of work rose at once to the exigencies of the new situation. Poor Méneval must have had a very hard time of it; but he speaks of his experiences with a cheerful fortitude which reveals the real loyalty and kindliness of his nature. "His activity," he says of Napoleon, "grew in proportion to the obstacles put in his way, and he sorely taxed my strength, which was by no means equal to my zeal."

"To give an idea of how the gravity of the situation had developed his faculties, and of the increase in work which had resulted therefrom, and that one may judge how his prodigious activity was equal to everything, it is necessary to acquaint the reader with the new order which Napoleon had established in the despatch of his numerous affairs. The Emperor used to have me waked in the night, when, owing either to some plan which he considered ripe for execution, and which had to be carried out, or to the necessity of maturing the preliminaries of some new project, or to having to send off some courier without loss of time, he was obliged to rise himself. It sometimes happened that I would hand him some document to sign in the evening. 'I will not sign it now,' he would say. 'Be here to-night at one o'clock, or at four in the morning; we will work together.' On these occasions I used to have myself waked some minutes before the appointed hour. As in coming downstairs I used to pass in front of the door of his small apartment, I used to enter to ask if he had been waked. The invariable answer was, 'He has just rung for Constant,' and at the same moment he used to make his appearance, dressed in his white dressing-gown, with a Madras handkerchief round his head. When by chance he had got to the study before me, I used to find him walking up and down with his hands behind his back, or helping himself from his snuff-box, less from taste than from preoccupation, for he only used to smell at his pinches, and his handkerchiefs were never soiled with the snuff. His ideas developed as he dictated, with an abundance and clearness which showed that his attention was firmly riveted to the subject with which he was dealing; they sprang from his head even as Minerva sprang, fully armed, from the head of Jupiter. When the work was finished, and sometimes in the midst of it, he would send for sherbet and ices. He used to ask me which I preferred, and went so far in his solicitude as to advise me which would be better for my health. Thereupon he would return to bed, if only to sleep an hour, and could resume his slumber as though it had not been interrupted. The solid *en cas* of food which used to be brought in at night at the Court before the Revolution, were not supplied at Napoleon's Court, for the Emperor had not inherited the enormous appetites of the princes of the ancient dynasty; but one of the Imperial cooks used to sleep near the larder to serve such refreshments as might be asked for in the night, and which were prepared in advance."

Sometimes Napoleon would not wake his zealous secretary ; as thus :

" When the Emperor rose in the night, without any special object except to occupy his sleepless moments, he used to forbid my being waked before seven in the morning. On those occasions I used to find my writing-table, in the morning, covered with reports and papers annotated in his writing. On his return from his levée, which was held at nine o'clock, he used to find, on his return to his cabinet, the answers and decisions which he had indicated drawn up and ready to be sent off."

" I never ceased to find him good, patient, and indulgent in his treatment of me," says Méneval, after he has told the story of the one row he ever had with his great master.

XIII.

NAPOLEON IN HIS STUDY.

MÉNEVAL is most interesting when he describes Napoleon in his study. There it was that the two saw most of each other; there Méneval is supreme as an authority. When Méneval speaks about general politics, he is nothing but a blind partisan; he retains throughout the curious misunderstanding of the English character and the English policy which created the master passion and the master mistake of Napoleon's mind and career; and all our poor Méneval has to say on these subjects may be skipped and dismissed. But when he brings us to the presence and to the side of the great man, he becomes once again fascinating. For instance, can you not see—nay, actually hear—Napoleon pacing up and down his study as you read this sketch?

"When some lengthy answer was rendered necessary by the reading of a report or despatch; when some spontaneous idea was suggested to him by his observations or comparisons; or when this idea having sprung up in his mind, elaborated by his meditations, had reached its maturity, and the moment to set it in motion had arrived, Napoleon could not keep still. He could not, like the pythoness, remain attached to his tripod. He collected his thoughts, and concentrated his

attention on the subject which was occupying him,
taking a strong hold on his mind.   He would rise
slowly, and begin to walk slowly up and down the
whole length of the room in which he found
himself.   This walk lasted through the whole of
his dictation.   His tone of voice was grave and
accentuated, but was not broken in upon by
any time of rest.   As he entered upon his subject,
the inspiration betrayed itself.   It showed itself by
a more animated tone of voice, and by a kind
of nervous trick which he had of twisting his
right arm and pulling at the trimmings of his
sleeve with his hand.   At such times, he did not
speak any faster than before, and his walk remained
slow and measured."

XIV.

NAPOLEON AS A MAN OF LETTERS.

THE extracts which I have given from Taine's
sketch of Napoleon will have removed from the
minds of my readers the idea—if ever they had it
—that Napoleon was simply the inarticulate or the
reticent soldier.   Frenchmen themselves are also
learning to have a new conception in this respect
of Napoleon.   Some time ago I heard M.
Jusserand, the brilliant and well-informed editor
of the French Men of Letters Series, speak of a
projected book on Napoleon as a Man of Letters.
I have no doubt that when the book comes to be

written, it will be found that Napoleon is entitled to as high a place in literature as Cæsar.

Here is a very vivid picture of him as he improvises:

"He had no difficulty in finding words to express his thoughts. Sometimes incorrect, these very errors added to the energy of his language, and always wonderfully expressed what he wished to say. These mistakes were not, moreover, inherent to his composition, but were created rather by the heat of his improvisation. Nor were they frequent, and were only left uncorrected when, the despatch having to be sent off at once, time was short. In his speeches to the Senate and to the Legislative Body; in his proclamations; in his letters to sovereigns, and in the diplomatic notes which he made his Ministers write, his style was polished and suited to the subject."

Méneval confirms Taine's statement as to the excessive nervous irritability which prevented Napoleon from writing with his own hand. Rarely, if ever, could he be got to do so.

"Writing tired him; his hand could not follow the rapidity of his conceptions. He only took up the pen when by chance he happened to be alone, and had to put the first rush of an idea on to paper; but after writing some lines he used to stop and throw away his pen. He would then go out to call his secretary, or, in his absence, either the second secretary, or the Secretary of State, or General Duroc, or sometimes the aide-de-camp on duty, according to the kind of work in which he was engaged. He made use of the first who answered his call without irritation, but rather with a visible satisfaction at being relieved from his trouble. His writing was a collection of letters unconnected with each other and unreadable. Half the letters to each word were wanting. He could not read his own writing again, or would not take the trouble to do so. If he was asked for some explanation he would take his draft and tear it up, or throw it into the fire, and dictate it over again—the same ideas, it is true, but couched in different language and a different style."

XV.

NAPOLEON'S ORTHOGRAPHY.

NAPOLEON, like other great men, had curious and almost unaccountable intellectual hiatuses. He was not correct in spelling—he was not perfect in arithmetic.

"Although he could detect faults in the spelling of others, his own orthography left much to be desired. It was negligence which had become a habit; he did not want to break or tangle the thread of his thoughts by paying attention to the details of spelling. Napoleon also used to make mistakes in figures, absolute and positive as arithmetic has to be. He could have worked out the most complicated mathematical problems, and yet he could rarely add up a sum correctly. It is fair to add that these errors were not always made without intention. For example, in calculating the number of men who were to make up his battalions, regiments, or divisions, he always used to increase the sum total. One can hardly believe that in doing so he wanted to deceive himself, but he often thought it useful to exaggerate the strength of his armies. It was no use pointing out any mistake of this kind; he refused to admit it, and obstinately maintained his voluntary arithmetical error. His writing was illegible, and he hated difficult writing. The notes or the few lines that he used to write, and which did not demand any fixed attention, were, as a rule, free from mistakes of spelling, except in certain words over which he invariably blundered. He used to write, for instance, the words 'cabinet,' 'Caffarelli,'—'gabinet,' 'Gaffarelli'; 'enfin que,' 'enfant que,'—'infanterie,' 'enfanterie.' The first two words are evidently reminiscences of his maternal language, the only ones which remained over from his earliest youth. The others, 'enfin que' and 'infanterie,' have no analogy with the Italian language. He had a poor knowledge of this language, and avoided speaking it. He could only be brought to speak it with Italians who did not know French, or who had difficulty in expressing themselves in our language. I have sometimes heard him conversing with Italians, and what he said was expressed in Italianised French with words terminating in i, o, and a."

XVI.

LAPSES.

IN Méneval Napoleon appears, as we have seen, as the most persistent and unsparing of workers. But there are very curious glimpses of Napoleon at intervals when that terrible brain was not working—or at least apparently not working—at its usual high pressure:

"He used sometimes to spend whole days without doing any work, yet without leaving the palace, or even his work-room. In these days of leisure—which was but apparent, for it usually concealed an increase of cerebral activity—Napoleon appeared embarrassed how to spend his time. He would go and spend an hour with the Empress, then he would return and, sitting down on the settee, would sleep, or appear to sleep, for a few minutes. He would then come and seat himself on the corner of my writing-table, or on one of the arms of my chair, or sometimes even on my knees. He would then put his arm round my neck and amuse himself by gently pulling my ear, or by patting me on the shoulder, or on the cheek.

He would speak to me on all sorts of disconnected
subjects, of himself, of his manias, of his constitution, of me, or of some plan that he had in his
head.   He was fond of teasing, never bitterly or
nastily, but on the contrary with a certain amount
of kindness, and accompanied with loud laughter.
He would glance through the titles of his books,
saying a word of praise or blame on the authors,
and would linger with preference over the tragedies
of Corneille and Voltaire.   He would read tirades
from these tragedies aloud, then would shut
up the book and walk up and down reciting
verses from 'The Death of Cæsar.' . . . When
he was tired of reading or reciting, he would
begin to sing in a strong, but false voice.   When
he had nothing to trouble him, or he was
pleased with what he was thinking about, it
was shown in the choice of his songs.   These
would be airs from 'Le Devin du Village,'
or other old operas. . . . When he was in a
more serious frame of mind, he used to sing
verses from the Revolutionary hymns and chants,
such as the *Chant du Départ* : '*Veillons au salut
de l'Empire.*'"

XVII.

WAS NAPOLEON SUPERSTITIOUS?

MÉNEVAL says emphatically, No; though he does
admit that Napoleon was something of a fatalist.
Josephine, being a Creole, was of course intensely

superstitious, and Méneval suggests that a good deal of the money she threw away so recklessly went into the pockets of Madame Lenormand, the famous conjurer of the period. If Napoleon, as is reported, ever did pay Lenormand a visit in Josephine's company, it was at the period when he was too much in love with Josephine to refuse even her most unreasonable request. But Napoleon retained from his early days the "habit of involuntarily signing himself with the cross, on hearing of some great danger; or on the discovery of some important fact, where the interests of France or the success of his plans were concerned, or at the news of some great and unexpected good fortune, or of some great disaster."

But though Napoleon believed in his star, he never trusted much to luck.

" He was always prepared in advance for every reverse he might meet."

" Before finally deciding upon his plans he would subject them to the minutest scrutiny ; every hazard, even the most improbable, being discussed and provided for. I saw Napoleon enjoying prosperity with the keenest pleasure, but I never once saw him betray any surprise. His measures were so well taken, and adverse chances so minimised by his calculations and arrangements, that if anything could have surprised him, it would have been the failure of plans which he had prepared with so much skill and so much care."

XVIII.

CURIOUS CHARACTERISTICS.

NAPOLEON'S constitution, Méneval declares, was "naturally robust; and the oath which he had taken from his youth to break off all bad habits had fortified it.   He had all the advantages of the bilio-sanguine temperament."

"I never saw Napoleon ill; he was only occasionally subject to vomiting bile, which never left any after effects. . . . He had feared, for some time, that he was affected with a disease of the bladder . . . but this fear was found to be without foundation. It has been noticed that men are rarely really suffering from the disease with which they imagine themselves to be affected. The existence of the disease which killed the Emperor was not suspected at that time, and I never heard him complain of pains in the stomach."

But like many robust people, Napoleon was extremely sensitive in certain respects. "The slightest evil smell was sufficient to upset him greatly," and he had "so keen a sense of smell that he could detect the vicinity of a subterranean passage, a cellar, or a sewer, a long way off."

Here is an even more peculiar instance of his sensitiveness :

"He had been anxious to gain some acquaintance with anatomy, and for this purpose Doctor

Corvisart had brought him some anatomical models
in wax, representing parts of the heart and
stomach. The Emperor had set aside the hour
which followed his luncheon for this study, but the
illusion produced by the attention given to these
parts of our animal organisation filled him with
such disgust that it used to make him sick. He
tried in vain to resist this revolt of his senses, but
he was forced to give up his lessons. Nevertheless,
the same man, riding over a field of battle after
a bloody fight, was not disgusted by the contact
of wounds of disgusting appearance and odour.
He often used to get off his horse and place his
hand on the chest of the wounded man to see
whether he still breathed ; he would raise him up,
with the help of his officers, and put to his lips
a bottle of brandy, which his servant Roustan
always carried with him."

Finally, as to Napoleon's physiognomy, here
is a curious fact which I see recorded for the first
time :

"When his coffin was opened at St. Helena,
twenty years after it was closed down, Napoleon
appeared to be sleeping. His teeth had preserved
their whiteness, his beard and nails seemed to
have grown since his death. His hands had the
colour of life—they were supple, and resisted
pressure."

XIX.

DAILY HABITS.

NAPOLEON, though he came from Corsica, and though he was the ruler of a nation which even yet leaves something to be desired in the practice of and provision for the bath, was extremely careful as to his personal cleanliness. All his intimates have called attention to his constant habit of taking hot-water baths—almost of boiling heat—whenever and wherever he could. Ultimately, as Méneval has recorded, he had to abandon this habit because it tended to increase the inclination to obesity which came to him after his fortieth year, and which, by the way, helped to change the whole face of the world by seriously diminishing his powers of work and of immediate decision. Here is Méneval's description of his daily toilet:

"He used to brush his arms and his broad chest himself. His valet finished by rubbing him very vigorously on the back and shoulders; but he often used to make Roustan, who was much stronger, do this for him. He formerly used to be shaved, but for a long time, that is to say, since about 1803, he had shaved himself—after he had changed his valet. A small mirror was held before him, and turned as required in the process of shaving. He then used to wash himself with a great quantity of water in a silver basin which, from its size, might have been taken for a vat. A sponge dipped in Eau de Cologne was passed over his hair, and the rest of the bottle was poured over his shoulders. His flannel singlets, his vests and pants of kerseymere, were changed every day. He never gave up wearing his green or blue uniform coats—the only coats he ever wore— until he was told that they were beginning to show signs of wear. His allowance for dress had at first been fixed at sixty thousand francs; he had reduced this amount to twenty thousand francs, all included. He was fond of saying that with an income of twelve hundred francs and a horse he should have all he wanted. He often referred to the times when he was an artillery lieutenant, and delighted in speaking of the order he put in his expenditure, and the economies which he attempted to avoid getting into debt, especially when the triumph of the English party in Corsica had cut off all supplies from home, and he had charge of his brother Louis, whom he was bringing up and maintaining on his pay. At such times he would censure the example of luxury which his aides-de-camp and the principal officers of his household gave to the officers of lower rank, who were attached to his person. Nevertheless, he liked to be surrounded with splendour and a kind of pomp. He often used to say to those on whom he lavished his money : ' Be economical and even parsimonious at home ; be magnificent in public.' He followed this maxim himself. Nobody was more modest in his dress, or less particular about his food, and all that concerned him personally. He told me one day that when he was quite a young officer he had sometimes travelled from Paris to Versailles in what used to be called the Court carriages, which were a kind of cheap coach; very comfortable, he used to add, and where he met very nice people. Only it was not a very expeditious way of travelling, for these carriages took five hours to do the journey."

XX.

NAPOLEON IN THE FIELD.

ONE of the grand secrets of Napoleon's influence with his army was the true spirit of *camaraderie* which he introduced the moment he went into the field. "In the camp," says Méneval, "all etiquette was banished in the entirely military relations between the sovereign and his comrades-in-arms:

"The private was authorised to leave the ranks, on presenting arms, and to lay any request he might have to make before the Emperor, either verbally or in writing. Such requests, whether they were granted or refused, were immediately attended to by the Emperor. When it happened that the petition could not be granted, the soldier was always told the reason of such refusal, which was explained to him with kindness. Very often

the refusal was compensated for by the grant of some
other favour. If any officer had a confession to
make to Napoleon, the Emperor was always ready
to hear him, and would listen to him in a paternal
manner."

It was one of the curiosities of this extraordinary temperament, that even in the midst of
his campaigns Napoleon insisted on doing the
work, and it might even be said, all the work, of
civil administration at home. His Ministers had
to write to him every day; he answered all their
reports, and a constant succession of messengers
were kept busy between him and Paris.

" Economical with his time, he calculated the
moment of his departure so as to find himself at
the head of his troops at the moment when his
presence there became necessary. He would then
proceed thither in his carriage in full speed. But
even during this journey he did not remain
idle, but busied himself in reading his despatches,
and very often received reports from his generals
and answered them forthwith. . . . By means of a
lamp which was placed at the back of his carriage,
and which lighted up the carriage during the
night, he was able to work as though he had been
in his work-room."

This picture of a great soldier on the way
to a bloody battle-field, and to the tremendous
issues of life and death, empire or disgrace, calmly
reading the details of administration, is certainly

one of the marvels of history. Let us follow him to the battle-field:

"Such was the privileged constitution of this extraordinary man that he could sleep an hour, be awakened to give an order, go to sleep again, be awakened anew, without suffering for it in his health or in his rest. Six hours of sleep were sufficient for him, whether taken consecutively or whether spread over intervals in the twenty-four hours. On the days which preceded the battle he was constantly on horseback, reconnoitring the enemy's forces, deciding upon the battle-field, and riding round the bivouac of his army corps. Even in the night he used to visit the lines to assure himself once more of the enemy's forces by the number of its fires, and would tire out several horses in the space of a few hours. On the day of the battle he would place himself at some central point, whence he could see all that was going on. He had his aides-de-camp and orderly officers by him, and used to send them to carry his orders in every direction. At some distance behind the Emperor were four squadrons of the guard, one belonging to each branch of the service, but when he left this position he only took a platoon with him as escort. He used usually to inform his Marshals of the place which he had chosen, so as to be easily found by the officers whom they might send to him. As soon as his presence became necessary he would ride off there at a gallop."

XXI.

THE DESCENT BEGUN.

I SHALL pass rapidly over much intervening ground, and bring the reader to the days when fortune had turned against Napoleon, and he sank, never again to rise.

In the midst of the disastrous retreat from Moscow, Napoleon for the first time thought of suicide as an outlet from his troubles. He feared above all things being taken prisoner by the Czar, and being paraded as part of his triumph:

"He asked his ordinary medical adviser, Doctor Yvan, in consequence, to give him a dose of poison, which was contained in a sachet which he could carry round his neck, and which was to spare him the humiliation of falling alive into the hands of the Cossacks, and of being exposed to the insults of these savages."

Napoleon carried the black taffeta sachet around his neck until he reached Paris. Then, in the midst of his cheerful surroundings, and of his engrossing occupations, he laid it aside, depositing it in one of his travelling bags. But 1814 came, and Napoleon, ruined, deserted, lonely, at Fontainebleau, remembered the sachet:

"One day, after having consulted Yvan on the various means of putting an end to one's life, he drew out the sachet in question before the doctor's eyes and opened it. Yvan, terrified by this action, seized part of its contents and threw it into the fire. It appears that on the morrow, a prey to the blackest thoughts, despair seized upon the Emperor's mind, and he rose without summoning anybody, diluted the rest of the poison in a goblet, and swallowed it. What remained of this lethal substance was no doubt insufficient in quantity or had been too much diluted to cause death. On April 11, 1814, towards eleven in the evening, the silence of the palace of Fontainebleau was suddenly disturbed by the sound of groans, and the noise of comings and goings. The Ducs de Bassano and de Vicence, and General Bertrand, rushed to the Emperor's side, whilst Yvan himself was sent for. Napoleon was stretched out on a sofa in his bedroom, with his head leaning on his hands. He addressed himself to Doctor Yvan: 'Death will have nothing to do with me. You know what I have taken.' Yvan, dumbfounded, troubled, stammered, saying that he did not know what His Majesty meant, that he gave him nothing; at last he lost his head altogether, and rushed out of the room to throw himself into an arm-chair in the adjoining room, where he had a violent fit of hysterics. Napoleon passed a fairly quiet night. On the morrow Doctor Yvan, M. de Turenne, and others, presented themselves at the Emperor's levée, and found him almost recovered from this

violent moral and physical shock.   He was calm,
deeply sad, and deplored the unhappy state in
which he was leaving France.   As to Doctor
Yvan, still troubled by the scene of the previous
night, and under the impression of the terror with
which Napoleon had filled him, he at once decided
to remain no longer in the palace.   And so, on
leaving the levée, he rushed down into the courtyard, and finding a horse tied to one of the gates,
jumped on its back and galloped away."

XXII.

NAPOLEON'S FORLORN YOUNG HEIR.

Two scenes, finally, I shall quote in the closing
hours of the great Napoleon drama.   Méneval
was attached to the person of Marie Louise for
some time after the abdication of the Emperor,
and only returned to France when Napoleon came
back from Elba and had again mounted the
throne.   Honest Méneval gives a pathetic picture
of his last interview with the poor boy who had
inherited Napoleon's name:

"Before leaving, I went to take leave of the
young Prince at the Imperial Palace of Vienna.
It grieved me to notice his serious and even
melancholy air.   He had lost that childish cheerfulness and loquacity which had so much charm in
him.   He did not come to meet me as he was
accustomed to do, and saw me enter without

giving any sign that he knew me. One might have said that misfortune was already beginning its work on this young head, which a great lesson of Providence had seemed to have adorned with a crown on his entrance into life, so as to give a fresh example of the vanity of human greatness. He was like one of those victims destined for sacrifice who are adorned with flowers. Although he had already spent six weeks with the persons to whom he had been confided, with whom I found him, he had not yet got accustomed to them, and seemed to look upon their faces, still strange to him, with distrust. I asked him in their presence if he had a message which I could take for him to his father. He looked at me in a sad and significant way, then gently freeing his hand from my grasp, he withdrew silently into the embrasure of a window some distance off. After having exchanged some words with the persons who were in the drawing-room, I approached the spot to which he had withdrawn, and where he was standing looking on with an attentive air. As I bent down to him to say farewell, struck with my emotion, he drew me towards the window, and looking at me with a touching expression, he whispered to me: 'M. Meva, you will tell him that I am still very fond of him!'"

XXIII.

A DOOMED MAN.

MÉNEVAL was not long with Napoleon without discovering that Napoleon, after the return from Elba, had lost his nerve, and knew he was a doomed man:

"He told me . . . that in making his attempt he had understood that he could appeal only to the courage and patriotism of the nation and to his sword. 'And for the rest,' he added, with a melancholy smile, 'God is great and merciful.' All his words were stamped with a calm sadness and a resignation which produced a great impression upon me. I no longer found him animated with that certainty of success which had formerly rendered him confident and invincible. It seemed as if his faith in his fortune, which had induced him to attempt the very hardy enterprise of his return from the island of Elba, and which had supported him during his miraculous march through France, had abandoned him on his entry into Paris."

Finally, after Waterloo, Méneval followed Napoleon to Malmaison, the scene of his early greatness and of his final overthrow:

"Walking one day with the Emperor in the private garden which adjoined his cabinet, he told me that he counted on me to follow him. I had no other intention. As I needed a little time to put my affairs in order, I asked him where I was to meet him. He told me that his first intention had been to go to America, but as there were some obstacles in the way of the realisation of this plan, he intended to go and live in England, and added that he meant to insist on the rights which were enjoyed by every English citizen. As I expressed some surprise at this resolution, he exclaimed: 'Without that condition I shall put myself at the head of affairs again.' My surprise increased on hearing this sudden revelation, and I could not help saying: 'But, sire, if such is your thought, do not wait until the time has passed; at some paces from here devoted generals and a faithful army call for you; you are not a prisoner, I suppose?' 'I have here,' he answered, 'a battalion of my guard who would arrest Becker, if I said one word, and would act as my escort. Young man,' he added, after a moment's silence, and with the gesture of pulling my ear, 'such resolutions are not improvised.' I then saw that the threat of placing himself at the head of affairs had only been torn from him by a flash of natural pride, and that it had never really been in his thoughts. This scene has remained engraved on my memory."

Méneval had to go back to Paris that night; when he was able to return to Malmaison, Napoleon had gone to Rochefort—his first milestone on the road that ended in St. Helena — and Méneval never saw him more.

CHAPTER III.

THE ESTIMATE OF AN OFFICIAL.*

So much for the estimate of Napoleon by an enemy and by a friend. Let us now take the more impartial estimate of a somewhat frigid official. While ready to do full justice to Napoleon's extraordinary genius as an administrator, Chancellor Pasquier had not Méneval's gift of admiration. Before giving those portions of Pasquier's memoirs which deal with Napoleon, I shall quote several passages of Pasquier's early life—partly because they are intensely interesting in themselves, and partly because they help one to understand the secret of Napoleon's long tenure of power, by describing the anarchic conditions to which his undisputed authority put an end.

I.

THE PASQUIER DYNASTY.

THE Pasquiers had been a family of officials for generations. They belonged to that curious and

* "Memoirs of Chancellor Pasquier." Translated by Charles E. Roche. (London : Fisher Unwin.)

hereditary race of judicial officers, which is a peculiarity of French official life. Young Pasquier, born in 1767, seemed destined to follow in the same track as his ancestors—to pass from office to office, from salary to salary — through all the well-ordered gradations which belong to such a class. But even in his early years he found himself surrounded by the signs of the coming strife. His mother, for instance, had passed, like other people, under the spell of the new gospel, preached by Jean Jacques Rousseau. Like so many other great ladies of the period, she had succeeded in obtaining an interview with that rather morose and shy philosopher by bringing him some music to copy, and it was under the influence of Rousseau that young Pasquier, while still an infant, was sent half naked into the garden of the Tuileries; "the result of this system," is his melancholy comment, "was to make me one of the most chilly of mortals."

II.

THE OLD RÉGIME.

THE Pasquiers had been able to acquire a pleasant country place near Le Mans, and we have several delightful glimpses of their career of prosperous public employment, and of what the old life of the provinces used to be before the storm burst. For instance, here is a very instructive picture of that

kind of prelate who helped to make life agreeable
for those who were prosperous, and still more
intolerable to those who were at the other end
of the social scale:

"The bishopric of Le Mans was one of those
most coveted. Its revenues were considerable;
the episcopal palace was a very fine one, which
had, as a dependency, a charming country seat
about one league distant from the town. This
seat had for some time been occupied by prelates
of high birth, grave men who scrupulously fulfilled
the duties of their holy ministry. Upon its becoming vacant in the last years of the reign of
Louis XV., it was given to the Abbé Grimaldi,
a young ecclesiastic, the scion of a great house,
distinguished by his agreeable personality, his
intellect, and his remarkably graceful manner.
A very pleasant companion, he showed himself
capable of a devoted friendship to those whom
he honoured by selecting as his friends, and he
proved his judgment by the choice of the vicars-
general with whom he surrounded himself. They
were, generally speaking, younger sons whom
fortune had not favoured much, and who had
entered the Church merely as a way to a happier
condition of affairs. While on terms of friendship
with them during the years he spent at the
Seminary of Saint-Sulpice, he had promised
to summon them to his side as soon as he
should be a bishop. He made good his promise,

and on his arrival at Le Mans, he was accompanied by a flock of vicars-general, who set the bishopric on a footing entirely different from that to which the people had hitherto been accustomed. They contracted acquaintances in the various social circles, specially attaching themselves to those with whom they could enter into the most agreeable relations. The bishop viewed this life of excitement, if not with a complacent, at least with a very indulgent eye. His pastoral excursions through his diocese were few and far between, and long did he tarry in the *châteaux* where he found society to his taste."

In the days before the Revolution, men entered upon professional life at an early age. At fifteen they entered either the army or navy; at twenty a man could be a well-instructed officer in the engineers; at twenty-one, could enter the magistracy; and it was at that age that Pasquier entered, as a Councillor into the Parliament of Paris. This was in January, 1787, just about that moment when the distracted Councillors of the King were beginning to think of some means of rescuing the kingdom from bankruptcy; and when Calonne was summoning the Assembly of the Notables which was the forerunner of the States General.

III.

PARIS BEFORE THE STORM.

I WILL pass over M. Pasquier's account of those conflicts between the old Parliament of Paris and the Court which were among the first heralds of the Revolution; I go on to quote a passage which is remarkable, though I do not think it can be correct. One of the disputed points in French history and in French political life to this hour, is the state of France before the Revolution. One can easily see why Conservatives are ready to proclaim that the country was progressing; while the Radical, who dates human progress from 1789, should draw just as black pictures of the ante-Revolutionary times. M. Pasquier was a Conservative, with certain Liberal leanings; and to that extent one must take his account as somewhat partial: but still here is his description, for what it is worth, of the appearance of Paris just before the breaking of the storm. The interest of the picture is largely enhanced by the contrast it suggests between Paris and its aristocracy in the days which preceded and those which followed the outbreak of the storm:

"I saw the splendours of the Empire. Since the Restoration I see daily new fortunes spring up and consolidate themselves; still, nothing so far has in my eyes equalled the splendour of Paris during the years which elapsed between 1783 and 1789. Magnificent residences stood then in the Marais quarter and in the Ile Saint-Louis. What is the Faubourg Saint-Germain of to-day compared with the Faubourg Saint-Germain of that period? And then with regard to outdoor luxury, let those who can remember a field day or a race day at Longchamps, or merely the appearance of the boulevard, ask themselves if the stream of equipages with two, four, or six horses, all vying in magnificence, and closely packed together at these places of rendezvous, did not leave far behind the string of private or livery coaches, among which appear a few well-appointed turn-outs, that are to be seen in the same localities nowadays?"

Similarly, Pasquier holds that the exactions of the Crown, and the abuses of power, were much exaggerated; and summing up the answer to the question, "Whence came that passion for reform, that desire to change everything?" he says, "it was due rather to a great stirring up of ideas than to actual sufferings," a statement I can hardly think correct. It is a statement, besides, in direct conflict with Taine, another very strong Conservative writer, one of whose points against the Revolution is the invasion of Paris by hordes of hungry and desperate men. Hungry and desperate men do not rush to a metropolis merely because there is " a great stirring up of ideas."

IV.

THE TAKING OF THE BASTILLE.

YOU will get some idea of all the momentous and picturesque sights which Pasquier saw, from this simple beginning of one of the chapters in his book: "I was present at the taking of the Bastille." His account differs very materially from that which one has formed in one's mind of that historic day. It makes the whole affair rather a playful and light burlesque than a hideous and portentous tragedy. Here is what M. Pasquier says:

"What has been styled the fight was not serious, for there was absolutely no resistance shown. Within the stronghold's walls were neither provisions nor ammunition. It was not even necessary to invest it.

"The Regiment of *Gardes Françaises*, which had led the attack, presented itself under the walls on the Rue Saint-Antoine side, opposite the main entrance, which was barred by a drawbridge. There was a discharge of a few musket-shots, to which no reply was made, and then four or five discharges from the cannon. It had been claimed that the latter broke the chains of the drawbridge. I did not notice this, and yet I was standing close to the point of attack. What I did see plainly was the action of the soldiers, the invalides, or others grouped on the platform of the high tower, holding their musket-stocks in air, and expressing by all means employed under similar circumstances their desire of surrendering.

"The result of this so-called victory, which brought down so many favours on the heads of the so-called victors, is well known. The truth is that this great fight did not for a moment frighten the numerous spectators who had flocked to witness its result. Among them were many women of fashion, who, in order to be closer to the scene, had left their carriages some distance away."

v.

THE GIRONDISTS.

PASQUIER saw the arrival of the Girondists in Paris; and it is interesting and pathetic to read his account of the hopes with which these men entered on their duties, when one knows how most of them ended on the guillotine. Pasquier had a friend in the Revolutionary party, a M. Ducos, and M. Ducos induced him to remain to breakfast with his fellow deputies from the Gironde. This breakfast is very different from the last supper of the Girondists with which history is familiar—the supper before the wholesale execution of the group:

"All of them were intoxicated with visions of future successes, and they did not take the trouble·

of hiding from me, although I had been introduced to them as an out-and-out Royalist, if not their plans, at least their ideas, which were of the Republican order. I was none the less struck with their madness. The eloquence of Vergniaud made itself felt even in the course of ordinary conversation, and it seemed to me destined to become the most formidable weapon of the party whose cause he was embracing."

VI.

THE ADVANCE OF THE STORM.

ONE of the curious things brought out in these Memoirs, is the strength of the hold the King and Queen had on many sections of the population, even at the moment when they were steadily advancing to their doom. Taine has proved pretty conclusively that the Jacobins, at the moment when they captured supreme power in the State, were in a minority; Pasquier's testimony tends to confirm this.

Here, for instance, is a scene in which the Queen figured :

"During these last months, I saw the unfortunate Queen at a performance of Italian opera, greeted with the cheers of a society audience which was eager to give her such small consolation. I saw this audience go wild when Madame Dugazon sang with Mermier the '*Evènements imprévus*' duo, which ends with the following words, 'Oh, how I love my master! Oh, how I love my mistress!' And upon her return to the Tuileries, there were those who did not hesitate to tell her that she had just listened to a genuine expression of the feelings of her subjects towards her."

Pasquier plainly shows that indecision was one of the main causes of the downfall of the Throne. For instance, there was no proper preparation for defending the Tuileries, though there were plenty of gallant young men ready to die in defending the entrance to the palace. Pasquier himself was of the number, and he gives a very vivid though brief picture of the dangers of the period by the following anecdote:

"The King had still at his disposal a regiment of the Swiss Guards and a few battalions of the National Guard, whose loyalty was undoubted. These ready means of defence were increased by a number of devoted followers, to whom free access to the *château* had been granted, and who had firmly resolved to make a rampart of their bodies in defence of the Royal Family.

"Together with the Prince de Saint-Maurice I resolved upon joining this faithful band. On the morning of August 9th we wrote to M. de Champcenetz to ask him for cards of admission. They had not reached us by evening, and during the night between August 9th and 10th we made several vain attempts to get into the *château*, which was then being threatened. If I make a note of this fact it is not because of its actual importance, but because of a couple of circumstances pertaining thereto, one of which was of a fatal nature, while the other was fortunate to a degree. The card which I had asked for on August 9th reached me by the local post two days later, when all was over. How was it that it should have been so long delayed in transmission without being intercepted? How was it that it did not then bring about my arrest? It was a piece of good luck which I have never been able to explain. Fate was not equally kind to the Prince de Saint-Maurice. His readiness to serve the King had no other result than mine, with the exception that his card did not reach him, and that he never discovered any trace of it. He lost his head on the scaffold, under the accusation of having been one of the defenders of the Tuileries."

VII.

A NARROW ESCAPE.

THE following picture gives even a more vivid glimpse of the perils which every friend of the Old Order ran at this period. It took place after the King had been compelled to take refuge in the Assembly:

"The inevitable consequences of this event were a fearful state of confusion and an actual dissolution of society. No longer did any one feel safe. No one expected to see the next day. My own safety was most seriously compromised by an imprudent detail of costume. On the morning of the 11th I made the mistake of going out with my hair trimmed and gathered up with a comb. I had forgotten that this mode of wearing the hair formed part of the uniform of the Swiss Guards. This slight indication was sufficient for two or three hundred angry men to pounce upon me on the Boulevard de la Madeleine. I was unable to make myself heard, and so was dragged to the Place Vendôme, where the mob was stringing up to lamp-posts all the Swiss and other fugitives from the *château* they could lay their hands on.

"I was rescued by a little drummer of the precinct who recognised me. It was he who was in the habit of notifying me when it was my turn to go on guard duty, and as I never answered the call, I was in the habit of paying him somewhat liberally for finding a substitute for me. He fought his way into the midst of the raving horde, commanded silence by a vigorous beating of the drum, shouted that I was not a Swiss, and gave my name and place of residence. On the strength of his testimony I was escorted home in triumph."

VIII.

A TERRIBLE PLAN.

THE fanaticism of the Revolutionary party—the strange mixture of the exaltation and self-sacrifice of a religious faith, and of a readiness to appeal to the most unscrupulous means for gaining their ends—all this is brought out by the following story. If we did not know what times these were, the story would be incredible; as it is, M. Pasquier only confirms what has appeared in the memoirs of the Revolutionary leaders. This is his story of an interview with his Revolutionary friend, Ducos:

"In the exultation of his triumph he revealed everything, and he told me a thing which the 'Memoirs of Madame Roland' have since confirmed, namely, the resolution reached at one of their caucuses to sacrifice one of their number, and to have him murdered, in order to impute his assassination to the Court, if no other means were forthcoming to excite the people against it. One Grangeneuve, I believe, had offered to sacrifice his life, and was to be the victim."

IX.

THE DEATH OF THE KING.

PASQUIER saw the execution of the King—unwillingly and accidentally. This is what happened:

"I lived in a house which faced on the Boulevard at the corner of the Madeleine Church. My father and I sat opposite each other all the morning buried in our grief, and unable to utter a word. We knew the fatal procession was wending its way by the Boulevards. Suddenly a somewhat loud clamour made itself heard. I rushed out under the idea that perhaps an attempt was being made to rescue the King. How could I do otherwise than cherish such a hope to the very last? On reaching the goal I discovered that what I had heard was merely the howling of the raving madmen who surrounded the vehicle. I found myself sucked in by the crowd which followed it, and was dragged away by it, and, so to speak, carried and set down at the scaffold's side. So it was that I endured the horror of this awful spectacle.

"Hardly had the crime been consummated when a cry of 'Long live the nation!' arose from the foot of the scaffold, and, repeated from man to man, was taken up by the whole of the vast concourse of people. The cry was followed by the deepest and most gloomy silence ; shame, horror, and terror were now hovering over the vast locality. I crossed it once more, swept back by the flood which had brought me thither. Each one walked along slowly, hardly daring to look at another. The rest of the day was spent in a state of profound stupor, which spread a pall over the whole city. Twice was I compelled to leave the house, and on both occasions did I find the streets deserted and silent. The assassins had lost their accustomed spirit of bravado. Public grief made itself felt, and they were silent in the face of it."

X.

THE REIGN OF TERROR.

ONE cannot help breathing hard while reading, amid all its baldness, many passages of this work, and especially those which give us pictures of the Reign of Terror. Poor young Pasquier had abundant opportunity of realising all the perils of that terrible time. Nearly all the old members of the Paris Parliament were classed as aristocrats and reactionaries ; and to have been one of them, unless Revolutionary fervour or atrocities came as a defence and an obliteration, amounted to a certainty of imprisonment, and an almost equal certainty of condemnation and death.

Pasquier's father was arrested with many of his colleagues, and was ultimately guillotined. Nothing can give a better idea of the horrors of the time than the simple narrative which Pasquier unfolds of his father's and his own adventures at this epoch. Here, for instance, is a curious picture of the state of mind which constant peril produced—the feeling that imprisonment was more welcome than liberty—a gaol safer than any other refuge :

" My father and I, therefore, went in different directions after a fond embrace, and with hardly the strength of uttering a word. We were never to meet again. I returned to Champigny. My father hid himself at La Muette, where he had dwelt during the course of the previous summer. Two days later he gave himself up, fearing that my mother might be arrested in his stead. Hardly was he within the walls of his prison, which had as inmates M. de Malesherbes, all the members of the Rosambo family, and a large number of his friends, when he experienced a feeling of relief. Indeed, outside of prison, one dared not meet, see, speak, nay, almost look at anybody, so great was the fear of mutually betraying each other. Relatives and the most intimate friends dwelt apart in the most absolute isolation. A knock at the door, and one supposed at once that the commissioners of the Revolutionary Committee had come to take one away. When once behind the bolts it was different. One found oneself, in a certain sense, once more enjoying social life, for one was in the midst of one's relations, of one's friends, whom one could see without hindrance, and with whom one could freely converse. The great judicial massacres (I am speaking of the month of January, 1794) had not yet taken place. Few days, however, went by without some victims, but the number of those behind the bars was so great, that to each one of them all danger seemed somewhat distant; and lastly, no sooner were many of them in gaol than they ended in believing that they were safer there than out of doors. One could no longer (so at least they imagined) accuse them of conspiring; and, were the foreign armies to make great progress, as there were good grounds for supposing, they would while in prison be more out of the reach of popular frenzy than elsewhere. So powerful a hold did these impressions take on the mind of my father, that having a few days later found the means of reaching me by letter, he urged me to reflect upon my situation, to well consider if the life that I was leading, and which he knew from experience, was not a hundred times worse than his own. Then, assuming that I would determine to get myself arrested, he informed me of an agreement that he had entered into with the porter of the prison to reserve for him alone, for a few days longer, the room which he occupied, so that we could dwell together."

XI.

ANOTHER NARROW ESCAPE.

BUT young Pasquier did not take this advice, and kept himself in hiding. However, he was not always to remain concealed, for if he did so he would have been denounced as an *émigré*, and his father, as the parent of an *émigré*, would have been more certain than ever of condemnation ; and so, says Pasquier, " I was compelled to send to my mother, every three months, certificates of residence, which she might produce in case of need." Let me pause for a moment in my extracts to point out how the beauty, devotion, self-sacrifice of French family life shine out in all the darkness of those hideous times. It is well to note the fact amid so much that is corrupt, unwholesome, and perilous in French society, that this beautiful ideal of a united and affectionate home has been preserved. Unhappy and hopeless, indeed, would France be if that pillar and ground-work of her national safety were imperilled or weakened.

Young Pasquier found several friends who were willing to conceal him during this period, and to run considerable risks in doing so. These friends also managed to get him the precious certificates, which protected both himself and his father. Several witnesses were required, and a Madame Tavaux, a mercer, who lived close to the house of the Pasquier family, and had been befriended by them, was the chief agent in getting these witnesses. Here is what happened one day :

" The greater number of those whom she thus brought together had no acquaintance with me whatever, and yet, on her mere word, they ventured to compromise themselves in the most dangerous fashion, so as to get me out of my difficulty. Thus did I reap the fruit of a few slight services rendered by my people in other days."

"I had just secured one of the precious certificates of residence which I had so eagerly sought. It had been granted to me by the General Assembly of the section, held in the church of the Trinité. I was about to depart when a little man approached me, and drew me aside under the pretence of saying a few words. I followed him without fear, believing him one of the witnesses procured on my behalf whom I did not know. He turned out to be a member of the Revolutionary Committee, and without further ado he handed me over to a guard close by. The latter was ordered to take me before the Committee, and I remained in his custody until the members of it had assembled. No sooner had I been questioned than it became an easy matter for them to elicit the fact that I was an ex-Councillor of the Paris Parliament, and that my father was already under arrest. There was consequently no room for doubt that I was a good capture, and I was notified, in spite of all my protestations, that I was to be taken to the Luxembourg prison."

XII.

A RESCUING ANGEL.

AND then came a scene which is probably only possible in France. Whatever may be going on there—farce, comedy, the high tension of tragedy— woman steps in and asserts her right of control. I don't know anything which makes upon me so strange an impression as the *frou-frou* of these French petticoats in the midst of slaughter, terror, and universal chaos. I read a book some time ago which had Zola and his acolytes for its contributors. It was a series of stories, all associated with the terrible war of 1870. It is the book which contains Zola's own splendid and pathetic little story, "The Attack on the Mill," and, if I mistake not, it is in the same volume that one finds that weird, amusing, appalling sketch, "Boule de Suif," Maupassant's most powerful, thrilling, and most pessimistic con- tribution to contemporary literature. There was another story, which was the history of an intrigue between Trochu and a high-class *demi-mondaine* in the very midst of the siege, and the sense of awe, horror, disgust, which you feel at this odious episode in the midst of the crash of bombs and the submergence in awful suffering of a whole world, is something that you can never forget.

All this I think of as I read the episode Pasquier tells in the history of his imprisonment:

"As it was necessary to make out a warrant for my arrest and order of committal, I was, while this was being done, taken into a room, where I was placed in custody of the same guard. Fortune willed that a young and rather good-looking woman should come into it just the same time. She was in a gay mood, and seeing me look rather disheartened, she could not resist the temptation of asking me the reason for being so downcast. I had no difficulty in enlightening her. As soon as I had told her my story, she exclaimed : 'What's that ? There was no personal charge against you, and they are going to send you to prison because you are your father's son ! What nonsense ! Wait a bit, I will go and talk to them.' No sooner said than she knocked at the door of the Committee-room, imperiously demanded admittance, and walked in as if in her own house. Now this woman was no less a person than the Citoyenne Mottei, the wife of the President of the Committee, and she exercised a powerful influence over her husband, who, on his side, held absolute sway over his colleagues. I soon heard an animated discussion, wherein the voice of Madame Mottei rose above all others. She came out at last, told me that she had done her best, and that there was a chance of my case taking a favourable turn."

But even yet Pasquier's case was not decided, his danger not yet over. Final rescue came, partly through an old townsman—Levasseur, a Revolutionary leader, whom Pasquier and his family had known in happier days—partly again through female agency. Petticoats and the tumbril—a woman's smiles, blandishments, appeals to the family affection and sexual love of these unchained tigers on the one side; and the cold relentlessness of the Revolutionary tribunals and the constant swish of the guillotine on the other—it is only France which could produce a combination so grotesque, appalling, ironic.

XIII.

STILL THE REIGN OF TERROR.

I MUST give one or two other pictures of the Reign of Terror before I go on to another section of Pasquier's Memoirs. The very acidity and almost brutal terseness of the style help to increase one's sense of the horrors of the time. After the escape to which I have already alluded, Pasquier once more buried himself in the provinces. Here came the dreadful news that his father had been guillotined, and many others who had been friends and colleagues:

"I spent two months of mental suffering in the locality where I had received the awful news. It was, I can never forget it, in the midst of some of the first days of a beautiful spring. All these dreadful misdeeds were being perpetrated with impunity under the rays of a most glorious sun. Alone with my grief, I would often wander for whole days through the woods and among the hills surrounding our retreat. I looked up to heaven, calling upon it to avenge the crimes of the earth."

After months of unsuccessful attempts to cross the frontier, of hiding in all kinds of refuges, Pasquier and his wife were arrested at Amiens by some members of the Revolutionary Committee of Paris. In separate post - chaises they were brought back to Paris.

There is something very weird in the account of this strange journey. It gives a picture of the times as vivid as any that I have ever read. I know no passage, indeed, which leaves so vivid an impression, except the chapters in that wonderful but little-known book of Balzac, "*Les Chouans.*" Pasquier's narrative is, of course, coloured by the prejudices of his class and of those awful times ; but these things add point to the portraits he gives of the persons and the incidents. One sees, living before one and as it were in a microscope, the upheaval of classes, the strange transformation of parties, and the seething ideas of that terrible Revolution, in the following description of Pasquier's journey between Amiens and Paris :

" My companion was a little cripple, physically as hideous as his soul was perverse. He greatly enjoyed telling me that he had known me since childhood, and that he had leased chairs in our parish church. He took pains to add that he would ever remember the generosity of my grandfather and father who had often given him a *louis* by way of a New Year's gift. He was a fervent disciple of the new philosophy, and his memory was stuffed with passages from the works of Voltaire and Jean Jacques. Thus, on passing a certain *château* which was being demolished, he remarked, 'No *château* ever falls but one sees twenty cottages arise in its stead.'

"On our passing through the village of Sarcelles, he gave me a curious example of the regeneration of morals towards which he and his compeers daily worked so zealously. On my pointing out to him a country residence of somewhat finer appearance and better kept than those we had seen so far, for everything in those days presented an appearance of decay and neglect, he replied, 'I should well think so. It is the house of our friend Livry. We often visit him. He still possesses, it is true, an annual income of fifty thousand livres, but he is a first-class fellow. We have just married him to the Citoyenne Saulnier, with whom he had so long cohabited. (She was *première danseuse* at the Opéra.) "Come now," we said to him, "it is time that this disgraceful state of affairs should cease. To the winds with family prejudice! The *ci-devant* marquis must marry the dancer." So he married her, and did wisely, for he might otherwise have already danced his last jig, or at the very least be rusticating in the shade of the walls of the Luxembourg prison.' Happily, our two guards combined with the lofty sentiments of which I have just given an idea a passionate fondness for money; and this was our salvation."

XIV.

A PRISON SCENE.

PASQUIER and his wife were confined for some days in a house in Paris before they were sent to the prison of Saint-Lazare; this was done with a view of abstracting from them all their remaining money; and official avarice saved their lives.

"Had I been imprisoned there two days earlier, I might possibly have been taken away in one of those carts which, during those two days, carried over eighty people from the prison to the foot of the scaffold. Every one connected with the Paris Parliament, one of my brothers-in-law, and several of my friends, perished on the day of my entering the prison. Had I arrived earlier, I could not have escaped their fate."

This is a sufficiently terrible picture, but a sentence that follows is even more terrible as a revelation of how families were swept off by the guillotine. " In this prison," says Pasquier, " were still two of my brothers-in-law and a brother, hardly more than a child, but who had, in spite of this, been a prisoner for eight months." Just fancy it—a father guillotined, a brother-in-law guillotined, two brothers-in-law standing under the shadow of the scaffold, a brother, likewise, who is still a child ; and Pasquier and his wife threatened with the same fate!

More terrible than almost any passage in these Memoirs is the description of a prison personage who played a prominent part in the economy of the gaols. One of the many grounds given for getting rid of obnoxious persons was a professed belief in prison conspiracies. "What added," says Pasquier, "to the horror of this mendacious invention was the means employed for giving practical effect to the principle." Here was the means :

"In every one of the large prisons were a certain number of scoundrels, apparently detained as prisoners like the others, but who were really there to select and draw up a list of the victims. Several of them had become known as spies, and, incredible as it may seem, their lives were spared by those in the midst of whom they fulfilled their shameful duty. On the contrary, the prisoners treated them gently and paid them court. I had scarcely passed the first wicket, and was following the jailer who was taking me to the room I was to occupy, when I found myself face to face with

M. de Montrou, already notorious through a few somewhat scandalous intrigues, and whose adventures have since created such a stir in society. He came close to me, and not pretending to notice me, whispered into my ear the following salutary bit of advice: 'While here do not speak a word to anybody whom you do not know thoroughly.'"

XV.

A PRISON TERRORIST.

AND now, here is a type of the creature which such a system produced. The picture is sufficiently appalling; but still more appalling to me is that of the state of terror and humiliation to which the proudest names in France were reduced :

"On reaching, with Madame Pasquier, the lodging destined for our use, and which had been vacated by the two victims of the previous day, we were soon surrounded by our relations and by a few friends who hastened to offer us all the assistance they could. We were enjoying, as far as one can enjoy anything when in a similar position, these proofs of kindly interest and friendship, when one of my brothers-in-law, who was looking out of the window, exclaimed, 'Ah, here is Pépin Dègrouttes about to take his daily walk. We must go and show ourselves. Come along with us.' 'Why so?' I queried, whereupon I was told that he was the principal one among the rascals whose abominable *rôle* I have described. They were designated by the name of '*moutons*,' a name consecrated by prison slang. Every afternoon he would thus take a turn in the yard, and it was for him the occasion of passing in review, so to speak, the flock which he was gradually sending to the slaughterhouse. Woe unto him who seemed to hide or to avoid his look! Such a one was immediately noted, and he could be sure that his turn would come next. Many a gallant man's death became a settled thing because he was a few minutes late in coming down into the yard and passing under the fellow's notice. The surrendering of oneself to his discretion was apparently a way of imploring mercy at his hands. We went through the formality, and it constituted a scene which I can never forget. I can still see him, a man four feet seven or eight inches high, hump-backed and twisted form, bandy-legged, and as red-headed as Judas. He was completely surrounded by prisoners, some of whom walked backward in his presence, earnestly soliciting a look from him."

The fall of Robespierre brought the release of Pasquier as well as others; and thus his sufferings ended. From this time forward he had a prosperous career, for he hailed the accession of Napoleon as the end of Anarchy, and soon was enrolled in the ranks of that lucky adventurer's chief officials.

XVI.

NAPOLEON.

THE extracts I shall now take from Pasquier will mainly refer to Napoleon. It is in this part of the narrative that the faults of these Memoirs come out most prominently. Here was an official, brought into almost daily contact with the most interesting figure in all human history; and yet he hardly adds anything to our knowledge of Napoleon's temperament or character. Pasquier does certainly give us an excellent account of the official workings of the Napoleonic machine. In all such descriptions there is nothing left unrecorded; the narrative is lucid, tranquil, and complete. But after all, it is Napoleon we want to hear about—Napoleon the man, not Napoleon the Emperor and the official; and for that information we mostly ask in vain. However, I must do my best to piece together passages from the Memoirs which bear on Pasquier's great master, and see if I can manage to get some addition to our knowledge of that intensely absorbing personality.

We get a first and rather amusing glimpse of Napoleon at the moment of his return after his victories in Italy. In this picture also we see beside Napoleon a man, his relations to whom form one of the most striking portions of this narrative :

"The General was presented to the Directoire in the courtyard of the Petit Luxembourg, where an *autel de la patrie* had been erected. He was introduced to the five directors by the Minister of Foreign Affairs, M. de Talleyrand, who took occasion to deliver a speech wherein, honouring in Bonaparte 'his undying love of country and humanity,' he praised 'his contempt of luxuriousness and pomp, this miserable ambition of ordinary souls! The day was at hand when it would become necessary to entreat him to tear himself away from the quiet peace of his studious retreat.' It was noticed that General Bonaparte hardly partook of any dish at the dinner which followed this ceremony. This abstinence was attributed to his feeling unwell, but I learned since from a confidential aide-de-camp, M. de La Valette, that Bonaparte had considered this precaution necessary in the face of the dangers which he believed threatened his existence. Whether or not his suspicions were based on any foundation, one cannot help recording them, for they must have greatly affected the resolution he was about to take."

XVII.

THE RETURN FROM EGYPT.

PASQUIER draws a different picture of the state of French feeling towards Napoleon on his return from Egypt from that which is generally accepted.

"Fate led me one evening to the theatre next to a box occupied by two very pretty women who were unknown to me. During the performance a message was brought to them. I noticed that it caused great and joyous commotion. They left, and I soon afterwards learnt that they were the sisters of Bonaparte, and that he had landed on French soil."

But Pasquier goes on to declare: "The effect produced on me by the knowledge of this fact, and on the greater number of those who received it simultaneously with me, was in no way prophetic of the consequences which were to follow." For at this period Napoleon was not thought so much of. "The expedition to Egypt, which has since appealed so strongly to the imagination, was then hardly looked upon as anything but a mad undertaking."

"What had especially struck people in these bulletins was a certain declaration in favour of the Mohammedan creed, the effect of which, though it might be somewhat great in Egypt, had in France only called forth ridicule. I state all this because a number of people, believing, apparently, that they were adding to their hero's greatness, have since sought to represent him as ardently and impatiently expected. I am of opinion that they have not spoken truly, and deceived themselves

with regard to the effect which they have sought
to produce. To my mind, Bonaparte is far greater
when he is considered as arriving when no one
expects him or dreams of him, when he faces the
disadvantages of a return bearing resemblance to
a flight, when he triumphs over the prejudices
which this return raises against him, and when in
the space of a month he lays hand on every form
of power. He is far greater, I maintain, when
surrounded by all the obstacles he has triumphed
over, than when an attempt is made to present him
as the cynosure of all eyes, and having but to come
forward to be lord of all."

XVIII.

NAPOLEON'S MOMENT OF FEAR.

IT was while he was breaking down the Legislative Assembly, which stood between him and
power, that Napoleon—as I have already told—
displayed one of the few moments of terror in his
whole lifetime. Curiously enough, his brother,
from the sheer fact of being a Parliamentarian,
was strong when the soldier was weak; and it
was the courage of the Parliamentarian that saved
the cowardice of the soldier.

"It is a known fact that on the 19th, at Saint-
Cloud, the firmness of General Bonaparte, so
often tested on the battle-field, was for a moment
shaken by the vociferous yells with which he was

greeted by the *Conseil des Cinq Cents*, in the face of which he deemed it prudent to beat a retreat. His brother Lucien was President of the Council, and the firmness of the Parliamentarian was in this instance more stable than that of the warrior. Lucien weathered the storm, and prevented the passing of a decree of outlawry. Bonaparte soon returned, supported by a military escort commanded by Generals Murat and Leclerc. The soldiers had been electrified by a rumour that the life of Bonaparte had been attempted in the Council Chamber. The appearance and the attitude of this faithful armed band quickly cut the Gordian knot. The Chamber was soon evacuated, and many of the members of the Council, anxious to take the shortest road, fled by the windows."

XIX.

TALLEYRAND.

I HAVE already said that the story of the relations between Napoleon and Talleyrand is one of the most interesting chapters in these Memoirs. Talleyrand, indeed, is sometimes a more prominent figure on M. Pasquier's canvas than Napoleon. It is a pity that M. Pasquier did not give us a full-length portrait of this extraordinary and repulsive personality; he gives instead somewhat disconnected glimpses. However, let us take

M. Pasquier as we find him; here is his first mention of the great *diplomat*:

"This is the place to dwell once more on the strange position of this man, who always seemed to enjoy the greatest confidence, and this at the time when, in reality, he did not inspire any, and did not really obtain it; who, on his side, appeared animated with the most sincere zeal, when it was impossible for those who had any intercourse with him to have any doubt as to his discontent. I often saw him in those days at the house of one of my relations, a woman of intellect, who, for some months past, had become very intimate with him, and in whose *salon* he spent many of his evenings; her social circle was small, and consequently no restraint was put upon him. Owing to this kind of intimacy, his actual frame of mind was readily penetrated, and I easily observed that, consumed as he was with a desire for fault-finding, he considered himself but little bound by any engagements, the result of his former deeds and utterances."

XX.

TALLEYRAND'S TREACHERY.

IT was during the negotiations at Erfurt that Napoleon reached the very zenith of his glory and his power. How often must he have looked back on those golden moments! M. Pasquier willingly recognises all the supreme skill happily displayed at this eventful hour.

"None of the seductions likely to impress favourably those whom it was necessary he should captivate had been neglected. The members of the Comédie Française had been ordered to Erfurt, where they played alternately comedy and tragedy; and so for a fortnight this little town enjoyed French plays nearly every night. Extravagance and magnificence could hardly go beyond this; and great was the delight of all those invited to enjoy so unexpected a treat. Napoleon, when giving his orders to Talma, previous to his departure from Paris, had promised him a *parterre* full of kings, and it will be seen that he had kept his word. He might have added that never would any *parterre* show itself so well disposed. Among the actresses forming part of the *troupe* were several pretty women, and if the Court chroniclers are to be believed, their merits did not pass unnoticed. Nay, it has even been stated that one of them had for some little time engaged the attention of the most eminent one of the personages among those whom Napoleon wished to win over to his side. Judging from all appearances, the happy result of his efforts in this respect must have been undoubted, and it can well be supposed that the attractions of Erfurt greatly surpassed those of Tilsit. It was at Erfurt that, during the performance of

Œdipe, the Emperor Alexander, by turning towards Napoleon, gave so pointed an application of the line: '*L'amitié d'un grand homme est un présent des dieux.*" On the part of Alexander, this meant not only a complete accord in political ideas, but a worship, and the devotion of the strongest friendship. On his side, Napoleon admirably exercised the art of deriving benefit from such demonstrations. His efforts ever tended towards not abating one jot of his pretensions to superiority, and he attained this object by caressing in a delicate manner the self-love of his powerful and august ally. His efforts in this direction were all the more constant for the fact that this superiority could alone explain and render secure the most astounding and most valuable of his triumphs. On no other occasion, perhaps, did the suppleness and craftiness of his Italian spirit shine to more brilliant advantage."

XXI.

HUMILIATION OF GERMANY.

ONE of the incidents of this time is narrated by Pasquier, and gives a very good idea of the dreadful humiliation to which Germany had been reduced by this successful conqueror.

"The *fête* given to Napoleon by the Duke of Saxe-Weimar during the Erfurt conferences cannot be passed over, for it characterises marvellously well the incredible obsequiousness of those on whom the burden of his omnipotence in Germany bore down. This Duke conceived the idea of inviting him to a hunting party on the very battle-field of Jena. The rout of the stags and deer represented that of the Prussians, and hecatombs of denizens of the forest took the place of human victims."

It is incidents like these that will explain to us the terrible revenge that Germany insisted on taking on France in 1870.

I return to Talleyrand's part in the conference at Erfurt. It throws a very curious light upon that *diplomat*. Talleyrand's "ardent desire was to attain personal importance," as Pasquier puts it. It will be understood, therefore, how miserable he was when Napoleon declared he would have no intermediary between himself and the Emperor Alexander of Russia, whom, as we have seen, Napoleon had so completely captured at this moment. Talleyrand, however, was equal to the occasion :

"Chance gave him the opportunity he was seeking. Having gone one day, after Napoleon had retired for the night, to the house of the Princess of Thurn and Taxis, where he intended to spend the rest of the evening, he met there the Emperor Alexander, who had come with the same intention. This chance meeting was a happy one for both of them; the conversation of the French courtier could not fail to be most agreeable to the Russian Sovereign. They soon contracted the habit of meeting in the evening, and this habit lasted as long as·the conferences. M. de Talleyrand had neglected nothing to convince Napoleon of the fact that he was using to his advantage only the facilities afforded to him by so precious a habit."

Talleyrand, in his Memoirs, states that the use he made of these confidences between himself and Alexander was to betray Napoleon:

"When Napoleon handed to Alexander the draft of the agreement which he was asking him to sign, it was M. de Talleyrand who pointed out to him the serious objections to it, and drafted for him the memorandum which he (Alexander) handed to Napoleon."

The explanation of all this, as Pasquier has no hesitation in declaring, was that Talleyrand was in the pay of the Emperor of Austria, and also that he obtained from him, as part of the price of his treason, the rich alliance of his nephew, Edmond de Périgord, and the daughter of the Duchess of Courland.

XXII.

THE TALLEYRAND INTRIGUE.

WHEN Napoleon embarked upon his Spanish campaigns, Talleyrand began to take means

to have his revenge on his master. One of
the first signs of the change in Talleyrand's
feelings was the close of the almost lifelong
struggle between himself and Fouché, Minister of
Police.

"Both men had apparently begun to look at
matters from the same stand-point, and losing all
confidence in the fortunes of Napoleon, had said
to themselves that if he were to disappear from
the scene, they would alone be in a position to
dispose of the Empire, and that it was consequently
necessary that they should determine upon his
successor, to their mutual and best advantage."

And now the confederates were so imprudent
as to warn the whole world of their reconciliation:

" It must either have been that they believed
themselves very powerful in their union, or that
they felt pretty well secure of the downfall of
the Emperor. I can still recall the effect produced
at a brilliant evening party given by M. de
Talleyrand by the appearance of M. Fouché on
the occasion when he entered his former foe's
drawing-room for the first time. No one could
believe his eyes, and the wonder was far greater
when the affectation of harmony was carried to
the point of the two men linking arms and
together walking from room to room during the
whole course of the evening."

Meantime the relatives and adherents of
Napoleon, whom he had left behind in Paris,

warned him of what was taking place, with the result that he became alarmed, and returned to Paris.

"It was, indeed, impossible not to notice that the rapidity with which he generally covered distances had been much greater than was his wont, and that, in spite of the difficulties presented to the traveller. He had been compelled to make several parts of the journey on horseback."

XXIII.

NAPOLEON IN A PASSION.

WHEN Napoleon came back he allowed his rage to slumber for a few days, but finally it burst, and there came one of the most repulsive scenes in history. The scene took place in presence of nearly all the Ministers and of several high officials, and lasted for over half an hour, during which Napoleon never ceased to violently declaim; and here are something like the terms of this remarkable address:

"You are a thief, a coward, a man without honour; you do not believe in God; you have all your life been a traitor to your duties, you have deceived and betrayed everybody; nothing is sacred to you; you would sell your own father. I have loaded you with gifts, and yet there is nothing you would not undertake against me. Thus, for the past ten months, you have been shameless enough, because you supposed, rightly

or wrongly, that my affairs in Spain were going
astray, to say to all that would listen to you,
that you always blamed my undertaking there,
whereas it was you yourself who first put it into
my head, and who persistently urged it. And that
man, that unfortunate (he was thus designating
the Duc d'Enghien), by whom was I advised of
the place of his residence? Who drove me to
deal cruelly with him? What, then, are you
aiming at? What do you wish for? What do
you hope? Do you dare to say? You deserve
that I should smash you like a wine-glass. I
can do it, but I despise you too much to take
the trouble."

M. Pasquier goes on to say:

"The foregoing is, in an abridged form, the
substance of what M. de Talleyrand was compelled to listen to during this mortal half-hour,
which must have been a frightful one for him if
one is to judge of it by the suffering felt at it by
those present, none of whom ever subsequently
referred to it without shuddering at its recollection."

But the most curious part of the transaction,
and what struck everybody who was present,
was :—

"the seeming indifference of the man who
had to listen to all this, and who, for nearly a
whole half-hour, endured, without flinching, a
torrent of invective for which there is probably

no precedent among men in such high positions and in such a place."

And there was even this more remarkable fact :—

"This man, who was thus ignominiously treated, remained at Court, and preserved his rank in the hierarchy of the highest Imperial dignities. Although in less close connection with the Emperor than heretofore, he did not for that reason become completely a stranger to affairs of State, and we are soon to see him called upon once more to give advice to his Sovereign on an occasion of the highest importance."

One of the most remarkable facts in connection with the whole story is the patience with which Talleyrand waited for his revenge; but when it came, the revenge was striking. It was Talleyrand's hand more than any other that was accountable for the final blow to Napoleon's power.

XXIV.

A CURIOUS BONAPARTE TRAIT.

PASQUIER confirms Taine's description of the character of Napoleon's family. The same strange self-confidence, the inflexibility of will, ran through them all.

"The Emperor had four brothers and three sisters. That indomitable stubbornness just referred to had already removed from his controlling power two of his brothers. The one known as Lucien, and afterwards as Prince de Canino, a title given to him by the Pope, had a fiery soul. He was ambitious and greedily fond of money. Public affairs had all the more attraction for him in that he had played an important part in them on the 18th Brumaire, and he could lay the flattering unction to himself that his firmness on that day so fraught with peril had greatly contributed to its success. He deserted the Court at the time his brother reached the summit of grandeur, and when he was in a position to promise the highest destinies to all the members of his family. On his becoming a widower, it was impossible to cause him to renounce his matrimonial views with a *divorcée*, who had been his mistress for some time past, and sooner than yield, he went into a voluntary exile, from which he did not return until after many trials, which finally led him to England, at the time of the misfortunes of 1815. During his stay in Italy, he seemed to make it a point of honour to show his loyalty to the Pontifical Government, whose subject he had become."

Joseph had exactly the same temperament:

" Joseph, the eldest of the family, had ascended the throne of Spain, after having occupied that of Naples. Witty, voluptuous, effeminate, although courageous, nothing in his incredible fortunes was to him a cause for surprise. I heard him in January, 1814, make the extraordinary claim that if his brother had not interfered with his affairs after his second entry into Madrid, he would be still governing Spain. This is explained by another striking trait of the character of the Bonapartes. No sooner had they set their feet on the path leading to Royal honours, than those most intimate with them were never to see them for a single instant belie the seriousness with which they took the highest positions; they even ended in believing that they had been called to them as a matter of course. They had the instinct of their greatness. Joseph displays at the very outset of the elevation of his brother such impatience to see himself in possession of a rank worthy of him that Napoleon was wont to say laughingly: 'I do believe that Joseph is sometimes tempted to think that I have robbed my eldest brother of the inheritance of the King, our father.'"

XXV.

THE FEMALE BONAPARTES.

AND Napoleon's sisters behaved in a similar way:—

"Of the three sisters the eldest almost reigned in Tuscany under the title of Grand Duchess. She made herself beloved there, and this fortunate province owed to her a gentle treatment denied to all other countries then united with France. She has left a pleasant memory behind her, in spite of the irregularities of her private life, which she did not take sufficient care to conceal. The Princess Pauline, wife of Prince Borghese, was perhaps the most beautiful woman of her time, and she hardly dreamt of giving prominence to any other advantage than this one. She had been to Santo Domingo with her first husband, General Leclerc. The sun of the tropics had, they do say, been astonished at the ardour of her dissipation. The fatigue consequent upon such an existence shattered her health, and for a long time she was carried about in a litter. In spite of her poor health, she was none the less beautiful.

" It remains for me to speak of Caroline, the wife of Murat, and Queen of Naples, who bore a great resemblance to the Emperor. Less beautiful than Pauline, although endowed with more seductive charms, she possessed the art, without being any more scrupulous than her sisters, of showing a greater respect for the proprieties ; besides, all her tastes vanished in presence of her ambition. She had found the Naples crown somewhat too small for her head, and greatly coveted the Spanish one, but in the end she became resigned to her fate, and wore with good grace that which had fallen to her lot. It may even be said that she did so with no little amount of dignity. She was insane enough to believe that her fortune could withstand the catastrophe which swept away that of Napoleon.

In that extraordinary race, the most sacred engagements, the deepest affections, went for nothing
as soon as political combinations 3eemed to advise
it ; nevertheless, each one of its members possessed
in the highest degree the family spirit. Caroline
took a hand in bringing about the downfall of her
brother, to whom she owed all her grandeur. It is,
perhaps, she who dealt the final blow."

CHAPTER IV.

AS NAPOLEON APPEARED TO A RELATIVE.*

LAVALETTE.

THE next estimate I shall give is that of
Lavalette.

Count Lavalette is the hero of one of the
most romantic stories in history. Few particulars
are given of that episode in his Memoirs which,
nevertheless, have an interest far beyond their
merely personal character. Lavalette was a
brave soldier, a successful Minister, and intimate
servant of Napoleon. But the great interest of
this book to me is the picture it gives of the
point of view of the average man during the
strange events that made up the passionate
drama of France from the beginning of the
Revolution to the end of the Empire. I don't
know how this book would strike a Frenchman;
but to me it reads as an extremely fair one.

* "Memoirs of Count Lavalette, adjutant and private
secretary to Napoleon, and Postmaster-General under the
Empire." (London : Gibbings.)

Events are set forth, it is true, without much
glow or inspiration; but on the other hand,
the moderation and simplicity of its tone enable
one to see events in their true light, and to
understand the feelings which took hold of the
minds of most Frenchmen, and made them pass
without much difficulty or much remonstrance
from one sort of government to another—governments so diverse as the old French Monarchy,
the wild Revolution, and then the iron despotism
of Napoleon.

I.

ABOUT THE BASTILLE.

LAVALETTE was the son of a respectable Paris
tradesman.   He received a good education, was
intended for the Church, and had got as far as
holy orders and a small position, when the
Revolution broke out and upset him, as everything else. He was soon a member of the
National Guard, and was present at many of
the stirring and terrible scenes which opened
the Revolution. As will be gathered from what
I have already said, he is a cool, unimpassioned
observer, had military instinct from his whole
temperament; and any description, therefore, which
he gives of the doings of the mob in that strange
period, is free from any enthusiasm, and rather
censorious than otherwise.   Thus, when he
describes what he saw at the taking of the

Bastille, you can clearly perceive that if he had been in command and such a monarch as Napoleon had been on the throne, the history of that event and of the whole world would have been very different. He confirms the impression, which has been got by every close student of the French Revolution, that the old Bastille was formidable and hateful rather for what it represented than what it was:

"Situated without the precincts of the city, beyond the Porte Saint-Antoine, it was evidently never intended as a check upon the metropolis. It was said the King meant to keep his treasure there, but the interior distribution clearly evinced that it was destined to serve as a State prison. This pretended fortress consisted of five towers, about one hundred and twenty feet high, joined together by strong high walls and surrounded by broad deep ditches. Its entrance was protected by drawbridges, and on July 14th it was commanded by a governor, and defended by about sixty Swiss veterans; a few old guns, of small size, were placed on the terraces of the towers. There was nothing very formidable in its appearance; but something like a superstitious terror pervaded the minds of the people, and most marvellous stories were told respecting the Bastille. For many ages the most noble victims of despotism groaned within its mysterious walls. Some prisoners, who had been fortunate enough

to escape from it, had published most terrifying
accounts. Those formidable towers, those vigilant
sentinels, who suffered no one, even by stealth,
to cast a look towards them ; those numerous,
ferocious - looking guards, frightful by their
appearance, and more frightful still by their
deep silence — all united to excite terror and
anxious curiosity. Nevertheless, the State prison
was not dangerous for the people ; it was designed
for persons of high birth, or for literary people
who ventured to displease the Ministry. But
to the wish of satisfying curiosity, was added a
noble feeling of pity for the numerous victims
supposed to be shut up in the fortress, and the
whole population of Paris resolved to make
themselves master of the Bastille."

II.

THE HANGING OF FOULON.

LAVALETTE saw the hanging of poor old Foulon.
He evidently does not believe that Foulon ever
used the phrase which had been attributed to
him: "Why don't the people eat grass?" or,
as Lavalette gives it, "Hay was good enough to
feed the Paris rabble." Anyhow, the sight of
his execution produced a great effect upon
Lavalette, and shaped his after career as it
did that of so many others.

"I crossed the Place de la Grève to the
Comédie Française; it rained, and there was

no tumult anywhere but facing the Hôtel de Ville. I was standing on the parapet when I saw raised above the crowd the figure of an old man with gray hair; it was the unfortunate Foulon being hanged at the lamp-post. I returned home to study my beloved Montesquieu; and from that moment I began to hate a revolution in which people were murdered without being heard in their defence."

There is something thrilling in this plain, blunt, terse narrative of that awful day. Familiar as the scene is to us all, these few lines seem to me singularly effective—above all things, by bringing out the fact, which is to be found in more than one scene in the Revolution, that this epoch-making tragedy passed through so narrow an area of disturbance. "There was no tumult anywhere but facing the Hôtel de Ville." By-and-by we shall see other and even more remarkable instances of this peculiar phenomenon of the Revolution. Lavalette, as a National Guard, was also present at the great march of the women to Versailles. His account of that day would gladden the heart of Taine. The Mœnads who headed the procession were "inebriated women, the refuse of humankind." Lavalette's company would have little to do with these creatures; and he was strongly of opinion that the whole manifestation could have been put down if the King had shown some firmness.

III.

" TO PARIS."

AND finally Lavalette accompanied the monarch in that journey back to Paris, which Carlyle and so many other writers have told us all about. Lavalette's narrative is excellent reading, though coloured by the Imperialist soldier's prejudices.

"The mob crowded in the marble court, and wandering on the outside of the palace, began to express again their designs with frightful howlings. 'To Paris! To Paris!' were the cries. Their prey was promised them, and then fresh cries ordered the unfortunate family to appear on the balcony. The Queen showed herself, accompanied by her children; she was forced by threats to send them away. I mixed in the crowd, and beheld for the first time that unfortunate Princess. She was dressed in white; her head was bare, and adorned with beautiful fair locks. Motionless, and in a modest and noble attitude, she appeared to me like a victim on the block. The enraged populace were not moved at the sight of woe in all its majesty. Imprecations increased, and the unfortunate Princess could not even find a support in the King, for his presence did but augment the fury of the multitude. At last preparations for departure did more towards appeasing them than promises could have done, and by twelve o'clock the frightful procession set off. I hope such a scene will never be witnessed again. I have often asked myself how the metropolis of a nation so celebrated for urbanity and elegance of manners, how the brilliant city of Paris could contain the savage hordes I that day beheld, and who so long reigned over it! In walking through the streets of Paris, it seems to me, the features even of the lowest and most miserable class of people do not present to the eye anything like ferociousness, or the meanest passions in all their hideous energy. Can those passions alter the features so as to deprive them of all likeness to humanity? or does the terror inspired by the sight of a guilty wretch give him the semblance of a wild beast? These madmen, dancing in the mire and covered with mud, surrounded the King's coach. The groups that marched foremost carried on long pikes the bloody and dishevelled heads of the Life Guards butchered in the morning. Surely Satan himself first invented the placing of a human head at the end of a lance. The disfigured and pale features, the gory locks, the half-open mouth, the closed eyes, images of death, added to the gestures and salutations the executioners made them perform, in horrible mockery of life, presented the most frightful spectacle rage could have imagined. A troop of women, ugly as crime itself, swarming like insects, and wearing grenadiers' hairy caps, went continually to and fro, howling barbarous songs, embracing and insulting the Life Guards."

This is certainly an appalling picture.

IV.

PARIS DURING THE MASSACRE.

LAVALETTE also saw some of the September massacres. He had succeeded—and with no great difficulty—in releasing a lady from the prison at the Hôtel de la Force; and then had tried to muster a body of National Guards to prevent the massacre of the rest. His efforts proved vain. His narrative brings out clearly the fact of this, as of other scenes, that a small, resolute, and violent minority are more potent than the mass of the overwhelming majority which opposes them. Lavalette went to "some of the National Guards, whom we looked upon as the most steady," but "notwithstanding my most pressing entreaties I could make no impression upon them." All he could do under the circumstances was to go to the prison of La Force and see what he could do himself. His description of the scene is very remarkable in more respects than one:

"Before the wicket that leads to the Rue de Ballets, I found about fifty men at most. These were the butchers; the rest had been drawn there by curiosity, and were perhaps more execrable than the executioners; for though they dared neither go away nor take part in the horrid deed, still they applauded. I looked forward, and at sight of a heap of bodies still palpitating with life, I uttered a cry of horror. Two men turned round, and, taking me abruptly by the collar, dragged me violently to the street, where they reproached me with imprudence, and then, running away, left me alone in the dark. The horrible spectacle I had witnessed deprived me of all courage; I went home overwhelmed with shame and despair for humanity so execrably injured, and the French character so deplorably disgraced."

I call this remarkable, because the number of the persons who took part in the massacre is put down at as low a figure as fifty; all the rest are spectators. But what follows is still stranger—confirming the statement which students of the Revolution have often heard—that Paris, outside a very restricted area, practically remained pretty much the same during the very worst times of the Revolution:

"The particulars of the massacre having all been recorded in the memoirs of the time, I need not repeat them here. I was, moreover, no spectator of them. They lasted three days, and—I blush while I write it—at half a mile from the different prisons nobody would have imagined that their countrymen were at that moment butchered by hundreds. The shops were open, pleasure was going on in all its animation, and sloth rejoiced in its vacuity. All the vanities and seductions of luxury, voluptuousness, and dissipation, peaceably swayed their sceptre. They feigned an ignorance of cruelties which they had not the courage to oppose."

v.

HOW A VILLAGE WAS AFFECTED BY THE OVERTURN.

IT will have been seen that Lavalette's sympathies were frankly Royalist in the early days of the Revolution, but when the foreign invasion enrolled every young Frenchman of spirit in the army, Lavalette was carried away like the rest, and determined to go to the front. His opinions, however, made even this rather difficult, and he was obliged to seek a volunteer corps. Two other friends, also of *suspect* opinions, adopted the same tactics; and here is one of the many adventures which befell them on the way—it is an extraordinary and vivid description of the kind of things which the great upheaval had made possible:

"We set off . . . for Autun, and we arrived next day at a village, not far from Vermanton, situated amidst woods, and the inhabitants of which got their livelihood by making wooden shoes. Two days before, a bishop and two of his grand-vicars, who were escaping in a post-coach, had been arrested by them. The coach was searched, and some hundred *louis-d'or* having been found in it, the peasants thought the best way to gain the property would be to kill the real owners. Their new profession being more lucrative than their former one, they resolved to continue it, and in consequence set themselves on the look-out for all travellers. Our sailors' dresses were not very promising, but we carried our heads high— our manners seemed haughty, and so a little hunchbacked man, an attorney of the village, guessed we might perhaps help to enrich them. The inhabitants being resolved not to make any more wooden shoes, applauded the hunchback's advice. We were brought to the municipality, where the mob followed us. The attorney placed himself on a large table, and began reading with emphasis in a loud voice all our passports— Louis Amédée Auguste d'Aubonne, André Louis Leclerc de la Ronde, Marie Chamans de la Valette. Here the rascal added the *de*, that was not in my passport. On hearing these aristocratic names a murmur began ; all the eyes turned towards us were hostile, and the hunch-back cried out that our knapsacks ought to be examined. The harvest would have been rich. I was the poorest of the set, and I had five-

and-twenty *louis* in gold. We looked upon ourselves as lost, when D'Aubonne, whose stature was tall, jumped on the table and began to harangue the assembly. He was clever at making verses, and knew besides at his fingers' ends the whole slang dictionary. He began with a volley of abuse and imprecations that surprised the audience; but he soon raised his style, and repeated the words 'country,' 'liberty,' 'sovereignty of the people,' with so much vehemence and such a thundering voice, that the effect was prodigious. He was interrupted by unanimous applause. The giddy-headed young man did not stop there. He imperiously ordered Leclerc de la Ronde to get upon the table. La Ronde was the cleverest mimic I ever saw. He was thirty-five years old, of a grotesque shape, and as dark as a Moor. His eyes were sunk in his head and covered with thick black eyebrows, and his nose and chin immeasurably long. D'Aubonne said to the assembly: 'You'll soon be able to judge whether we are or are not Republicans from Paris.' And turning to his companion he said to him: 'Answer to the Republican catechism: What is God? What are the people? What is a King?' The other, with a contrite air, a nasal voice, and winding himself about like a harlequin, answered: 'God is nature; the people are the poor; a king is a lion, a tiger, an elephant, who tears to pieces, devours, and crushes the poor people to death.' It was not possible to resist this. Astonishment, shouts, enthusiasm, were carried to the highest pitch. The orators were embraced—hugged—carried in triumph. The honour of lodging us grew a subject of dispute. We were forced to drink, and we were soon as much at a loss how to get away from these brutal wretches, now our friends, as we had been to escape out of their hands while they were our enemies. Luckily, D'Aubonne again found means to draw us out of this scrape. He gravely observed that we had no time to stop, and that our country claimed the tribute of our courage. They let us go at last."

VI.

A FIRST VIEW OF NAPOLEON.

I MAKE a big skip in the life of Lavalette, and bring him to the time when he made the acquaintance of Napoleon, with whom he was destined afterwards to be so closely associated. He was introduced to Napoleon when the young General was winning those victories in Italy that first created his fame, and he was immediately appointed an aide-de-camp. This is his account of his first interview with Napoleon:

"I went to the General-in-Chief, who lodged in the Palazzo Serbelloni. He was giving audience. His saloon was filled with military men of all ranks, and high civil officers. His air was affable, but his look so firm and fixed that I turned pale when he addressed himself to me. I faltered out my name, and afterwards my thanks, to which he listened in silence, his eyes fastening on me with an expression of severity that quite disconcerted me. At last, he said, ' Come back at six o'clock, and put on the sash.' That sash, which distinguishes the aides-de-camp of the General-in-Chief, was of white and red silk, and was worn around the left arm."

VII.

NAPOLEON AND JOSEPHINE.

THIS was at Milan; and it was at the moment when Napoleon, still in the early flush of his passion for Josephine, had succeeded in getting her to leave her beloved Paris and follow him to the army. Lavalette describes a curious and characteristic scene :

" The General-in-Chief was at that time just married. Madame Bonaparte was a charming woman; and all the anxiety of the command—all the trouble of the government of Italy—could not prevent her husband from giving himself wholly up to the happiness he enjoyed at home. It was during that short residence at Milan that the young painter Gros, afterwards so celebrated, painted the picture of the General. He represented him on the Bridge of Lodi, at the moment when, with the colours in his hand, he rushed forward to induce the troops to follow him. The painter could never obtain a long sitting. Madame Bonaparte used to take her husband upon her lap after breakfast, and hold him fast for a few minutes. I was present at three of these sittings. The age of the newly-married couple, and the painter's enthusiasm for the hero, were sufficient excuses for such familiarity."

Lavalette was united to Napoleon by family ties, for he married a Beauharnais—a relative of the Empress—and Napoleon seems to have had great confidence in him. There is not quite as much about Napoleon as one might have expected from such intimacy, and the glimpses of the great General are few and far between.

VIII.

LABOURS AND FATIGUES.

NAPOLEON sent for Lavalette one evening, after his return to Paris from the disastrous expedition to Russia, and here is what took place :

"On my arrival he commanded me to come every evening into the bath-room next to his bed-chamber. He then had me called in to him, while he warmed himself undressed before the fire. We talked familiarly together for an hour before he went to bed. The first evening I found him so cast down, so overwhelmed, that I was frightened. I went to see his secretary, who was my friend. I communicated to him my fears that his mind, formerly so strong, had begun to sink. 'You need not fear,' he replied; 'he has lost nothing of his energy; but in the evening you see him quite bent down with fatigue. He goes to bed at eleven o'clock, but he is up at three o'clock in the morning, and till night every moment is devoted to business. It is time to put an end to this, for he must sink under it.' The principal subject of our conversation was the situation of France. I used to tell him, with a degree of frankness the truth of which alone could make him pardon its rudeness, that France was fatigued to an excess—that it was quite impossible to bear much longer the burthen with which she was loaded, and that she would undoubtedly throw off the yoke, and according to custom, seek an alleviation to her sufferings in novelty, her favourite divinity. I said in particular a great deal of the Bourbons, who, I observed, would finally inherit his royal spoil if ever fortune laid him low. The mention of the Bourbons made him thoughtful, and he threw himself on his bed without uttering a word; but after a few minutes, having approached to know whether I might retire, I saw that he had fallen into a profound sleep."

IX.

THE RETURN FROM ELBA.

I PASS on to Lavalette's description of the return of Napoleon from Elba. He was in the Tuileries on the night when Napoleon made his re-entry, and his description is very vivid of that remarkable scene:

" Five or six hundred officers on half-pay were walking in the extensive courtyard, wishing each other joy at the return of Napoleon. In the apartments the two sisters-in-law of the Emperor, the Queens of Spain and Holland, were waiting for him, deeply affected. Soon after, the ladies of the household and those of the Empress came to join them. The *fleurs-de-lis* had everywhere superseded the bees. However, on examining the large carpet spread over the floor of the audience-chamber where they sat, one of the ladies perceived that a flower was loose: she took it off, and the bee soon reappeared. Immediately all the ladies set to work, and in less than half an hour, to the great mirth of the company, the carpet again became Imperial. In the meanwhile time passed on; Paris was calm. Those persons who lived far from the Tuileries did not come near it; everybody remained at home; and indifference seemed to pervade the minds of all. But it was not the same in the country. Officers who arrived at Fontainebleau, preceding the Emperor, told us it was extremely difficult to advance on the road. Deep columns of peasants lined it on both sides, or rather made themselves master of it. Their enthusiasm had risen to the highest pitch. It was impossible to say at what hour he would arrive. Indeed, it was desirable that he should not be recognised, for, in the midst of the delirium and confusion, the arm of a murderer might have reached him. He therefore resolved to travel with the Duc de Vicence in a common cabriolet, which, at nine o'clock in the evening, stopped before the first entrance near the iron gate of the quay of the Louvre. Scarcely had he alighted when the shout of 'Long live the Emperor!' was heard; a shout so loud that it seemed capable of splitting the arched roofs. It came from the officers on half-pay, pressed, almost stifled in the vestibule, and who filled the staircase up to the top. The Emperor was dressed in his famous gray frock-coat. I went up to him, and the Duc de Vicence cried to me, 'For God's sake place yourself before him, that he may get on!' He then began to walk upstairs. I went before, walking backwards, at the distance of one pace, looking at him, deeply affected, my eyes bathed with tears, and repeating, in the excess of my joy, 'What! It is you! It is you! It is you, at last!' As for him, he walked up slowly with his eyes half closed, his hands extended before him, like a blind man, and expressing his joy only by a smile. When he arrived on the landing-place of the first floor, the ladies wished to come to meet him; but a crowd of officers from the higher floor leaped before them, and they would have been crushed to death if they had shown less agility. At last the Emperor succeeded in entering his apartments; the doors were shut, not without difficulty, and the crowd dispersed, satisfied at having seen him. Towards eleven o'clock in the evening, I received an order to go to the Tuileries; I found in the saloon the old Ministers, and in the midst of them the Emperor, talking about the affairs of government with as much ease as if we had gone ten years back. He had just come out of his bath, and had put on his undress regimentals. The subject of the conversation, and the manner in which it was carried on, the presence of the persons who had so long been employed under him, contributed to efface completely from my memory the family of the Bourbons and their reign of nearly a year."

X.

A CHANGED FRANCE.

BUT Napoleon found a different France from that over which he had ruled so long :

" The eleven months of the King's reign had thrown us back to 1792, and the Emperor soon

N

perceived it ; for he no longer found the submission, the deep respect, and the Imperial etiquette he was accustomed to. He used to send for me two or three times a day, to talk with me for hours together. It happened sometimes that the conversation languished. One day, after we had walked up and down the room in silence, tired of that fancy, and my business pressing me, I made my obeisance and was going to retire. 'How!' said he, surprised, but with a smile; 'do you then leave me so?' I should certainly not have done so a year before ; but I had forgotten my old pace, and I felt that it would be impossible to get into it again. In one of those conversations, the subject of which was the spirit of Liberty that showed itself on all sides with so much energy, he said to me, in a tone of interrogation, ' All this will last two or three years?' 'That your Majesty must not believe. It will last for ever.' He was soon convinced of the fact himself, and he more than once acknowledged it. I have even no doubt that if he had vanquished the enemy and restored peace, his power would have been exposed to great danger by civil broils. The Allies made a great mistake in not letting him alone. I do not know what concessions he would have made, but I am well acquainted with all those the nation would have demanded, and I sincerely think he would have been disgusted with reigning, when he must have found himself a constitutional king after the manner of the patriots. Nevertheless, he submitted admirably well to his situation—at least in appearance. At no period of his life had I seen him enjoy more unruffled tranquillity."

XI.

WATERLOO.

THERE are some other scenes which I shall pass by until I reach the departure for Waterloo, and the awful moment when Napoleon returned from his last and disastrous battle. The scenes are described tersely, but the fearsome hope of the first, and the awful despair of the second, come out from the cold language with a strange lucidity and impressiveness. Here is what happened in the Champ de Mars :

"After the celebration of mass, to which, by-the-bye, everybody turned their backs, the Emperor went down and took his place on an amphitheatre in the middle of the Champ de Mars, from whence he was to distribute the eagles to all the cohorts of the departments. This was a beautiful scene, for it was a national one. The situation, besides, was true. The Emperor took care to address a word to each of the corps that received these colours, and that word was flattering and full of enthusiasm. To the department of the Vosges, he said : 'You are my old companions.' To those of the Rhine : 'You have been the first, the most courageous, and the most unfortunate in our disasters.' To the departments of the Rhone: 'I have been bred amongst you.' To others: 'Your bands were at Rivoli, at Arcola, at Marengo, at Tilsit, at Austerlitz, at the Pyramids.' These magic names filled with deep emotion the hearts of those old warriors, the venerable wrecks of so many victories. . . . A few days afterwards the Emperor set off. I left him at midnight. He suffered a great deal from a pain in his breast. He stepped, however, into his coach with a cheerfulness that seemed to show he was conscious of victory."

And now for the second scene:

" At last I learned the fatal news of the battle of Waterloo, and the next morning the Emperor arrived. I flew to the Elysée to see him; he ordered me to his closet, and as soon as he saw me he came to meet me with a frightful epileptic laugh. 'Oh! my God!' he said, raising his eyes to heaven, and walking two or three times up and down the room. This appearance of despair was, however, very short. He soon recovered his coolness, and asked me what was going forward at the Chamber of Representatives. I could not attempt to hide that exasperation was there carried to a high degree, and that the majority seemed determined to require his abdication or to pronounce it themselves if he did not send it in willingly. 'How is that?' he said. 'If proper measures are not taken, the enemy will be before the gates in eight days. Alas!' he added, 'I have accustomed them to such victories, that they know not how to bear one day's misfortune. What will become of poor France? I have done all I could for her.' Then he heaved a deep sigh."

Lavalette saw Napoleon at Malmaison, but there is little of interest in what he says—except that he confirms the testimony of other witnesses as to the completeness of Napoleon's collapse after the crushing defeat of Waterloo.

CHAPTER V.

NAPOLEON, AS HE APPEARED TO A SOLDIER.*

LET us now see how Napoleon impressed a mere soldier—Marbot. He saw Napoleon Bonaparte in the midst of his greatest battles, at almost the most critical moments of his career, and was brought into the closest and most intimate contact with him. There are abundant stories of Napoleon throughout his volumes, and Baron Marbot can tell a story often with a great deal of point. And yet the impression of Napoleon is a blurred one. Did you ever read the description of Scobeleff after the failure of the great assault on Plevna, which was written by MacGahan—that brilliant journalist whom cruel death untimely destroyed? I recall the passage from memory after some fifteen years; I can still remember that terrible portrait of war, with Scobeleff, his face stained with blood and powder, his sword twisted, des-

* "The Memoirs of Baron de Marbot." Translated by Arthur John Butler. Two Vols. (London : Longmans.)

peration and fury in his bloodshot eyes; and then later on Scobeleff washed, scented, dressed like a dandy; and then a third picture—Scobeleff waking up in his sleep to weep bitter tears over the deaths of the brave fellows he had led in thousands to destruction. *There* was a picture that stands out in the memory for ever, and that reveals war in a flash, as a black sky shows its battlements and turrets, its banks and seas of cloud when lightning bursts forth and opens up its darkness. There is no such passage in all Marbot. There are scenes, some of them very vividly described; and there are plenty of good stories; but somehow or other inspiration is wanting, and you do not feel that you have got inside Napoleon one bit more than you have done before. And yet I can understand the extraordinary popularity which the book has attained. If Marbot fails with Napoleon, he is more successful with his marshals, and you get some very clear and correct notions of what some of them were like.

The book, too, is wonderfully effective as a description of what war is like in the details as distinguished from general results and plans. The author is so candid and so simple that you are able to live his life with him from day to day. He is distinctly egotistic, though there is an utter absence of braggadocio; and he is utterly frank in taking more interest in his own affairs and adventures than in anything or anybody else. The result is that you often, through this description of individual experiences, get an extraordinarily clear idea of a movement, a great episode, or a decisive battle. I share also in the pleasant impression the book has universally made as to the personality of the author. His honesty, bravery, and good faith shine out in every page of the book : and it can be easily understood why Marbot—though he served under the Bourbons. —was dear enough to Napoleon to be especially mentioned in his last will, and to get a small legacy all to himself.

I.

GLIMPSES OF THE TERROR.

I DO not purpose to devote much of my space to the author. His career has an interest of its own ; but the chief interest of the book is his descriptions of the men bigger than himself with whom he was brought in contact. Suffice it to say that he was the son of a distinguished French general. He was born in 1782, and in his childhood he had an opportunity of getting some glimpses of the Reign of Terror under the men of the Convention. In 1793, when eleven years of age, he and his father made a stoppage at Cressensac on their way to Toulouse. He goes on to say :

" While we were halting here I saw a sight that I had never seen before. A marching column of gendarmes, National Guards, and volunteers entered the little town, their band playing. I thought it grand, but could not understand why they should have in the middle of them a dozen carriages full of old gentlemen, ladies, and children, all looking very sad. My father was furious at the sight. He drew back from the window, and as he strode up and down the room with his aide-de-camp I heard him exclaim: 'Those scoundrels of the Convention have spoilt the Revolution, which might have been so splendid! There is another batch of innocent people being taken off to prison because they are of good family, or have relations who have gone abroad! It is terrible!' I understood him perfectly, and like him, I vowed hatred to the party of terror who spoilt the Revolution of 1789. I may be asked, why, then, did my father continue to serve a Government for which he had no esteem? Because he held that to repel the enemy from French territory was under all circumstances honourable, and in no way pledged a soldier to approval of the atrocities committed by the Convention in its internal administration.

"What my father had said awakened my lively interest in the persons whom the carriages contained. I found out that they were noble families who had been that morning arrested in their houses, and were being carried to prison at Souilhac. I was wondering how these old men, women, and children, could be dangerous to the country, when I heard one of the children ask for food. A lady

begged a National Guard to let her get out to buy
provisions ; he refused harshly. The lady then held
out an assignat, and asked him to be so kind as to
get her a loaf ; to which he replied : ' Do you
think I am one of your old lackeys ? '   His
brutality disgusted me ; and having noticed that
our servant Spire had placed in the pockets of the
carriage sundry rolls, each lined with a sausage, I took
two of them, and approaching the carriage where the
children were, I threw these in when the guard's
back was turned.   Mother and children made
such expressive signs of gratitude that I decided
to victual all the prisoners, and accordingly took
them all the stores that Spire had packed for the
nourishment of four persons during the forty-eight
hours which it would take us to reach Toulouse.
We started without any suspicion on his part of
the way in which I had disposed of them.   The
children kissed their hands to me, the parents
bowed, and we set off.   We had not gone a
hundred yards, when my father, who, in his haste
to escape from a sight which distressed him, had
not taken a meal at the inn, felt hungry and asked
for the provisions.   Spire mentioned the pockets
in which he had placed them.   My father and
M. Gault rummaged the whole carriage, and found
nothing.   My father pitched into Spire ; Spire
from the coach-box swore by all the fiends that he
had victualled the carriage for two days.   I was
rather in a quandary ; however, not liking to let

poor Spire be scolded any more, I confessed what I had done, fully expecting a slight reproof for having acted on my own authority. But my father only kissed me, and long afterwards he used to delight to speak of my conduct on that occasion."

II.

THE REVOLUTION IN THE SCHOOL.

YOUNG Marbot was sent to school at the College of Sorèze. It was a military school taught by Benedictine monks. Owing to the popularity of the Benedictines and the prudence of Dom Ferlus, the principal, the school was spared by the revolutionaries. And now, here is an interesting glimpse of what a school was like in the days when the Republic reigned:

"The monks wore lay clothes, and were addressed as 'citizen'; but otherwise no change of any importance had taken place in the routine of the school. Of course it could not but show some traces of the feverish agitation which prevailed outside. The walls were covered with Republican 'texts.' We were forbidden to use the term 'monsieur.' When we went to the refectory, or for a walk, we sang the 'Marseillaise,' or other Republican hymns. The exploits of our armies formed the chief subject of conversation; and some of the elder boys enrolled themselves among the volunteers. We learnt drill, riding, fortification, etc. This military atmosphere tended to make the manners of the pupils somewhat free-and-easy; and as for dress, thick boots, only cleaned on the tenth day, gray socks, brown coat and trousers, shirts tattered and ink-stained, no necktie or cap, untidy hair, hands worthy of a charcoal-burner, gave them a rough appearance enough. . . . As I have said, when I entered the college at the end of 1793, the sanguinary rule of the Convention was at its heaviest. Commissioners were travelling the provinces, and nearly all those who had any influence in the South came to visit the establishment of Sorèze. Citizen Ferlus had a knack of his own for persuading them that it was their duty to support an institution which was training, in great numbers, young people who were the hope of the country. Thus he got all that he wanted out of them. Very often they allowed him to have large quantities of faggots which were destined for the supply of the armies, on the plea that we formed part of the army, and were its nursery.

"When these representatives arrived they were received like Sovereigns; the pupils put on their military uniforms; the battalion was drilled in their presence; sentries were placed at every door, as in a garrison town; we acted pieces inspired by the purest patriotism; we sang national hymns. When they inspected the classes, especially the history classes, an opportunity was always found of introducing some dissertation on the excellence of Republican government, and the patriotic virtues which result from it. I remember in this connection that the Deputy Chabot, who had been a Capuchin, was questioning me one day on Roman history. He asked me what I thought of Coriolanus, who, when his fellow-citizens, forgetful of his old services, had offended him, took refuge with the Volsci, the Romans' sworn enemies. Dom Ferlus and the masters were in terror lest I should approve the Roman's conduct; but I said that a good citizen should never bear arms against his country, nor dream of revenging himself on her, however just grounds he might have for discontent. The representative was so pleased with my answer that he embraced me, and complimented the head of the college and his assistants on the good principles which they instilled into their pupils."

III.

FIRST SIGHT OF NAPOLEON.

MARBOT was destined to make the acquaintance at an early age of the mighty genius who was to model his whole career and to shape the history of all mankind. His father received a command in Italy, and on his way there stopped at Lyons. He was surprised to find the city *en fête*, and was informed that Napoleon had arrived. Napoleon was supposed, at the time, to be in Egypt; as a matter of fact he was rushing to Paris in response to a summons from the Abbé Sieyès. The sights and scenes which he beheld at this period produced a lasting effect on Marbot, as they did on the mind of Daniel O'Connell, and made Marbot—as they made O'Connell—a confirmed enemy of revolutionary government. Marbot's description will, perhaps, enable one, even in the present day, to understand the sickness, the revolt, and the reaction which destroyed the Republic, and brought Napoleon and the Empire. The scene, which I am about to quote, is exquisite. It shows the father of Marbot meeting the man who was then but a brother-officer with that mixture of courtesy and distrust in which men all treat each other when from equality, the one is just rising to the higher position :

"The houses were all illuminated and beflagged; fireworks were being let off; our carriage could hardly make its way through the crowd. People were dancing in the open spaces, and the air rang with cries of 'Hurrah for Bonaparte! he will save the country!' This evidence was irresistible; we had to admit that Bonaparte was in Lyons. My father said, 'Of course I thought they would bring him, but I never suspected it would be so soon; they have played their game well. We shall see great events come to pass.

Now I am sure that I was right in getting away from Paris; with the army I shall be able to serve my country without being mixed up in a *coup d'état*. It may be as necessary as it seems, but I dislike it altogether.' With that he fell into deep thought, lasting through the tedious interval required to make our way through the crowd, which grew thicker at every step, and reach our hotel.

"Arrived there, we found it hung with lanterns and guarded by a battalion of grenadiers. They had given General Bonaparte the apartments ordered a week before for my father. Quick-tempered though he was, he said nothing, and when the landlord made somewhat confused apologies to the effect that he had been compelled to obey the orders of the Town Council, my father made no answer. On hearing that a lodging had been taken for us in a good hotel of the second class kept by a relation of the landlord's, my father confined himself to bidding M. Gault order the postilions to drive there. When we got there we found our courier; he was an excitable man, and being well-warmed by the numerous drams which he had taken at every halting-place on his long journey, had kicked up the devil's own row on learning, when he preceded us at the first hotel, that the apartments engaged for his master, had been given to General Bonaparte. The aides-de-camp, hearing this fearful uproar and learning the cause of it, went to let their chief know that General Marbot had been thrown over for him. At the same moment Bonaparte himself, through the open window, perceived my father's two carriages standing before the door. Up to then he had known nothing of his landlord's shabby behaviour towards my father, and seeing that General Marbot, recently Commandant of Paris, and at that moment at the head of a division of the army in Italy, was too important a man for any off-hand treatment, and that, moreover, he himself was returning with the intention of being on a good footing with everybody, he ordered one of his officers to go down at once and offer General Marbot to come and share his lodging with him in soldier fashion. But the carriages went on before the aide-de-camp could speak to my father; so Bonaparte started at once on foot in order to come and express his regret in person. The cheers of the crowd which followed him as he drew near our hotel might have given us notice, but we had heard so much cheering since we entered the town that it occurred to none of us to look out into the street. We were all in the sitting-room, and my father was pacing up and down plunged in meditation, when suddenly a waiter, throwing open both folding-doors, announced General Bonaparte.

" On entering he ran up to my father and embraced him; my father received him courteously but coldly. They were old acquaintances, and between persons of their rank a few words were sufficient to explain matters with regard to the lodging. They had much else to talk of, so they went alone into the bedroom, where they conferred together for more than an hour.

"General Bonaparte and my father returned into the sitting-room, and introduced to each other the members of their respective staffs. Lannes and Murat were old acquaintances of my father's, and he received them very cordially. He was somewhat cold towards Berthier, whom he had seen in old days at Marseilles when he was in the body-guard and Berthier an engineer. General Bonaparte asked me very courteously for news of my mother, and complimented me in a kind manner on having taken up the military career so young. Then gently pinching my ear— the flattering caress which he always employed with persons with whom he was pleased—he said, addressing my father: 'He will be a second General Marbot some day.' His forecast has been verified, though at that time I had little hope of it. All the same, his words made me feel proud all over—it doesn't take much to awaken the pride of a child.

"The visit came to an end, and my father gave no indication of what had passed between General Bonaparte and himself; but I learnt

later on that Bonaparte, without actually betraying his schemes, had endeavoured by the
most adroit cajoleries to enlist my father on
his side. My father, however, steadily evaded
the question.

"So shocked was he at the sight of the people
of Lyons running to meet Bonaparte, as if he
were already Sovereign of France, that he expressed a wish to get away next morning at
daybreak; but his carriages required repair, and
he was forced to stay an entire day at Lyons.
I took the opportunity of getting a new forage
cap made, and in my delight at this purchase
I paid no sort of heed to the political conversation which I heard all about me, nor, to tell the
truth, did I understand much of it. My father
went to return General Bonaparte's visit. They
walked for a long time alone in the little garden
of the hotel, while their staffs kept at a respectful distance. We saw them at one time
vigorously gesticulating, at another talking more
calmly; presently Bonaparte, coming close to
my father with a coaxing air, took his arm in
a friendly fashion. His motive probably was
that the authorities, who were in the courtyard,
and the many curious spectators who were
crowding the neighbouring windows, might say
that General Marbot assented to General
Bonaparte's plans. For this clever man never
overlooked any means of reaching his end;

some people he gained, and wished to have it believed that he had also won to his side those whose sense of duty led them to resist him. Herein his success was wonderful.

"My father came out from this second conversation even more thoughtful than from the first, and on entering the hotel he gave orders that we should proceed on the following day. But General Bonaparte was going to make a visit of inspection of the points in the neighbourhood of the town suitable for fortification, and all the post-horses had been engaged for him. For the moment I thought that my father would be angry, but he confined himself to saying: 'There's the beginning of omnipotence.'"

IV.

NAPOLEON OFTEN DECEIVED.

THE next passage I will quote will show how attentive Napoleon was to details, and yet how, in spite of all his precautions, he was deceived. The very terror which he inspired was often the cause of his being kept in ignorance:

"The Emperor used as a rule to treat his officers with kindness, but there was one point on which he was, perhaps, over severe. He held the colonels responsible for maintaining a full complement of men in the ranks of their regiments, and as that is precisely what is most difficult to achieve on a campaign, it was just on this point that the Emperor was most often deceived. The corps commanders were so afraid of displeasing him, that they exposed themselves to the risk of being set to fight a number of enemies out of proportion to the strength of their troops, rather than admit that illness, fatigue, and the necessity of procuring food had compelled many of the soldiers to fall to the rear. Thus Napoleon, for all his power, never knew accurately the number of combatants which he had at his disposal on the day of battle. Now it befell that, while we were staying at Brunn, the Emperor, on one of the rounds which he was incessantly making to visit the positions of the different divisions, noticed the mounted chasseurs of his guard marching to take up new lines. He was particularly fond of this regiment, the nucleus of which was formed by his Guides of Italy and Egypt. His trained eye could judge very correctly the strength of a column, and finding this one very short of its number, he took a little note-book from his pocket, and, after consulting it, sent for General Morland, colonel of the mounted chasseurs of the guard, and said to him in a severe tone: 'The strength of your regiment is entered on my notes at twelve hundred combatants, and although you have not yet been engaged with the enemy, you have not more than eight hundred troopers there. What has become of the rest?' General Morland, at fighting an excellent and very brave officer, but not gifted with the faculty of ready reply, was taken aback, and answered, in his Alsatian French, that only a very small number of men were missing. The Emperor maintained that there were close upon four hundred short, and to clear the matter up he determined to have them counted on the spot; but knowing that Morland was much liked by his staff, and being afraid of what their good nature might do, he thought that it would be safer if he took an officer who belonged neither to his household nor to the guard, and, catching sight of me, he ordered me to count the chasseurs, and to come and report their number to him in person. Having said this, he galloped off. I began my operation, which was all the more easy that the troopers were marching at a walk and in fours."

It is a proof of the wonderful accuracy of Napoleon's eye that his estimate on this occasion turned out to be correct almost to a unit. But Marbot, unable to withstand the appeal of the commander, backed up by that of the surgeon who had stood beside his father's death-bed, declared to the Emperor that they were only eighty instead of four hundred short. Marbot delayed his report until evening, fearing that if he told his lie to the Emperor during the day,

and while he was on horseback, he would go back
to the chasseurs and himself count the regiment.
When nightfall came Marbot approached the Imperial head-quarters:

"I was taken in, and found him lying at full
length on an immense map spread on the floor.
As soon as he saw me he called out, 'Well,
Marbot, how many mounted chasseurs are there
present in my guard? Are there twelve hundred
of them, as Morland declares?' 'No, sir, I only
counted eleven hundred and twenty, that is to say,
eighty short.' 'I was quite sure that there were a
great many missing.' The tone in which the
Emperor pronounced these last words proved that
he expected a much larger deficit; and, indeed, if
there had been only eighty men missing in a
regiment of twelve hundred which has just
marched five hundred leagues in winter, sleeping
almost every night in the open air, it would have
been very little. So when the Emperor, on his
way to dinner, crossed the room where the
commanders of the guard were assembled, he
merely said to Morland, 'You see now you've got
eighty chasseurs missing; it is nearly a squadron.
With eighty of these fellows one might stop a
Russian regiment. You must keep a tight hand
to stop the men from falling out.' Then passing
on to the commander of the foot grenadiers, whose
effective strength had also been much weakened,
Napoleon reprimanded him severely. Morland,

deeming himself very fortunate in getting off with a few remarks, came up to me as soon as the Emperor was at table, and thanked me warmly, telling me that some thirty chasseurs had just rejoined, and that a messenger arriving from Vienna had fallen in with more than a hundred between Znaym and Brunn and a good many more this side of Hollabrunn, so that he was certain that within forty-eight hours the regiment would have recovered most of its losses. I was quite as anxious for it as he, for I understood the difficulty in which I had been placed by my excess of gratitude towards Fournier. Such was my dread of the just wrath of the Emperor, whose confidence I had so gravely abused, that I could not sleep all night.

" My perplexity was still greater the next day, when Napoleon, during his customary visit to the troops, went towards the bivouac of the chasseurs, for a mere question addressed to an officer might have revealed everything. I was, therefore, giving myself up for lost, when I heard the bands in the Russian encampment on the heights of Pratzen, half a league from our outposts; therefore, riding towards the head of the numerous staff accompanying the Emperor, among whom I was, I got as near to him as I could and said in a loud voice, ' There must surely be some movement going on in the enemy's camp, for there is their band playing marches.' The Emperor heard my remark, abruptly quitted the path leading to the guard's bivouac, and went towards Pratzen to observe what was going on in the enemy's advance guard. He remained a long time watching, and at the approach of night he returned to Brunn without going to see his chasseurs. Thus I remained several days in mortal anxiety, although I heard of the successive return of sundry detachments. Finally, the battle being at hand, and the Emperor being very busy, the idea of making the verification which I had so much dreaded passed out of his thoughts, but I had had a good lesson. So when I became colonel and the Emperor questioned me on the number of combatants present in the squadrons of my regiment, I always told the exact truth."

v.

NAPOLEON'S DIPLOMATIC METHODS.

MARBOT, having told how Napoleon could be deceived, proceeds to give an instructive instance of how Napoleon could deceive. The scene, which is about to be described, took place at the critical moment when the King of Prussia was still wavering between peace and war— between joining in the coalition against Napoleon or remaining neutral. To get some idea of what Napoleon was doing, the King sent Herr von Haugwitz on a diplomatic mission invented for the occasion. It was just after the battle of

Bregenz, in which the army of Jellachich had been beaten and captured; and Napoleon's purpose was to get information of this decisive victory to the King of Prussia as soon as possible. Here was the strategy employed:

"Duroc, the marshal of the household, after giving us notice of what we were expected to do, had all the Austrian colours which Massy and I had brought from Bregenz, replaced privately in the quarters which we were occupying. Some hours afterwards, when the Emperor was talking in his study with Herr von Haugwitz, we repeated the ceremony of presentation in precisely the same manner as the first time. The Emperor, on hearing music in the court of his house, feigned astonishment, and went to the window, followed by the ambassador. Seeing the trophies borne by the sergeants, he called the aide-de-camp on duty, and asked what it all meant. The answer was that there were two aides-de-camp of Marshal Augereau, who were coming to bring the Emperor the colours of Jellachich's Austrian army which had been captured at Bregenz. We were ordered to enter, and there, without winking, and as if he had never seen us, Napoleon received the letter of Augereau, which had been sealed up, and read it, although he had known the contents for four days. Then he questioned us, making us enter into minutest details. Duroc had cautioned us

to speak loud, because the Prussian ambassador
was a little deaf. This was unlucky for my
comrade and superior, Massy, since he had lost
his voice and could hardly speak; so it was I
who had to answer the Emperor, and seeing
his plan, I depicted in the most vivid colours
the defeat of the Austrians, their dejection, and
the enthusiasm of the French troops. Then,
presenting the trophies one after another, I
named all the regiments to which they had
belonged, laying especial stress upon two, the
capture of which was likely to produce the
greatest effect upon the Prussian ambassador.
'Here,' said I, 'are the colours of the Emperor
of Austria's own regiment of infantry; there is
the standard of his brother, the Archduke
Charles's, Uhlans.' Napoleon's eyes sparkled, and
seemed to say, 'Well done, young man.' Then
he dismissed us, and as we went out we heard
him say to the ambassador, 'You see, Count,
my armies are winning at all points; the Austrian
army is annihilated, and very soon the Russian
army will be so.' Von Haugwitz appeared
greatly upset, and as soon as we were out of
the room, Duroc said to me, 'This evening the
diplomat will write to Berlin to inform his
Government of the destruction of Jellachich's
army. This will somewhat calm the minds of
those who are keen for war with us, and will
give the King of Prussia fresh reasons for

temporising, which is what the Emperor ardently desires.'

"The comedy having been played, the Emperor wished to get rid of an awkward witness who might report the positions of his army, and so hinted to the ambassador that to stay between two armies all ready for an engagement might be a little unsafe for him. He bade him go to Vienna to M. de Talleyrand, his Minister for Foreign Affairs—advice which Herr von Haugwitz followed that same evening. The next day the Emperor said nothing to us about yesterday's performance, but, wishing no doubt to evince his satisfaction at the way in which we had seized his idea, he asked tenderly after Major Massy's cold, and pinched my ear, which was with him a sort of caress."

VI.

AUSTERLITZ.

ONE of the most vividly-described battles in the whole book is Austerlitz. Even the non-military reader can feel himself carried away by the briskness, vividness, and horror of the narrative. I give one or two extracts :

"Marshal Soult carried not only the village of Pratzen, but also the vast tableland of that name, which was the culminating point of the whole country, and consequently the key of the battle-field. There, under the Emperor's eyes, the sharpest of the fighting took place, and the Russians were beaten back. But one battalion, the 4th of the line, of which Prince Joseph, Napoleon's brother, was colonel, allowing itself to be carried too far in pursuit of the enemy, was charged and broken up by the Noble Guard and the Grand Duke Constantine's cuirassiers, losing its eagle. Several lines of Russian cavalry quickly advanced to support this momentary success of the guards, but Napoleon hurled against them the Mamelukes, the mounted chasseurs, and the mounted grenadiers of his guard under Marshal Bessières and General Rapp. The mêlée was of the most sanguinary kind; the Russian squadrons were crushed and driven back beyond the village of Austerlitz with immense loss. Our troopers captured many colours and prisoners, among the latter Prince Repnin, commander of the Noble Guard. This regiment, composed of the most brilliant of the young Russian nobility, lost heavily, because the swagger in which they had indulged against the French having come to the ears of our soldiers, these, and above all the mounted grenadiers, attacked them with fury, shouting as they passed their great sabres through their bodies: 'We will give the ladies of St. Petersburg something to cry for!'"

Here one sees the hideous and bestial ferocity which war begets. And then comes a passage in which there is a glimpse of the curious limitations which soldiers place on themselves :

" The painter Gérard, in his picture of the battle of Austerlitz, has taken for his subject the moment when General Rapp, coming wounded out of the fight, and covered with his enemies' blood and his own, is presenting to the Emperor the flags just captured and his prisoner, Prince Repnin. I was present at this imposing spectacle, which the artist has reproduced with wonderful accuracy. All the heads are portraits, even that of the brave chasseur who, making no complaint, though he had been shot through the body, had the courage to come up to the Emperor, and fell stone dead as he presented the standard which he had just taken. Napoleon, wishing to honour his memory, ordered the painter to find a place for him in his composition. In the picture may be seen also a Mameluke, who is carrying in one hand an enemy's flag and holds in the other the bridle of his dying horse. This man, named Mustapha, was well known in the guard for his courage and ferocity. During the charge he had pursued the Grand Duke Constantine, who only got rid of him by a pistol-shot, which severely wounded the Mameluke's horse. Mustapha, grieved at having only a standard to offer to the Emperor, said in his broken French as he presented it : 'Ah! if me catch Prince Constantine, me cut him head off and bring it to Emperor!'

Napoleon, disgusted, replied : ' Will you hold your tongue, you savage ? ' "

And now, here is another scene in which, once more, ferocity has the upper hand :

" The Emperor, whom we left on the plateau of Pratzen, having freed himself from the enemy's right and centre, which were in flight on the other side of Austerlitz, descended from the heights of Pratzen with a force of all arms, including Soult's corps and his guard, and went with all speed towards Telnitz, and took the enemy's columns in rear at the moment when Davoust was attacking in front. At once the heavy masses of Austrians and Russians, packed on the narrow roadways which lead beside the Goldbach brook, finding themselves between two fires, fell into an indescribable confusion. All ranks were mixed up together, and each sought to save himself by flight. Some hurled themselves headlong into the marshes which border the pools, but our infantry followed them there. Others hoped to escape by the road that lies between the two pools; our cavalry charged them, and the butchery was frightful. Lastly, the greater part of the enemy, chiefly Russians, sought to pass over the ice. It was very thick, and five or six thousand men keeping some kind of order, had reached the middle of the Satschan lake, when Napoleon, calling up the artillery of his guard, gave the order to fire on the ice. It broke at countless points, and a mighty cracking was heard. The water, oozing through the fissures, soon covered the floes, and we saw thousands of Russians, with their horses, guns, and waggons, slowly settle down into the depths. It was a horribly majestic spectacle which I shall never forget. In an instant the surface of the lake was covered with everything that could swim. Men and horses struggled in the water among the floes. Some—a very small number—succeeded in saving themselves by the help of poles and ropes, which our soldiers reached to them from the shore, but the greater part were drowned."

VII.

THE PATH OF GLORY.

IN the fight General Morland—the commanding officer for whose sake Marbot had lied to the Emperor—was killed ; the subsequent fate of his remains gives Marbot the opportunity for telling one of the most sardonic stories in the whole book :

" The Emperor, always on the look-out for anything that might kindle the spirit of emulation among the troops, decided that General Morland's body should be placed in the memorial building which he proposed to erect on the Esplanade des Invalides at Paris. The surgeons, having neither the time nor the materials necessary to embalm the general's body on the battle-field, put it into a barrel of rum, which was transported to Paris. But subsequent events having delayed the construction of the monument destined for General Morland, the barrel in which he had been placed was still standing in one of the rooms of the School of Médicine when Napoleon lost the Empire in 1814. Not long afterwards the barrel broke, through decay, and people were much surprised to find that the rum had made the general's moustaches grow to such an extraordinary extent that they fell below his waist. The corpse was in perfect preservation, but in order to get possession of it, the family were obliged to bring an action against some scientific man who had made a curiosity of it. Cultivate the love of glory and go and get killed, to let some oaf of a naturalist set you up in his library between a rhinoceros horn and a stuffed crocodile!"

VIII.

NAPOLEON AND HIS TROOPS.

THE main interest of these volumes, of course, is their picture of Napoleon; and, accordingly, I extract by choice the passages which refer to him and help to complete his portrait. Here, for instance, is an example of the manner in which he managed to win the hearts of his soldiers:

"Our road lay by Aschaffenburg, whence we went on to Wurzburg. There we found the Emperor, who held a march-past of the troops of the 7th corps, amid great enthusiasm. Napoleon, who was in possession of notes about all the regiments, and knew how to use them cleverly so as to flatter the self-esteem of every one, said, when he saw the 44th of the line, 'Of all the corps in my army you are the one in which there are most stripes, so your three battalions count on my line for six.' The soldiers replied with enthusiasm, 'We will prove it before the enemy.' To the 78th Light Infantry, composed mainly of men from Lower Languedoc and the Pyrenees, the Emperor said : 'These are the best marchers in the army ; one never sees a man of them fallen out, especially when the enemy has to be met.' Then he added, laughing, 'But to do you justice in full, I must tell you that you are the greatest rowdies and looters in the army.' 'Quite true, quite true !' answered the soldiers, every one of whom had a duck, fowl, or goose in his knapsack."

IX.

THE RISE OF THE HOUSE OF ROTHSCHILD.

IN the course of his narrative of war and war's alarms, Marbot stops to tell the well-known story of the rise of the house of Rothschild. When Napoleon had beaten the Prussians, he confiscated the estates of the Elector of Hesse-Cassel as a punishment for his vacillation between the two warring monarchs :

"The avaricious sovereign had amassed a large treasure by selling his own subjects to the English.

They were employed to fight the Americans in the War of Independence. Disloyal to his relations, he had offered to ally himself to the French, on condition that the Emperor would give him their states, so nobody regretted him. But his hurried departure was the cause of a remarkable incident which as yet is little known.

"When forced to leave Cassel in a hurry to take refuge in England, the Elector of Hesse, who was supposed to be the richest man in Europe, being unable to bring away the whole of his treasures, sent for a Frankfort Jew, named Rothschild, an obscure banker of the third rank, known only for the scrupulous practice of his religion. This seems to have decided the Elector to entrust to him 15,000,000 francs in specie. The interest of the money was to be the banker's, and he was only to be bound to return the capital.

"When the palace of Cassel was occupied by our troops the agents of the French Treasury seized property of great value, especially pictures, but no coined money was found, yet it appeared impossible that in his hasty flight the Elector could have carried away the whole of his immense fortune. Now, since, by what are conventionally called the laws of war, the capital and the interest of securities found in a hostile country belong of right to the conqueror, it became important to know what became of the Cassel treasure. Inquiry showed that before his departure the Elector had passed a whole day with the Jew Rothschild. An Imperial commission visited him and minutely examined his safes and books; but it was in vain; no trace of the Elector's deposit could be found. Threats and intimidation had no success until the commission, feeling sure that no personal interest could induce a man so religious as Rothschild to perjure himself, proposed to administer an oath to him. He refused to take it. There was talk of arresting him, but the Emperor, thinking this a useless act of violence, forbade it. Then they had resource to a not very honourable method. Unable to overcome the banker's resistance, they tried to gain him over by the bait of profit. They proposed to leave him half the treasure if he would give up the other half to the French administration. A receipt for the whole, accompanied by a deed of seizure, would be given him to prove that he had only yielded to force and to prevent any claim from lying against him; but the Jew's honesty rejected this suggestion also, and his persecutors, tired out, left him in peace. Thus the 15,000,000 francs remained in Rothschild's hands from 1806 till the fall of the Empire in 1814. Then the Elector returned to his states, and the banker returned him his deposit as he had received it. You may imagine the sum which a capital of 15,000,000 francs would produce in the hands of a Jew banker of Frankfort. From this time dates the opulence of the Rothschilds, who thus owe to their ancestor's honesty the high place which they now hold in the finance of all civilised countries."

x.

NAPOLEON AND QUEEN LOUISE.

AFTER Napoleon's victory at Friedland, there came, as is known, the interview between him and the Emperor of Russia and King of Prussia at Tilsit. Here took place an historic and characteristic scene between Napoleon and the Queen:

" One day Napoleon went to call on the unfortunate Queen of Prussia, who was said to be in great grief. He invited her to dinner on the following day, which she accepted, doubtless much against the grain. But at the moment of concluding peace, it was very necessary to appease the victor. Napoleon and the Queen of Prussia hated each other cordially. She had insulted him in many proclamations, and he had given it her back in his bulletins.

" Yet their interview showed no traces of their mutual hatred. Napoleon was respectful and attentive, the Queen gracious and disposed to captivate her former enemy. She had all need to do so, being well aware that the treaty of peace created, under the title of Kingdom of Westphalia, a new state whose territory was to be contributed by electoral Hesse and Prussia.

" The Queen could resign herself to the loss

of several provinces, but she could not make up her mind to part with the strong place of Magdeburg, the retaining of which would be Prussia's safeguard. On his side, Napoleon, who proposed to make his brother Jerome King of Westphalia, wished to add Magdeburg to the new state. It is said that in order to retain this important town, the Queen of Prussia, during dinner, used all the methods of friendliness until Napoleon, to change the conversation, praised a superb rose that the Queen was wearing. The story goes that she said: 'Will your Majesty have this rose in exchange for Magdeburg?' Perhaps it would be chivalrous to accept, but the Emperor was too practical a man to let himself be caught by a pretty offer, and it is averred that while praising the beauty of the rose and of the hand which offered it, he did not take the flower. The Queen's eyes filled with tears, but the victor affected not to perceive it. He kept Magdeburg, and escorted the Queen politely to the boat which was to take her across to the other side."

XI.

NAPOLEON WOUNDED.

THERE is a popular and widespread delusion that Napoleon was never wounded; indeed, this is taken as one of the many signs and tokens of that demoniacal luck which for a long time marked his destiny. Marbot dissipates this, as well as some other illusions. Here is a scene which took place during the attack on Ratisbon:

"While waiting till everybody was ready, Marshal Lannes had gone back to the Emperor to receive his final orders. As they were chatting, a bullet—fired, in all probability, from one of the long-range Tyrolese rifles—struck Napoleon on the right ankle. The pain was at first so sharp that the Emperor had to lean upon Lannes, but Dr. Larrey, who quickly arrived, declared that the wound was trifling. If it had been severe enough to require an operation, the event would certainly have been considered a great misfortune for France; yet it might perhaps have spared her many calamities. However, the report that the Emperor had been wounded spread through the army. Officers and men ran up from all sides; in a moment Napoleon was surrounded by thousands of men, in spite of the fire which the enemy's guns concentrated on the vast group. The Emperor, wishing to withdraw his troops from this useless danger, and to calm the anxiety of the more distant corps, who were getting unsteady in their desire to come and see what was the matter, mounted his horse the instant his wound was dressed, and rode down the front of the whole line amid loud cheers."

XII.

NAPOLEON AND THE GRENADIER.

HERE is another scene which gives a good picture of the relations between Napoleon and his soldiers. Marbot is still talking of the events before Ratisbon :

"It was at this extempore review held in presence of the enemy that Napoleon first granted gratuities to private soldiers, appointing them knights of the Empire and members, at the same time, of the Legion of Honour. The regimental commanders recommended, but the Emperor also allowed soldiers who thought they had claims to come and represent them before him; then he decided upon them by himself. Now it befell that an old grenadier who had made the campaigns of Italy and Egypt, not hearing his name called, came up, and in a calm tone of voice, asked for the Cross. 'But,' said Napoleon, 'what have you done to deserve it?' 'It was I, sir, who, in the desert of Joppa, when it was so terribly hot, gave you a water-melon.' 'I thank you for it again; but the gift of the fruit is hardly worth the Cross of the Legion of Honour.' Then the grenadier, who up till then had been as cool as ice, working himself up into a frenzy, shouted, with the utmost volubility, 'Well, and don't you reckon seven wounds received at the

Bridge of Arcola, at Lodi and Castiglione, at the Pyramids, at Acre, Austerlitz, Friedland ; eleven campaigns in Italy, Egypt, Austria, Prussia, Poland——" but the Emperor cut him short, laughing, and mimicking his excited manner cried : ' There, there, how you work yourself up when you come to the essential point ! That is where you ought to have begun; it is worth much more than your melon. I make you a knight of the Empire, with a pension of 1,200 francs. Does that satisfy you ?' ' But your Majesty, I prefer the Cross.' ' You have both one and the other, since I make you knight.' ' Well, I would rather have the Cross.' The worthy grenadier could not be moved from that point, and it took all manner of trouble to make him understand that the title of knight of the Empire carried with it the Legion of Honour. He was not appeased on this point until the Emperor had fastened the decoration on his breast, and he seemed to think a great deal more of this than of his annuity of 1,200 francs. It was by familiarities of this kind that the Emperor made the soldiers adore him, but it was a means that was only available to a commander whom frequent victories had made illustrious; any other general would have impaired his reputation by it."

XIII.

DETECTION OF A SPY.

THERE is an episode which shows Napoleon's extraordinary readiness and fertility of resource. It occurred just before the great battle of Wagram. The scene is also interesting as showing the curious fluctuations of feeling in Napoleon's character :

"Knowing that the enemy was expecting him to cross as before, between Aspern and Essling, and that it was important to conceal his plan of turning their position by crossing opposite Enzersdorf, Napoleon had a careful watch kept over all who entered the island by the great bridges connecting it with Ebersdorf. Every one on the island must have learnt the secret towards the end of the time; but as it seemed certain that none were on it but French soldiers or officers' servants, who were all guarded, no danger was apprehended from inquisitiveness on the enemy's part. This, as it turned out, was a mistake; for the Archduke had contrived to introduce a spy among us. Just when he was about to give information of the point which we were going to attack, an anonymous letter, written in Hungarian, was brought by a little girl to the Emperor's Mameluke, Roustan, with the warning that it was important and urgent. It was at first supposed to be a begging letter; but the interpreters soon translated it, and informed the Emperor. He came at once to the island, and ordered every soul—troops, staffs, commissaries, butchers, bakers, canteen men, even officers' servants—to be drawn up on parade. As soon as every one was in the ranks, the Emperor announced that a spy had found his way into the island, hoping to escape notice among 30,000 men; and, now that they were all in their places he ordered every man to look at his neighbour to right and left. In the midst of the dead silence, two soldiers were heard to cry, 'Here is a man we don't know.' He was arrested and examined, and admitted that he had disguised himself in a French uniform taken from men killed at Essling. This wretch had been born at Paris, and appeared very well educated. Having ruined himself at play, he had fled to Austria to escape his creditors, and there had offered himself as spy to the Austrian staff. A small boat used to take him across the Danube at night, landing him a league below Ebersdorf, and fetch him back the next night on a given signal. He had already been frequently on the island, and had accompanied detachments of our troops going to fetch provisions or materials from Ebersdorf. In order to avoid notice, he always went to places where there was a crowd, and worked with the soldiers at the entrenchments.

He got his meals at the canteen, passed the night near the camps, and in the morning, armed with a spade as though on his way to join a working party, he would go all over the island and examine the works, lying down among the osiers to make a hurried sketch of them. The next night he would go and make his report to the Austrians, and come back to continue his observations. He was brought before a court-martial and condemned to death; but the bitter regret which he expressed for having served the enemies of France disposed the Emperor to commute the penalty. When, however, the spy proposed to deceive the Archduke by going to make a false report on what he had seen, and coming back to tell the French what the Austrians were doing, the Emperor, disgusted at this new piece of infamy, abandoned him to his fate, and let him be shot."

XIV.

NAPOLEON AS HAROUN-AL-RASCHID.

AMID the many unpleasant impressions which Taine's tremendous indictment of Napoleon leaves on the mind, none is more odious than that left by Taine's picture of the Emperor in his Court. Rude, boorish, vulgar, inconsiderate to malignity, mischievous to brutality, he is drawn—passing from courtier to courtier, and even from lady to lady, with a look that froze, a sneer that wounded, a question that was like a poisoned arrow. It is only fair, then, to quote the following passage from Marbot, which, though it does not present Napoleon in a particularly amiable light, yet gives an impression of naïveté, good-humour, and affability, not altogether consistent with Taine's lurid and shocking picture.

Napoleon used to insist that his great officials, to whom he gave magnificent salaries, should entertain largely in order to encourage trade and so keep Paris in good humour. Marescalchi, who—as Marbot puts it—was ambassador for Napoleon, King of Rome, to Napoleon, Emperor of the French, was one of the most brilliant of these entertainers, and he was especially remarkable for his fancy-dress balls. At these balls Napoleon was a constant visitor. He had just been divorced from Josephine—it was the year 1810—but had not yet married Marie Louise :

" Wearing a plain black domino and common mask, and with Duroc, similarly disguised, on his arm, Napoleon used to mix with the crowd and puzzle the ladies, who were rarely masked. The crowd, it is true, consisted of none but trustworthy persons, because M. Marescalchi always submitted his list to the Minister of Police; and also because the assistant-adjutant-general, Laborde, so well-known for his talents in scenting a conspirator, was at the entrance of the rooms, and allowed no one to enter without showing his face and ticket and giving his name. Agents in disguise went about, and a battalion of the guard furnished sentries to every exit. These precautions, however, were so well managed by Duroc that, once in the room, the guests were unconscious of any supervision."

It was at one of these balls that poor Marbot was almost ruined by an importunate and accidental acquaintance. Madame X——, the widow of an official, thought that her pension was insufficient, and, having made vain application to all the other members of the Imperial family, she resolved finally to get at the Emperor himself. By an oversight she managed to make her way to the masked ball:

"The ball was on the ground-floor, card-tables being on that above; when I entered, the quadrilles were going on, and a crowd was gazing at the magnificent costumes. Suddenly, in the midst of the silk, velvet, feathers, and embroideries, appeared a colossal female figure, clad in plain white calico, with red corset, and bedizened with coloured ribbons in the worst taste. This was Madame X——, who had found no better way of displaying her magnificent hair than dressing as a shepherdess, with a little straw hat over one ear, and two large tresses down to her heels. Her curious get-up, and the strange simplicity of the dress in which she appeared in

the brilliant assembly, drew all eyes towards her.
I had the curiosity to look that way, having
unluckily taken off my mask. Madame X——,
feeling awkward in the crowd of strangers, came
to me, and took my arm without more ado,
saying aloud, ‘Now I shall have a partner.’”

XV.

MARBOT IN A TIGHT PLACE.

MARBOT managed, however, to make his escape,
and then this is what happened :

“Rid at length of this dreadful incubus, I
hastened up to the first floor, where, going through
the quiet card-rooms, I went and established
myself in a room at the far end, dimly lighted
by a shady lamp. No one being there, I took
off my mask, and was resting and consuming an
excellent ice, rejoicing in my escape, when two
masked men, short and stout, in black dominoes,
entered the little room. ‘Here we shall be out of
the crowd,’ said one; then calling me by my name
without prefix, he beckoned me to him. I could
not see his face, but as I knew all the great
dignitaries of the Empire were in the house, I
felt sure that a man who could so imperatively
summon an officer of my rank must be an
important personage. I came forward, and the
unknown said in a whisper, ‘I am Duroc: the
Emperor is with me. He is overcome by the

heat, and wishes to rest in this out-of-the-way room; stay with us, to obviate any suspicion on the part of a chance enterer.' The Emperor sat down in an arm-chair, looking towards a corner of the room. The general and I placed ours back to back with his so as to cover him, facing the door, and began to chat, by the general's wish, as if he were one of my comrades. The Emperor taking off his mask, asked the general for two handkerchiefs, with which he wiped his face and neck; then, tapping me lightly on the shoulder, he begged me (that was his term) to get him a large glass of cold water, and bring it myself. I went at once to the nearest buffet, and filled a glass with iced water; but as I was about to carry it to the room where Napoleon was, I was accosted by two tall men in Scotch costume, one of whom said in my ear, 'Can Major Marbot answer for the wholesomeness of that water?' I thought I could, for I had taken it at random from one of the many decanters standing there for the use of all comers. Doubt-less, these two persons were some of the police agents who were distributed about the house under various disguises to look after the Emperor without worrying him by too ostentatious attention, and moved about at a respectful distance, ready to fly to his help if they were wanted. Napoleon received the water which I brought him with so much satisfaction that I thought he must be parched with thirst; to my surprise, however, he swallowed only a small mouthful, then, dipping the two handkerchiefs in the iced water, he told me to put one on the nape of his neck while he held the other to his face, repeating, 'Ah! that's good, that's good!' Duroc then resumed his chat with me, chiefly about the recent campaign in Austria. The Emperor said, 'You behaved very well, especially at the assault on Ratisbon and the crossing of the Danube; I shall never forget it, and before long I will give you a notable proof of my satisfaction.' I could not imagine what this new reward was to consist of, but my heart leapt for joy. Then, oh woe! the terrible shepherdess appeared at the end of the little room. 'Oh! there you are, sir! I shall complain to your cousin of your rudeness,' she exclaimed. 'Since you deserted me I have been all but smothered ten times over. I had to leave the ball-room, the heat is stifling. It seems comfortable here; I will rest here.' So saying, she sat down beside me.

"General Duroc said nothing, and the Emperor, keeping his back turned and his face in the wet handkerchief, remained motionless; more and more so as the shepherdess, given free play to her reckless tongue, and taking no notice of our neighbours, told me how she thought she had more than once recognised the personage whom she sought in the crowd, but had not been able to get at him. 'But I must speak to him,' she said; 'he absolutely must double my pension. I know that people have tried to injure me by saying that I was free in my youth. Good heavens! go and listen for a moment to the talk down there between the windows. Besides, what about his sisters? What about himself? What does he come here for, if not to be able to talk as he likes to pretty women? They say my husband stole; poor devil! he took to it late, and was pretty clumsy at it. Besides, have not his accusers stolen too? Did they inherit their town houses and their fine estates? Didn't he steal in Italy, Egypt, everywhere?' 'But, madame,' said I, 'allow me to remark that what you say is very unseemly, and I am all the more surprised you should say it to me, that I never saw you till this morning.' 'Oh! I speak the truth before any one. And if he does not give me a good pension, I will tell him, or write to him, what I think of him pretty plainly. Oh! I am not afraid of anything.' I was on tenterhooks, and would willingly have exchanged my situation for a cavalry charge or a storming party. However, my agony was alleviated by feeling that Madame X——'s chatter would clear my character with my two neighbours when they heard that I had never seen her till that morning, had not brought her to the ball, and had got away from her as soon as I could."

XVI.

THE END OF THE ADVENTURE.

"NEVERTHELESS, I was rather anxious about the
way in which this scene would end, when Duroc,
leaning towards me, said: 'Don't let this woman
follow us.' He rose. The Emperor had replaced
his mask while Madame X—— was raving at him,
and as he passed in front of her he said to me,
'Marbot, people who take an interest in you
are pleased to know that you never met this
charming shepherdess till to-day, and you would
do well to send her off to feed her sheep.' So
saying, Napoleon took Duroc's arm and went
out. Madame X——, astounded, and thinking she
recognised them, wanted to dart after them. I
knew that, strong as I was, I could not hold
this giantess by the arm, but I seized her by the
skirt, which tore at the waist with a loud crack.
At the sound the shepherdess, fearing that if
she pulled she would presently find herself in
her shift, stopped short, saying, 'It's he! it's he!'
and reproaching me bitterly for having hindered
her from following. This I endured patiently
until I saw in the distance the Emperor and
Duroc, with the two Scotchmen following a little
way off, come to the end of the long suite of
rooms and reach the staircase. Judging, then, that
Madame X—— would not be able to find them

in the crowd, I made her a low bow without a word, and went off as quick as I could. She was ready to choke with rage, but feeling that the lower part of her garment was about to desert her, she said to me, 'At least, try to get me some pins, for my dress is falling off.' But I was so angry at her freaks that I left her in the lurch, and I will even admit that I was mischievous enough to rejoice at her awkward position. I quickly left the house and returned home. I passed a disturbed night, seeing myself in my dreams pursued by the shepherdess, who, in spite of my remonstrances, kept insulting the Emperor horribly. Next day I went to cousin Sahuguet to tell her the extraordinary conduct of her dangerous friend. She was disgusted, and forbade her house to Madame X——, who a few days after received orders to leave Paris, nor do I know what became of her.

"The Emperor, as is well known, attended a state mass every Sunday, after which there was a grand reception at the Tuileries, open to every one who had reached a certain rank in the civil or judicial service, and to officers in the army. As such I had the entrée, of which I only availed myself once a month. The Sunday following the day on which the scene I have related took place I was in perplexity. Ought I to show myself to the Emperor so quickly, or would it be better to let some weeks pass? I consulted my mother, and her opinion was that as I was in no way to blame in the affair, I had better go to the Tuileries, and show no signs of embarrassment, which advice I followed. The people who came to court formed a rank on each side of the way to the chapel. The Emperor passed in silence between them, returning their salutes. He replied to mine by a good-natured smile, which seemed to me of good omen, and completely reassured me. After the mass, as Napoleon went through the rooms again, and, according to his custom, addressed a few words to the people who were there, he stopped in front of me, and being unable to express himself freely in presence of so many hearers, he said to me, sure that I should take his meaning: 'I am told that you were at Marescalchi's last ball; did you enjoy yourself very much?' 'Not the least bit, sir.' 'Ah!' replied the Emperor, 'if masked balls sometimes offer agreeable adventures, they are apt also to cause very awkward ones. The great thing is to get well out of them, and no doubt that is what you did.' As soon as the Emperor had passed on, General Duroc, who was behind me, said in my ear: 'Confess that there was a moment when you were in a considerable fix! So was I, indeed, for I am responsible for all the invitations; but it won't happen again. Our impudent shepherdess is far away from Paris, and will never come back.'"

XVII.

AFTER MOSCOW.

THERE is a vivid description of some of the horrors of the Russian campaign, but the mention of Napoleon is not frequent, and there is no picture of him that stands out in bold relief. But here is a passage which throws a singular and clear light on France and her attitude to Napoleon after these disasters. It is a picture the more striking because it is drawn, not by a politician or a philanthropist, but by a soldier who revelled in war's perils and glories:

"The majority of the French nation still confided in Napoleon. No doubt well-informed persons blamed him for having forced his army on to Moscow, and especially for having waited there till winter; but the mass of the people, accustomed to regard the Emperor as infallible, and having, moreover, no idea of what had really happened, or of the losses of our army in Russia, saw only the renown which the capture of Moscow had shed on our arms; so they were eager to give the Emperor the means of bringing victory back to his eagles. Each department and town was patriotically ready to find horses; but the levies of conscripts and money soon chilled their enthusiasm. Still, on the whole, the nation sacrificed itself with a good grace, squadrons and '

battalions rising as if by magic from the ground.
It was astonishing that, after all the drafts of men
which France had undergone in the last twenty
years, never had soldiers of such good quality
been enlisted. This was due to several causes;
first, there had been for some years in each of
the hundred and twenty existing departments a
so-called 'departmental' company of infantry—
a kind of prætorian guard to the prefects, and
formed by their picked men, who, being well
looked after and not overworked, had time to
grow to their full strength, and being regularly
drilled and exercised, needed only their 'baptism of
fire' to make them perfect troops. The companies
varied in strength from one hundred to two
hundred and fifty men; the Emperor sent them
all to the army, where they were merged in line
regiments. Secondly, a great number of conscripts
from previous years, who, for one reason or
another, had obtained leave to be placed at the
'tail' of their depôts, to wait until they were
required, were called up. They, too, as they
grew older, had nearly all become strong and
vigorous."

XVIII.

THE BLOOD TAX.

THERE is something strangely moving and
pathetic in this picture of the readiness of the
people of France to place themselves at the

mercy of their terrible ruler. Here is a continuation of the picture which will show how thoroughly merciless were the exactions with which Napoleon demanded the full tax of blood :

"These were legal measures; but not so was the recalling of persons who had drawn a lucky number at the conscriptions and thus escaped service. All of these below the age of thirty were required to serve. This levy, therefore, furnished a number of men fit to undergo the fatigues of war. There was some grumbling, especially in the south and west; but so great was the habit of obedience, that nearly all the contingent went on duty. This submission on the part of the people led the Government to take a still more illegal step, which, as it touched the upper class, was the more dangerous. After having made men serve whom the ballot had exempted, they compelled those who had quite lawfully obtained substitutes to shoulder their muskets all the same. Many families had embarrassed and even ruined themselves to keep their sons at home, for a substitute cost from 12,000 to 20,000 francs at that time, and this had to be paid down. There were some young men who had obtained substitutes three times over, and were none the less compelled to go; cases even occurred in which they had to serve in the same company with the man whom they had paid to take their place. This piece of iniquity was owing to the advice of Clarke, the War Minister, and Savary, the Police Minister, who persuaded the Emperor that, to prevent any movement of opposition to the Government during the war, sons of influential families must be got out of the country and sent to the army, to act in some sort as hostages. In order, however, to reduce the odium of this measure somewhat, the Emperor created, under the name of Guards of Honour, four cavalry regiments formed of young men of good education. They wore a brilliant hussar uniform, and had generals for their colonels.

"To these more or less legal levies, the Emperor added the produce of a forestalled conscription, and there were excellent battalions formed of sailors, and artificers or gunners of marine artillery, all well-set men trained in handling arms, who had long been weary of their monotonous life in ports, and were eager to go and win glory along with their comrades of the land forces. They soon became formidable infantry, and amounted to 30,000. Lastly, the Emperor further weakened the army in Spain by taking from it not only some thousands of men to replenish his guard, but whole brigades and divisions of seasoned veterans."

XIX.

THE DEFEAT AT LEIPSIC.

EVERYBODY knows the story of the great battle of Leipsic. Marbot reveals the secret of that utter absence of any preparation for retreat, which explained so much of the horrible bloodshed, by which Napoleon's retreat after the battle was followed.

"The Emperor's chief of the head-quarters' staff was Prince Berthier, who had been with him since the Italian campaign of 1796. He was a man of capacity, accuracy, and devotion to duty, but he had often felt the effects of the Imperial wrath, and had acquired such a dread of Napoleon's outbreaks, that he had vowed in no circumstance to take the initiative or ask any question, but to confine himself to executing orders which he received in writing. This system, while keeping the chief of the staff on good terms with his master, was injurious to the interests of the army; for great as were the Emperor's activity and talents, it was physically impossible for him to see to everything, and thus, if he overlooked any important matter, it did not get attended to.

"So it seems to have been at Leipsic. Nearly all the marshals and generals commanding army corps pointed out to Berthier over and over again the necessity of providing many passages to secure a retreat in the event of a reverse, but he always answered, 'The Emperor has given no orders.' Nothing could be got out of him, so that when, on the night of the 18th, the Emperor gave the order to retreat on Weissenfels and the Saale, there was not a beam or a plank across a single brook."

This is one of the many instances in history of the demoralisation which the uncontrolled and despotic temper of a leader is apt to produce in his subordinates. There is a significant passage in the course of this description which shows how far the Emperor had begun to lose his popularity, even in the army:

" The Emperor came by, but as he galloped along the flank of the column he heard none of the acclamations which were wont to proclaim his presence. The army was ill-content with the little care which had been taken to secure its retreat."

XX.

NAPOLEON AS A FRIEND.

THROUGHOUT Marbot's narrative there is scarcely a reflection which shows any strong reprobation of Napoleon's methods or character; indeed, our Marbot is almost as free from any penetrating sense of the horrors of war as though the soul of old Froissart had passed into his. Nevertheless, he cannot help, now and then, giving us glimpses of the red and hideous ruin which Napoleon had brought on France. Here is a passage of sober but effective eloquence in which Marbot paints France as she was in 1814:

" Several military writers have expressed surprise that France did not rise as in 1792 to repel the invaders, or at least form, like the Spaniards, a focus of national defence in every province. To this the answer is, that twenty-five years of war, and the conscription too frequently anticipated, had worn out the enthusiasm which in 1792 had improvised armies. The example of Spain does not apply to France. Paris has been allowed to gain too much influence, and unless she puts herself at the head of the movement, France is helpless. In Spain, on the other hand, each province, being a little government, could act and raise an army, even when the French held Madrid. France was ruined by centralisation."

Marbot, as well as the other chroniclers, shows Napoleon's softer side. He was very indulgent to some of his lieutenants, especially to General Lasalle, who seems to have been one of the greatest scamps as well as one of the most brilliant soldiers in the army.

" Lasalle had intimate relations with a French lady in high society, and while he was in Egypt their correspondence was seized by the English and insultingly published by order of the Government—an act which even in England was blamed. A divorce followed, and on his return to Europe Lasalle married the lady. As general, Lasalle was placed by the Emperor in command of the advanced guard of the Grand Army. He distinguished himself at Austerlitz and in Prussia; having the audacity to appear before Stettin and summon the place with two regiments of hussars. The Governor lost his head and brought out the keys, instead of using them to lock the gates, in which case all the cavalry in Europe could not have taken it. This feat brought Lasalle much credit, and raised the Emperor's liking for him to a high point. Indeed, he petted him to an incredible degree, laughing at all his freaks, and never letting him pay his own debts. Just as he was on the point of marrying the lady to whom I have referred, Napoleon had given him 200,000 francs out of his privy purse. A week later, meeting him at the Tuileries, the Emperor asked, 'When is the wedding?' 'As soon as I have got some money to furnish with, sir.' 'Why, I gave you 200,000 francs last week! What have you done with them?' 'Paid my debts with half, and lost the other half at cards!' Such an admission would have ruined any other general. The Emperor laughed, and, merely giving a sharp tug to Lasalle's moustache, ordered Duroc to give him another 200,000 francs."

CHAPTER VI.

NAPOLEON'S CHIEF DETRACTOR.*

NAPOLEON interfered with and ruined many careers; but in the long gallery of those on whom he trampled in his march to greatness, none is so remarkable as Barras.

This Barras was so utter and tremendous a blackguard that one is tempted, in reading these Memoirs of his, to forget that he was also very brave, adroit, resourceful, and that he went within an inch of being a very great man. This book is intended to be a tremendous indictment of Napoleon, but it turns out a tremendous indictment of Napoleon's greatest enemy and assailant. Most of the blows of Barras at the person of Napoleon fall short, and even recoil on himself; but between Barras and Napoleon there was probably less to choose than some critics have said. To read the hot encounters of the two is to be reminded of what a desperate game it

* "Memoirs of Barras." (London : Osgood & McIlvaine.)

was—how unprincipled, how reckless, and how selfish were the men who fought over the body of France. And finally, this book confirms the opinion that Napoleon in real greatness was much superior to all the rivals whom he cast down, and especially to this one, who rises, as it were, from the dead to continue the conflict.

I.

NEARLY A GREAT MAN.

I HAVE said that Barras went very near to being a great man. I base this statement mainly on the part he played against Robespierre. Make what deductions you like—allow for change of circumstances, for the growing disgust and revolt against the cruelties of the Dictator and his universal guillotine—the fact remains that Barras succeeded where other of the mightiest spirits of the French Revolution failed. Instead of following Danton to the scaffold, as everybody would have thought probable, Barras sent Robespierre there, and undoubtedly he was the inspirer, the leader, and the spirit without whom the movement against the omnipotent Dictator would have collapsed. Corrupt, pleasure-loving, unprincipled—all these things Barras was; but, on the other hand, he was capable, fearless, ready-witted, a born leader of men. And while one must loathe his vices, is there not, on the other hand, something singularly

human and picturesque in his strange, terrible,
and contradictory nature—with love and laughter
on the one side, and a struggle on the edge of the
precipice and at the foot of the guillotine on the
other—with the beautiful Madame Tallien and
Josephine Beauharnais on his arm, and on the
other hand, the tiger-eyes of Robespierre to face
and to subdue?

II.

BARRAS AND ROBESPIERRE—A CONTRAST.

WHAT merit these Memoirs have is not in the
least due to grace of style.   Barras was not a
very articulate man.   He was, above all things,
a man of action.   In the tribune he was rarely
effective; his pen is clumsy, cold, uninspired.   But
to a certain extent that is one of the charms of
these Memoirs.   I find it thrilling and convincing
to read an account such as he gives—dry, unpretentious, matter-of-fact—of some of the wildest
and most terrible scenes of the Revolution—
notably of that day of days when he and
Robespierre were in the death-grip.   And indeed,
I find something else in the absence of all grace
from these accounts.   Napoleon used to say that
he was always on his guard against generals who
made pictures to their imaginations.   He wanted
the man who saw what was right in front of him
without haze or illusion, or thoughts coloured by
wishes.   Barras made no pictures to his imagina-

tion. Around Robespierre he saw none of the halo, either of worshipping reverence or awe-struck horror, with which either admiration or hatred endowed him. Barras simply saw an enemy who would kill if he weren't killed; he went for the enemy with straight, direct, and clear-eyed simplicity, while others paused, vacillated, and debated; and so was successful where others had failed. Of the two men, Robespierre was in private virtuous, spotless, and the other, in private vices, almost unsurpassable. It is, indeed, the revolt of a corrupt, vicious, laughter-loving man of the world against saintly austerities, that is in action in the fight between Barras and Robespierre; but whatever the faults and crimes of Barras, posterity shares the joy of his contemporaries at his victory over the Sea-green Incorruptible, for it was, after all, the victory of humanity over the pitiless cruelty of a fanatic.

III.

THE INCORRUPTIBLE AT HOME.

WHEN Barras returned to Paris after the successful siege of Toulon, where first he and Napoleon were brought into contact, there were already rumours that he had begun that career of peculation in which he was to surpass all his contemporaries. Robespierre had no toleration for any such form of political crime; and, doubtless, he had marked out Barras as one of the " corrupt men " of whom the sanguinary guillotine was to rid the nation.   Barras, doubtless, felt this too, and this adds a terrible interest to the account which these Memoirs give of the interview between the two men.   One can almost read between its lines the deadly hate, the mutual terror, the severe examination of each other's resources, which these duellists were already feeling before they crossed swords in the fight to the death.

Here is the account Barras gives of the interview :

" I finally resolved on calling upon this almightiness, this representative of Republican purity, the incorruptible one *par excellence.*   I had never had more than a passing glimpse of Robespierre, either on the benches or in the hall-ways of the Convention; we had never had any personal intercourse.   His frigid attitude, his scorn of courtesies, had imposed on me the maintenance of a reserve which my self-pride dictated to me when in face of an equal.   Fréron considered our safety depended on this visit, so we wended our way to the residence of Robespierre.   It was a little house situated in the Rue Saint-Honoré, almost opposite the Rue Saint-Florentin.   I think it no longer exists nowadays, owing to the opening made to create the Rue Dupont just at that spot.   This house was occupied and owned by a carpenter, by name

Duplay. This carpenter, a member of the Jacobin Club, had met Robespierre at its meetings; with the whole of his household, he had become an enthusiastic worshipper at the shrine of the popular orator, and had obtained for himself the honour of securing him both as boarder and lodger. In his leisure moments Robespierre was wont to comment on the 'Emile' of Jean Jacques Rousseau, and explain it to the children of the carpenter, just as a good village parish priest expounds the Gospel to his flock. Touched and grateful for this evangelistic solicitude, the children and apprentices of the worthy artisan would not suffer his guest, the object of their hero-worship, to go into the street without escorting him to the door of the National Convention, for the purpose of watching over his precious life, which his innate cowardice and the flattery of his courtiers were beginning to make him believe threatened in every possible way by the aristocracy, who were seeking to destroy the incorruptible tribune of the people. It was necessary, in order to reach the eminent guest deigning to inhabit this humble little hole of a place, to pass through a long alley flanked with planks stacked there, the owner's stock-in-trade. This alley led to a little yard from seven to eight feet square, likewise full of planks. A little wooden staircase led to a room on the first floor. Prior to ascending it we perceived in the yard the daughter of the carpenter Duplay, the owner of the house. This girl allowed no one to take her place in ministering to Robespierre's needs. As women of this class in those days freely espoused the political ideas then prevalent, and as in her case they were of a most pronounced nature, Danton had surnamed Cornélie Copeau 'the Cornelia who is not the mother of the Gracchi.' Cornélie seemed to be finishing spreading linen to dry in the yard ; in her hand were a pair of striped cotton stockings, in fashion at the time, and which were certainly similar to those we daily saw encasing the legs of Robespierre on his visits to the Convention. Opposite her sat Mother Duplay between a pail and a salad-basket, busily engaged in picking salad-herbs."

IV.

A MEMORABLE INTERVIEW.

BUT I must hurry on to the interview :

"Robespierre was standing, wrapped in a sort of chemise peignoir; he had just left the hands of his hairdresser, who had finished combing and powdering his hair ; he was without the spectacles he usually wore in public, and piercing through the powder covering that face, already so white in its natural pallor, we could see a pair of eyes whose dimness the glasses had until then screened from us. These eyes fastened themselves on us with a fixed stare, expressive of utter astonishment at our appearance. We saluted him after our own way, without any embarrassment, and in the simple fashion of the period. He showed no recognition of our courtesy, going by turns to his toilet-glass hanging to a window looking out on the courtyard, and then to a little mirror, intended, doubtless, as an ornament to his mantelpiece, but which nowadays set it off; taking his toilet-knife, he began scraping off the powder, mindful of observing the outlines of his carefully-dressed hair; then, doffing his peignoir, he flung it on a chair close to us in such a way as to soil our clothes, without apologising to us for his action, and without even appearing to notice our presence. He washed himself in a sort of wash-hand basin which he held with one hand, cleaning his teeth, repeatedly spat on the ground right at our feet, without so much as heeding us, and in almost as direct a fashion as Potemkin, who, it is known, did not take the trouble of turning the other way, but who, without warning or taking any precaution, was wont to spit in the faces of those standing before him. This ceremony over, Robespierre did not even then address a single word to us. Fréron thought it time to speak, so he introduced me, saying, ' This is my colleague, Barras, who has done more than either myself or any military man to bring

about the capture of Toulon.   Both of us have
performed our duty on the field of battle at
the peril of our lives, and we are prepared to
do likewise in the Convention.   It is rather
distressing, when men have shown themselves
as willing as ourselves, not to receive simple
justice, but to see ourselves the object of the
most iniquitous charges and the most monstrous
calumnies. 'We feel quite sure that at least
those who know us as thou dost, Robespierre,
will do us justice, and cause it to be done us.'
Robespierre still remained silent; but Fréron
thought he noticed, by an almost imperceptible
shadow which flitted over his motionless features,
that the *thou*, a continuation of the revolutionary
custom, was distasteful to him, so, pursuing the
tenor of his speech, he found means of immediately substituting the word *you*, in order
to again be on good terms with this haughty
and susceptible personage. Robespierre gave no
sign of satisfaction at this act of deference; he
was standing, and so remained, without inviting
us to take a seat. I informed him politely that
our visit to him was prompted by the esteem
in which we held his political principles; he
did not deign to reply to me by a single word,
nor did his face reveal the trace of any emotion
whatsoever. I have never seen anything so
impassible in the frigid marble of statuary or
in the face of the dead already laid to rest. . . .

Such was our interview with Robespierre. I cannot call it a conversation, for his lips never parted; tightly closed as they were, he pursed them even tighter; from them, I noticed, oozed a bilious froth boding no good. I had seen all I wanted, for I had had a view of what has since been most accurately described as the *tiger-cat*."

It would be a waste of the time of the reader to dwell on the points in this narrative which are intensely interesting. The simplicity and even squalor of the surroundings of the mighty master of life and death, his sinister looks, his appalling silence—all these things the most hurried reader can find for himself in the passage. Its sense of reality and of life is overwhelming.

v.

DANTON.

I CANNOT dwell on the passages in which Barras describes the closing conflicts between Robespierre and the other Revolutionaries, but there is not a line in this portion of the Memoirs which is not intensely vivid; the more so for the reason I have already given—that the narrative has the matter-of-fact unpretentiousness of daily life.

Take as an example this scene, which occurred just a few days before Danton's execution:

"As I was leaving the Convention one day in the company of Danton, Courtois, Fréron, and

Panis, we met in the Cour du Carrousel several deputies who were members of the secret committees. Danton, going towards them, said to them, 'You should read the Memoirs of Philippeaux. They will supply you with the means of putting an end to this Vendean war which you have undertaken with the view of rendering your powers necessary.' Vadier, Amar, Vouland, and Barrère charged Danton with having caused these Memoirs to be printed and circulated. Danton merely replied, 'I am not called upon to vindicate myself.' Thereupon an angry discussion ensued, degenerating into personalities. Danton threatened the members of the Committee that he would take the floor in the National Convention, and charge them with malversations and tyranny. The others withdrew without replying, but bearing him no goodwill. I said to Danton, 'Let us at once return to the National Convention; take the floor; you may rest assured of our support, but do not let us wait until to-morrow, for there is a likelihood of your being arrested to-night.' 'They would not dare to,' was Danton's contemptuous rejoinder; then addressing himself to me, he said, 'Come and help us to eat a pullet.' I declined. Brune, the friend, and up to that time the inseparable aide-de-camp of Danton, was present. I remarked to Brune, 'Guard Danton carefully, for he threatened where he should have struck.' "

In this "Come and help us to eat a pullet," there is that human touch necessary to remind us that even in those apocalyptic times, men, who were in the very heart of the cyclone, went about their business and their pleasures pretty much as we all do in ordinary times.

VI.

ROBESPIERRE'S LUST FOR BLOOD.

THE account of the execution of Danton adds nothing to the details we have already known ; but there are some statements about Robespierre which I have not seen anywhere before. They strike me as not like the truth — as mere invention :

"It has been stated that, not content with having seen the victims pass his house, Robespierre had followed them to the place of execution, that he had contemplated them with ferocious satisfaction in the different phases of their agony; lastly, that the insatiable tiger, rendered more bloodthirsty by the sight, appeared to be licking his jaws and gargling his throat with the blood flowing in torrents from the scaffold into the Place de la Révolution. But if his joy was complete at the very moment when Danton's head fell, he is said by some mechanical instinct to have put his hand to his neck, as if to make sure that his own head was on his shoulders. He was making no mistake in believing that his head was now more than ever in jeopardy since that of Danton had fallen. It may be said that at that moment the power of Robespierre renounced its main support —that of the trust reposed in him by the patriots. He sought to conceal himself amid the masses surrounding the guillotine, but, as if already pursued by a celestial vengeance, he was seen to wend his way homewards with tottering steps, as if he had lost his balance."

Here is a small but eloquent proof of the terrible ascendency Robespierre exercised over the Convention:

" Such was the terror produced by Robespierre that a member of the National Convention who thought the gaze of the Dictator was fixed upon him, just as he was putting his hand to his forehead in musing fashion, quickly withdrew it, saying : ' He will suppose that I am thinking of something.' "

VII.

FOUQUIER-TINVILLE.

FINALLY, from this portion of the Memoirs I must quote the passages in which Barras, with a terrible and grim humour—which gives us some idea of the iron nature of the man, and of its haughty scorn of human nature—describes the obsequiousness of-Fouquier-Tinville, and the other wretches who had been the joyous instruments of Robespierre's tyranny.

"When Robespierre, together with Couthon and Saint-Just, were arraigned before the Revolutionary Tribunal, merely for the purpose of having their identity established, since they were outlawed and nothing remained but to hand them over to the executioner, Fouquier-Tinville, the Public Prosecutor (performing the duties of the officer of the law nowadays called *procureur-général*), was in a state of agitation hardly to be imagined—he who up to that very moment had gone every day, even but yesterday, to take the orders of Robespierre and Saint-Just in regard to all the unfortunate people whom it pleased them to send to the scaffold, to see himself directly, and by a superior and inevitable will, entrusted with the duty of bringing to the same scaffold the men who had been first chosen, so to speak, as organisers of slaughter, and, to say the very least, actual dictators! Fouquier's embarrassment in so critical a conjunction may be conceived; he doubtless could say to himself with some show of reason and presentiment: 'Mutato nomine de te. . . .' I could not blame him for the sort of embarrassment I noticed in his whole person at the moment of fulfilling a like duty. Fouquier-Tinville had already made an attempt to apologise for his behaviour with regard to the condemned men themselves. 'I am well aware that it is not

I,' he said, 'who am sentencing ces messieurs' (for this was the only allowable appellation, the word monsieur having been struck out of the language), 'since they are outlaws, and that in the present case the tribunal merely applies the penalty; I am well aware that it is my duty, and even my right, to urge on justice and to guide it; what I am doing to-day is in one respect less than what I was doing yesterday, for yesterday we gave judgments on our own responsibility, while to-day we are merely executing the decree of the National Convention; but yet——' I could not see when this 'but yet' was going to stop, and in what way Fouquier-Tinville would get rid of his hesitation; there was a danger of its increasing during the surrounding confusion. I saw that there was no time to be lost, and that it was necessary to instil courage into the head of the Revolutionary Tribunal. I am thus designating Fouquier-Tinville; I would have called him the soul of it, could one believe such monsters possessed a soul. 'Come now, citizen Fouquier,' I exclaimed in a loud but cold, imperious voice, 'the National Convention have commissioned me to see its orders carried out; I give you the one to proceed without further delay with the fulfilment of your mandate. This is the day to show oneself a patriot by sending the guilty ones forthwith to the scaffold awaiting them.' Fouquier did not require a second warning. He at once took his place

on the bench, doffed his little cape, his hat with
the brim turned up *à la* Henri IV., summoned
the judges, repeated the fatal formula against
Robespierre, Couthon, Saint-Just, and the whole
of the frightful band with as much firmness as on
the previous day he had pronounced the formula
' by and in the name of Robespierre.'   All the
forms of the ceremonial were completed in short
order ; in less than half an hour the condemned
men had, to use the judge's phraseology, ' their
toilet made, their boots greased,' and could go to
their destination. . . . So I urged on Fouquier,
saying, ' Come now, let us make a start.' ' We
will start at once,' replied Fouquier quickly, and
even with really triumphant alacrity ; ' but where
shall we take them to ? ' ' Why, to the usual
place, where so many have preceded them.' ' But,'
said Fouquier to me in an undertone, with an air
of respectful and intimate confidence, ' for a week,
citizen representative, we have been sending our
condemned to the Barrière du Trône ; we have
given up using the Place de la Révolution.'
' Return to it, then,' I said, with a determined
gesture ; ' the way to it shall be past Robespierre's
house ; the prophecy must be fulfilled ! ' ' Poor
Danton,' said Fouquier-Tinville, with an air of
being moved to pity, ' there was a patriot for
you ! ' believing, the knavish and cruel Fouquier,
that he could obliterate by this appearance of
regret the fact that he, Fouquier, had been

Danton's primary murderer! . . . Fouquier bowed humbly, and said to the Clerk of the Court and the escort of gendarmes, 'To the Place de la Révolution!' In less than two hours, the clerk, the ushers, the gendarmes, with Fouquier-Tinville still at their head, arrived at the Committee of Public Safety, and all, speaking almost together and with combative eagerness, gave me an account of the execution as of a triumph thoroughly accomplished. The terrible Robespierre was at last launched into the eternal night, and slept side by side with Louis XVI. . . . The spectators, impatient of and, it may truly be said, hungering for the death of Robespierre, had not allowed the sigh of deliverance to escape their bodies until after they had convinced themselves of the consummation of the execution by the unquestionable evidence of the head severed from the trunk and rolling into the basket of the executioner. Well, then, even after the execution there seemed to reign an almost general kind of fear of the possible resurrection of the implacable man whose inexorable speeches and sentences, without appeal, had so cruelly tortured human minds. The newspapers were uncertain whether they should venture to publish even the fact. The *Moniteur*, already more than official (for it has always belonged to the victorious side), especially shrank from this its primary duty; it was only twenty-six days later, *i.e.* on the 6th Fructidor following, that this

Moniteur made up its mind to record the most colossal and decisive fact of modern times, not only for France, but for Europe and the whole human race."

VIII.

TWO NOTORIOUS WOMEN.

NOT a member of the whole family of Napoleon is spared by Barras. There is a picture of the mother and sisters of Napoleon which seeks to confirm some of the worst charges made against the Imperial family. It is a squalid and an odious picture, but I am not prepared to say of it, as of other pictures in the book, that it is untrue. A lack of morality of any kind was undoubtedly one of the marked characteristics of the Napoleonic race.

However, it is on poor Josephine that Barras is most severe. The pages which he devotes to her are among the most infamous in literature. But it is my business to let Barras speak for himself.

The two women who were credited with exercising the greatest influence over him at the moment when he was practically Dictator of France, were Madame Tallien and Madame Josephine de Beauharnais. This is how he speaks of them:

"Madame Tallien, since the ninth Thermidor, had shown herself in all public places, even at the theatres, winning undisputed supremacy over her

sex. She was the feminine dictator of beauty.
As I was one of those who had been instrumental
in saving her life previous to the ninth Thermidor,
I had remained on a footing of intimacy with her,
not to be interrupted by my accession to the
Directorate. Those who, in all the relations of
life, consider only the means which can procure
them access to those in power, believed that
Madame Tallien, having possibly granted certain
favours, consequently exercised a certain sway
over me, and appealed to her, some under the
cloak of passion, others under that of devotion,
friendship, enthusiasm, or admiration. Madame
Tallien did not abuse this position to any too
great extent, seeking, it is true, in all this a happy
way of supplementing her fortune—a very small
one at the time, and one she was compelled to
share with her husband, who possessed none,
either because he had earned little money, or
from the reason that he had run through it quickly.
Madame Tallien might, therefore, busy herself in
good earnest to pick up the money she judged
necessary for her maintenance; but it must be
admitted that money, in the case of Madame
Tallien, was not the main object, but the means of
obtaining the pleasures she was fond of or which
she procured for others. I must in this connection
point out a distinction which the acquaintances of
Madame Tallien and Madame Beauharnais agreed
n establishing between these two gentlewomen, to

wit, that the *liaisons* of Madame Tallien were for her genuine enjoyment, to which she brought all the ardour and passion of her temperament. As for Madame Beauharnais, it was the general belief that her relations, even with the men whose physical advantages she best appreciated, were not so generous as those of Madame Tallien. Even although the physical basis appeared to be with Madame Beauharnais the origin of her *liaison*, determined by an involuntary impulse, her libertinism sprang merely from the mind, while the heart played no part in the pleasures of her body ; in a word, never loving except from motives of interest, the lewd Creole never lost sight of business, although those possessing her might suppose she was conquered by them and had freely given herself. She had sacrificed all to sordid interests, and, as was said of a disreputable woman who had preceded her in this style of turning matters to account, 'she would have drunk gold in the skull of her lover.' When compared to Madame Tallien, it did not seem possible that Madame Beauharnais could enter into competition with her in the matter of physical charms. Madame Tallien was then in the height of her freshness ; Madame Beauharnais was beginning to show the results of precocious decrepitude."

IX.

THE SYMMETRY OF BARRAS'S VILLAINY.

I AM sure every reader of this, and of the passages I shall have still to quote, will feel a sentiment of intense disgust. Of all dishonours, there is none so base as that known as "kissing and telling." Barras does more. He not only tells, but he makes the weakness or the affection which women displayed to himself the basis of a charge and an enduring hatred against them. Up to the present he has given no instance of any wrong—either of ingratitude or desertion—which he suffered at the hands of the beautiful Madame Tallien; and yet he not only reveals his relations with her, but goes out of his way to represent her as self-seeking, lewd, and base. In the code of honour among men with any pretence to heart, or even to decency, I should put it as almost the first article that association with a woman had made her ever afterwards—amid change, after separation, even after desertion—a sacred being to be protected, above all things to be respected and to be spared.

But what a light these revelations of Barras throw on the meanness of his dark and cold soul! There is something to me positively appalling in this bit of self-portraiture. When I come across a man complete and perfect in vice, I at once feel as if I were face to face with some terrible portent of nature. And this man—willing to receive the

endearments of words and of acts of some of the
most beautiful, fascinating, and tender women of
the period, and maintaining amid every scene of
passion and affection, with the background of the
guillotine, and all the horrors and abysses of the
time—maintaining amid all this the same coldness
of heart, the same frigid outlook of the eye—it
is a picture of a human being which makes me at
once bewildered and aghast! Robespierre must
have been blind in that great interview between
him and Barras not to have seen the depths of
inflexibility, cruelty, and resolve which were in the
eyes of Barras. Or would it not be more correct
to say that Robespierre was too clear-sighted, and
that his frozen silence—his refusal to utter even
one word, to give an indication by one look—was
his instinctive sense of the kind of man with
whom he was dealing? Robespierre was a highly
nervous and sensitive man; his enemies declare
that he was an arrant coward. He certainly had
not firmness of nerve. In the weeks that preceded
the final struggle for his life he went to a shooting-
gallery to steady his nerves by pistol practice.
He fainted after the first shot!

X.

TWO PORTRAITS—BARRAS AND ROBESPIERRE.

LOOK at the portraits of the two men which are
in these volumes; and, perchance, they may

modify, if not revolutionise, your conception of them, and of the events in which they took part. The portrait confirms the feeling of surprise I remember to have experienced when first I saw that authentic likeness of Robespierre of which Lord Rosebery is the owner. I loathe Robespierre, and thus I have to confess that this portrait is unpleasantly startling to me. To my imagination the Sea-green Incorruptible always appeared as having a long face, with straight, regular, icy-cold features. The portrait that looks on one from this book is that of a man with a short, rather chubby face; the cheeks are full and round; the nose is irregular, with broad nostrils, and a slight tendency to the snub; the air is almost boyish, and is gentle, even tender and rather sad. In short, if I had been shown the portrait without knowing the name or the nationality, I should have said it was the portrait of an Irishman; and I might have even gone the length of guessing that it was the portrait of John Philpot Curran, the celebrated Irish orator and patriot, beautified and idealised. And I may mention, as some extenuation of this impression, that I have read somewhere that Robespierre had some Irish blood in his veins.

The portrait of Robespierre faces the first volume of these Memoirs, that of Barras faces the second. And what a contrast! I am convinced that any physiognomist in the world who was asked to say which was the cruel monster and which the kindly and genial nature, would at once reverse the verdict of history, and see in Robespierre the hero of mercy, and in Barras the embodiment of cruelty. There is the distinction of the aristocrat about Barras. He appears tall, shapely, erect; a haughty and hard self-confidence in his attitude. And then, that face! The mouth is large, well-shaped, as tight as a rat-trap; the nose is long, regular, distinguished; and even through the spectral black and white of an engraving, the eyes still seem to burn and stare with brilliant and steel-like glitter. It is a terrible face.

In "A Strange Story"—Bulwer Lytton's best story—there is a spectre that strikes death as it passes. It is called the *Scin-læca*, if I remember rightly after nearly a quarter of a century, and the doomed one shudders as it passes and strikes. Barras was the *Scin-læca* of Robespierre. It was no wonder that he was awed and paralysed into a frozen silence as Barras passed.

XI.

NAPOLEON AND JOSEPHINE.

FROM Josephine, Barras passes to Napoleon, and he is as severe on the future husband as on the wife :

" Bonaparte, who knew of all her adventures just as well as I did, had often heard the story

of them told in my presence; but in consequence
of his intention, not to say his eagerness, to reach
his goal by all possible means, he had looked
upon the two gentlewomen whom I mention in
the light of means to this end; and whether it was
that Madame Tallien's beauty had, at the same
time, captivated him, or whether he believed, as
reputed, that she possessed greater influence than
Madame Beauharnais, it was to Madame Tallien that
he in the first place addressed his vows and respectful
attentions.   This was soon followed by a declaration of what he called his unconquerable passion.
Madame Tallien replied to the little enamoured
Corsican in a contemptuous fashion, which left
him no hope.   She even went so far as to say
to him ironically that 'she thought she could do
better. . . .'   After such a defeat Bonaparte considered that, beaten in one direction, he might
do better in another, so he conceived the idea
of paying his court to Madame Beauharnais, and
as he had some knowledge of her interested character and her cupidity, that prominent feature of
it with which he was acquainted, he bethought himself of opening the door with the key that never
finds any door closed.   He therefore began to
make Madame Beauharnais presents which suited
her courtesan's taste in matters of dress and
jewellery.   Not only did he give her shawls and
expensive and elegant jewellery, but diamonds of
considerable value.   This would have constituted

an act of madness had it not been one of speculation. Something of this came to my ears, so censuring the young man, however amiable a personage he might be, for subjecting himself to the necessity of beginning by paying an old woman, I said to Bonaparte, 'It seems that you have taken La Beauharnais for one of the soldiers of the thirteenth Vendémiaire, whom you should have included in the distribution of money. You would have done better to have sent this money to your family, which needs it, and to whom I have just rendered further assistance.' Bonaparte blushed, but did not deny having made presents of considerable value. As I was bantering him about his generosity, wherein I pretended to see the effects of a boundless passion, he himself began to laugh, and said to me, 'I have not made presents to my mistress; I have not sought to seduce a virgin; I am one of those who prefer love ready made than to make it myself. . . . Well, then, in whichever of these states Madame Beauharnais may be, if the relations between us were really serious, if the presents which you blame me for having made were wedding presents, what, then, would you have to find fault with, citizen Director?—"This woman whom you accuse," said Tallien, after the ninth Thermidor, "this woman is mine!"—I do not intend to give you absolutely the same answer just now, but I might say to you, Were this woman to become mine, what would be the objection?' 'I have no objection to make ; still, it is a matter deserving some thought.' At the time of the siege of Toulon, 'theeing and thouing' had taken the place of *you*, from the soldier to the general and from the general to the soldier. Hence it was that I had acquired the habit of 'theeing and thouing' Bonaparte. I said to Bonaparte as familiarly as heretofore : 'Is it seriously meant, what thou hast just told me ? I have just thought over thy idea of marriage, and it seems less ridiculous to me than at first sight.' 'In the first place, Madame Beauharnais is rich,' answered Bonaparte with vehemence. He had been deceived by the lady's external luxury, ignorant of the fact that the unfortunate creature depended for her existence on loans contracted in Paris on the imaginary credit of property in Martinique, which she was far from possessing, since her mother still lived ; and, as the latter troubled herself very little about her daughter, whose dissoluteness she was acquainted with, she contented herself with sending her a meagre allowance, which she had of late cut down and even suspended remitting, owing to a series of poor harvests. The widow Beauharnais lived at Fontainebleau in a state bordering on misery. The greater part of the year she quartered herself on Madame Doué, a Creole like herself, without whose relief she would have lacked the first necessaries. She would come to Paris by the public stagecoach (*petites voitures*), her daughter Hortense was apprenticed to a dressmaker, and her son to a carpenter; this was either very philosophical or very unmotherly of her, since she could find means for her toilette, which, at all periods, was ever that of a courtesan. 'Well,' said I to Bonaparte, 'since you are seriously asking my advice, I will answer you in your own words; why should you not? Your brother Joseph has shown you the way to marriage; the X—— dowry has put an end to his financial straits. You tell me that you are at your wits' end for money, and that you cannot afford to lose any more time over the matter; well, then, marry; a married man has a standing in society, and can better resist the attacks of his enemies; you think you have many of them amongst the Corsicans; if you have luck you will make friends of them, beginning with Saliceti, whom you dread. There is nothing like success to win over everybody to one's side.'"

XII.

JOSEPHINE'S TEARS.

THE next passage I shall quote has a certain comic force that almost relieves its blackguardism:

"A few days later it was Madame Beauharnais' turn to come and confide in me. Actuated as she was by motives of interest, she did not display any reserve in confessing them to me at the very outset of her visit; she began by laying down in most plain terms that no impulse of the heart was at the bottom of this new bond; that the little 'puss in boots' is assuredly the very last she could have dreamed of loving, as he had no expectations. 'He belongs to a family of beggars,' she said, 'which has failed to win respect wherever it has dwelt; but he has a brother who has married well at Marseilles, who promises to help the others, and him. He seems enterprising, and guarantees he will soon carve his fortune.' Madame Beauharnais confesses to me that he has made her presents of a magnificence which has led her to believe that he is possessed of greater means than people wot of. 'As regards myself,' she says to me, 'I have not seen fit to inform him of my straitened circumstances; he believes I am now in the enjoyment of a certain fortune, and is under the impression that I have great expectations over in Martinique. Do not impart to him anything you know, my good friend; you would be spoiling everything. Since I do not love him, you can understand my going into the business; 'tis you I will ever love, you may depend on it. Rose will always be yours, ever at your disposal, you have only to make a sign; but I know full well that you no longer love me,' she proceeded, suddenly bursting into tears, which she had the power of summoning at pleasure; 'this is what grieves me most ; never will I console myself for it, do what I may. When one has loved a man like you, Barras, can one ever know another attachment ?' 'How about Hoche?' I replied with very little emotion, and almost laughing; 'you loved him above all others, and yet there was the aide-de-camp, Vanakre, *e tutti quanti!* . . . Come now, you are a mighty fine cajoler.' This was the mildest and truest word that could be spoken to her ; to cajole all who came in contact with her was the trade of Madame Beauharnais, a veritable *chevalier d'industrie*, so to speak, in town and at Court, from the day she had been imported from her island of Martinique into France. My answer took her breath away, and unable to utter any reply in the face of such positive facts, she contented herself with shedding some more tears, seizing my hands with all her might, and carrying them to her eyes, so as to bedew them with her tears. I was getting tired of this scene, and, not knowing how to put an end to it, I adopted the course of ringing, so as to have my valet as a third party. This compelled her to cease ; Madame Beauharnais was a true actress, who knew how to play several parts at one and the same time. She told my valet that she had suddenly felt poorly, that her nerves troubled her, and that on such occasions she could not hold back her tears; that I had just ministered to her as a brother would to his sister, and that she now felt a great deal better.

I took advantage of this improvement to order my carriage, to send Madame Beauharnais home in it, and thus I was rid of her. 'In your indisposed state you cannot return home alone,' I said to her. I ordered one of my aides-de-camp to accompany her. Her tears had suddenly dried up; her features so discomposed but a moment ago had resumed their placidity and pretty ways, and their habitual coquettishness. On returning my aide-de-camp told that the lady reached her house in excellent health. A few sighs had escaped her during the drive homeward, and the only words spoken by her had been, 'Why do people have a heart over which they have no control? Why did I ever love a man like Barras? How can I cease loving him? How can I tear myself from him? How can I think of any other but him? Tell him from me, I entreat you, how deeply I am devoted to him; that I will never love but him, whatever happens to me in this world. . . .' My aide-de-camp further informed me that just as the carriage reached Madame Beauharnais' house, Bonaparte was there waiting for her at the door. Embarrassed at being accompanied by my aide-de-camp, Madame Beauharnais hurriedly steps out of the carriage, asks Bonaparte to give her his arm, and tells him hastily in the presence of my aide-de-camp, whom she called to witness, that she had just 'had a fainting fit at my house; that she had so suffered that I would not hear of her returning home alone, and that she had hardly recovered her strength. Give Barras my best thanks,' she adds, on dismissing my aide-de-camp, 'and tell him that you left me with his best friend.'"

XIII.

HER STORY TO NAPOLEON.

I PASS on to some scenes that are so atrocious in language and in thought that I have hesitated for a long time whether I should have them or not; but, after all, the characters of Napoleon and Josephine have passed into history, and there is no room left for any reticence about them. And I believe they will injure most their author:

"My best friend was there waiting impatiently to learn the result of the step he had been the first to advise. Everything had been fully concerted between the pair, but each of them was vying in deceiving the other with astounding readiness. The following is an illustration of the way in which they played their farce. As a consequence of having told Bonaparte of her alleged indisposition, it was necessary to give some reason for this indisposition to the man who was about to become her protector for life. I heard some time afterwards of the story the cajoling courtesan had invented. According to her I had a long while courted her without success; she had constantly repulsed my advances because I was not the man to appeal to her so delicate soul.   In consequence of her harsh treatment of me I had sought to console myself with Madame Tallien, whom I had selected out of spite only, remaining attached to her out of *amour propre* alone; and I so little cared for her, she went on to say, that I had offered to give her up at once for Madame Beau- harnais, if the latter would become my mistress; were she to be believed I had been more pressing than ever on this last occasion, and my violence had led to a struggle during the course of which she had fainted; but the recollection of the one she loved, the mere thought of Bonaparte, had restored all her strength to her, and she had come out victorious, desirous of bringing to the near bond to which she had given her consent all the purity of a widow faithful to the memory of her husband, and a virginity often more precious than the first, since it represents a resolution of the heart and the will of reason.   Bonaparte listened, with no small emotion, to this lying concoction, worthy, indeed, of the most artful of women, but whom he, artful as he was himself, looked upon as an angel of candour and truth.   All this made such an impression on him that he flew into a passion against me, ready in his fury to go to extremes, even to call me out for having attempted an assault on the virtue of his future wife.   Madame Beauharnais quieted him with caresses and words, which plainly showed that she dreaded nothing so

much as a scandal which would have revealed the
secret of the comedy played by her, and proved,
besides, that so far from my seeking to do violence
to Madame Beauharnais, I was long since tired of
and bored with her. 'I am quite sure,'said Bonaparte
to her, 'from what you tell me, that Barras failed
in his attempts on your virtue, madame, in spite
of his not having the reputation of a sentimental
lover in the habit of sighing at the feet of cruel
beauties. But I have for so long seen you on a
certain intimate footing with him that doubts
might truly have arisen in any other mind than
mine; you will admit, madame, that it is allowable to think, without showing oneself too severe,
that women seeking to hold him at arm's length
should at least take earlier steps, so as not to be
exposed to a scene like the one you have just told
me of. There are accidents for which a woman is
responsible when she has not taken means to
prevent them.' It would be thought that Madame
Beauharnais would have been abashed by such
excellent reasoning, but it will be seen what ruses
were at the service of the courtesan. 'Why,' she
argued, 'had she not called at Barras' house would
she have been fortunate enough to meet Bonaparte? If she had of late gone there more frequently than before, had it not always been from
a desire to meet him more often? If she had
perchance overlooked many things repugnant to
the elegance and delicacy of her morals, would she

ever have done so had it not been for the consideration, ever present to her mind, of rendering some
service to her future husband? For, when all is
said and done, if Barras' manners are somewhat
rough and outspoken, he is, on the other hand, a
good sort of fellow, and very obliging; he is a true
friend, and if once he takes an interest in you, you
may feel sure he will not desert you, but give you
a warm support. Let us, therefore, take men and
things as we find them. Can Barras be useful to
us in his position? Undoubtedly he can, and to
good purpose. Let us, therefore, get all we can
out of him, and never mind the rest!' 'Oh,'
exclaimed Bonaparte with enthusiasm, 'if he will
but give me the command of the Army of Italy I
will forgive everything. I will be the first to show
myself the most grateful of men ; I will do honour
to the appointment, and our affairs will prosper ;
I guarantee that ere long we shall be rolling in
gold.' Later on, taking a higher stand-point,
Bonaparte has called this glory. But 'gold' was
the naïve expression uttered in the presence of the
woman he considered a meet person to become
his partner in life ; quite independently of his
personal need and desire of making a fortune, the
artful Corsican had guessed aright that the means
of winning Josephine was money. He had begun
his success by giving her presents ; this success was
assured when he promised that he would make
her 'roll in gold were he but commander-in-

chief.' 'Let us work together,' they thereupon said mutually; 'let us keep our secret to ourselves, act together, and do our best to obtain the appointment promptly.'"

XIV.

BARRAS'S MOST DEADLY CHARGE.

BARRAS proceeds to give another scene in which the statements are even more detestable and shocking. His statements amount to this: that Josephine, accompanied by Napoleon, came to see Barras, penetrated into his cabinet, and there invited her own dishonour. And this is followed by the even more atrocious suggestion that Napoleon not only knew, but approved this hideous traffic for the sake of getting the command in Italy. This is the deadliest of all the charges Barras makes against Napoleon; is it true?

I have not a high opinion of the morality of Napoleon, or of any of his family, but I do not believe this charge. It is possible that Josephine was frail—it is the almost universal belief that she was; but I believe the evidence shows that at this moment at least, in his life, Napoleon was really in love with her. I will give later on the love-letters in which Napoleon poured forth from Italy all the passion and tenderness which this woman inspired in him—a passion and tenderness largely due, probably, to the fact that she was the first lady he had ever met in the course of his squalid and poverty-stricken youth. It is not in the least likely that Napoleon would have consented to buy even a prize so lofty as the command in Italy at the price of that woman's honour.

And, indeed, Barras is contradictory of his own story. In one page Napoleon figures as a dupe, in the next as a conscious intriguer; now he is madly jealous; the next moment he is more indifferent to the acts of his future wife than the beast in the field.

I agree with the summary of this part of the case which I find in the preface by M. Duruy, the unwilling editor of these Memoirs. It appears to me as true, kind, and judicious.

"True, Bonaparte may have later entertained doubts, suspicions as to Josephine's virtue. And, indeed, it must be confessed that the indiscretions of this most charming, but also most frivolous, of women, furnished matter enough for grievous discoveries. Look at her portrait by Isabey, which dates precisely from that period. This bird-like head, all dishevelled, expresses coquetry, thoughtlessness, an undefinable frailty and incon-sistency, characteristic, perhaps, even then, as it had been in the past, of her virtue. It is none the less a certainty that Bonaparte believed in her, and loved her ardently and blindly; that passion alone made him wish for and resolve upon this marriage; and that, if any one calculated in

T

this affair, it might possibly have been Josephine, but at all events it was not the man of genius, desperately smitten, smitten 'like a fool,' who was dying with love at the feet of this pretty doll."

I have sufficiently indicated my opinion of Barras. He was undoubtedly one of the greatest men of his time, but it was a greatness founded on utter baseness. The vindication which he has published of himself only tends to confirm the impression which posterity was inclined to form of him with the materials already at its disposal. It is curious that a man should, under his own hand, have supplied the evidence by which conjecture should be turned into certainty, suspicion into unquestioning conviction.

CHAPTER VII.

JOSEPHINE.*

THE memoirs of Barras leave so bad a taste in the mouth that it is necessary to seek some violent relief; and my next essays will be taken from the writings of those whose admiration for him was unstinted.

With the first of the volumes which supply the material for this portion of the volume, I shall have to deal briefly. The Count de Ségur is very interesting, especially to military readers, but he goes over ground which I have already traversed.

The volume is mainly interesting as an antidote to the "Memoirs of Madame de Rémusat," whose pictures of Napoleon's personality and Court supplied Taine with the chief material for his indictment.

The reader will not have forgotten the truly

* "An Aide-de-Camp of Napoleon: Memoirs of General Count de Ségur." Translated by H. A. Patchett Martin. (London: Hutchinson.) "Napoleon and the Fair Sex." Translated from the French of Frédéric Masson. (London: Heinemann.) "The Private Life of Napoleon." Translated from the French of Arthur Lévy. (London: Bentley.)

odious picture of Napoleon's Court which I quoted from Taine. I put in contrast with this the picture which is drawn by M. de Ségur. Writing of 1802, M. de Ségur exclaims: "No epoch was more glorious for Paris. What a happy and glorious time! The whole year has left on my memory the impression of a realisation of the most brilliant Utopias, a spectacle of the finest galas, and that of a grand society restored to all good things by the presiding genius."

And then he goes on to give this interesting and agreeable picture of Napoleon at home:

"The First Consul in his more personal surroundings had initiated many ingenious amusements, and given the signal for an almost universal joy.

"True, his household was divided into two parties, but kept in check by the firmness of their chief, they remained in the shade. These were, on one hand, the Beauharnais; on the other, Napoleon's own family. The marriage of Louis Bonaparte with Hortense de Beauharnais on July 17th, 1802, appeared to have put an end to these differences, so that peace seemed to pervade everything, a domestic peace which was not one whit more durable than the other peaces of this epoch. But at first this alliance, and several other marriages amongst the younger members of Napoleon's family, increased the general cheerful disposition of mind by the addition of their honeymoon happiness. The well-known attractions and wit of the sisters of the First Consul, the many graces of Madame Bonaparte and her daughter, and the remarkable beauty of the young brides who had just been admitted into this fascinating circle, above all the presence of a real hero, gave an indefinable charm and lustre to this new. Court, as yet unfettered by etiquette, or any other tie than the former traditions of good society.

"Our morning amusements at Malmaison consisted of country-house diversions in which Napoleon used to take part, and in the evening of various games, and of conversations, sometimes light and sparkling, sometimes profound and serious, of which I still find records in my note-book. The Revolution, philosophy, above all, the East, were the favourite topics of the First Consul. How often, as night drew on, even the most youthful amongst these young women, losing all count of time, would fancy they could see what he was describing, under the charm of his admirable narratives, so vividly coloured by a flow of bold and novel illustration, and his piquant and unexpected imagery."

The reader will also remember the passage in which Taine describes the infectious weariness of Napoleon at the play. Ségur has a different story to tell:

"The other amusements of his household consisted in private theatricals, in which his adopted children and ourselves took part. He sometimes would encourage us by looking on at our rehearsals, which were superintended by the celebrated actors, Michaud, Molé, and Fleury. The performances took place at Malmaison before a select party. They would be followed by concerts, of Italian songs principally, and often by little dances where there was no crowding or confusion, consisting, as they did, of three or four quadrille sets with plenty of space between each. He would himself dance gaily with us, and would ask for old-fashioned tunes, recalling his own youth. These delightful evenings used to end about midnight."

There is an anecdote which presents Napoleon in a pleasant light:

"One evening, at St. Cloud, when he was describing the desert, Egypt, and the defeat of the Mamelukes, seeing me hanging on his words, he stopped short, and taking up from the card-table, which he had just left, a silver marker—a medal representing the combat of the Pyramids—he said to me, 'You were not there in those days, young man.' 'Alas, no,' I answered. 'Well,' said he, 'take this and keep it as a remembrance.' I need hardly say that I religiously did so, the proof of which will be found by my children after me."

And, finally, here is Ségur's summary of Napoleon's demeanour to his dependents, illustrated by quite a pretty story :

"Such was his usual amenity, concerning which I remember that one day when our outbursts of laughter in the drawing-room were interrupting his work in the adjoining study, he just opened the door to complain that we were hindering him, with a gentle request that we should be a little less noisy."

There are many passages in Ségur which show the Marshals of Napoleon in a far from favourable light. Their ambition, their selfishness, their murderous jealousy of each other, shock and appal—especially when one sees thousands of the lives of brave men sacrificed to passions so ignoble. These pictures also enable one to take a different view of Napoleon's treatment of these men than that to which Taine has given such fierce expression. It will be remembered that Taine bitterly complains that Napoleon appealed only to the basest elements in these men ; that he exploited their selfishness, their ambition, their vices, and their weaknesses. After one has read Ségur and some other authorities, one is tempted to come to the conclusion that if Napoleon acted on these motives in his subordinates, it was because these motives were the only ones to which he could appeal.

I pass from this point and from Ségur to another and an even more fervid eulogist of the great Emperor.

M. Albert Lévy devotes two bulky volumes to

the record of the smallest incidents of Napoleon's life, with extracts from not scores but hundreds of memoirs in which he forms the central figure; and this work—evidently the result of years of patient labour—is devoted to proving that of all men who have lived Napoleon was the most generous, the most unselfish, and the most patriotic.

I cannot accept this estimate; but in the pages of M. Lévy's intensely interesting volumes there is the satisfaction of feeling that Napoleon is restored to something of human shape. He is there neither god, nor demon, nor angel—though M. Lévy would have him angelic—but a human being, with plenty of human weaknesses, affections, and even considerateness, athwart all his iron strength, callousness, and voracious ambition.

I.

EARLY YEARS.

NAPOLEON'S early years were, as we already know, full of all the straits and miseries of genteel poverty. His father, as everybody knows, was an easy-going, thriftless, helpless creature, who died at an early age of cancer in the stomach—the only heritage, as Taine sardonically remarks, which he left to his great son. It was from his mother that Napoleon inherited most of his qualities. She came of a commercial family, partly Swiss in origin, and at an age " when most girls are thinking of marriage she was studying order, economy, and careful management." It was from her that Napoleon inherited what M. Lévy calls "those instincts of honesty, of excessive carefulness in all matters in which money plays a part, which is one of the most characteristic features of Napoleon."

The education of the children was the first point to be determined. In those days anybody with influence with the clergy or at the Court could get a free education, and young Napoleon, having the first, was enabled in this way to get into the Royal College at Brienne, where boys were trained for the Navy. He had first, however, to spend some time at Autun to learn French—so thoroughly Italian was the man who became afterwards the most absolute ruler of Frenchmen the world has seen. In three months at Autun Napoleon had "learned sufficient French to enable him to converse easily and to write small essays and translations." At Brienne there were many things to make him unhappy: his foreign birth, his foreign accent, doubtless his foreign mistakes; but, above all things, his poverty. Even at school the inequalities of life make themselves bitterly felt; and Napoleon, with all his pride, love of command, and sensitiveness to slights, must have suffered more than most boys.

"At Brienne," he writes afterwards himself, " I was the poorest of all my schoolfellows. They always had money in their pockets, I never. I

was proud, and was most careful that nobody
should perceive this. . . . I could neither laugh
nor amuse myself like the others." Bonaparte
the schoolboy was out of touch with his comrades,
and he was not popular.

It will be seen from this passage that Napoleon
was made early acquainted with those traits of
human nature which gave him his permanently
and instinctively low opinion of it, and which
helped to make him regard life as simply a personal struggle, where you destroy or are destroyed.
Napoleon was five years and a half in this school;
and, curiously enough, though he must really have
been unhappy, he saw it afterwards through the
gauze of retrospect as being very different. One
day, when he was First Consul, and was walking
with Bourrienne—the one schoolfellow whom he
loved in Brienne—in the gardens of Malmaison,
the residence of his office, he heard the chiming of
bells, which always had a remarkable effect upon
him ; he stopped, listened delightedly, and said in
a broken voice: "That reminds me of my first
years at Brienne ; I was happy then." M. Lévy is
able to prove that the tenderness of these recollections showed itself in another way also. Napoleon befriended nearly everybody who was ever
connected with the school unless they had treated
him badly. Napoleon was one of the worst writers
of his time. His script was undecipherable, even
to himself ; sometimes he found it hard to write

his own name; but old Dupré, who was his writing-master, came to him once at St. Cloud and reminded the Emperor—as Napoleon then was—that "for fifteen months he had had the pleasure of giving him lessons in writing at Brienne." Napoleon could not help exclaiming to the poor man, who was quite aghast: "And a fine sort of pupil you had! I congratulate you."

After a few kindly words he dismissed Dupré, who received a few days later a notification of a pension of one thousand two hundred francs (forty-eight pounds).

II.

IN THE ARTILLERY.

NAPOLEON was unable to get a place in the Navy, for his influence was not sufficiently great; so he besought his family to try and get him into the artillery or engineers. He was sent to the Military School in Paris, and arrived there in 1784—that starting-point of the great events that led the King to the scaffold and himself to an Imperial throne. The descriptions of the period show that he is like most other new-comers to a great city.

He gaped at everything he saw, and stared about him. His appearance was that of a man whom any scoundrel would try to rob after seeing him.

But even at that age—he was then fifteen—he had the instincts of order and activity. There is extant a letter written at that period, in which he very cleverly criticises the luxury and the laxity of the discipline which existed in the Military School. He found that the pupils had a large staff of servants, kept an expensive stud of horses and a number of grooms ; and to his realistic and practical mind all this was abomination.

"Would it not be better," he exclaimed, "of course without interrupting their studies, to compel them to buy enough for their own wants, that is to say, without compelling them to do their own cooking, to let them eat soldiers' bread, or something similar, to accustom them to beat and brush their own clothes, and to clean their own boots and shoes ? "

In thus writing young Napoleon was describing the things he had to do himself, then and afterwards, for a long time. It was these hardships of his childhood that helped to make him and to, at the same time, mar his nature.

"All these cares spoiled my early years," he himself said in 1811. "They influenced my temper and made me grave before my time."

Unlike some of the boys around him, Napoleon refused to run into debt. A friend of his family, seeing him in low spirits, offered to lend him money so as to be able to make a better show.

Napoleon grew very red and refused, saying : " My mother has already too many expenses, and I have no business to increase them by extravagances which are simply imposed upon me by the stupid folly of my comrades."

At sixteen he passed his examination without any particular distinction. He was forty-second out of fifty-eight pupils who passed. His German master's comment upon him at the time was that "the pupil Bonaparte was nothing but a fool."

On September 1, 1785, he was named Second Lieutenant in the Bombardiers garrisoned at Valence. His new uniform was in proportion to the slenderness of his purpose.

His boots were so inordinately large that his legs, which were very slender, disappeared in them completely. Proud of his new outfit, he went off to seek his friends, the Permons. On seeing him the two children, Cecilia and Laura (the latter was afterwards Duchesse d'Abrantès), could not restrain their laughter, and to his face nick-named him "Puss in Boots." He did not mind, it appears, for, according to one of these little wits, the lieutenant took them a few days later a toy carriage containing a puss in boots, and Perrault's fairy story.

III.

EARLY POVERTY.

AT Valence—part of the journey to which Napoleon had to perform on foot from having spent his money—he had to live a very modest life. It is said that he was "a great talker, embarking, on the smallest provocation, into interminable arguments;" that he developed "those powers of pleasing which he possessed in a remarkable degree;" and applied himself, above all, "to pleasing the fair sex, who received him with acclamation." I doubt the correctness of this latter statement. Throughout his entire life we have seen Napoleon was *gauche* and constrained and dumb before women; his flirtation was of the barrack-room grossness, directness, and simplicity—horseplay . rather than play of wit.

He obtained leave of absence after the easy fashion of those times, and visited his home in Corsica. This visit must have left sad impressions, for we can trace from that period the disappearance of even the slight gaiety which was to be found in his life at Valence. When he went into garrison at Auxonne — his new station — he began that ferocious system of work which he continued for so many years afterwards. He never went out except to a frugal dinner, and then he had to be summoned, so absorbed was he in his studies. Immediately dinner was over he went back to his room. He lived most humbly. Milk was his chief food. He himself, writing to his mother, said :

" I have no resources here but work; I only dress myself once a week; I sleep but very little since my illness; it is incredible. I go to bed at ten o'clock, and get up at four in the morning. I only eat one meal a day—at three o'clock."

But he broke down under the work, and had once again to seek refuge in his Corsican home. He returned to Auxonne after a longer vacation than would have been possible with any but the ill-disciplined troops of France. And now comes a period of Napoleon's life which must always stand out in his history, and cannot permit any impartial person to regard him as a wholly selfish man. He brought back with him his brother Louis, and for some time supported this brother and himself on his wretched pay. That pay amounted to three pounds fifteen shillings a month:

"The two brothers, therefore, had to lodge, clothe, and feed themselves upon three francs five centimes (two shillings and sixpence) a day; and, moreover, Louis's education, which Napoleon had undertaken, had to be provided for."

Even on these restricted means Napoleon was able to live without getting into debt, but he had to do it at the sacrifice of every comfort. It is recorded that he cooked their broth with his own hands, and broth formed the chief meal of the day. Napoleon never forgot the privations of this time, nor the lessons it taught. Louis was afterwards—as we know—King of Holland, but, like every other relative of Napoleon, made but a poor requital to his illustrious relative. In rage at one of these acts of Louis, Napoleon cried out:

"That Louis whom I educated out of my pay

as a sub-lieutenant, God knows at the price of what privations! Do you know how I managed it? It was by never setting foot in society or in a café; by eating dry bread, and by brushing my clothes myself, so that they should last longer."

An Imperial official once complained to him that he could not live on a salary of forty pounds a month. Said Napoleon:

"I know all about it, sir. . . . When I had the honour to be a sub-lieutenant I breakfasted off dry bread, but I bolted my door on my poverty. In public I did not disgrace my comrades."

One proof of the scrupulousness of his examination of his expenses is to be seen in a tailor's bill, still extant, on which he had obtained a reduction of twopence.

IV.

A YOUTHFUL CYNIC.

THE period between Napoleon's earliest military days and his appearance at Toulon belongs to Corsica rather than to France. He spent nearly an entire year on furlough there. He was reprimanded, and at one time seemed likely permanently to lose his position in the regular army. A biographer who does not love him declares that he was guilty during this period of crimes of insubordination and want of discipline enough to have shot him a hundred times over in ordinary times. It is certain that he had to go to Paris to justify himself. Here, again, he had to face the privations and humiliations of extreme poverty. He owed fifteen francs to his wine merchant, and he had to pawn his watch. Bourrienne, his old college chum—afterwards his secretary—thus describes Napoleon at this period.

" Our friendship of childhood and college days," says Bourrienne, " was as fresh as ever. I was not very happy ; adversity weighed heavily upon him, and he often wanted money. We passed our time like two young men with nothing to do, and with but little money—he had even less than I. Every day gave birth to some new plans; we were always on the look-out for some useful speculation. At one time he wanted to hire with me several houses then being built in the Rue Montholon, intending to make money by sub-letting them."

The two comrades often dined together, Bourrienne usually paying for the dinner—at least so Bourrienne says, though, as he became infamous for avarice and peculation, the statement must be taken with reserve. It is certain that sometimes poor Napoleon had to dine at a restaurant where a dish cost but a modest threepence.

While the future ruler of France was thus in the depths, France herself was marching through the terrific events that ended in the overthrow of the monarchy. Napoleon was never a democrat, but what little traces of democracy there might have been in him were destroyed by what he then saw. It is known that he saw the march on the Tuileries on June 20th. When he saw the ragged and fierce crowd going in the direction of the Palace, "Let us follow these scoundrels," was his comment. And when the poor King put on the red cap he was equally disgusted. "Why did they allow these brutes to come in? They ought to have shot down fifty or sixty of them with cannon, and the rest would have run."

This youthful cynic has already weighed and found wanting the men who are at the head of affairs. "You know those who are at the head," he writes to his brother Joseph, "are the poorest of men. The people are equally contemptible when one comes in contact with them. They are hardly worth all the trouble men take to earn their favour." "You know the history of Ajaccio," he continues; "that of Paris is exactly the same, only that there, perhaps, men are more petted, more spiteful, more censorious." And finally here is his judgment of the French people as a whole— a judgment given, it will be observed, with the detachment and with the calm contempt of a foreigner: "The French people is an old people, without prejudices, without bonds. Every one seeks his own interest, and wishes to rise by means of lying and calumny; men intrigue more contemptibly than ever." And finally, from this period, here is an extract worth giving—it is Napoleon's comment on a proclamation to the Corsicans which had been written by his brother Lucien:

"I have read your proclamation; it is worth nothing. It contains too many words and too few ideas. You run after pathos; that is not the way to speak to nations."

Here already we see the final philosophy of Napoleon. His view of human nature is low; self-interest is the one guiding motive—unchecked, uncrossed, unmixed by other and higher impulses; the people, when they attack constituted authorities, are rabble to be shot down, and the one art of government is to rule men through their base passions. After all, the sternest critic of Napoleon is himself; the portrait he draws with his own hand, is very like that of M. Taine. M. Lévy—if he wanted to make his hero a saint— should have omitted his hero's own letters.

V.

FLIGHT FROM CORSICA.

NAPOLEON was restored to his rank, and then he rushed back home again—still filled by that strong sense of family obligation which may be distinctively Corsican—as it is distinctively Irish— and making sacrifices at this period, as throughout his life, for his relatives, which, as I have said

U 2

before, do not permit us to regard him as wholly selfish. In Corsica he came into collision with Paoli —for Napoleon wished Corsica to remain French— and Paoli retorted by giving orders for the arrest and expulsion of the Bonaparte family; and with their property pillaged and burned behind them, the large and poverty-stricken family fled from their native island to Marseilles. In Marseilles Napoleon's pay was the chief support of the family; this was supplemented by the public relief given to distressed patriots who had suffered for the cause.

I pass rapidly over the episode at Toulon— which first gave Napoleon prominence—with the observation that his action was not so highly regarded at the time as at a subsequent date. Bonaparte's name is scarcely mentioned in the bulletins, but he succeeded, in those days of improvised soldiers and quick promotions, in being made a General of Brigade.

Then there is another interval, during a portion of which he is imprisoned, and in some danger, as everybody was in the days of the Terror; and finally he is called to Paris in order to take part in the Vendean war. He is asked, however, to descend from the artillery to the infantry; he declines, and for some months he is in Paris— without employment, without money, without much hope. All kinds of projects hovered before his mind. There was an idea of his being sent to Turkey to put the troops of the Grand Sultan in order; he tried to make money as an exporter of books; he got his dinner either at the expense of his friends in arms, or at the house of some Corsicans; he was wretched bodily and mentally; and his wretchedness appeared in his exterior and in his manners.

" He was to be met wandering about the streets of Paris in an awkward and ungainly manner, with a shabby round hat thrust down over his eyes and with his curls (known at that time as *oreilles de chien*) badly powdered, badly combed, and falling over the collar of the iron-gray coat which has since become so celebrated ; his hands, long, thin, and black, without gloves, because, he said, they were an unnecessary expense; wearing ill-made and ill-cleaned boots." " But his glance and his smile were always admirable, and helped to enliven an appearance always sickly, resulting partly from the yellowness of his complexion, which deepened the shadows projected by his gaunt, angular, and pointed features."

And mentally he was in the same condition as externally. Bourrienne and his wife meet him in the Palais Royal; together they go to the theatre. "The audience was convulsed with laughter; Bonaparte — and I was much struck by it — preserved an icy silence."

" Another time he disappeared from us without saying a word, and when we thought he must have left the theatre, we espied him seated in a

box on the second or third tier, all alone, looking
as though he wished to sulk."

The fact, of course, is that Napoleon was
consumed by all that volcanic activity which was
to burst forth very soon in such lava tide; and
neither then nor at any other time has he the
power of idling gracefully. Either he is in fierce
activity or he mopes and despairs.

VI.

A FIRST CHANCE.

AND then all these periods of gloomy and despondent
expectation are put an end to, after the anarchic
and unaccountable manner of human affairs, by a
slight chance acquaintance. M. de Pontecoulant,
when he was appointed a member of the War
Committee of the Committee of Public Safety,
found things in dreadful disorder, and did not
know where to turn, and a chance conversation
with M. Boissy d'Anglas elicited this remark:

"I met yesterday a general on half-pay. He
has come back from the Campaign of Italy, and
seemed to know all about it. He might give you
some good advice."

"Send him to me," said M. Pontecoulant; and
the next day there came to the Minister on the
sixth floor—where he had his office—"the leanest
and most miserable-looking creature he had ever
seen in his life"—a young man, with a wan and

livid complexion, bowed shoulders and sickly appearance. Bonaparte was a name so strange and so unknown that the War Minister could not remember it; but when the young man spoke, he recognised the acquaintance of Boissy d'Anglas. Bonaparte was told to draw up a memorandum setting forth the views he had expressed verbally; but he went out, and thinking this a polite dismissal, sent no memorandum. But he was induced to present his ideas, and got work in the War Office as a sort of secretary to the Minister. But even this position he did not long retain. He asked for the command of a brigade, a demand which at five-and-twenty struck the superior powers as audacious; and when Pontecoulant retired from office, Napoleon was again without employment.

And finally he had to seek promotion through the lady who, in even virtuous Republican days, played the part of the Pompadour or the Du Barry with the monarchs—Madame Tallien, the mistress of Barras. The reader has heard so much of this episode already that I need not recapitulate it.

There I leave M. Lévy for the moment, and pass to another eulogist of Napoleon, who is even more lifelike in his description of this period in his hero's life.

The work of M. Frédéric Masson deals entirely with one side of Napoleon's life and character—his relations, namely, to women. The book has

an outspokenness that may prove a little trying
even to an age that has grown so much less
squeamish than it used to be. I should say at
once that M. Masson is a devoted and almost
blind worshipper of the central figure of his book;
and that if one were to believe the picture which
he presents—I am sure in perfect good faith—one
would be obliged to regard Napoleon as one of
the gentlest, sweetest, and most amiable men.
His faults would be an excess—instead of a defect
—of sensibility. Of that other side of Napoleon—
which we know from many pages—in his relations
to women, M. Masson gives us not even a trace.

Let us take M. Masson's very interesting and
very industriously compiled volume as we find it;
if we cannot accept his conclusions or his portrait,
at least let us be grateful to the superabundance
of material for forming our own conclusions and
our own image which his marvellous industry has
placed at our disposal.

In spite of all I have already written about
Josephine, I make no apology for quoting largely
from M. Masson's description of her.

There is an everlasting fascination about the
story of her life with that strange and marvellous
creature whom she married. Even her defects of
character lend an additional interest to the subject; a woman quiet, decorous, certain, stable,
would have been a much worthier person, and,
perchance, would have made Napoleon much

more tranquil in his mind; but neither on him nor on us could she have exercised the same continual fascination as this wayward, fickle, frail Creole, that still smiles out upon us with her empty and kindly look from the grave on which the grass has been growing for little short of a century!

It is one of the many proofs of the fascination which the story exercises on the French mind that every detail of her life, of her courtship and her union with Napoleon, is known and recorded with such extraordinary care. Take this volume which lies before me. I declare that I read the account M. Frédéric Masson gives of the first interview between Napoleon and Josephine de Beauharnais, as though it were something that had occurred but yesterday; and as though I were standing and looking on at the whole scene between the two, at their half-stammered words, their exchange of half-timid, half-searching glances, at the very furniture in the rooms; and this love scene took place a hundred years ago! The passages in the book which deal with the episode are a marvellous instance of the power which a good writer, with his facts and details ample and well arranged, can exercise in realising for himself and for you a long-forgotten and long-dead scene.

VII.

HE.

THERE are various and conflicting accounts of the events which led to Napoleon's first acquaintance with Josephine. The story usually told is that a short time after he had put down the attack on the Convention, Napoleon was visited by a young man who begged to be excused from obeying a decree which the victorious General had just published—the decree ordering the disarmament of the civil population. The youth remarks that the sword which he desires to preserve had belonged to his father, and as he mentions the father's name Napoleon realises how different is his position from that of a few months ago, when he was pawning his sword and half starving, or picking up meals by taking "pot-luck" at the houses of old friends, not much richer than himself. For the youth was the son of Viscount Beauharnais, and Viscount Beauharnais was a nobleman of ancient descent; had even been, like Mirabeau and other fathers of the Revolution, once President of the great Constituent Assembly which had made the Revolution ; had been Commander-in-Chief of one of the armies of the Republic ; and, finally, after the manner of such highly-distinguished aristocrats in those days, had been guillotined. Napoleon is interested and flattered by the request of the lad, grants it quite cordially, and a few days afterwards a lady comes to offer him her thanks—it is Josephine de Beauharnais, the mother of the boy.

For the first time this rustic of twenty-six years, who knows only the revolutionary armies, to whom no woman has ever paid any particular attention, sees before him one of those beautiful, elegant, and attractive women whom hitherto he has only seen from the distance of the pit of a theatre, and he finds himself in the position which most flatters his pride—that of offering protection; and with this *rôle*, which he plays for the first time, he is delighted beyond all words.

VIII.

SHE.

JOSEPHINE, on the other hand, was at this moment in desperate case. She had narrowly escaped guillotining, as everybody knows, by the overthrow of Robespierre; released from prison she found herself a widow of more than thirty years, with two children, and with scarcely anything left from the ruin of her fortune. A Creole, unable at any period of her life to take any account of money, extravagant, fond of elegance, dress and pleasure, there is nothing for her but to beg for money from her relatives in far Martinique; to borrow some from those nearer home; to borrow from others who are not friends; and above all, to make debts—in confidence in the future which in those strange days offered all kinds of possibilities to pretty and elegant women. All the large fortune of her husband in land had been confiscated when he was executed; her own fortune had existed rather on paper than in solid coin of the realm; her father was dead, her mother was very poor; and the English, in any case, had blockaded the island and stood between her and remittances. Even the furniture of her house had been pledged; in short, poor Josephine at this moment was at the very end of her tether. This was her position when the following scene took place. I trust the vividness of the description will make as profound an impression on others as it does on me.

IX.

BONAPARTE KNOCKS.

"JUST then, to return the visit he had received from the Viscountess de Beauharnais, General Bonaparte rings at the entrance gate of the mansion in the Rue Chantereine. He does not know that the house belongs to Citizeness Talma, who, while she was Demoiselle Julie, got it from a man whose mistress she was. He does not see that the house, with one hundred metres of grounds, situated in a remote quarter, just at the extremity of Paris, a couple of steps from the Rue Saint-Lazaire, surrounded even still by gardens, is hardly worth fifty thousand francs—the price paid in 1781, and the price which will be again paid in 1796.

"The door being opened by the concierge, for there is a concierge, the General goes through a sort of long passage; at one side he sees the stable with two black horses, going on seven years old, and a red cow; on the other, the coach-house, in which there is but one shattered vehicle, is closed. The passage leads into a garden. In the centre stands the living room; a ground floor with four very high windows, and surrounded by a low attic. The kitchen is under-ground. Bonaparte goes up the four stone steps which turn to a sort of simple balustraded terrace, and penetrates into an antechamber sparsely furnished with a copper fountain and low cupboard of oak, and a deal press."

X.

THE ROOM.

" THE obliging Gonthier introduces him into a little apartment, a dining-room, where, near the round mahogany table, he could sit down on one of the four black horse-hair chairs, unless he prefers to look at some engravings on the wall, framed in black and gold. Not much luxury, but here and there tables and consoles of mahogany and rosewood with marble supports and gilt ornamentation, give tokens of former elegance, and in the two large glass presses built into the wall, a tea urn, vessels, all the accessories of the table in English electro-plate which does duty for silver-plate. As for plate, in the true sense of the word, there are in the house only fourteen spoons and five forks, one soup spoon, six dessert spoons, and eleven little coffee spoons.

" But he does not know that."

XI.

ENTER JOSEPHINE.

" JOSEPHINE, decked out by her lady's-maid, Citizeness Louise Compoint, leaves her room and hurries to the dining-room to greet this visitor who is to lead to fortune ! She can hardly receive him anywhere else, for the ground floor contains, besides this dining-room, only a little drawing-room which she has turned into a dressing-room, and her own bedroom. This bedroom is pretty but simple, with its upholstery of blue chintz, with red and yellow tufts, its sofa, some tasteful articles of furniture in mahogany and rosewood; its only artistic object is a little marble bust of Socrates, standing near a harp, by Renaud. As for the dressing-room, except a grand piano by Bernard, there is nothing in it but mirrors ; a mirror on the large dressing-table, a mirror on the mahogany chest of drawers, on the night table, and on the mantel-piece a mirror composed of two little glasses.

"What! is this all the furniture of this elegant lady? Yes; and she eats off earthenware plates, except on great occasions for which she has a dozen of blue and white china ones; the table-linen comprises eight table-cloths, all so worn that in the inventory, serviettes and table-cloths are valued at four pounds. But Bonaparte does not notice all this; he does not know that this uncommon and elegant woman who is before him, whose infinite grace disturbs his brain, whose recherché toilette is a feast to his eyes, has only in her wardrobe four dozen chemises partly worn out, two dozen handkerchiefs, six petticoats, six nightdresses, eighteen fichus, twelve pairs of stockings of different colours. In addition she has for outward wearing, six muslin shawls, two taffeta robes (one brown, the other violet), three fine, coloured, embroidered muslin dresses, three plain muslins, two book-muslin dresses, three Jouy linen dresses, and one of white embroidered lawn. This underclothing so really poor, and these outward coverings so relatively numerous, though the stuffs are shabby and cheap, show the whole disposition of Josephine—it is Josephine all over to have sixteen dresses and six petticoats."

XII.

THE FASCINATION BEGINS.

"BUT what matter? Bonaparte only sees the dress, or rather he only sees the woman, the soft chestnut hair, slightly made up, dyed, it is true—but it is then the time of white powdered wigs—a skin brown enough, already lined from care, but smoothed, whitened, pinked by cosmetics; teeth, already bad, but no one ever sees them, for the small mouth is always ready to melt into a slight, sweet smile, which agreed with the infinite mildness of her long-lashed eyes, with the tender expression of her features, with a tone of voice so touching that later on servants would stop in the passages to hear it. And with that a mobile, delicate nose, with ever-quivering nostrils, a nose a little raised at the end, engaging and roguish, which provoked desire.

"Nevertheless the head is scarcely to be mentioned in comparison with this body, so free, so stately, not yet spoiled by stoutness, and which ends in little, straight, arched feet—feet so plump and soft as to invite a kiss. On the body no restraint, no corsets, not even a neck-band to support the throat, which is, however, short and expressionless. But her general attractiveness goes beyond defining. This woman has a grace which belongs only to herself: 'She even goes to bed gracefully.' This grace results from such a just proportion of build that one forgets she is of mediocre stature, so easy and elegant are all her movements. A long and careful study of her body, a coquetry which has refined all her gestures, that loses no advantage, and is constantly on the defensive, leaves nothing to chance; this unde-finable nonchalance which makes the Creole woman the essence of womanhood; this sensu-ality which, like a light perfume, floats around these languid attitudes of the supple and easy limbs, was it not enough to turn the brain of everybody, and most of all of him who was newer and less experienced than any other? The woman seduces him from the first moment, while at the same time the lady dazzles him by, as he says himself, 'that calm and noble dignity of the old French society.'"

XIII.

IN THE TOILS.

"SHE feels that he is ensnared, that he belongs to her, and when he comes back on the next day, the day after, and then every day, when he sees about Madame de Beauharnais men who belonged to the ancient Court, who are great lords in comparison with him, 'petit noble' (the word is his own), a Ségur, a Montesquieu, a Caulaincourt, who treat her as a friend, an equal, somewhat as a comrade, he does not notice the dark side; he does not realise that these men, who will always have for him a certain prestige, come there as bachelors, and do not bring their wives. After the Jacobin surroundings in which he lived, and which in Vaucluse, Toulon, Nice, and Pa s had been an advantage to him, he experienced a n infinite satis-

x

faction in finding himself in such company. All
the appearances (and nothing here was more than
appearance, the luxury of the lady as well as her
nobility, her society, and the place she occupied in
the world), all these appearances he accepted for
realities, and saw them so, his senses aiding.

"Fifteen days after the first visit a *liaison* com-
menced. In writing to each other they still talk only
friendship, but in the confusion of that time, says a
witness, shades, transitions, were but little observed.

"'They loved one another passionately.' As
to him, it is quite easy to believe it; as to her,
why should we not believe that she was then
sincere? This Bonaparte was new ground, a
savage to tame, the lion of the day to show about
in her chains. For the woman, already beginning
to age, this ardour of passion, these kisses, as
under the Equator, prove to her that she is still
beautiful, and that she will always please. Good
enough as a lover, but what of a husband? He
makes an offer of his hand—he supplicates her to
marry him. After all, what has she to lose? She
is at the last extremity, and it is the throwing of
a card that she risks. He is young, ambitious, he
is Commander-in-Chief of the Interior; during
the Directoire it is remembered that he furnished
plans for the last Italian campaign, and Carnot is
going to give him the chief command in the
approaching campaign. It means, perhaps, salvation. Then what does she commit herself to?

A marriage? But divorce is a remedy ready to hand, for there is no question of priest or religious ceremony. What is it in reality? A contract which will last as long as it pleases the parties to observe the conditions, but which is of no value either in the conscience of the wife or in that of her old world; which will bring something big if well played, for this young man may mount high; which will bring, in any case, a pension if he is killed."

XIV.

VENIAL MENDACITIES.

" NEVERTHELESS, she has precautions to take; first of all, her age to dissemble, for she does not want to avow, either to this youth of twenty-six or to any one else, that she is more than thirty-two years old. So Calmelot, her confidential man, at present tutor of her children, goes, accompanied by a friend named Lesourd, to a notary's: "They certify that they know Marie-Joseph Tascher, widow of the citizen Beauharnais, intimately, know that she is a native of the Island of Martinique, and that at the present moment it is impossible for her to procure a certificate of birth on account of the island being occupied by the English." That is all; no other declaration, no date. Armed with this, Josephine can declare to the Civil officer that she was born on June 23, 1767, whilst in reality she was born on June 23, 1763. People

do not examine her more closely. As to fortune,
she intends there shall also be illusion. Here, one
would believe, there must be some difficulty, but
Bonaparte accepts all that she does, and then in
private, in the presence only of Lemarrois, aide-
de-camp of the General, the strangest contract of
marriage that notary ever received, is prepared ;
no community of goods under any form nor in
any manner whatsoever; absolute separation of
means ; all authority given in advance by the
future husband to the future wife; guardianship
of the children by the first marriage exclusively
to be held by the mother; a jointure of fifteen
hundred pounds if she becomes a widow, and in
the latter case also the right to get back all that
she could justly claim as belonging to her.

"Of documents relating to personal property
not a single one. All that the future wife possesses
is a claim to the property which was common to
herself and the late M. Beauharnais. He did not
make an inventory, and until the inventory was
made she could not decide whether to accept or
renounce. The inventory was made two years
later, and she renounced, but these two years had
brought something better. Bonaparte made no
secret of the smallness of his fortune. 'On his
side the future husband declared he possessed no
real estate nor personal property other than his
wardrobe and his military equipage, the whole
valued by him at ——, and then he signed the

nominal value.' Just as the notary of Madame de Beauharnais had said, his 'cape and sword' were his fortune. But the General found the declaration superfluous, and in the contract he purely and simply had the paragraph scratched out.

"The contract is dated 18 Ventôse, An IV. (March 8, 1796). The next day the marriage took place before the Civil officer, who complaisantly gave to the husband twenty - eight years instead of twenty-six, and to the wife twenty-nine instead of thirty-two. This mayor seems to have a passion for equalising. Barras, Lemarrois, who is not a major, Tallien and Calmelot, the inevitable Calmelot, are witnesses. There is no mention of the consent of the parents; they were not consulted.

" Two days after, General Bonaparte goes alone to join the army in Italy; Madame Bonaparte remains at the Rue Chantereine."

There is something weird, is there not, in this revivification of the past, even to the numbering of the articles of underclothing in poor Josephine's wardrobe. The details may seem squalid, but somehow or other they do not so impress me. There is something in their accumulation that adds so much to the reality and familiarity of the picture, and nothing that thus brings us face to face with the daily life of so portentous a figure as Napoleon, can ever cease to interest mankind.

XV.

DITHYRAMBIC LOVE.

I GO back to M. Lévy's volume for a description of the epoch which followed.

It is a stage in Napoleon's life which it is very hard to understand, the existence of which many people have forgotten, and which is in contrast with the strange lawlessness, heartlessness, frigidity of temper which supreme power finally begat in Napoleon's character. We have extant his correspondence with his wife during his campaign in Italy; it is the correspondence of an impassioned boy with his first love. Its warmth of language, its hysterical joy, its strange despair, all its quick alternation of the liveliest and most acute feelings, stand, as it were, outside that stern man we know, with that impassive face in the midst of the wholesale carnage of the battle-field. The daring conspirator who was ready to stake his head in the fight for a crown—the man whose settled frown, cold and steady gaze, and imperious demeanour affright the bravest general into an awed silence—this man is to be seen in these letters falling on his knees, clasping his hands, tearing his hair, sobbing in the outbursts of jealous and almost tenderly submissive love. It is certainly one of the most curious contradictions between the outer demeanour, the general character, and

the inner nature which history presents. Above
all, it confirms the theory of many shrewd observers of human nature, that it is women after all
who alone understand men, for it is they who
alone see them as they really are.

I will give some specimens of these letters.
It will be seen that I in no way exaggerate their
character.

At Chanceaux, on his way to Italy, he has to
stop to exchange horses; he takes advantage of
the pause to write a letter.

"Every instant," he writes, "takes me farther
from you, adorable creature, and every instant I
feel less that I can bear being separated from you.
You are perpetually in my thoughts; I rack my
brains to imagine what you are about. If I think
you are sad, my heart feels broken; if I fancy
you gay, laughing with your friends, I reproach
you for having forgotten our grievous separation
of three days ago.

"If I am asked whether I have slept well, I
feel that, before answering, I ought to receive
news from you as to whether you have had a good
night. Sickness, man's fury, affect me not, except by the idea that they may come upon you.
. . . Ah! be not gay, but rather somewhat melancholy, and, above all, may your soul be exempt
from grief as your body from illness."

XVI.

SUSPICION.

UNDERNEATH all these outbursts of passion one
can detect, as M. Lévy points out, a vague sense
of apprehension and coming danger. Napoleon
had not failed to see the "tepidity" which his
wife felt towards him, and he knew, perhaps, that
her past had not been altogether without reproach.
In any case, he is tormented all through his campaign; and in the midst of those mighty victories
which were dazzling the world, amid all the
acclaims of that triumphant army—in the midst,
too, of the dangers which Napoleon madly ran—
his innermost heart is constantly tortured with the
idea that his love is not returned, that his confidence is betrayed. It is impossible not to tarry
with some pleasure at this stage of Napoleon's
career; it is somewhat like the early, innocent
maidenhood of a woman that has ended disastrously.

Here is what is said of Napoleon by one of his
secretaries of this period:

"General Bonaparte, however taken up he
might be with his position, with the matters entrusted to him, and with his future, had yet time
to give himself up to thoughts of another kind.
He was thinking constantly of his wife. He
longed for her, and watched for her coming with
impatience. He often spoke to me of her and his

love, with the expansions and the illusions of a very young man. The continual delays that she interposed before her departure were torture to him, and he occasionally gave way to fits of jealousy, and to a kind of superstition, which was strong in his nature. One day the glass of Josephine's portrait, which he always wore about him, broke, and he turned dreadfully pale. 'Marmont,' he exclaimed, 'either my wife is ill or unfaithful.'"

XVII.

FRIVOLOUS JOSEPHINE.

JOSEPHINE, meantime, is not much touched by these outbursts. Josephine may or may not have been the abandoned woman Barras declares, but her letters about her curious lover—so wan, awkward, abrupt, so devoid of drawing-room graces—give a curious picture of the conflicting emotions of her mind. Here is the first paragraph of one of them :

"You have seen General Bonaparte at my house. Well, it is he who is good enough to act as stepfather to the orphans of Alexandre de Beauharnais, as husband to his widow ! Do you love him ? you ask me. No. . . . I do not. Then you dislike him ? No ; but my state is one of tepidity towards him that is displeasing to me."

It is clearly evident from this that when Josephine married, it was not from love. The next paragraph shows, however, the method by which Napoleon was able to procure influence over her mind. It is also a curious and instructive proof of how early was that perfect self-confidence which was one of the secrets of his final triumph and glory. There is also an allusion to Barras which would seem to lend some confirmation to the un-favourable view of the alliance on which that arch-enemy of Bonaparte has insisted:

"Barras assures me that if I marry the General he will obtain for him the command in Italy. Yesterday Bonaparte was talking to me about this favour, which is already causing some of his brothers-in-arms to grumble, although it has not yet been granted. 'Do they imagine,' he said, 'that I need protection in order to rise? They will only be too glad when I accord them mine. My sword is by my side, and with that I will do anything."

And finally comes this delicious passage, which shows at once the indecision of the woman and the weapon by which she was finally overcome— the weapon of Napoleon's thorough confidence in himself:

"I do not know how it is, but sometimes this ridiculous assurance gains upon me to such an extent as to make me believe possible all that this man suggests to me; and, with his imagina-tion, who can tell what he may not attempt?"

Similarly after her marriage, her comment on

these extraordinary letters—more extraordinary because of the character of the man who wrote them and of his surroundings—her comment is one of the most fatuous utterances . recorded in history : "What an odd creature Bonaparte is ! " she says. "What an odd creature Bonaparte is" is really delightful in its sublime unconsciousness—in its naïveté, in its tragic forecast of her subsequent fate. M. Lévy—who is a simple man himself—describes the phrase as "vulgar and unseemly." His comment is as simple as the original phrase. It is not specially vulgar or specially unseemly ; it is gigantically stupid.

Above all things, Josephine did not wish to leave her beloved Paris. And life in that delightful city was now more delightful than ever, for the victories of her husband, producing mighty street demonstrations, reflected their glory on her ; she is cheered as she rides through the triumphant crowds ; she is at last in a steady and brilliant social position. She tries all kinds of expedients to excuse her delay in departing for her husband's camp, until at last she takes refuge in the splendid invention that she is *enceinte*.

At once Napoleon is pacified, and he bursts out into a profusion of apologies, regrets, almost grovelling palinodes. As thus :

" My life is a perpetual nightmare. A horrible presentiment prevents me from breathing. I live no more. I have lost more than life, more than happiness, more than rest. . . . Write me ten pages; that alone may console me a little. You are ill, you love me; I have afflicted you; you are *enceinte*. I have sinned so much against you that I know not how to palliate my crimes. I accuse you of remaining in Paris, and you are ill there. Forgive me, my dearest; the love with which you have inspired me has taken away my reason. I shall never find it again."

And so it goes on, gathering force and fire as it proceeds; tumultuous, impassioned, like the improvisation of the Italian stock from which he has come. Whatever else Napoleon is, at this period of his existence he is not cold; the volcano emits lava continuously. Here, for instance, is another passage in the same letter:

" I have always been fortunate; my fate has never resisted my will ; and to-day I am struck in what touches me most closely. Without appetite, without sleep, indifferent to friends, glory, and country—you, you alone—the rest of the world no more exists for me than if it were annihilated. I care for honour because you care for it, for victory because it gives you pleasure; otherwise I should have quitted all to throw myself at your feet. My darling, mind you tell me that you are convinced that I love you more than it is possible to imagine; that you are persuaded that every moment of my time is consecrated to you; that never an hour passes without my thinking of you ;

that in my eyes all other women are without charm, beauty, or wit; that you and you alone, such as I see you now, can please me and absorb all the faculties of my soul, that you alone have sounded all its depths; . . . that my strength, my arms, my mind—all is yours; . . . that my soul is in your body; and that the day when you change, or the day on which you cease to live, would be that of my death; that nature and the earth are only beautiful in my eyes because you inhabit them."

And finally the letter, after pages of this kind of thing, winds up with this impassioned outburst:

" A child, adorable as his mother, is about to see the light in your arms! Unhappy that I am, I would be satisfied with one day! A thousand kisses on your eyes, your lips! Adorable woman, what is your power? I am ill with your illness; fever is burning me! Do not keep the courier more than six hours, and let him return straight-way to bring me the cherished letter from my sovereign."

XVIII.

THE FIRST QUARRELS.

ALL these outpourings did not make it a bit easier for Josephine to leave Paris; it was not until she feared that her little invention about being *enceinte* would be betrayed by Junot—

Napoleon's faithful servant—that she consented to go; and then, says a contemporary observer, "Poor woman, she burst into tears, and sobbed as though she were going to execution." At last she reaches Milan. "General Bonaparte," says Marmont, "was very happy, for then he lived only for her. This lasted for a long time. Never had a purer, truer, more exclusive love possession of the heart of man." But he has to rush from her arms to continue his fights with the enemy; and his letters, instead of cooling, grow warmer:

"I turn over and over in my mind your kisses, your tears, your charming jealousy, and the charms of the incomparable Josephine light unceasingly in my heart a warm and bright flame. When shall I be free from all worry, from all business, and at liberty to pass my time near you, and nothing to think of but the happiness of saying and proving it. .... I thought I loved you a few days ago, but since I have left you I feel that my love has increased a thousandfold. .... I implore you to show me your defects sometimes; be less beautiful, less gracious, less tender, less loving especially; above all, never be jealous, never cry—your tears distract me, burn my blood. .... Come and join me, so that before we die we may be able to say: 'We were happy so many days.'"

And the next day he writes in a similar strain:

"I have been to Virgil's village, on the edge

of a lake, by moonlight, and not one instant passed without my thinking of Josephine. I have lost my snuff-box, and beg you to choose me one— rather flat, and to have something rather pretty written upon it, with your hair. A thousand kisses, as burning as you are cold."

And meantime poor, lazy, tepid Josephine proves a very poor correspondent. Letter after letter from Bonaparte begins with some such phrase as this: "Two days without a letter from you. Thirty times to-day have I said that to myself." "I hope that on arriving to-night I shall receive a letter from you." "I am starting immediately for Verona. I had hoped for a letter from you, and am in a state of the utmost anxiety." "No letter from you. I am really anxious." "I write to you frequently, my dear one, and you but little to me. You are haughty and unkind, as unkind as you are heedless."

And so it goes on in reproach after reproach:

"I have received your letters and have pressed them to my heart and my lips, and the grief at my absence, divided from you as I am a hundred miles, has vanished. But your letters are as cold as if you were fifty ; they might have been written after fifteen years of married life."

Here is another:

"I love you no longer; on the contrary, I detest you. You are a wretch, very clumsy, very stupid, a Cinderella. You never write to me;

you do not love your husband. You know what pleasure your letters give him, and you never write him even six miserable lines."

And still Napoleon goes on protesting the vehemence of his love:

"I hope soon to be in your arms. I love you to distraction. All is well. Wurmser has been defeated at Mantua. Nothing is wanting to your husband's happiness save the love of Josephine."

And three days after this letter, when he comes to Milan to join his wife, his love gets a shock greater than her silence and the coldness of her letters. The Palazzo where he had expected to find her is empty, Josephine has gone to Genoa; and then Napoleon, unable to control his grief, disappointment, the wound inflicted on his love and self-love, pours forth his feelings in two letters eloquent in their grief. The first is written immediately after his arrival:

"I reach Milan, I rush to your room; I have quitted all to see you, to press you in my arms. You were not there; you are travelling about in search of amusement; you put distance between us as soon as I arrive; you care nothing for your Napoleon. A caprice made you love him, inconstancy renders him indifferent to you."

And on the next day there comes another letter equally agonised in tone:

"To love you only, to render you happy, to do nothing that can annoy you, that is my destiny, and the object of my life. Be happy, do not reproach me, care nothing about the fidelity of a man who lives only through you; enjoy only your own pleasures and your own happiness. In asking for a love equal to mine, I was wrong. How can I expect lace to weigh as heavily as gold? In sacrificing to you all my desires, all my thoughts, every instant of my life, I simply yield to the ascendency that your charms, your character, and your whole heart have obtained over my unhappy heart. I am unhappy if nature did not endow me with attractions sufficient to captivate you, but what I deserve at the hands of Josephine is at least consideration and esteem, for I love you madly and solely. . . . Ah! Josephine, Josephine!"

Josephine, meantime, was surrounded by young officers, who adored and flattered and courted her, and the memoir writers have no hesitation in declaring that she was unfaithful to Napoleon; but this may not be true, for French memoir writers are not sparing of women's reputations. At all events, Napoleon banished several officers from his army who were suspected of paying too much devotion to his wife; and from the moment when, returning to Milan, he found that she had gone and not awaited him, there is a gradually increasing coldness in his letters. The romance was over; Josephine herself had killed it.

XIX.

HIPPOLYTE CHARLES.

AMONG the officers of the army of Italy, when
Napoleon was Commander-in-Chief, was a young
man named Hippolyte Charles. I suppose there is
nothing more curious—nor inexplicable—in some
respects more saddening, in others more satis-
factory, than the difficulty the greatest men of
history have found in gaining real and faithful
love. George Eliot in one of her early stories
stands up for the man, with poor stumbling gait
and commonplace mind, who wins the love of some
woman far superior to himself ; and asks whether
the straight-limbed young gods have not enough
from life without begrudging to the poor devil,
who is neither fair of form nor brilliant of mind,
the great good the gods have given him of a
perfect woman's devotion. Catherine of Russia
had wondrous charm in addition to her vast gifts
of courage, resolve, clear vision—and yet Catherine,
as her biographer tells us, was as much deceived
by the various men on whom she bestowed so
profusely the riches of her own nature and of her
Empire, as the veriest grisette. And, similarly,
Napoleon—the god of his own time, the god of
so many successive generations of men—Napoleon
never succeeded until it was too late in winning
the devotion of his own wife. And to make the

tragedy the more grotesque, a Hippolyte Charles was his successful rival. Hippolyte Charles, who had not great external advantages, being small and thin, very brown of skin, with hair black as jet, but very careful of his person, and very smart in his fine Hussar uniform laced with gold, showed the greatest attention to the wife of his Commander-in-Chief. He was a man of the kind most dangerous to a woman who is rather bored, and does not love her husband. Charles was what is called amusing. He made puns, and was somewhat affected. The keen interest that Josephine took in this young Hussar was known to every one in the Army of Italy, and when what M. de Ségur calls "Napoleon's jealous displeasure" burst forth, no one was surprised to see Charles, at that time aide-de-camp to General Leclerc, "banished from the Army of Italy by order of the Commander-in-Chief."

XX.

IN EGYPT.

WHEN Napoleon went to Egypt he was accompanied a portion of the way by Josephine. The separation between them is said to have been touching. It is not known whether Josephine offered to accompany him or not. It is certain, however, that Napoleon still continued to have a warm affection for her. In the midst of all his preparations for his great campaigning—in the midst of the discussions with the scientific men whom he had brought with him—Napoleon, says Bourrienne, "passionately devoted to France, anxious for his own glory, though his heart was so full, there was still a large place kept for Josephine, of whom he almost always spoke to me in our familiar conversation."

But Josephine still was tepid, and was terribly indiscreet. In the correspondence of Napoleon with his brothers we see the anxiety gradually turning into certainty, and despair is transformed into rage and repulsion. To his brother Joseph he writes from Cairo: "Look after my wife; see her sometimes. I beg Louis to give her good advice." In the same letter he says: "I send a handsome shawl to Julia; she is a good woman, make her happy." Soon after, however, there is a very different note in the letters, and in a letter to Josephine there occurs this phrase—the epitaph on his lost confidence in his wife's fidelity: "I have many domestic sorrows, for the veil is entirely lifted." The latter part of this phrase was omitted in the earlier memoirs of Josephine; it has since been restored. In this same letter there is another passage which speaks a sorrow as profound as even these first words:

"Your affection is very dear to me. Were I to lose that, and to see you betray me, I should turn misanthrope; it alone saves me. One is in a sad plight when all one's affections are centred upon one person. Arrange that I should have active employment on my return, either near Paris or in Burgundy. I wish to pass the winter there, and to shut myself up; I am tired of human nature. I want solitude and isolation; grandeur wearies me, my affections are dried up."

Prince Eugène—Josephine's son—has in his Memoirs to confess that his mother's conduct disturbed Napoleon. He puts down the reports that reach his stepfather to malice and calumny; but, nevertheless, he has to give us a picture of Napoleon which is not without pathos:

"Although I was very young, I inspired him with so much confidence that he made me a sharer in his sorrows. It was generally at night that he thus unbosomed himself, walking with great strides up and down his tent. I was the only person to whom he could talk openly. I sought to soften his resentment, I comforted him as best I could, and as much as my age and the respect I felt for him permitted."

At last there came one of those violent explosions of wrath which were the terror of Napoleon's surrounding. He addressed Bourrienne in a voice stifled with rage; reproaches him that he has not repeated the reports which Junot had brought fresh from Paris—Junot might have been better employed—and then went on:

" Josephine . . . . and I am six hundred leagues

away . . . . Josephine to have thus deceived me. She, she . . . . woe to them . . . . I will exterminate the whole tribe of fops and puppies. As for her divorce. Yes . . . . a public overwhelming divorce . . . . I know all."

Poor Bourrienne seeks in vain to stop this torrent of wrath, and recalls to Napoleon the fact that whatever might be his domestic misadventures, he had at least the comfort of the mighty glory that his Egyptian campaign had gathered around him. There is something extremely human, something really that makes Napoleon less of the scarcely human monster of the Taine portrait, in the passage which follows:

"My glory!" exclaimed Napoleon in despair. "What would I not give if only what Junot has told me were not true, so dearly do I love that woman!"

The origin of all these outbursts was the behaviour of Josephine with Hippolyte Charles. That young gentleman, after his expulsion from the Army of Italy, had entered into business in a large provision firm, was prospering, had money to spend, kept up a fine establishment, and Josephine again listened to him. He paid her visits at Malmaison, her residence as the General's wife; and, finally—it is scarcely credible that a woman could be so imprudent and expect to retain her reputation and her husband's love—"ended by living there altogether as its master."

This is what had been reported to Napoleon. He took his revenge. To this period belongs that well-known intrigue between Napoleon and Madame Pauline Faures, which suggests to Taine one of his most remarkable passages; and from this time forward Napoleon's confidence in his wife was gone. When Josephine heard that he was returning, she determined to forestall her enemies, and to win back his love by going to meet him. Possibly she recollected that most unhappy day when she left Milan, and Napoleon, rushing, as he thought, to her loving and expecting arms, found nothing but emptiness and absence. But fortune was against her this time; she went to meet him by one route, he arrived by another.

So it happened that on October 16th, 1798, at six in the morning, Napoleon found no one when he reached his house in the Rue Chantereine, and his irritation and jealousy were thereby increased.

To make this unexpected solitude in his own home the more exasperating, Napoleon had passed through France amid the mad acclamations of the people — the forerunners of that inexhaustible popularity which very soon was to enable him to mount the throne. After all these wild crowds of almost idolatrous admirers—after all this tumult —to come home and find this silence, this apparent neglect! Napoleon was so exasperated that he refused for some time to even see Josephine, and took measures for having the divorce proceedings set in motion; and what must have made the whole business the more exasperating for Napoleon was that just at that moment, when this wretched domestic complication came to disturb and pre-occupy him, he was on the eve of the events which were to lead him—if he only had the nerve and the resource—to the loftiest pinnacle of human glory; which, with loss of nerve—by one slight mistake—might end in death on the scaffold.

Under these circumstances, Josephine adopted a desperate but a wise expedient. She used her two children as the intermediaries between her and her husband. The scene which followed is described by more than one contemporary, but the best accounts are those of Prince Eugène, who of course was present, and of Bourrienne, Napoleon's secretary. Prince Eugène says that Napoleon gave his mother a "cold reception." Bourrienne describes the reception as one of "calculated severity" and the "coldest indifference." But when Napoleon saw Josephine, her eyes streaming with tears, in despair, conducted to his presence by Hortense and Eugène, he broke down—"he opened his arms and forgave his wife."

It is hard to say what judgment we should pronounce on this episode. M. Lévy, of course, has no difficulty in seeing in it a sublime gene-rosity; it may have been the cynical indifference which made Napoleon finally regard Josephine as merely a pretty woman—not to be cast off because of her prettiness—to be simply used and despised. There is much more respect to a woman in a jealousy that will not be appeased than in a reconciliation which has its roots in the senses and in contempt.

And now there comes the second epoch in the lives of Napoleon and Josephine. As married people go, they got on pretty well together. There are abundant proofs that Napoleon was in his way a fairly good family man. He certainly desired to be so considered himself.

"At home," he said to Roederer, "I am an affectionate man; I play with the children, talk to my wife, read novels to them."

And certainly there are proofs that he was very fond of children. We have seen already how intoxicated he was by the prospect of Josephine's being *enceinte*. Later on, his delight was keen when that poor infant was born with so tragic a destiny—so pitiful an end—the Duke of Reichstadt. Here are two very pretty pictures of Napoleon with the children of Queen Hortense, daughter of Josephine, wife of his brother Louis, the father of the Napoleon whom we knew in our days as Emperor of the French:

"Uncle Bibiche! Uncle Bibiche!" This exclamation came from a child of scarcely five years of age, running breathlessly in the park of Saint-Cloud after a man visible in the distance followed by a troop of gazelles, to whom he was distributing

pinches of snuff, disputed eagerly. The child was
the eldest son of Hortense, and the distributor of
snuff was Napoleon, who had earned the name of
" Uncle Bibiche" by the pleasure that he took in
setting the boy on the back of one of the gazelles
and walking him about, to the intense joy of the
child, who was carefully held on by his uncle.
The child, it appears, was charming, and, moreover, possessed a great admiration for his uncle.
When he passed in front of the grenadiers in the
Tuileries gardens, the boy would call out : " Long
live grandpapa, the soldier!" " It used to be,"
says Mademoiselle Avrillon, " a real holiday for the
Emperor when Queen Hortense came to see her
mother, bringing her two children. Napoleon
would take them in his arms, caress them, often
tease them, and burst into laughter, as if he had
been their own age, when, according to his custom,
he had smeared their faces with cream or jam."

Finally, there were plenty of things to show
that ordinarily he was kind and considerate to
Josephine. Napoleon himself said: " If I found
no pleasures in my home life, I should be too
miserable." " Once the quarrels of the first years
were over," says Thibaudeau, " it was on the whole
a happy household."

" The Emperor," says Mademoiselle Avrillon,
" was, in reality, one of the best husbands I have ever
known. When the Empress was poorly, he passed
near her every hour that he could spare from his

work. He always went into her room before going to bed, and very often, when he woke in the night, he would send his mameluke for news of Her Majesty, or else come himself. He was tenderly attached to her." "How touching was the peace that reigned in the Imperial household!" says Constant. "The Emperor was full of attentions for his wife, and used to amuse himself by kissing her on the neck and the cheeks, tapping her face, and calling her his 'great stupid.' She often read new books to him; he liked her to read to him, as she read admirably and much enjoyed reading aloud. When the Emperor showed an inclination to go to sleep, the Empress used to descend a little staircase and rejoin the company in the drawing-room just as she had left them."

XXI.

HOPELESS JOSEPHINE.

TWO or three more details will help us to form a correct view of the relations between Napoleon and Josephine. One of the husband's peculiarities was the interest he took even in the small details of his wife's toilet. He used sometimes to assist at her preparations; "and," writes one of the intimates of the household, "it was strange to us to see a man whose head was so full of great things going into all sorts of details, and pointing out the gowns or the jewels he wished her to wear

on such and such occasion. He one day spilled
some ink over one of the Empress's gowns because he did not like it, and to force her to put on
another."

"On the morning of the consecration," says
the Duchesse d'Abrantès, "the Emperor himself
tried on the Empress the crown she was to wear.
During the ceremony he was most attentive,
arranged this little crown, which surmounted a
coronet of diamonds, altered it, replaced it, and
moved it again."

But, nevertheless, there were occasional quarrels
between the two, mainly owing to the incurable
extravagance of Josephine. Napoleon inherited
from his mother, and from his days of struggle,
a most careful regard for the value of money. Of
that I shall give some curious stories by-and-by.
Poor Josephine, on the other hand, never was
capable of counting the cost of anything, and she
was so fond of spending money that she frequently
bought things quite useless to her for the mere
sake of buying. The result was that she was
always being cheated, always in debt, always in
terror and tears when the time came round to
meet her bills and she had to appeal to her stern
taskmaster for money. Says Sismondi :—

" Josephine . . . . was always surrounded by
people who robbed her; she denied herself no
whim, never reckoned the cost, and allowed prodigious debts to accumulate. It happened on one

occasion, when the settlement of the budget was
approaching, that Napoleon saw the eyes of Josephine and of Madame de la Rochefoucauld (principal lady-in-waiting) very red. He said to Duroc:
' These women have been crying; try to find out
what it is about.' Duroc discovered that there
was a deficit of six hundred thousand francs
(twenty-four thousand pounds). Napoleon, incredulous, immediately wrote an order for one
million francs (forty thousand pounds), and exclaimed: ' All this for miserable trifles! Simply
stolen by a lot of scoundrels! I must send away
so-and-so, and forbid certain shopkeepers to present themselves at the Palace.' "

XXII.

NAPOLEON'S INFIDELITIES.

POOR Josephine had further and graver causes of
complaint. For the infidelities, the coldness, the
neglect with which she afflicted Napoleon when he
was a raw young soldier, and for the first time
knew the graces and charms of a pretty woman,
she had to pay the penalty of years of misery,
helpless jealousy, sometimes even violence. By
a process which is not uncommon in married life,
and especially among those whose fortunes have
undergone considerable modification, the woman's
love grew as the man's waned. Napoleon sometimes was decent enough to endeavour to conceal

his infidelities, at others he seems to have been cynically indifferent to the feelings of his wife ; and on one occasion he treated her as only a brute could do. Sometimes, as Taine has told us, he went the length of telling her the details of his amours, replying to her tears and her reproaches with, "I have a right to answer all your objections with an eternal ' Moi.' "

When in 1806–7 Napoleon was in Poland, there was a reversal of the parts which the husband and wife played towards each other in the other epoch of their married life, when Josephine was in Paris and Napoleon was in Italy. The reader will remember the letters of impassioned ardour in which the young soldier addressed in those days the tepid wife—how he pressed her to follow him, to be always near him. When Napoleon went to Poland there is a repetition of the same thing ; but it is Josephine that longs to go to Napoleon, it is Napoleon that likes their separation. When Josephine did not get the summons she so eagerly longed for, poor Josephine—she was only a superstitious, weak Creole creature after all—would try to master her feverish impatience and her apprehensions in a characteristic way :

" Every evening," says the Duchesse d'Abrantès, " she used to consult the cards in order to learn whether she would receive the desired orders or not."

Josephine sends letter after letter, resorts to

every species of tender coquetry. Much of all this is to be found in the following little extract from one of Napoleon's letters:

"An officer brings me a carpet from you. It is rather short and narrow, but I thank you none the less for it."

Meantime Napoleon keeps protesting that there is only one woman in the world for him. "All these Polish women are French, but to me there is but one woman in the world." "In the deserts of Poland one thinks little of beauties," he writes in another letter. Following this description of Poland was the announcement—not altogether consistent—that the noblesse of the province had given a ball in his honour: "Very beautiful women, very rich, dressed in Paris fashion." This, at least, was a tolerable and an inhabited "desert."

XXIII.

MADAME WALEWSKA.

POOR Josephine's apprehensions turned out to be well founded. Napoleon met in Warsaw the only woman who ever made a real impression upon him since the days when his fiery young fancy so glowed with love for Josephine. And it was here, also, that Napoleon met the only woman, except Josephine, who showed any desire to be faithful to him in disaster as in the days of his glory. Napoleon first saw Madame Walewska at that

very ball which he mentioned in his letter to
Josephine. Napoleon afterwards said of her:
"She was a charming woman, an angel. One
might say that her soul was as beautiful as her
face." She is thus described at the moment
when Napoleon saw her for the first time:

"She was two-and-twenty, fair, with blue eyes,
and a skin of dazzling whiteness ; she was not tall,
but perfectly formed, with an exquisite figure. A
slight shadow of melancholy lay on her whole
person, and rendered her still more attractive.
Recently married to an old nobleman of bad
temper and extremely rigid views, she seemed
to Napoleon like a woman who has been sacrificed
and who is unhappy at home. This idea increased
the passionate interest the Emperor felt in her as
soon as he saw her."

The records of the time show that in this case
Napoleon was prompt and strong; but his love-
making was never of a very refined order. Thirty-
seven years of age, a great General, with Europe
gradually falling at his feet, he conducted his
siege of a woman after the fashion of an attack
on a fortified town. The courtship, indeed, is one
of the most curious in history; I can but glance
at it for more reasons than one. Says Constant:

"The day after the ball the Emperor seemed
to me in an unusually agitated state. He walked
about the room, sat down, got up, and walked
about again. Immediately after luncheon he sent

a great personage to visit Madame Walewska for him, and to present to her his homage and his entreaties. She proudly refused proposals made too brusquely, or was it perhaps the coquetry innate in woman that suggested to her to refuse?"

Napoleon, however, wrote a letter which in some degree made up for his brusqueness, and the young Countess promised to visit him.

The Emperor, while waiting for her, walked about the room and displayed as much impatience as emotion. Every moment he inquired the time. Madame Walewska arrived at last, but in what a state!—pale, dumb, her eyes bathed in tears.

Everybody knows the end of the story. Madame Walewska, after the disappearance of Napoleon from her native country, remained in shadow; she made her presence felt for the first time when reverses began to come. Then she wrote to her old lover, and she visited him in the island of Elba after his first dethronement. But perhaps the favour she conferred on him that he valued most was that she gave him a son. In due time the son lived to be one of the chief advisers and Ministers of Napoleon III., and died before the war in which the whole Napoleonic dynasty went down.

In the meantime poor Josephine comes part of the way to her husband, but he tells her to go back; the weather, he says, is bad, the roads unsafe. "Return to Paris," he writes to her; "be

happy and contented."   In another letter containing the same advice, he says : " I wish you to be
gay and to give a little life to the capital."   And,
finally, one can see to the depths of the tragedy
when one reads between the lines of this sentence
in one of these letters :

" I wish you to have more strength.   I am told
you are always crying. Fie ! How ugly that is ! "

Josephine might well be " always crying."   It
was the visit to Poland and the love of Countess
Walewska that led to her own final downfall.   It
gave Napoleon the idea of having children, founding a dynasty—in other words, of divorcing his
wife.

XXIV.

THE DIVORCE.

NAPOLEON contemplated a divorce from Josephine, it will be remembered, at an early period
of their married life.   However, he and she got
over their difficulties, and divorce did not finally
come from any rupture of affection.   I find it hard
to decide what Napoleon really felt at this period
of his life.   His present apologist sees in his
conduct in this, as in almost every other circumstance, nothing but sublime unselfishness ; sublime
unselfishness was not in Napoleon's nature.   On
the other hand, even Taine admits that he had
sensibility, though he contends that it was a
sensibility rather of nerves than of heart.   At all

events, there are plenty of passages to show that he did not separate from Josephine without considerable wrench of feeling. When it was suggested to him in 1804 that he ought to look for an heir, he cried out :

" It is from a feeling of justice that I will not divorce my wife. My interests, perhaps the interests of the system, demand that I should marry again. But I have said to myself: 'Why should I put away that good woman simply because I have become greater?' No, it is beyond me. I have the heart of a man, I am not the offspring of a tigress. I will not make her unhappy."

Knowing how much of an actor Napoleon was, it is hard to say whether these excellent sentiments were what he really felt, or desired other people to think he felt; or may not these sentences be the compensation he thought himself bound to make for what he was contemplating? One of the subtle tricks of self-love and selfishness is to imagine that verbal remorse is a sufficient justification for unworthy acts. In 1809, however, the decision so often contemplated was finally made, and was the result of the *liaison* with Madame Walewska. When Napoleon was in the apogee of his power and glory he spent three months at Schönbrunn, and during that period Madame Walewska was his companion. When she became *enceinte* Napoleon's hesitation came to an end ; he determined to have an heir to his throne.

There is a curious domestic scene—told with French *verve*, and also with that slight spice of cynicism which one finds in most things French—when Napoleon was making his final announcements to Josephine. She had fought against the divorce for a long time; but finally, weak-willed, luxury-loving, very much afraid of her husband, she began to yield. When the final moment approached, however, she could not resist bringing into the last action all the batteries of her woman's arts. Napoleon had dined, and then had been left alone with the Empress. M. de Bausset tells what followed :

"Suddenly I heard loud cries proceeding from the Emperor's drawing-room, and emitted by the Empress Josephine. The usher, thinking she was ill, was about to open the door, but I prevented him, saying that the Emperor would call for help if he thought right. I was standing near the door when Napoleon opened it, and, perceiving me, said hastily: 'Come in, Bausset, and shut the door.' I entered the drawing-room and saw the Empress lying on the floor uttering piercing cries. 'I shall not survive it,' she kept repeating. Napoleon said to me : 'Are you strong enough to lift Josephine and carry her to her apartments, by the private staircase communicating with her room, so that she may have all the care and attention her state requires ?' With Napoleon's help I raised her in my arms, and he, taking a candlestick off the table, lighted me and opened the door of the drawing-room. When we reached the head of the staircase, I pointed out to him that it was too narrow for me to carry her down without running the risk of a fall. Napoleon called an attendant, gave him the candle, and himself took hold of Josephine's legs to help me to descend more gently. When she felt the efforts I was making to save myself from falling, she said, in a low voice: 'You are holding me too tightly.' I then saw that I need be under no uneasiness as to her health, and that she had not lost consciousness for a moment. The Emperor's agitation and anxiety were extreme. In his trouble he told me the cause of all that had occurred. His words came out with difficulty and without sequence, his voice was choked and his eyes full of tears. He must have been beside himself to give so many details to me, who was so far from his councils and his confidence. The whole scene did not last more than seven or eight minutes."

M. Lévy does not give the curious scene which took place when the divorce was being decided on; it is one of the instances in which Napoleon exhibited that extraordinary sensibility which is one of the contradictions in his strange make-up. I quote the passage as given by Taine:

"He tosses about a whole night, and laments like a woman; he melts and embraces Josephine; he is weaker than she. 'My poor Josephine, I can never leave you;' folding her in his arms he declares that she shall not quit him; he abandons himself wholly to the sensation of the moment; she must undress at once, sleep by his side, and he weeps over her. 'Literally,' she says, 'he soaked the bed with his tears.'"

On the evening of December 15, 1809, Napoleon and his wife signed the deed annulling the marriage. ": The Emperor," says Mollien, "was no less moved than she, and his tears were genuine."

XXV.

AFTER THE DIVORCE.

AND it is in the few days after the divorce that for the first time in all that strangely busy career —every moment of which was devoted to work in some form or another—Napoleon for the first time lets sentiment get the better of him, and falls into the idle languor of regret and grief. He left the Tuileries on the very night of the divorce "as if he could not endure the solitude," and went "almost alone" to the Trianon. He spent three days there all by himself, refusing to see even his Ministers, the first and the last time in all his reign when business was suspended; and two or three days after the divorce he could not keep away from Josephine, and went to visit her at Malmaison, whither she had retired. She returned the call a few days later by coming to the Trianon; indeed, the position had that mixture of tragedy and comedy which one sees in those dramas that set forth the strange surprises that the divorce laws of America sometimes produce.

"During dinner," says Mademoiselle Avrillon, "the Empress seemed happy and quite at ease, and any one would have thought that their Majesties had never parted."

He also provided a magnificent income for her —eighty thousand pounds, afterwards increased to one hundred thousand pounds. Poor Josephine was not thereby saved from herself; as in the days of her married life she continued to make debts, and over and over again Napoleon had to remonstrate with her. Once he sent M. Mollien as the messenger of his reproaches.

On his return from Malmaison the Minister informed the Emperor of Josephine's wretchedness at having displeased him ; Napoleon interrupted Mollien, exclaiming, "You ought not to have made her cry ! "

Josephine, on her side, asked after the child which Napoleon had by his new wife, had it brought to see her ; and, finally, when disaster came upon her husband, offered to rejoin him once more. She died in 1814, before his final overthrow.

There have been many better women than Josephine, but the same softness, womanliness, weaknesses that gave her the empire she once held over Napoleon's heart, have enabled her to retain a tender place in the memory of posterity. She is one of the popular heroines of the great historic drama.

CHAPTER VIII.

MARIE LOUISE.*

IT is time to tell something of the other woman who played a great part in Napoleon's career: Marie Louise, his second wife.

I.

THE CORSICAN OGRE.

I FIND a very good picture of her in an interesting little book called " The Three Empresses." The three Empresses are Josephine, Marie Louise, and Eugénie. The volume is simple, unpretentious, rather uncritical; but the writer is pleasant, sympathetic, and womanly; and one can spend several pleasant hours in her society and that of the three rather hapless women who are her heroines.

Nothing could have seemed more unlikely in human affairs than that Marie Louise should become the wife of Napoleon. Here is one of the first incidents in her life:

* " Three Empresses," by Caroline Gearey. (London : Digby, Long, & Co.) " Napoléon et les Femmes," by Frédéric Masson. (Paris : Paul Ollendorff.) " The Private Life of Napoleon," by Arthur Lévy. (London : Richard Bentley.)

"Some time during the early spring of the year 1797, a party of Royal fugitives might have been seen leaving the Austrian capital and hurriedly making their way along the road to Hungary; the progress of their attendants being somewhat impeded by the many packages of valuable property which they were endeavouring to save from the enemy. Making one of this party of refugees of the Imperial House of Hapsburg was the little Archduchess, Marie Louise, then a child between five and six years old, 'whom our imagination,' writes Sir Walter Scott in his 'Life of Napoleon,' 'may conceive agitated by every species of childish terror derived from the approach of the victorious general, on whom she was at a future and similar crisis destined to bestow her hand."

And her education, besides, had been carefully devoted towards increasing the hatred of the man who had inflicted this humiliation on her family. For she was brought up "with the truest respect for religion, while she learned to eschew revolutionary ideas, more especially as exemplified in the conduct of Napoleon Bonaparte."

To such an extent was the latter feeling carried, that when Marie Louise used to play as a child with her little brothers and sisters, they were accustomed to select the blackest and ugliest of their dolls, which they dressed in uniform and stuck full of pins, in denunciation of the ogre who was an incarnation of terror to their childish minds. The young Archduchess had, too, a lively remembrance of the war in the year 1805, which also brought Austria to the very verge of ruin. The Imperial family had on that occasion been again compelled to flee from their capital, and writing from Hungary, where they had taken refuge, to her father, Marie Louise had endeavoured to console him by the assurance that she prayed daily and hourly that the power of the usurper might be humbled in the dust, cheerfully suggesting that perhaps the Almighty had let him get so far that his ruin might be more complete when it came.

Later on, when Marie Louise heard that Napoleon had lost the battle of Eckmuhl, she wrote to her father.

"We have heard with joy," she writes, "that Napoleon was present at the great battle which he lost. May he lose his head as well!" She then goes on to refer to a prophecy which was current that he would die that year at Cologne, adding: "I do not attach much importance to these prophecies, but how happy I should be to seem them fulfilled."

"Napoleon appeared to her on a background of blood, a kind of fatal being, a wicked genius, a satanic Corsican, a sort of Antichrist," thus a clever French writer sums up the girl's early impressions of her future husband.

To her he was the murderer of the Duke

d'Enghien, the enemy of every crowned head in Europe, the author of the treachery at Bayonne, the persecutor of the Pope, the excommunicated sovereign.

Finally there was the great, and, as we would have thought, the insuperable obstacle that Napoleon was the child and embodiment of the French Revolution, and the French Revolution had guillotined Marie Antoinette, the aunt of Marie Louise, but fifteen or sixteen years before.

II.

THE REARING OF MARIE LOUISE.

BUT the rearing of Marie Louise had been of a kind that made her accept pliantly whatever her father thought it her duty to do. I don't know a picture much more repulsive than that of the girlhood of this woman. The French author tells it with the plainness of speech characteristic of his race, and though the passage leaves much to be desired in point of delicacy, it is so true, so lifelike, and so instructive a picture, that I cannot refrain from giving it:

"She was taught a number of languages, German, English, Turkish, Bohemian, Spanish, Italian, French, even Latin, for she is ignorant of where destiny will take her. The more her vocabulary is extended, the more words she has to express the same idea. That is all she wants.

She has many accomplishments, music and drawing, which make a decent and high occupation for idle Princesses. She has just the semblance of religion, restraining her to its minutest practices, but she has been taught how to dispute on the dogmas, for her future husband may be schismatic. As for morals, by a carefully arranged mystery, the Archduchess is allowed to ignore the fact that in nature there exist beings of different sexes. With precautions which only the casuists of the great Spanish schools could conceive of, they strove in every way to safeguard her innocence, going to refinements of modesty that became pruriency. In the yards there were only hens, not a single male bird amongst them; there were only hen canaries in the cages, no songsters; there were no male dogs in the rooms, nothing but females. And the books—such contemptible books—are expurgated, scissors in hand, pages, lines, even words, cut out, without it ever occurring to the cutters that, in the face of these gaps, even Archduchesses would think. It is true that a governess, an ayah, who afterwards became a great lady, kept a tight rein on even dreams. It was she who held complete sway indoors, assisted at the lessons, directed and controlled the games, kept watch over the domestics and the junior schoolmistresses. She did not quit the pupil either day or night. As the care of the Princess was an important matter, and belonged to the domain of politics, the holder of this office changed if the ministers went out of office; Marie Louise had five governesses in eighteen years, but her education was controlled by laws so severe and so strict that, beyond the mutations in the *personnel* of the establishment, there was no variety for her.

"For amusement she had those forms which belong to convent life : flowers to cultivate, birds to take care of, sometimes a little frolic on the lawn with the governess's daughter ; on days when she went out she had a familiar intimacy, very sweet, but very plebeian, with the old uncles who dabbled in painting and music. There was no toilet, no jewellery, no dancing, nor any participation in the gaieties of the Court—only some journeys to and from the Diet. The thing which was the most memorable to Marie Louise— that which afforded her the greatest break in the routine of life—was an occasional flight before a French invasion ; discipline then lost something of its regularity, and her tasks were somewhat slackened. Therefore it is not a woman whom they deliver to Napoleon, it is a child bent to a control so severe, so uniform, and so narrow, that any discipline will be sweet in comparison, and even the least pleasure will be new.

"But if education has in her case so compressed nature, it need not be feared that nature will not in due course take its revenge. This is the education that the daughters of Marie Thérèse have received, and we have seen Marie Antoinette at work at Versailles, Marie Caroline at Naples, and Marie Amélie at Palma. Doubtless! But Napoleon imagined that the husbands had not set the right way to work, and he has his plans. The schoolgirl whom he has received will simply pass out of the convent at Schönbrunn into the convent of the Tuileries or Saint-Cloud. There will only be added the husband. There will be the same inflexible regulations, the same rigorous surveillance; no liberty of action, no literature which has not been chosen; no visits will be allowed to male friends, the ayah will be replaced by a duenna, and four feminine guards will be perpetually on the watch, two at the door, two in the apartment, night and day, like sentinels before the enemy."

III.

IPHIGENIA.

UNDER such circumstances, and with such a training, how could poor Marie Louise regard the marriage to Napoleon as anything but an act of self-sacrifice? And her own people so fully shared this view that they rather shrank from mentioning the subject to her. Her father excused himself from even hinting at it on the ground of not desiring to even seem to influence her decision; her young stepmother "utterly declined to have anything to do with it," and when Metternich "first put the proposal before the young Arch-duchess, she is said to have listened with much distaste and dismay;" but she presently asked him: "What does my father wish?" And that, after all, was the one decisive question for her.

At first Marie Louise, who was much attached to her home and family, could look only on the gloomiest side of the picture, the having to part from them to journey to a country that was strange to her, as the affianced bride of a man whom she had never seen, and whose very name had been a terror to her. But Metternich did his very utmost to reassure her by turning her thoughts to the gaiety and grandeur which awaited her at the French Court, where she would occupy a position in which she would have the whole world at her feet; while shortly afterwards Napoleon despatched Count Montesquieu to Vienna with his portrait — one of Isabey's exquisite miniatures set in diamonds—when gazing at it long and attentively, she observed with an air of relief: "After all, he is not ill-looking."

IV.

EVERLASTING PEACE.

MEANTIME, every good Austrian thought that the marriage would ensure permanent alliance between France and Austria, and there was a tremendous reaction in Napoleon's favour. Metternich, as the chief manager of the marriage, was especially popular. To his wife, who had remained in Paris, the diplomatist wrote:

"All Vienna is interested in nothing but this marriage. It would be difficult to form an idea of the public feeling about it and its extreme popularity. If I had saved the world I could not receive more homage for the part which I am supposed to have played in the matter. In the promotions that are sure to follow I shall have the Golden Fleece."

The Archduchess herself, too, soon became an object of intense popular interest. Count Otto de Mesloy, the French representative at Vienna, was especially rapturous over the marriage; for to his eyes it meant that the alliance would "ensure lasting tranquillity to Europe, compel England to make peace, and give the Emperor the necessary leisure for organising the vast empire he has created in accordance with his lofty conceptions. . . . All humanity will repose beneath the shadow of the laurels of our august Emperor; and after having conquered half Europe he will add to his numerous victories the most difficult and most consolatory of all—the conquest of a general peace."

It is from his dithyrambic pages that we get the most glowing descriptions of the effect of the prospect on the Viennese.

"Every morning," writes this enthusiastic

courtier, " one may see thousands of curious people station themselves before the Palace, to watch the Archduchess pass on her way to mass. The people are delighted to see her radiant with health and happiness."

There are several pathetic little circumstances in the period that elapsed between the acceptance of the marriage and the arrival of Marie Louise in France. Thus, what could give a better picture of her girlishness than the following account of an interview she had with Marshal Berthier, who had come to Vienna as Napoleon's representative?

" The Archduchess conversed in the most spontaneous and unaffected manner with Marshal Berthier, telling him that she liked playing the harp, and asking if she would be allowed to take lessons, saying that she was fond of flowers, and so hoped that the Emperor would permit her to have a botanical garden. She also spoke of Fontainebleau, and the wild and picturesque scenery of the forest, adding : ' I like nothing better than beautiful scenery.' She went on to say that she trusted that the Emperor would be indulgent to her, as she did not know how to dance quadrilles, but added that she would be quite willing to take dancing lessons if he wished it."

V.

THE BRIDEGROOM.

MEANTIME the expectant bridegroom presents us
at this period of his life with a picture which is
very unlike that which most of us had formed of
him in our imaginings ; a picture in which we can
scarcely recognise the cruel, terrible, and fateful
being who was able to retain a face impassive as
marble in the midst of the carnage of battle-fields,
and who sent lightly so many hundreds of thousands of human beings to slaughter. The childish
excitement, the keen anxiety, the curious outbreaks, even of self-distrust, and what I may call
the antics and frivolities of Napoleon at this
epoch, are useful as helping to make us understand how thoroughly human he was after all.
And yet it is a picture which is, on the whole,
repellent to me. One of Napoleon's critics described him as Jupiter Scapin—half demigod,
half " Merry Andrew." The grotesque puerilities
under all this iron mask and in this heart of steel,
rather add to the sense of horror at all the gigantic
evil he was capable of creating. A man of
doom, who was at least consistently grave, self-
controlled, and terrible, would be less repellent
than this creature of contradictions, at once so
lofty and so mean, so awful and so grotesque, so
proud and so grovelling.

But let me tell the story of his acts and

thoughts from contemporary records, and leave to the reader the conclusions as to his character. Catherine, daughter of the King of Wurtemberg, who was with Napoleon at the time in Paris, gives an excellent description of Napoleon in a letter to her father :

"You will never believe, my dear father, how much in love he is with his future wife. He is excited beyond anything I could have imagined, and every day he sends one of his chamberlains, charged, like Mercury, with the missives of Great Jove. He showed me five of these epistles, which certainly were not written by St. Paul, but which really might have been dictated by an ardent lover. He talks of nothing but her, and what concerns her; I will not enumerate for you all the pleasures and presents he is preparing for her, of which he has given me a detailed account. I will content myself with showing you the disposition of his mind by repeating that he told me that, once married, he would give peace to the whole world, and all the rest of his time to Zaïre."

VI.

AS A WESTERN ODALISQUE.

NAPOLEON'S other acts showed his curious self-distrust and incurable suspicion of women —a suspicion founded not merely on his unhappy experiences with Josephine, but also on his low, brutal view of the sex. Accordingly, his plans with regard to his new wife are a singular mixture of precaution and indulgence. M. Masson declares that "no man, however high or low in the social scale, was to be allowed to remain even for a moment with the Empress." In short, his idea is that his wife should lead in the West the life of the dwellers in the harem in the East, except that the duenna took the place of the eunuch. But the other side of the system is that Napoleon offers to his young wife all material comforts, just like those that "a Sultan would bestow on his favourite Odalisque."

"At Vienna Marie Louise never knew what it was to have elegant dresses, exquisite laces, rare shawls, or luxurious underwear. She will have now—on condition, however, that no male *modiste* approaches her, that the selections are made by her ladies-in-waiting—everything French industry can produce, all that is novel, that is dear. He gives her a foretaste of all these by the trousseau and jewel-cases which he sends her, every article of which he has seen himself, and has had packed under his own eyes."

It will make some of the ladies who read this article almost envious when I mention even some of the presents of which Berthier was the bearer to the young bride.

Among other splendours, says Baron Peyrusse, were a necklace composed of thirty-two groups of

stones, valued at 900,000 fr. (£36,000), some ear-
rings which had cost 400,000 fr. (£16,000), and
the portrait of Napoleon set in a circle of sixteen
single diamonds, valued at 600,000 fr. (£24,000).
Napoleon, we see, could be lavish on behalf of a
betrothed whose dowry was, after all, a modest
one, amounting only to 500,000 fr. (£20,000).

VII.

THE GILDED CAGE.

IF I had the space I might give a good many
other details from the extraordinarily minute and
laborious pages of M. Masson with regard to the
gilding of Marie Louise's cage. With the same
deadly and appalling quantity of detail which I
observed when quoting from him with regard to
Josephine, M. Masson has counted up the number
of Marie Louise's chemises, dressing-gowns, stockings, etc.; for her toilet alone the new Empress
was to have an allowance of 30,000 fr. (£1,200) a
month, or 360,000 fr. (£14,400) a year.

"In Vienna she had nothing but a few poor
jewels, which the wife of a bourgeois in Paris would
have despised : a few ornaments for her hair, a few
small pearls, a few in paste—in short, the jewel-
case of a ruined Princess. She will have in Paris
diamonds such as no Princess ever had before. In
Austria she had modest rooms ; in France she will
occupy apartments the decoration of which the

Emperor has superintended himself—from which everything has been removed that might recall the former occupant—apartments which, in whatever palace she may reside, will always have the same little articles of daily use, so that she may everywhere find the same things close to her hands and follow the same habits. He himself has superintended the selection of all these things also, and their arrangement. He is so proud of his work that he invites everybody to see it. . . . Marie Louise, under the system of training to which she was subjected, was never allowed by her governesses to take sweets lest they should injure her digestion; as Napoleon knows that she is a bit of a glutton, and, like all Viennese women, would like to eat sweets and drink coffee every hour, he transforms his table, multiplies there sweets, bonbons, confectionery, and provides daily a lunch of pastry alone. . . . She cannot say whether she likes the play or not, for she has never been allowed to go to the theatre; but she would not be a true daughter either of her age or her country if she did not love it. She will now have all kinds of entertainment—drama or music as often as she likes, either going with him to the theatres or having private theatricals in her own palaces. Is there anything else she wants? She can have it—dogs, birds, masters of music, painting, or embroidery, all kinds of stamps, every sort of Dunkirk ware—everything, in short, on the one condition that she bows to the discipline of the harem, and leads a life similar to that which she has been brought up to expect. She will only go out for great ceremonies, civil and religious, to great balls and theatres, to clubs, to *salons*, to vacations, to State journeys. She will appear then lofty, almost like a goddess, in her great robes, heavy with diamonds, surrounded by a procession of ladies-in-waiting, officials—seen from afar off by the people like an idol. Thus does he gild the cage and adorn the prison ; thus does he take precautions for keeping her still a child by amusing her with toys ; thus does he regulate minutely her whole life in order that she may pass without any shock from the state of the captive Archduchess at Schönbrunn to the state of the captive Empress at Paris. Thus does he ensure her continence, and thus does he place his wife with Cæsar's, above and outside of suspicion."

VIII.

THE NEMESIS OF NATURE.

I CANNOT say whether one should laugh at or weep over all these things when one knows how it all ended ; and is Napoleon to be admired or despised as he goes through all these preparations for his young bride ? On the whole I cannot— though it makes him appear rather more good-natured than one had pictured him—I cannot say that the picture makes me feel a higher respect for his character. There is something essentially vulgar, and perhaps even a little brutal, in it all. Underneath it all lies the idea which pervades his whole existence—which is the basis of all his philosophy—which makes him in many respects the truest type of the Mephistopheles that real life has created—namely, the contempt and the disbelief in everything in human nature except its low baseness and its selfishness. He wants to win the heart of a young woman. "Come, jewellers, architects, dressmakers, pastry-cooks, and prepare all your wares to set before her. Her vanity, her gluttony, her love of all creature comforts—these are the only things in her which I know; and as for her passions, the only way by which I can safeguard her and myself from her longing to gratify them is by shutting her up in a French harem"—this is the language he really holds to himself about this young girl. If she has a soul, or a heart, Napoleon either does not know or care for their existence. To him at least they have no reality. Has this woman affections? She has, as a matter of fact, plenty of affection, for it is related of her that she sends to her father, her stepmother, and her brothers and sister everything she can extract out of all those brilliant presents which her husband is showering upon her—articles of toilet, furniture, books, precious bits of china—amounting

in value, it is said, to two hundred thousand francs
a year. But Napoleon does not care to think—
perhaps is incapable of thinking of all this, and
makes no attempt to appeal to this worthier,
better side of the young girl's nature. It is well
to remember all this at this particular moment in
the lives of the two; it throws a curious light on
the character of Napoleon; it is the key to their
subsequent relations; above all, it represents the
triumph of the simplicity and the spiritual and
the humane in human nature over the cold
calculations, the material and gross conceptions
of its motives and factors by the cynical and the
corrupt.

IX.

THE FIRST MEETING.

WE can find no better revelation, both of
Napoleon's essential vulgarity and of his dis-
tinctive misunderstanding of the human heart,
than his conduct at his first meeting with his
wife. His apologists do their best to extenuate
and even to eulogise his conduct on this occasion.
I shall be surprised if my readers take the same
view of the transaction.

Let us listen, first, to M. Lévy, and see how
he opens the story of the transaction:

" As politics had given Napoleon a new wife,
he undertook to make the conquest. With this
object he invented all sorts of romantic ways of

pleasing Marie Louise at their first meeting. In the opinion of rigorous observers of Court etiquette, it was no light affair to regulate the first interview. All the technical works bearing on the subject were consulted, precedents were hunted up, the dusty archives sleeping peaceably in corners were routed out, and finally Prince Schwarzenberg discussed with Napoleon, line by line, all these questions of form. Eventually the following solemn dispositions were made: Tents were raised between Compiègne and Soissons, two leagues from the latter town, for the interview between their Majesties. These tents were placed beside the road, with two flights of steps to each, whether from Compiègne or from Soissons. . . . The Emperor, on receiving notice of the Empress's approach, was to leave Compiègne with five carriages, and accompanied by the Princes and Princesses of his family, and by the grand officers of state and of his staff who were to travel with him. . . . The Emperor, on reaching the place intended for the interview, was to leave his carriage, and pass through the first tent on the Compiègne side, in which all the persons of his suite were to remain. The Empress was to pass through the first tent on the Soissons side, leaving there all her suite. It was also arranged that the Emperor and Empress were to meet in the middle tent, where would be placed a cushion, before which the Empress should stop ; that she should curtsey, and that the Emperor, raising her, should embrace her. That a few minutes later their Majesties should enter a carriage holding six persons, with the Princesses; that the grand officers of state and the officers of the staff should accompany the carriage on horseback. Finally, that the two processions should unite, so as to make but one with that of their Majesties at Compiègne."

Such was the programme; this is how it was carried out.

X.

AN ESCAPADE.

THE scene in the three tents was entirely omitted. As soon as the Emperor heard the Empress had left Vitry for Soissons, "indifferent to his dignity and to formality, he jumped into a carriage with the King of Naples and started off *incognito* and without his suite." And it should be added that a heavy shower of rain was falling at the same time, and that when he reached the carriage of the Empress at Courcelles, Napoleon was soaked through. I quote the remainder of the scene from M. Lévy:

"He approached her carriage without being recognised, but the equerry, not aware of his intentions, opened the door, let down the steps, and cried 'The Emperor.' Napoleon fell on Marie Louise's neck, who was quite unprepared for this somewhat rough and gallant greeting, and then immediately ordered them to drive at full speed to Compiègne, which was reached at ten o'clock at night. They passed at full gallop in front of the tents solemnly erected, and under the very eyes of the arrangers of Court etiquette, who, parchments in hand, saw with amazement these violators of Royal proprieties rush past them. It will, of course, be imagined that the delicate point of the relations between the Emperor and Empress from March 28th (date of the arrival at Compiègne) to April 1st (date of the consecration of the civil marriage), had been carefully thought out. It was expressly stipulated that the Emperor should sleep at the Hôtel de la Chancellerie, and not at the Palace, during the stay at Compiègne. On March 28th, at ten o'clock at night, the procession drove up to the Palace. Supper was prepared for their Majesties and all the Court in the Gallery of Francis I. Under the patronage of that gallant monarch, Napoleon addressed to his bride words which were emphasized by imploring looks. Marie Louise blushed, and was dumb with astonishment. To overcome the scruples of her who was only his wife by proxy, Napoleon called in the authority of Cardinal Fesch, to whom he said, in presence of the Empress: "Is it not true that we are really married?" "Yes, sire, according to the civil law," replied the Cardinal, little dreaming of the use to

which his answer would be put. The breakfast
which Napoleon caused to be served next morning
in the room of Marie Louise by her waiting women
dispenses us from explaining how the latter part
of the protocol was eluded, and why the apartments in the Hôtel de la Chancellerie did not
shelter their august tenant. His valet says: 'After
his conversation with the Empress, Napoleon retired to his room, scented himself with eau de
Cologne, and, clothed only in a dressing-gown,
returned secretly to the Empress.' To complete
his story, Constant adds: 'Next morning, while
dressing, the Emperor asked me whether any one
had noticed the way he had broken through
the programme.' By his enthusiasm the most
powerful monarch in Europe shows us that his
temperament has not changed since 1796. The
impatience of the Emperor for the arrival of Marie
Louise is the same as that of General Bonaparte
for Josephine."

I leave the reader to form his own opinion of
the apologies for this strange scene which the
eulogist of Napoleon gives. It does not alter
my view of the transaction. I will not weary,
and perchance disgust, the reader by adding the
even more audacious and franker defences of
M. Masson.

It is pleasanter to be able to record that
Napoleon had the apartments at Compiègne
arranged so as to give them a home-like ap-

pearance to the young bride; she found there her favourite dog, "which she had been persuaded to discard," "some pet birds, and a piece of unfinished tapestry which she had been working when she left the Hoff burg for Vienna."

XI.

A PORTRAIT.

AND now for a portrait of the young bride. I quote from Miss Gearey :

" A tall, stately maiden, fresh and youthful, abounding in health and strength, with blue eyes, blonde hair, a pink-and-white complexion, and an expression of innocence and candour. Marie Louise could hardly be styled pretty, and her figure was too much inclined to *embonpoint* to be really graceful, but she possessed the indefinable charm of youth and the attractions which may be derived from a clear complexion, an abundance of chestnut hair, and an exquisite set of teeth. She is said to have been so indifferent to her personal appearance, and so little fond of dress, that the Emperor himself insisted on superintending the bridal toilet, and stood by while the mistress of the robes placed the crown upon the head of the Empress and arranged the Imperial mantle upon her shoulders."

There can be [no doubt that Napoleon did his best to recommend himself to his young bride ;

his efforts were of the same mixed character as
those by which he preceded their marriage. As
during his courtship he sought the aid of the tailor
and the dancing-master, so during the early days
of his marriage he oscillated between grotesque
exploits and a considerateness which in one so
hard is interesting, and even a little touching.

"At Court and in society," says Fouché, "the
instructions were to please the young Empress,
who, without any return, had captivated Napoleon; he was quite infatuated about her. The
Empress Marie Louise, his young and insignificant wife, was the object of his tenderest care.
Napoleon followed her everywhere with loving
looks. She saw that he was proud to show her
everywhere to everybody." Madame Durand,
wife of the General of that name, and principal
lady-in-waiting to the Empress Marie Louise,
says: "During the first three months following
his marriage, the Emperor was day and night
with the Empress. The most urgent business
could hardly drag him away from her for a few
moments." "The Emperor," says Monsieur de
Champagny, "was the best husband in the world.
It would be impossible for any one to display more
delicate and loving attention."

XII.

SELF-DISTRUST.

METTERNICH tells a curious story which reveals the strange self-distrust of Napoleon before a daughter of the Hapsburgs:

"I found Napoleon with the Empress. Conversation turned upon commonplace topics, when Napoleon said to me: 'I wish the Empress to speak openly to you, and tell you candidly what she thinks of her position. You are a friend, and she ought to have no secrets from you.' As he concluded this remark Napoleon locked the door of the drawing-room, put the key in his pocket, and disappeared through another door. I asked the Empress what this scene meant; she replied by putting the same question to me. Seeing that she had not been prepared beforehand by the Emperor, I guessed that he wished to enable me to gather from the mouth of the Empress herself some ideas upon her domestic life, so that I might give a favourable report to the Emperor her father. We remained locked up together for nearly an hour, when Napoleon returned, laughing, into the room. 'Well,' said he, 'have you had a good talk? Did the Empress say good or bad things about me? Did she laugh or cry? I do not ask you for a report; these are secrets between you two, and do not concern any third person, even when that third person is the husband.' Next day Napoleon found an opportunity of speaking to me. ' What did the Empress say to you, yesterday ? ' he asked. ' You told me,' I answered, ' that our conversation did not concern a third person. Permit me to keep it a secret.' ' The Empress told you,' exclaimed Napoleon, ' that she was happy with me, and that she had no complaints to make. I hope that you will repeat it to your Emperor, and that he will believe you rather than other people."

Indeed, it would appear that for once Napoleon was conquered, and stood in awe of another human being. This was probably what elicited from his wife the curious, astonishing, historic phrase : " I am not afraid of Napoleon, but I begin to think he is of me."

XIII.

NAPOLEON'S FOIBLES.

AND, indeed, she had abundant reason for coming to this view. He indulges her every whim—indeed, he is on the look-out to anticipate them. He learns that she wants a second set of Brazilian rubies, but finds her purse unequal to the price. The Emperor, "highly pleased with the wisdom of the Empress, and with her methodical disposition, commanded that a second set should be prepared similar to the first, but of the value of between 300,000 fr. and 400,000 fr. (£12,000 to £16,000), and desired that nothing should be said about what he had heard, or of what he intended to do."

When New Year's Day approaches, he asks her whether she is not going to send some presents to her sisters. She answers that she had already thought about it, and that she had ordered jewels to the amount of about 25,000 fr. (£1,000). As he thinks that rather small, she answers that her sisters were not spoiled as she was, and that they would think their presents magnificent. The Emperor then tells her that he had intended to give her 25,000 fr. for her presents, but that he had thought it over and would give her double that amount (£2,000). Eventually the Empress receives 100,000 fr. (£4,000) from him.

There is nothing which so much tests the love of married people as the small occurrences of daily domestic life. Even in these things Napoleon yielded to his wife. Child of the warm South, Napoleon was always chilly, could never endure a cold room ; when he was exhausted and wanted to be refreshed, he always found refuge in a par-boiling bath. Even on this point he had to give way to his wife, accustomed to the icy spaciousness of Austrian palaces.

"During the autumn following his marriage," says Madame Durand, "the Court went to spend some time at Fontainebleau. Fires were lighted everywhere, except in the Empress's room, and she, accustomed to stoves, said that the fire was disagreeable to her. One day the Emperor came to sit with her; on leaving her room he complained of the cold, and desired the lady-in-waiting to have a fire lighted. When the Emperor was gone the Empress countermanded the fire. The lady-in-waiting was Mademoiselle Rabusson, a young lady who had recently come from Ecouen, very simple and outspoken. The Emperor came back two hours later, and asked why his orders had not been executed. 'Sire,' said the lady, 'the Empress will not have a fire. She is in her own rooms here, and I must obey her.' The Emperor laughed heartily at this answer, and, on returning to his own room, said to Marshal Duroc, who happened to be there: 'Do you know what has just happened to me in the Empress's apartments? I was told that I was not at home there, and that I could not have a fire.' The answer provided the Castle with amusement for several days."

XIV.

HOUSEHOLD CHANGES.

NAPOLEON made even greater sacrifices to his wife; he changed his table and his method of taking his meals. The incessant love of work which was one of his peculiarities, and one of the secrets of his prosperity, never, as we know, had permitted him to spend on his meals even an approach to a proper length of time. Here is a

description of him which M. Lévy has drawn up
from several different sources, at the period when
he was at the zenith of his glory and his power:

"The 'pleasure of the table' did not exist
for the Emperor. The simplest food was what
pleased him best, such as *œufs au miroir* (a form
of poached egg); French beans in salad, no
made dishes, a little Parmesan cheese, a little
Chambertin mixed with water, was what he liked
best. 'In a campaign or on a march,' he wrote to
Duroc, Grand Marshal of the Palace, 'let all the
tables, including mine, be served with soup, boiled
beef, a roasted joint, and some vegetables; no
dessert.' Twelve minutes was the time allowed
at Paris for dinner, which was served at six
o'clock. Napoleon used to quit the table, leaving
the Empress and the other guests to continue
their repast. His breakfast, which he ate alone
at half-past nine, never lasted more than eight
minutes. It was served on a little round mahogany
table, without a napkin."

Now let me contrast with this picture of
Napoleon this other, after he had passed under
subjection to Marie Louise:

"He who has hitherto regulated his existence
by his business, was now compelled to conciliate,
sometimes even to sacrifice his business to the
tastes, to the desires, sometimes even the caprices
of his wife. His habit had been to lunch alone,
rapidly, at the corner of a table, when business

permitted him to think of eating at all. Now, at least during the years 1810 and 1811, after which he liberated himself, there was a regular big breakfast at a fixed hour with his wife, a breakfast with one soup, then entrées, one roast, two sweets, four hors-d'œuvre, and a complete dessert, instead of the four little dishes with which, up to then, he had been content."

XV.

HORSEPLAY.

AND now I complete the picture of Napoleon at this period by an extract which will show him, I will not say in a ridiculous light, but in a grotesque one. This picture reveals that curious mixture of greatness and levity which makes him one of the most astounding amalgams of qualities in human history—that amalgam which produced for him the paradoxical epithet of Jupiter Scapin, to which I have already alluded.

" Since his poverty-stricken youth, solitary and melancholy, there has remained with him—when chances of development arrived too late—a taste for hand games, noisy and active playfulness. This could not express itself at the right time, and the result is now seen. His forty-one years endeavour to accommodate themselves to the eighteen years of Marie Louise. He is more of a child than she is, with a species of passion for the amusements of a schoolboy. See him on horseback pursuing her in a gallop along the terraces of Saint Cloud. The horse bucks, the rider falls and gets up laughing, and crying, 'Breakneck.' See him playing a game of baseball at Malmaison, kicking a football, or amusing himself as 'catch-who-can.' To the life of the cloister prepared for her and which she had wholly accepted, she only proposes one amendment—she wishes to ride on horseback, a time-honoured custom for the Princesses of Lorraine ever since they were freed from maternal tutelage. Marie Antoinette has done the same, and one may remember the similar remonstrance of Marie Thérèse. Napoleon will not leave to anybody else the task of teaching her to manage a horse. It is he who places the Empress in the saddle, and holding the horse by the bridle, runs alongside. When the learner has to some extent found her seat, each morning after breakfast, he orders one of his horses to be made ready, jumps on its back without taking time to put on his boots, and in the large courtyard where, every ten paces, a stableman is stationed on orderly duty to guard against every fall, he prances near his wife in silk stockings, amusing himself during the gallop with exciting cries, urging on the horses to make them stride out, falling himself more frequently than he wishes.

" . . . Marie Louise, up to that time, had only one society trick of which she was proud, that was to be able to move her ear without stirring a muscle of her face. Poor trick! At present she plays at billiards, for which she has conceived a great liking, and provokes the Emperor, who makes such bad shots that—in order to show his superiority—he seeks lessons from one of his chamberlains.

"And always, when she wishes to draw a profile of her husband, for which he poses himself to please her, as he would never do for any painter when she sits at the piano and plays for him German sonatas, which he likes a little; or when she shows him her needlework, the sash or belt which she has embroidered—as a matter of fact, her sewing mistress has done the most of it— he is there attentive, absorbed in her, trying to enlighten her, to amuse her, 'his good Louise Marie,' and by his middle-class 'theeing' and 'thouing' astonishes his stiff-necked Court, for the husbands of the Faubourg Saint-Germain take care not to use the second person singular to their wives."

XVI.

DELICACY.

ANOTHER story from Metternich reveals another example of Napoleon's curious delicacy in remonstrating with his wife, as well as that morbid suspicion by which he was constantly haunted. Napoleon had appointed the Duchess of Montebello as her duenna. One day Napoleon hears that, while walking in the park at Saint Cloud, the Duchess has presented to the Empress one of her cousins. At once Napoleon sends Metternich to remonstrate. And this is how the account of Metternich goes on. Napoleon is speaking:

"'The Empress spoke to him, and was wrong in so doing; if she allows all sorts of young men to be presented to her, she will soon fall a prey to intriguers. Every one in France has always a favour to ask. The Empress will be deceived, and, without being able to do any good, will be exposed to a great many annoyances.' I told Napoleon that I shared his views, but that I failed to understand his motives for taking me into his confidence. 'It is,' he replied, 'because I want you to speak to the Empress.' I expressed surprise that he did not speak to her himself. 'The advice is good and wise,' I added, 'and the Empress has much too much sense not to see it.' 'I prefer,' he broke in, 'that you should undertake the commission. The Empress is young; she might think me disagreeable. You are her father's minister and a friend of her childhood, and what you say to her will make more impression upon her than anything that comes from me.'"

XVII.

A SON.

AND now, within three months after the marriage, Marie Louise gave signs that she was going to become a mother; and Napoleon is transported. At eight in the morning, on March 20th, 1811, after a painful time and some danger, Marie Louise gave birth to the poor child who is known to history as the Duke of Reichstadt.

The child remained seven minutes without giving a sign of life; Napoleon glanced at him, thought him dead, and occupied himself solely with the Empress. At last the child emitted a cry, and then the Emperor went and kissed his son. The crowd assembled in the Tuileries gardens awaited with anxiety the delivery of the Empress. A salute of twenty-one guns was to announce a girl, a hundred a son. At the twenty-second report, delirious joy spread among the people. Napoleon, standing behind a curtain at one of the windows of the Empress's room, enjoyed the spectacle of the general intoxication, and was profoundly moved by it. Large tears rolled down his cheeks, of which he seemed to be unconscious, and in that state he came to kiss his son a second time.

XVIII.

NAPOLEON AS A FATHER.

NAPOLEON was an indulgent father. Here is a picture of the terrible man whose existence was fatal to so many human beings, on which it is well for a few moments to dwell.

"Entrance to his study," says Méneval, "was forbidden to every one. He would not allow the nurse to come in, and used to beg Marie Louise to bring in her son herself; but the Empress was so little sure of her strength when she took him from the arms of the nurse, that the Emperor, who stood waiting for her at the door, used to hasten to meet her, take the child in his arms, and carry him off, covering him with kisses. If he were at his writing-table, about to sign a despatch, of which each word had to be weighed, his son lying on his knees, or pressed against his chest, did not leave him. Sometimes he would drive away the important thoughts that occupied his mind, and, lying down on the ground, would play with this darling son like another child, careful to discover what would amuse him, and to avoid anything that teased him. His devotion to and patience with his boy were inexhaustible. The Emperor loved his son passionately; he took him in his arms every time he saw him, picked him up quickly from the ground, then put him down again, and picked him up again, laughing at the child's amusement. He teased him, carrying him in front of the looking-glass, and making grimaces at him, at which the child laughed till he cried. At luncheon-time he would take him on his knee, and dipping his finger in the sauce, smear his face with it."

XIX.

MARIE LOUISE'S TREASON.

I MUST pass rapidly over the remainder of the story; it is not edifying. When Napoleon's misfortunes came, Marie Louise reverted to her old allegiance, and became the dutiful daughter of her father—the loyal subject of Austria—once again. When Napoleon was defeated, and had to fly to Elba, he hoped, or professed to hope, that his exile would be shared. "In the island of Elba," he said, "I may still be happy with my wife and my son." When his letters from Elba received no answer, he took alarm, and sent messengers, and wrote letter after letter to his absent wife. "I expect," he says in one, "the Empress at the end of August. I desire her to bring my son, and . . . I am surprised at not receiving any news of her." And when he left Elba to begin the gigantic but brief struggle of the Hundred Days, he appealed to the Emperor of Austria not to separate husband and wife, father and son :

"I am too well acquainted with the principles

of your Majesty—I know too well what value you attach to family ties, not to feel a happy conviction that you will hasten, whatever may be the inclinations of your Cabinet and your policy, to help me in pressing forward the moment of meeting between a wife and her husband, and a child with his father."

XX.

NEIPPERG.

MARIE LOUISE had found another man who obtained over her an ascendency which Napoleon never could attain. The intrigue which ended in making Marie Louise the mistress of Count Neipperg, is obscure; but there is a general impression that Metternich and her own father were responsible for it. Neipperg was a professional lady-killer, was brave, agreeable, a musician, and apparently an amiable man at bottom. While Napoleon was at Elba, Marie Louise was at Aix-les-Bains, with Neipperg in her train. Later on they took an excursion to Switzerland together, and before Napoleon died, she had borne Neipperg at least one child.

The Powers had bestowed upon her the Duchy of Parma. Neipperg was her Prime Minister, and governed the kingdom well enough to give it prosperity, and to make himself much beloved. She did not see much of her son by Napoleon— an unhappy and interesting boy, over whose early death sinister rumours have been secretly current ever since. I have no time to tell that poor lad's pathetic story. The scanty pictures we have of him leave a pleasant impression. He was always attached to the memory of his father, showed an early love for a soldier's life, and dreamed constantly of a great future. But his tiny life was brief—he died of consumption. The best epitaph on his career was his own. A cradle had been presented to him when he was a new-born baby by the Viennese, and it was restored to the Schatzzimmer, or Treasury, at Vienna; and the Treasury was not far from the Capuchin Church in Vienna, where the bodies of the Hapsburg family lie. This will explain the saying of the young Prince.

"My cradle and my grave will be near to each other," said the Prince, when he was lying ill. "My birth, and my death, that is my whole history."

XXI.

IL SERENISSIMO.

THE memory of Napoleon seems to have made little impression on Marie Louise. She declared afterwards that she had never loved him. Years after Napoleon's death, referring to her first marriage, she said, "I was sacrificed." When somebody asked her how she felt the change from the dignity of an Empress to the poor status of a Grand Duchess, she exclaimed:

"Ah, my God, I am happier here; and that period of my life only lives in my memory as a miserable dream."

She herself gave the best explanation of the kind of character which the training of a Court produces in its women.

"We Princesses," she said, "are not brought up as other women, nor with the same family sentiments. We are always prepared for events which may transport us from our relatives and give us new and sometimes antagonistic interests. Look at my poor sister who went to live in Brazil, unhappy and far from all belonging to her."

It was, perhaps, this training that enabled her to so easily change her allegiance, to so calmly bear her transformations of fortune. Even the death of Napoleon seems to have made little impression on her.

"According to a letter written by Count Neipperg to Prince Metternich, and quoted by M. Saint-Amand, she puts on mourning (but not widow's weeds), while the members of her household were ordered to wear it for three months. Two funeral services were celebrated in honour of the man who had once stood in the relation of husband to the Duchess of Parma, while a notice of his death was at the same time inserted in the *Gazette de Parme*. The astute and diplomatic Neipperg actually wrote to inform Prince Metternich that this insertion had appeared without any reference to the title of Emperor or ex-Emperor, or the names of Napoleon or Bonaparte, which he was pleased to remark were 'inadmissible,' and could only serve to wound the heart of Her Majesty the Duchess. It had therefore been arranged that the mighty conqueror, before whose prowess all Europe had once trembled, should have a funeral service held in his honour under the style and title of *Il Serenissimo!* a conveniently vague term which, according to Neipperg, might be indiscriminately applied to any degree of princely gradation."

"Nothing could be more delicious than this—Napoleon's name masked under the *alias* of *Il Serenissimo!* Perhaps the irony is even greater that his death gave his widow welcome relief, allowed her first to marry Neipperg, and afterwards to descend, after Neipperg's death, on Count Bombelles, a French officer in the Austrian service. To Bombelles she left the greater part of her fortune when she died in 1847, at the age of fifty-six. Meantime, 1840 had come, and the second funeral of Napoleon; the apotheosis that ended in that tomb in the Invalides, at which I stood gazing the other day. And so even Neipperg and Marie Louise and the *Gazette de Parme* proved of no avail. Napoleon's name is still spoken. *Il Serenissimo!* It was sublime!"

CHAPTER IX.

NAPOLEON'S LAST VOYAGES.*

ADMIRAL USSHER was one of the many gallant Irishmen who have served the British Empire on sea. He took a prominent and a brave part in the naval engagements between England and France during the reign of Napoleon. In April, 1814, he was stationed off Toulon, and so he came unexpectedly to play a prominent part in one of the closing scenes of Napoleon's life. It was he who took Napoleon to Elba after the first abdication.

I.

AN ADVENTUROUS ENTERPRISE.

THE narrative in which he described this great adventure is simple, straightforward, often sublimely and heroically unconscious. I cannot imagine anything more striking than the calm way in which the author describes what must have appeared, to any but a fearless man, a dare-devil and almost certainly fatal enterprise. As thus: On

* "Napoleon's Last Voyages," the Diaries of Admiral Ussher and John R. Glover. (London : Fisher Unwin.)

April 24th, 1814, he observed, at ten o'clock at night, a brilliant light in the direction of Marseilles, "which," he says, "I conjectured was an illumination for some important event." This was all he had to go upon, yet he made no hesitation as to his proper course ; and here is what followed : .

"Every sail was then set on both ships, and every exertion was made to work up the bay. At daybreak we were close off the land. All was apparently quiet in the batteries, and not a flag flying ; nor were the telegraphs at work, which was uniformly the case on the approach of the enemy. Everything betokened that some great change had taken place. The morning was serene and beautiful, with a light wind from the southward. Eager to know what had happened, but above all anxious to hear (for who that has once experienced the horrors and miseries of war can wish for. its continuance ?) that peace had been restored, I sailed in toward the island of Pomégue, which protects the anchorage of the bay of Marseilles. To guard against a surprise, however, should such be attempted, I took the precaution of clearing the ship for action, and made signal to the *Euryalus* to shorten sail, that in the event of the batteries opening unexpectedly upon the *Undaunted* my friend Captain Napier, by whose judgment and gallant conduct I had on other occasions profited, might render me any assistance, in the event of my being disabled. We now

2 C

showed our colours, and hoisted at the main a flag
of truce, and the Royal Standard of the Bourbons, which the ship's tailor had made during the
night. This flag had not been displayed on the
French coast for a quarter of a century. Thus
equipped, we were allowed to approach within
gunshot, when we observed men coming into the
battery, and almost immediately a shot struck us
on the main deck. Finding it was not their
intention to allow us to proceed, I gave orders to
wear ship, and hauled down the flag of truce and
standard. While wearing, a second shot was
fired, which dropped under the counter. This
unusual and unwarrantable departure from the
rules of civilised warfare I resolved to notice in
the only way such attacks ought to be noticed,
and determined at once, in the promptest and
most energetic way, to convince our assailants
that under no circumstances was the British flag
to be insulted with impunity. I therefore again
wore round, and, arriving within point-blank shot
of the battery, poured in a broadside that swept
it completely, and in five minutes not a man was
to be seen near the guns. It was entirely abandoned. I now made sail for a second battery,
and by a signal directed the *Euryalus* to close,
intending to anchor off the town. Shortly after-
ward, observing a boat with a flag of truce
standing out of the harbour, I shortened sail to
receive it. On coming alongside, I found she had

on board the mayor and the municipal officers of Marseilles, who had come from the town to apologise for the conduct pursued by the batteries, intimating that it was an unauthorised act of some of the men. They informed me of the abdication of Napoleon."

What splendid rashness—this entrance into a great and well-guarded city with a single ship, simply because "I conjectured" there had been some "important event"!

II.

MARSEILLES AFTER THE ABDICATION.

HOWEVER, fortune favoured the brave, and Captain Ussher soon had abundant evidence that the invader was welcome. I know few pictures which bring home to the mind so clearly the absolute horror and despair which Napoleon's career had at last produced, as that to be found in the pages of Admiral Ussher. The gallant officer landed, and here is what happened :

"Never did I witness such a scene as now presented itself, as, almost choked by the embraces of old and young, we were hoisted on their shoulders and hurried along we knew not whither. I certainly did not envy the situation of my friend Captain Napier, whom I saw most lovingly embraced by an old lady with one eye, from whom he endeavoured in vain to extricate himself, not using, I must say, the gentlest terms our language affords. In this way we arrived at the Hôtel de Ville, amid loud cries of 'Vive les Anglais!' We were received by our friends who had come with the flag of truce in the morning, but who were evidently not prepared for such a visit from us now. . . . They now politely requested us to wait upon the general in command. We found that officer attending High Mass at the cathedral, and it is hardly possible to describe his astonishment, and the excitement caused by seeing two British naval officers, in their uniforms, in the midst of the congregation. I went up to the general, who received me with much apparent cordiality, and with considerable tact (for we were at the time the greater 'lion' of the two) invited us to join the procession (I think it was that of the Virgin), for which preparations had been made, and which was about to set out from the church where we then were. The streets through which we passed were excessively crowded, so much so that it was with the utmost difficulty the procession could make its way at all. The predominance of old people and children among the crowd was remarkable. Commenting upon this to some of the municipal officers, I was told that this was caused by the conscription, which had swept off without distinction (like another plague) all the young men who were capable of bearing arms, causing indescribable misery not only here, but everywhere throughout France. Happy indeed were these poor people at seeing us among them, the harbinger of peace, which many of them had so long and ardently desired. That this was the prevailing feeling among them their whole demeanour amply testified, as with loud vociferations of 'Vive les Anglais!' they plainly told us that we were not unwelcome visitors."

It is well to always bring into relief the terrible consequences of Napoleon's campaigns in the decimation of the French population. People who, in despair at the divisions, the squalors, and the helplessness of French political life, sigh for the return of a great autocrat, always ignore this feature in the career of Napoleon. When somebody said that the picture of Napoleon still occupied a place in every cottage in the land, the obvious and just retort was made that if it had not been for Napoleon the place would have been occupied by the picture of the eldest son of the family, whom Napoleon had sent to premature and awful death.

III.

THE FALLEN EMPEROR.

FROM Marseilles Admiral Ussher went on to Fréjus, from which Napoleon was to embark for Elba. He found the fallen Emperor in "Le

Chapeau Rouge," the small and solitary inn of
the place.

"Napoleon was dressed in the regimentals
of the Old Guard, and wore the star of the
Legion of Honour. He walked forward to meet
us, with a book open in his hand, to which he
occasionally referred when asking me questions
about Elba and the voyage thither. He received
us with great condescension and politeness; his
manner was dignified, but he appeared to feel
his fallen state. Having asked me several
questions regarding my ship, he invited us to
dine with him, upon which we retired. Shortly
afterwards I was waited upon by Comte Bertrand,
who presented us with lists of the baggage,
carriages, horses, etc., belonging to the Emperor.
I immediately made arrangements for receiving
them, and then demanded an interview with the
several envoys of the allied Sovereigns, feeling
that, being placed in a position of such peculiar
responsibility and delicacy, it was necessary to
hear from them the instructions they had received from their respective sovereigns that I
might shape my conduct accordingly, and particularly that I might learn from them what ceremony was to be observed at Napoleon's embarka-
tion, and on arriving on board the *Undaunted*, as
I was desirous to treat him with that generosity
toward a fallen enemy which is ever congenial to
the spirit and feelings of Englishmen."

Napoleon always kept a friendly recollection of Admiral Ussher; one can see in these sentences the origin of the feeling.

IV.

DEPARTURE FOR ELBA.

IT was characteristic of the desire of France to get rid of Napoleon that Ussher was woke up at four o'clock in the morning after he had dined with Napoleon, "by two of the principal inhabitants," "who had come into my room to implore me to embark the Emperor as quickly as possible," intelligence having been received that the army of Italy, lately under the command of Eugène Beauharnais, was broken up; that the soldiers were entering France in large bodies.

These fears were not, apparently, altogether groundless, for Ussher observed that Napoleon "was in no hurry to quit the shores of France." Under the circumstances, Ussher was requested by the representatives of the Powers to gently force the Emperor to leave, and this he did with much combined firmness and tact:

" I demanded an interview, and pointed out to the Emperor the uncertainty of winds, and the diffi- culty I should have in landing in the boats should the wind change to the southward and drive in a swell upon the beach, which, from the present appearance of the weather, would in all probability happen before many hours; in which case I should be obliged, for the safety of His Majesty's ship, to put to sea again. I then took leave and went on board. . . . Napoleon, finding that it was my determination to put to sea, saw the necessity of yielding to circumstances. Bertrand was accordingly directed to have the carriages ready at seven o'clock. I waited on the Emperor at a quarter before seven to inform him that my barge was at the beach. I remained alone with him in his room at the town until the carriage which was to convey him to the boat was announced. He walked up and down the room, apparently in deep thought. There was a loud noise in the street, upon which I remarked that a French mob was the worst of all mobs (I hardly know why I made this remark). 'Yes,' he replied, 'they are fickle people;' and added: 'They are like a weathercock.' At this moment Count Bertrand announced the carriages. He immediately put on his sword, which was lying on the table, and said: 'Allons, Capitaine.' I turned from him to see if my sword was loose in the scabbard, fancying I might have occasion to use it. The folding-doors, which opened on a pretty large landing-place, were now thrown open, when there appeared a number of most respectable-looking people, the ladies in full dress, waiting to see him. They were perfectly silent, but bowed most respectfully to the Emperor, who went up to a very pretty

young woman in the midst of the group and asked
her, in a courteous tone, if she were married, and
how many children she had.   He scarcely waited
for a reply, but, bowing to each individual as he
descended the staircase, stepped into his carriage,
desiring Baron Koller, Comte Bertrand, and me to
accompany him.   The carriage immediately drove
off at full speed to the beach, followed by the
carriages of the envoys.   The scene was deeply
interesting.   It was a bright moonlight night,
with little wind ; a regiment of cavalry was drawn
up in a line upon the beach and among the trees.
As the carriages approached the bugles sounded,
which, with the neighing of the horses, and the
noise of the people assembled to bid adieu to
their fallen chief, was to me in the highest degree
interesting."

v.

NAPOLEON'S POWERS OF OBSERVATION.

NAPOLEON soon began to reveal that extraordinary
power of observation, tenacity of memory, and
mastery of detail which did so much to account
for his greatness in war. " Nothing," writes Ussher,
" seemed to escape his observation."   When a
question arose as to where the ship should anchor
on the Corsican shore, Napoleon " proposed Calvi,
with which he was perfectly acquainted, mentioning the depth of the water, with other remarks on
the harbour, etc., which convinced me that he

would make us an excellent pilot had we touched there." Talking to an English lieutenant who had been in charge of the transports that brought to Elba Napoleon's horses, baggage, etc., he "gave a remarkable proof of his retentive memory." Lieutenant Bailey informed him that after the Guards had embarked a violent gale of wind arose, with a heavy sea, which at one time threatened the destruction of the transports, and that he considered Savona a dangerous anchorage. Napoleon remarked that if he had gone to a small bay (I think it was Vado) near Savona, he might have lain there in perfect safety.

VI.

RULER OF ELBA.

THE other quality of Napoleon which comes out most vividly from Ussher's narrative, was the facility with which he settled down to the work of governing his little island. Think of the awful strain through which he had passed for all these years, and especially in those which immediately preceded his overthrow, and then wonder at the vast power of recovery he showed when he was able to sit down for hours and discuss with an English naval officer the new flag which he was going to give to Elba! And when the time came for him to land, he went through the ceremony of taking possession of his little territory as imperially as though he were entering Paris. And immediately he set to practical work, as though the smallest affairs of this little kingdom were as much worthy of attention as even the world-stirring events in which he had been playing the principal part for nearly twenty years. Take this entry, for instance:

"*May* 5.—At four a.m. I was awakened by shouts of 'Vive l'Empereur!' and by drums beating; Napoleon was already up, and going on foot over the fortifications, magazines, and store-houses. At ten he returned to breakfast, and at two mounted his horse, and I accompanied him two leagues into the country. He examined various country houses, and gave some money to all the poor we met on the road. At seven he returned to dinner."

And, again, on May 6, the following day, we have a somewhat similar entry:

"Already he had plans in agitation for conveying water from the mountains to the city. It appears always to have been considered by him of the first importance to have a supply of good water for the inhabitants of towns, and upon this occasion it was evidently the first thing that occupied his mind, having, almost immediately after arrival, requested me to go with him in the barge in search of water."

And, again, watch him on May 7:

"*May* 7.—Napoleon was employed visiting the

town and fortifications. After breakfast he again embarked in the barge, and visited the different storehouses round the harbour."

And two final extracts will give an even better idea of how this marvellous creature could rise superior to the worst reverses of fortune. It is the entry under date May 9 :

"*May* 9.—This day I accompanied Napoleon to Longone, where we lunched amid repeated cries of 'Vive l'Empereur!' . . . Instead of returning by the same road, he turned off by goat-paths to examine the coast, humming Italian airs, which he does very often, and seemed quite in spirits."

And on the evening of the second day "he entered upon the subject of the armies and their operations at the close of the last campaign, and continued it for half an hour, until he rose from table. After passing into the presence-chamber, the conversation again turned on the campaign, his own policy, the Bourbons, etc., and he continued talking with great animation till midnight, remaining on his legs for three hours."

In this last scene Napoleon is quite himself. Everybody familiar with his character and demeanour will know that he was a tremendous talker. It was only on the battle-field that he maintained the immobile face and the sphinx-like silence which he believed necessary to maintain the morals of his army; in private he had all the excessive mobility, the great love of conversation, and the high powers of rhetoric which came to him from his Italian blood.

VII.

THE VOYAGE TO ST. HELENA.

IT will be seen that Napoleon made almost a conquest of the heart of Ussher, that he was treated still as a Royalty, and that accordingly the narrative of the British officer is sympathetic and even eulogistic. The other narrative—that which describes the voyage to St. Helena—is written in a very different spirit. Even those who do not love Napoleon cannot feel altogether pleased with the almost studied rudeness with which the fallen Emperor was treated on board the *Northumberland*. Here, for instance, is how Napoleon was treated on the question of cabin accommodation :

" The Admiral after this went into the after-cabin with some of the officers, and finding Bonaparte seemed to assume an exclusive right to this cabin, he desired Maréchal Bertrand to explain that the after-cabin must be considered as common to us all, and that the sleeping cabin could alone be considered as exclusively his. Bonaparte received this intimation with submission and apparent good-humour, and soon after went on deck, where he remained a considerable time, asking various questions of each officer of trifling import. He particularly asked Sir George Bingham and Captain Greatly to what regiments they belonged, and when told that Captain Greatly belonged to the Artillery, he replied quickly, 'I also belong to the Artillery.' After conversing on deck for some time, this ex-Emperor retired to the cabin allotted him as a sleeping cabin, which is about nine feet wide and twelve feet long, with a narrow passage leading to the quarter-gallery. The Admiral had a similar sleeping cabin on the opposite side. The after-cabin is our general sitting-room, and the fore-cabin our mess-room; the others of the party are accommodated below by the captain and some of the officers giving up their cabins, and by building others on the main-deck. Thus this man, who but a short time since kept nations in dread, and had thousands at his nod, has descended from the Emperor to the General with a flexibility of mind more easily to be imagined than described. He is henceforth to be styled General, and by directions from our Government, he is to have the same honours and respect paid him as a British General not in employ."

VIII.

A CAGED LION.

THE picture of Napoleon at table is not inviting. It seems that he there preserved his bad manners to the end :

"At six p.m. dinner was announced, when we all sat down in apparent good spirits, and our actions declared our appetites fully equal to those spirits. General Bonaparte ate of every dish at table, using his fingers instead of a fork, seeming to prefer the rich dishes to the plain-dressed food, and not even tasting vegetables. Claret was his beverage, which he drank out of a tumbler, keeping the bottle before him. He conversed the whole of dinner time. . . . After dinner he did not drink wine, but he took a glass of noyau after his coffee, previous to rising from table. After dinner he walked the deck, conversing principally with the Admiral. . . . After walking for some time he proposed a round game at cards, in compliance with which the Admiral, Sir George Bingham, Captain Ross, and myself assembled with General Bonaparte and his followers in the after-cabin, where we played at vingt-un [*sic*] (which was the game chosen by the Emperor) till nearly eleven o'clock, when we all retired to our beds."

I have given one specimen of the kind of petty humiliations to which Napoleon was exposed ; here is another :

"He sat but a short time at dinner, and then went on deck, where he walked, keeping his hat off, and looking round steadfastly and rather sternly to see if the British officers did the same. However, as the Admiral, after saluting the deck put his hat on, the officers did the same (the Admiral having previously desired that the officers should not be uncovered), and thus not a British head was uncovered, at which he was evidently piqued, and soon retired to the after-cabin. His followers were constantly uncovered in his presence, and watched his every motion with obsequious attention. About eight p.m., General Gourgaud begged of us to join the vingt-un party, which the Admiral, Sir George Bingham, Captain Ross, and myself did, and played until about half-past nine, when Bonaparte retired to bed. During this evening he talked but little and appeared sulky ; however, this produced no alteration in our manner toward him, neither was he paid more respect than any other officer present."

And here comes a delicious revelation of the difficulties with which human nature repressed itself in spite of violent political prejudices. I have italicised a sentence in this passage :

" His fellow prisoners are ever uncovered in his presence, and in speaking to him invariably address him either ' Sire ' or ' Votre Majesté,' but the Admiral, as well as the officers, at all times addressed him as General. *However, the difficulty of repressing the inclination to pay him marked attention is evident*, and the curiosity of both officers and men in watching his actions is very easily perceived."

IX.

LIFE IN ST. HELENA.

IN this narrative, as in that which I began, there is the same remarkable evidence of an almost complete recovery of spirits by Napoleon. There are constant entries to the effect that he seemed in excellent spirits, and spoke constantly to the Admiral. Sometimes he is spoken of as in "uncommonly high spirits," and sometimes, when he plays cards, he is one of as " noisy a group as ever assembled on such an occasion."

After his landing in St. Helena, his real decline of health and spirits began, and there is something saddening in the contrast between the comparative tranquillity, and even liveliness, of his spirits on board the vessel, and the beginning of that fight with not too chivalrous guardians, which broke him down and killed him at a comparatively early age. One of his susceptibilities was as to the presence near him of British soldiers.

Talking of Longwood House, this is what the narrator says :

" From the house you have a commanding view to the eastward of the sea and the shipping, and to the northward the camp of the 53rd forms a pleasing object in the foreground to any one except Bonaparte, who seems to loathe the sight of a British soldier, and at whose particular request great pains were taken to place the camp out of his sight. But this could not be done without giving up the very best situation for a camp."

Finally, Napoleon began to be even forgotten by the people among whom his lot was cast:

"Bonaparte leads a secluded life, few or none ever going near him, although no person of respectability has been refused a pass when asked for; but so little is he now thought of that his name is seldom or never mentioned, except on the arrival of a ship. Indeed, the inhabitants express so little curiosity that two-thirds of them have not yet seen him (although he has been to St. Helena eight months), nor do they ever seem inclined to go a hundred yards out of their way for that purpose. Even Mrs. Wilkes, the wife of the late Governor, although she was six months in the island after he arrived, went away without seeing him, whereas the curiosity of the passengers going home from India has almost exceeded credibility."

X.

NAPOLEON'S SELFISHNESS.

FINALLY, our bluff English observer is disgusted by Napoleon's selfishness in the small affairs of daily life, and this is his estimate of his character and manners:

" Greatness of mind or character, in my opinion, he does not possess, very frequently acting like a mere spoilt child. Feeling I consider him devoid of. Every religion is alike to him, and did I believe there existed such a being as an Atheist, I should say Bonaparte is that being. Of those about him, he seems neither to care nor feel for the privations they undergo from their blind and infatuated attachment to him, which many of his actions prove, and which the following cir- cumstance, which occurred during the passage out, will show. Madame Bertrand had been con- fined to her cabin by serious illness for ten days or a fortnight. On her appearing in the cabin, we all congratulated her on her recovery. This was in the forenoon, and about two o'clock Bonaparte came into the cabin, and sat down to play at chess with General Montholon. At this time Madame Bertrand was below, but soon after made her appearance, seemingly to pay her devoirs to this once great man. Putting on one of her best smiles, she approached the table where he was playing, and where she stood by his side silent for some time, no doubt in anxious expectation of receiving the Emperor's con- gratulations, which would have amply repaid all sufferings she had undergone. But in this, dis- appointment alone was her portion, for he merely stared her steadfastly in the face, and then con- tinued his game of chess without taking the slightest further notice. She, evidently piqued, quitted the table, and came over to the other side of the cabin, where she sat by me on the sofa until dinner was announced, when the Admiral, as he usually did, handed her to her seat. Even sitting down at table he took not the slightest notice of her, but began eating his dinner. During the dinner, missing the bottle of claret which usually stood before him, and Madame Bertrand, ever watchful of his motions, having handed him one which was near her, he very condescendingly exclaimed, 'Ah! comment se porte madame?' and then very deliberately continued his meal. This, and this alone, was all the notice the long and serious illness of his favourite drew forth."

It will be seen that these two narratives, though they cannot be described as inspired or luminous, are valuable additions to our knowledge of a man whose tyranny over the imagination and the interest of mankind Time seems to have no power of diminishing.

CHAPTER X.

A FINAL PICTURE.

ONE afternoon I stood by the tomb of Napoleon in the Invalides in Paris, and I can never forget the strange, weird, indescribable feeling which came over me as I looked down amid the surrounding silence on the mass of brown-red marble which enclosed his remains. What brings so strong a sense of the emptiness and transitoriness of life as standing face to face with the unbreakable stillness of death—especially when the ashes, laid low and still, created such wild and cyclonic tumult in their living day as those of Napoleon? In the cold and majestic isolation of his tomb— far from the side of Josephine, who lies in quiet and gentle rest; far from that other consort who never really loved him—far from the Countess Walewska—one of the most pathetic and touching figures in his strange and fierce life; far from the poor boy over whose cradle he more than once was seen to be in mournful forecast of his joyless destiny; above all, far from those wild shouts and hurrahs of mighty armies which found in his word and eye that inspiration to meet and defeat numbers, dangers, and death—alone he lies in death as he lived in life. The whole scene struck me as significant, eloquent, almost a revelation, and an appeal by dead Napoleon to that recognition from history which history has been so ready to give him.

I.

WATERLOO.

NEXT to this scene, the most impressive picture I have ever been enabled to form in my mind of Napoleon's personality, was from a story of Kielland, the great Norwegian writer. In his "Tales of Two Countries,"* there is a description of Napoleon at the battle of Waterloo. I omit nearly all the setting, for it is irrelevant to my purpose. Suffice it to say that a young man named Cousin Hans desires to become acquainted with a pretty young woman, and that the only way he can contrive to do so is to make himself the victim of the man he supposes to be her father, a retired captain, who has bored more than one generation by his accounts of the battle of Waterloo. Cousin Hans places himself in the way of the captain, and to attract the old soldier's interest, makes believe that he is studying military manœuvres by drawing strokes and angles in the sands. This is what follows :

" The whole esplanade was quiet and deserted. Cousin Hans could hear the captain's firm steps approaching; they came right up to him and stopped. Hans did not look up; the captain

* "Tales of Two Countries." From the Norwegian of Alexander L. Kielland. Translated by William Archer. (London : Osgood, McIlvaine.)

advanced two more paces and coughed. Hans drew a long and profoundly significant stroke with his stick, and then the old fellow could contain himself no longer. 'Aha, young gentleman,' he said, in a friendly tone, taking off his hat, 'are you making a plan of our fortifications ?' Cousin Hans assumed the look of one who is awakened from deep contemplation, and bowing politely, he answered with some embarrassment: 'No, it's only a sort of habit I have of trying to take my bearings wherever I may be.' 'An excellent habit, a most excellent habit,' the captain exclaimed with warmth. 'It strengthens the memory,' Cousin Hans remarked modestly. 'Certainly, certainly, sir,' answered the captain, who was beginning to be much pleased by this modest young man. 'Especially in situations of any complexity,' continued the modest young man, rubbing out his strokes with his foot. 'Just what I was going to say !' exclaimed the captain, delighted. 'And, as you may well believe, drawings and plans are especially indispensable in military science. Look at a battle-field, for example.' 'Ah, battles are altogether too intricate for me,' Cousin Hans interrupted, with a smile of humility. 'Don't say that, sir !' answered the kindly old man. 'When once you have a bird's-eye view of the ground and of the positions of the armies, even a tolerably complicated battle can be made quite comprehensible. This sand, now, that we have before us here, could very well be made to give us an idea in miniature of, for example, the battle of Waterloo. . . . Be so good as to take a seat on the bench here,' continued the captain, whose heart was rejoiced at the thought of so intelligent a hearer, 'and I shall try to give you in short outline a picture of that momentous and remarkable—if it interests you ?' 'Many thanks, sir,' answered Cousin Hans ; 'nothing could interest me more.'"

II.

THE BATTLE.

WATERLOO is an old story ; but I must give it, as our poor good-natured captain did, in order to bring out the great passage to which I have alluded :

"The captain took up a position in a corner of the ramparts, a few paces from the bench, whence he could point all around him with a stick. Cousin Hans followed what he said closely, and took all possible trouble to ingratiate himself with his future father-in-law. 'We will suppose, then, that I am standing here, at the farm of Belle-Alliance, where the Emperor has his head-quarters ; and to the north—fourteen miles from Waterloo—we have Brussels, that is to say, just about at the corner of the gymnastic school. The road there along the rampart is the highway leading to Brussels, and here ' (the captain rushed over the plain of Waterloo), 'here in the grass we have the Forest of Soignies. On the highway to Brussels, and in front of the forest, the English

are stationed—you must imagine the northern
part of the battle-field somewhat higher than it is
here. On Wellington's left wing, that is to say,
to the eastward—here in the grass—we have the
Château of Hougoumont; that must be marked,'
said the captain, looking about him. The service-
able Cousin Hans at once found a stick, which
was fixed in the ground at this important point.
'Excellent!' cried the captain, who saw that he
had found an interested and imaginative listener.
'You see it's from this side that we have to expect
the Prussians.' Cousin Hans noticed that the
captain picked up a stone and placed it in the
grass with an air of mystery. 'Here, at Hougoumont,' the old man continued, 'the battle began.
It was Jerome who made the first attack. He
took the wood; but the château held out,
garrisoned by Wellington's best troops. In the
meantime Napoleon, here at Belle-Alliance, was
on the point of giving Marshal Ney orders to
commence the main attack upon Wellington's
centre, when he observed a column of troops
approaching from the east, behind the bench, over
there by the tree.' Cousin Hans looked round,
and began to feel uneasy: could Blucher be here
already? 'Blu— Blu——' he murmured ten-
tatively. 'It was Bulow,' the captain fortunately
went on, 'who approached with thirty thousand
Prussians. Napoleon made his arrangements
hastily to meet this new enemy, never doubting
that Grouchy, at any rate, was following close on

the Prussians' heels. You see, the Emperor had
on the previous day detached Marshal Grouchy
with the whole right wing of the army, about fifty
thousand men, to hold Blucher and Bulow in
check. But Grouchy—but of course all this is
familiar to you,' the captain broke off. Cousin
Hans nodded reassuringly. 'Ney accordingly
began the attack with his usual intrepidity. But
the English cavalry hurled themselves upon the
Frenchmen, broke their ranks, and forced them
back with the loss of two eagles and several
cannons. Milhaud rushes to the rescue with his
cuirassiers, and the Emperor himself, seeing the
danger, puts spurs into his horse and gallops down
the incline of Belle-Alliance.' Away rushed the
captain, prancing like a horse in his eagerness to
show how the Emperor rode through thick and
thin, rallied Ney's troops, and sent them forward
to a fresh attack."

III.

NAPOLEON.

AND now comes the great passage of the sketch :

" Whether it was that there lurked a bit of the
poet in Cousin Hans, or that the captain's repre-
sentation was really very vivid, or that—and this
is probably the true explanation—he was in love
with the captain's daughter, certain it is that
Cousin Hans was quite carried away by the situation. He no longer saw a queer old captain
prancing sideways ; he saw, through the cloud of
smoke, the Emperor himself, on his white horse

with the black eyes, as we knew it from the engravings. He tore away over hedge and ditch, over meadow and garden, his staff with difficulty keeping up with him. Cool and calm, he sat firmly in his saddle, with his half-buttoned greatcoat, his white breeches, and his little hat crosswise on his head. His face expressed neither weariness nor anxiety; smooth and pale as marble, it gave to the whole figure in the simple uniform on the white horse, an exalted, almost a spectral aspect. Thus he swept on his course, this sanguinary little monster, who in three days had fought three battles. All hastened to clear the way for him, flying peasants, troops in reserve or advancing—ay, even the wounded and dying dragged themselves aside, and looked up at him with a mixture of terror and admiration as he tore past them like a cold thunderbolt. Scarcely had he shown himself among the soldiers before they all fell into order as though by magic, and a moment afterwards the undaunted Ney could once more vault into the saddle to renew the attack. And this time he bore down the English, and established himself in the farmhouse of La Haye-Sainte. Napoleon is once more at Belle-Alliance. 'And now here comes Bulow from the east—under the bench here, you see—and the Emperor sends General Mouton to meet him. At half-past four —the battle had begun at one o'clock—Wellington attempts to drive Ney out of La Haye-Sainte. And Ney, who now saw that everything de-

pended on obtaining possession of the ground in
front of the wood—the sand here by the border of
the grass,' the captain threw his glove over to the
spot indicated — 'Ney, you see, calls up the
reserve brigade of Milhaud's cuirassiers, and
hurls himself at the enemy. Presently his men
were seen upon the heights, and already the
people around the Emperor were shouting
'Victoire!' 'It is an hour too late,' answered
Napoleon. As he now saw that the Marshal in
his new position was suffering much from the
enemy's fire, he determined to go to his assistance, and, at the same time, to try to crush
Wellington at one blow. He chose, for the
execution of this plan, Kellermann's famous
dragoons and the heavy cavalry of the guard.
Now comes one of the crucial moments of the
fight. You must come out here upon the battle-
field!' Cousin Hans at once arose from the
bench, and took the position the captain pointed
out to him. 'Now you are Wellington!' Cousin
Hans drew himself up. 'You are standing there
on the plain with the greater part of the English
infantry. Here comes the whole of the French
cavalry rushing down upon you. Milhaud has
joined Kellermann; they form an illimitable
multitude of horses, breastplates, plumes, and
shining weapons. Surround yourself with a
square!' Cousin Hans stood for a moment
bewildered; but presently he understood the
captain's meaning. He hastily drew a square

of deep strokes around him on the sand. 'Right!' cried the captain, beaming. 'Now the Frenchmen cut into the square; the ranks break, but join again; the cavalry wheels away and gathers for a fresh attack. Wellington has every moment to surround himself with a new square. The French cavalry fight like lions; the proud memories of the Emperor's campaigns fill them with that confidence of victory which made his armies invincible. They fight for victory, for glory, for the French eagles, and for the little cold man who, they know, stands on the height behind them, whose eye follows every single man, who sees all and forgets nothing; but to-day they have an enemy who is not easy to deal with. They stand where they stand, these Englishmen, and if they are forced to step backwards, they regain their position the next moment. They have no eagles and no Emperor, and when they fight they think neither of military glory nor of revenge; but they think of home. The thought of never seeing again the oak-trees of Old England is the most melancholy an Englishman knows. Ah, no, there is one which is still worse—that of coming home dishonoured. And when they think that the proud fleet, which they know is lying to the northward waiting for them, would deny them the honour of a salute, and that Old England would not recognise her sons, then they grip their muskets tighter, they forget their wounds and their flowing blood; silent and grim, they clench their teeth, and hold their post and die like men.' Twenty times were the squares broken and reformed, and twelve thousand brave Englishmen fell. Cousin Hans could understand how Wellington wept when he said, 'Night or Blucher!'"

IV.

NAPOLEON IN RETREAT.

AND quite as vivid is the remainder of the picture —the picture of Napoleon in retreat:

"The captain had in the meantime left Belle-Alliance, and was spying around in the grass behind the bench, while he continued his exposition, which grew more and more vivid: 'Wellington was now in reality beaten, and a total defeat was inevitable,' cried the captain in a sombre voice, 'when this fellow appeared on the scene!' And as he said this, he kicked the stone which Cousin Hans had seen him concealing, so that it rolled in upon the field of battle. 'Now or never,' thought Cousin Hans. 'Blucher!' he cried. 'Exactly!' answered the captain, 'it's the old werewolf Blucher, who comes marching upon the field with his Prussians.' So Grouchy never came; there was Napoleon, deprived of his whole right wing, and facing 150,000 men. But with never-failing coolness he gives his orders for a great change of front. But it was too late, and the odds were too vast. Wellington, who by Blucher's arrival was enabled to bring his reserve into play, now ordered

his whole army to advance. And yet once
more the Allies were forced to pause for a
moment by a furious charge led by Ney—the
lion of the day. 'Do you see him there?'
cried the captain, his eyes flashing. And Cousin
Hans saw him, the romantic hero, Duke of El-
chingen, Prince of the Moskowa, son of a cooper
in Saarlouis, Marshal and Peer of France. He
saw him rush onward at the head of his battalions
—five horses had been shot under him—with his
sword in his hand, his uniform torn to shreds,
hatless, and with the blood streaming down his
face. And the battalions rallied and swept ahead;
they followed their Prince of the Moskowa,
their Saviour at the Beresina, into the hopeless
struggle for the Emperor and for France. Little
did they dream that, six months later, the King
of France would have their dear Prince shot as
a traitor to his country in the gardens of the
Luxembourg. There he rushed around, rallying
and directing his troops, until there was nothing
more for the general to do; then he plied his
sword like a common soldier until all was over,
and he was carried away in the rout. For
the French army fled. The Emperor threw
himself into the throng; but the terrible hubbub
drowned his voice, and in the twilight no one
knew the little man on the white horse. Then
he took his stand in a little square of his Old
Guard, which still held out upon the plain; he
would fain have ended his life on his last

battle-field.   But his generals flocked around him, and the old grenadiers shouted, ' Withdraw, sire!   Death will not have you.'   They did not know that it was because the Emperor had forfeited his right to die as a French soldier. They led him half-resisting from the field; and, unknown in . his own army, he rode away into the darkness of the night, having lost everything. 'So ended the battle of Waterloo,' said the captain, as he seated himself on the bench and arranged his neckcloth."

I shall be in despair, and forfeit all my poor claims to being a judge of literature, if my readers do not read this splendid narrative with the same breathless interest as I did; and if that awful figure of " the little man on the white horse " does not haunt their imaginations, as it did mine, for many an hour after they have read it.   I thought the description of Waterloo in Stendhal's " Chartreuse de Parme " was the last and greatest word that literature had to speak on that historic day; but really Kielland is finer, to my mind, than even Stendhal.   At all events, I have never read anything which brought home to my imagination with the same vividness the terrible central figure of that day ; and all the godlike genius and demoniac power, all the horror and glory and despair which were embodied in his person in the battle-field.

THE END.

F. M. EVANS AND CO., LIMITED, PRINTERS, CRYSTAL PALACE, S.E.